THE COMPLETE BOX SET

CASSA DAUN

Midnight Moon Series Box Set

Copyright © 2022 Cassa Daun

All rights reserved. No part of this book may be reproduced, transmitted, downloaded, distributed, stored in or introduced into any information storage and retrieval system, in any form or by any means, whether electronic or mechanical, without express permission of the author, except by a reviewer who may quote brief passages for review purposes.

This book is a work of fiction and any resemblance to any person, living or dead, events, occurrences, or locales is purely coincidental. The characters and the storylines are created from the author's imagination or are used fictitiously.

Cover pictures from Depositphotos®

Cover design by Q Design

Contents

	VI
Runt	1
1	2
2	14
3	23
4	37
5	45
6	53
7	61
8	69
9	77
10	87
11	97
12	106
13	117

Stray	122
1	123
2	130
3	140
4	148
5	158
6	166
7	176
8	184
9	194
10	202
11	212
12	220
13	231
Bait	244
1	245
2	254
3	264
4	275
5	284
6	293

7	301
8	310
9	318
10	327
11	334
12	341
13	350
Stud	362
1	363
2	370
3	378
4	386
5	395
6	402
7	410
8	419
9	427
10	436
11	443
12	449
13	458

Midnight Moon isn't a sleepaway camp for pups. And it definitely isn't an academy for the youth of privileged packs.

It's for adult rejects. The runts. The unwanted. The loners.

So which am I? After my family died, all of the above. I suppose that makes me a perfect fit, even if I shouldn't be. I was sent here, not only in hope of forcing my transition but also for protection from an outcast aiming to stop me from claiming my rightful spot. While it might be the best place to hide, I quickly discover I'm not invisible.

The Four have pinned their eyes on me.

runt

1

The Uber lurched away, spinning tires briefly on the dirt road and leaving me at the entrance of Camp Midnight Moon in a cloud of dust. I coughed as the dirt settled, my warm breath pushing smoky puffs into the frigid air. As the headlights disappeared and the night closed in, my eyes readjusted and took in the place I'd be calling home for ... who knew how long. The rest of December? A full month? Maybe more. Winter in The Great Smoky Mountains of Tennessee? Sounded as isolating as home, only a different setting. It was far enough from Alabama to keep me stranded. And hidden. That was the idea.

The camp was settled along the edge of the national park, down an obscure road, purposely separate from all the other park camps to prevent accidental human interaction from the Gatlinburg locals and tourists. Keep us concealed. Keep them away.

A single light cast over the main pathway, barely showing the secluded cabins off in the distance. I adjusted my Kate Spade backpack, gripped the handle of the wheeling suitcase my aunt gave me, then stepped up on the first wooden tier post of the rail fence and looked around before hopping over. Carvings marked the fence—witch made, for security no doubt. The camp sign hung crooked on the locked gate. Camp Midnight Moon. Pup Camp, as the rumor mill calls it. It wasn't an endearing nickname. It was derogatory and mocking, like when us southerners use "bless your heart" as a sarcastic nicety. Not really nice or sweet. It's a fucking joke. There are other places considered boarding schools and academies where the privileged and respected packs send their young to learn life lessons they can't be bothered to teach themselves. But that's not this camp. This place is comprised of loners, late transitioning runts, and anyone just plain ole unwanted, where the over-eighteen are sent in hopes to hide or change the family disappointment, maybe squelch some family guilt. Well ... *we're*. A place where *we're* sent. *I am here. I'm part of this now.* So which category did I fit in? I supposed all of them. Even having a large pack family, being the youngest set me up to be a bit of a loner. Also, while most wolves shed their human skin for the first time around when humans hit puberty, I still hadn't made my transition at twenty. Ergo, continued runt status with all the limitations involved. And recently, I had also become unwanted by everyone acquainted with my deceased family.

I was also late. While I'd heard the camp's enrollment was revolving—adding new people whenever space allowed—I was under the impression most arrived on Mondays. And here I was strolling in just after dark—and probably after dinner—on Wednesday. My stomach flip-flopped at the thought, rumbling almost loud enough to alert anyone in the closest cabins. Hopefully, since I'd missed the beginning of the day, I'd get some grace with no actual torture of introductions until tomorrow.

After dragging the worthless wheeled suitcase down the dirt path, I knocked on the chipped green door of the cabin with the plaque indicating "Office" and the number one, then glanced around at the dark surrounding forest. Nothing. My finger traced over the name stamps on the door plaque. Tim. Rosie. They were the alpha pair, the leads who ran the camp. They maintained a basic form of guidance and authority, to help train and hone wolf traits and report behaviors back to any pack families who actually care to know about their attendees. My Aunt Sonya had spilled this minimal information the previous night when she'd also dropped the news of my enrollment. We had been leaving the parking lot of the vampire bar Purgatory, there for the mandatory multi-species gathering for discussions about the recent battle and decisions for the future of our amicable supernatural lifestyles. They had voted temporary leaders, for our pack territory and for the area vampires. As my dad's sister and only remaining active member of our pack—since I hadn't yet transitioned—all had elected Aunt Sonya to be the interim pack alpha for the territory.

See, I was never supposed to come to this camp, or any camp, even with being a runt. In fact, I'd never even traveled before. I was the daughter of Jin Wellis, the Alpha Lead of all pack territories in southern Alabama, and he kept me home, kept me mostly hidden during my extended wait for transition. Taking online classes and working at our family restaurant—The Back Burner—was my everyday life. When I was younger, even after my mother's death, he'd trained me in the techniques and skills of our kind, as much as he could while I still donned my initial human skin. Every year after sixteen with no change, time slipped faster and faster away along with his patience, instruction, and attention.

But all of that was before he chose to back a power-hungry vampire in a strike against our local reapers and got himself and our pack—our family—killed.

My eyes stung, and I blinked rapidly to squash the threat of tears. It'd been two weeks since most of my family had died. Not long at all. I'd cried the entire first day, with what felt like a waterfall's worth of salty drops to mourn the family I loved, the family I'd once known them to be, who I'd already been mourning for several years because of their detachment. More tears came when I'd learned my father's reason for joining the vampires' fight against the reapers was about me. But I'd cried very few tears since, and I wouldn't let more fall now.

"Not here," I whispered to myself. Tears would only show weakness. Aunt Sonya told me coming here would be better than withering away at home. "It'll wake you up," she'd said. She hoped it would force my transition—being around different people from different packs. She'd heard it had been true for others. But that wasn't the only reason. Being the offspring of Jin, I had alpha claim of our territory as soon as I transitioned. I could always be challenged or choose to step aside after, but it was my position to hold. With my family's death, I also got the house and The Back Burner. All of it made me a target. Aunt Sonya knew it would take more than a few prayers from her local church group to keep me safe, especially from Uncle Raif—my late mother's younger brother, who once had been part of our pack but had been cast out. When and if he found out our family was gone, there was a chance he'd return and try to claim it all. So Aunt Sonya promised me she'd manage the restaurant as she usually did and watch over everything else while I was gone. I couldn't exactly refuse her since she had handled everything when my world had shattered, when there were three fresh graves dug beside my mother's, and twelve others from our pack alone buried the very same day. I owed her for her clear, logical thoughts, for forcing me to breathe, and for trying to protect me.

Loud voices echoed into the night, coming from the largest cabin down the row, likely the dining hall and main gathering spot.

It was time to jump in.

I delayed the walk down the trail for as long as possible, my stride small enough to rival a toddler's. Voices still spewed out from the expansive building, loud and energetic.

Maybe the place wasn't as bad as the random rumors I'd heard growing up. Maybe I would find whatever I needed to move on. Maybe it would be a salvation.

I watched my breath turn to smoke in the lamplight above the entrance and shivered as a cold breeze cut through my weak clothing. The journey was already off to an unprepared start.

The door burst outward right as I reached for the handle, nearly knocking me over. I stumbled out of the way while two massive bodies exited, followed closely by two more. Boys ... er, guys. *Whoa.* They were big. I mean big, big. Doubtful they were runts.

And given their proximity to each other, also doubtful they were loners.

Unwanted, then.

With my sudden clamor to get out of the way and the soft squeak I emitted, their heads snapped in my direction, eyes narrowing, scrutinizing. All their gazes dragged from my shocked face straight down to the suitcase beside my blue Checkerboard Vans then slowly made the return trip up my five-foot frame, taking in the ripped jeans, tight tank, and the half-zipped thin hoodie before settling again on my face and dirty blond hair with shoulder-length, choppy strands. I was instantly glad I'd only grabbed basic clothes. What would be the reason for pretty dresses or jewelry at this camp, anyway? But despite my normal-looking attire, their eye trips lasted far longer than they should have. And if that fact wasn't worrisome enough, all of their upper lips curled a bit during their rough perusal. Repulsion? Annoyance? Yeah, they had definitely scented me, knew I was a runt who smelled more human than wolf and lacked the ability to scent them so acutely in return.

Apparently, I'd thought too quickly about all the rumors. The place was going to be hell, worse than my sheltered high school experience and dealing with the local pack assholes who threw attitude my way whenever I was around, driving me into reclusiveness even more. I was still the short, odd-smelling outsider. Fun.

"You done with the eye fuckin'?" I snapped, immediately on the defensive, a bit of my Alabama twang slipping out with my anger. I straightened my spine and glared right back at them—up at them—though not truly making eye contact for fear they'd see through the fragile bravado hiding the fact that my usual ferocity had been recently snuffed. Not wanting to give them any more time to react, I gripped my suitcase in one hand and shoved the closest chest blocking my way, ready to push through him and the door quickly. Only, when my hand connected with the plain white T-shirt and the solid wall of muscle beneath, I made the mistake of focusing on the owner. Big mistake. Chest Number One had short black hair up top, the sides shaved close to his skull, with a squared, pale face and a clenched, angry jaw. And scars. Many scars. Long, scattered lines of delicate white-pink skin streaked his jaw and neck. His narrowed hazel eyes blinked once with a slight twitch of his lips, breaking my brief trance and spurring me back into motion.

Before I could manage two steps past him, his hand halted me, dropping onto my shoulder. The grip wasn't a grip at all, not heavy or containing. Not exactly threatening. It simply rested there, causing me to ignore my initial instinct to grab hold and twist.

"Feisty runt." His voice held no accent and was as hard and sharp as his body looked. I probably should have been terrified, but I wasn't. While I knew things could technically happen at Pup Camp, maybe even bad things, the chances of anything going down right in front of the main building with others inside was pretty slim. Plus, I knew enough to defend myself. Though, four huge guys might be a bit more of a challenge to escape than a single attacker. The thought almost made me shiver.

Chest Number Two stepped into view. "Eye fuckin'?" He attempted to mimic my accent, though it sounded more northern.

A Yank, Italian American maybe. It was also smoother with its anger, like a sneaky lullaby that drifted right into a nightmare. He chuckled, the tone rich inside my ears. I didn't want to look, but dammit, there was no way to ignore them now, and it was probably a good idea to identify them in the event I lived through the encounter. Under the dull lamplight, I noticed his olive skin and tapered brown hair with a thicker length on top. His face was longer, more rectangle-shaped, sporting a manly dimple in the chin, full enough lips to make all the Kardashians jealous, and low, heavy brows over soulful brown eyes. He had scars along his neck, too. Not as prominent as the first guy but noticeable.

I ducked away from the hand on my shoulder and dipped to the side, trying to break for the door. The other two chests had beat me to it, chuckling but not adding any more commentary to the group welcoming. One was the thinnest of them all, though still appearing solid. Wavy locks of brown hair sweeping down to his shoulders shadowed the copper-toned skin of his face more. At my assessment of him, one side of his lips quirked, his amber eyes narrowed, and the pointed tip of his nose lifted a bit as he sniffed the air. The final chest had arms crossed over it, the owner sporting a permanent golden summer tan beneath his scruffy face. His pouty lower lip betrayed the vacant look in his eyes, which were different colors—one blue, one brown. And while his dark blond hair was cropped close on the sides, the top had longer length that was slicked back, except for a single chin-length strand that had escaped and settled over his cheek. Silver glinted from many places around his face. Piercings. Several of them. A hoop through the pouty lower lip, a bar above his eyebrow, several more in his ears. He was the shortest, possibly a runt, but still large enough to be intimidating.

Damn. At camp for only a few minutes and I was already a mess. For the past two weeks, numbness had contained me. I'd had no motivation. No concept of life or feeling. I'd felt even more alone than I usually had, grieving a family that, while close in physical proximity, had been so distant they'd often felt a world away. And now, it was as if all of my emotion was reawakening. Sadness. Irritation. Anger. And bothered as I was by these assholes' attitudes, the wolf testosterone surrounding me had gotten thick and heady really fast, bringing an intoxication that churned up other feelings inside. That much man-wolf hormone was impossible to ignore, even though I couldn't actually smell it. I could sense it. All over. I needed to leave before I offered to climb one without even having my cabin assignment. Because … wow! I wasn't a girl who had sex so freely, even in the best of emotional states. To be honest, I wasn't usually so interested, but mostly, the guys weren't, especially any who had met me through my family. First, they all respected my father, so not many would chance using me for a quick lay, if they even held a mild interest at all, let alone consider a full-on coupling with a runt girl. Everyone always looks for alpha material. It was in our nature to level up. Being the biggest, boldest, and most beautiful wasn't an alpha requirement—my father wasn't even considered large—but a majority of the time, yeah, that was the case. Or at least that was what most looked for. Dominant. Commanding. Protective.

All of my sexual encounters had been of the quickie variety. Rushed. Twice from visiting packs with brave guys who had dared to seduce me during brief stays with my family. My actual first time was with a human my senior year of high school. He thought I was pretty. And while he'd unknowingly sensed my differences, like other humans, he ultimately ignored his subconscious warnings to keep away and listened to his dick instead. It had been a blissful night until he shot his load and his brain re-engaged its flight instinct. He'd avoided me after. C'est la vie.

Giggling lightly at my thoughts, probably making them think I was crazy—but whatever, I'd gotten that back home too—I flipped around the last one's body and reached for the door, only for it to swing wide again, knocking the suitcase from my hand and throwing me backward, directly into one of the solid bodies.

A leggy brunette with a high ponytail, a lotus throat tattoo, and a septum piercing stepped out, looking down at me as I awkwardly righted myself against the body at my back. I didn't want to turn around to face them again. I knew they were all still there by their amused grunts, one obviously holding really still while I wiggled myself back into an upright position.

Two other brunettes exited behind her, both also tall, slim, with designer-dream model builds made for the streets instead of the runways. Same hair. Practically the same face with wide-set dreamy eyes, pert noses, though with basic ear piercings and no visible tattoos.

"This a street-chic designer show or something?" I muttered to myself.

"The fuck are you?" Brunette One spat the words through a thin-lipped scowl as her eyes looked over the scene. "Get out of their way, Princess." Her hand reached out and grabbed hold of my arm, yanking me off the body at my back. Was she something to him? To them?

Few people had the balls to touch me back home. Aside from the occasional daring human in the schools I'd attended, people usually avoided me. I was Jin's daughter—too short, too feisty, too off-limits, too fill-in-another-blank. Not that I'd never been involved in a few scraps, because, duh, for all those same reasons too.

When my body jerked forward by her forceful hand, I bit my teeth together audibly in warning and yanked my arm from her grasp. "Best to keep your hands to yourself."

She huffed a laugh, catching her friends' eyes conspiratorially before reaching out again. She thought she could best me. Bless her heart.

"Nope," I said, beating her to the punch by grasping her hand and twisting her arm behind her back. Hard.

Although she tried to hold it back, she released a pained hiss. As the other two stepped closer, I twisted higher and tighter, drawing another tiny hiss and a mumbled plea to stop.

"I hate repeating myself, but I will this once with words you'll understand. Back. The. Fuck. Off."

And they did. I spun the girl with my body, shifting toward the door, catching sight of the guys' eyes pinned on me, the look not exactly impressed or surprised, but not totally aloof either.

The door opened again. This time two sighs emitted from behind me, followed by a perky female voice. "Oh boy. You must be Teenie, right? Teagan Wellis?"

Before I could confirm, the first guy with the scars smirked. "Teenie." My family nickname—obviously exchanged from my aunt to the guides upon enrollment—oozed through his scowl. "You should probably let her go, or ..." He let the warning hang, not caring about the camp guides behind me.

"Yes, please release Nima. While we encourage friendly, competitive challenges during events here, we don't tolerate verbal or physical assaults," the male guide—Tim, I gathered—added. "That includes threats, Loch."

I dropped my hands from Nima and stepped away, eyeing Chest Number One. Loch, huh?

"Good girl," Loch said, ignoring Tim. All the guys released puffs of air that could barely be considered laughs and walked away, and the girls trailed behind them, like thirsty pups.

I rolled my eyes. *Super.*

2

"Ah. Fuck." A mumbled voice traveled out from behind the darkened shed close to both the lake and the cabin where I'd been assigned.

After talking more with Rosie and Tim at their office, they had instructed me to walk ahead while they informed others of the sleep assignment change-up. Unfortunately, the only two empty cabins were not in a suitable condition for tenants—missing roof pieces, broken floorboards—due to age and a few transition mishaps. And since the girls' cabins were all filled, they were pulling at least one girl to bunk with me in the smallest cabin by the lake. They were also shifting the two males currently staying there into another place.

Hearing a long, pleasured groan and a repetitive garbled sound, like a choking duck, I stopped and peered at the shadows beside the shed curiously. A guy leaned against the side where kayaks and other lake equipment too big to fit inside were stacked along storage racks. His shaved head tipped back, and his hands threaded into a mass of hair at his waist. A girl knelt in front of him, face curtained by her long strands, bobbing on the dick I couldn't see. The choking and slurping sounds came from her.

The guy grunted, calling my eyes back up to his face, where his turned head and opened eyes now stared right at me.

Shit.

The whites of his teeth gleamed brightly through the darkness as he smiled, watching me watch them. "Oh, shit yeah, sexy. Wanna join?"

The girl released his dick with an audible pop and her face shifted toward me, her hands taking over where her mouth had left off, twisting and stroking. I could see her teeth too as she sneered at me, which made her recognizable as one of the girls from outside the dining hall, her hair now loose.

"Yes. Keep going, Nerine. Ahh," the guy urged, closing his eyes again.

It seemed more of the rumors were true then. This place was also known as being a sex camp. I supposed it made sense, given that so many degenerates of our kind were smashed together, away from their packs, free to explore and not be judged while they were basically being banished or whatever. From what I'd heard, though, it wasn't often that couples bonded here. If they did, they kept their inferior pack positions and returned to one of their families. Most sent here wouldn't be alphas. They weren't cut to lead. They struggled with some aspect of being a wolf and were here to be trained to fit in somewhere, or simply survive in ordinary society at the very least if they chose to stay alone in the end. So yeah … sex here was understandable. And there was no need to worry about protection since our wolf bodies didn't contract most human diseases. Pregnancy was a rare concern, too. Conception only occurred during a female's heat, which didn't happen until after our first transition and only a few times a year after.

I shook my head, adjusted my backpack and suitcase, and hurried past the shed, taking the path to the cabin closest to the lake. As I rounded the side, soft light from windows spilled out to the ground and trailed faintly to the lake—Midnight Lake. A tiny smile crept onto my face for the first time since … well, for a while. The view at night was gorgeous. A line of moonlight barely rippled on the water's still surface. I was almost giddy, eager to see what everything looked like in the daylight.

Turning from the lake, I placed a hand on the wooden handrail and took the first of three steps up to the tiny porch deck of cabin number five.

"Why the fuck do we need to move? This is bullshit," a harsh, gravelly voice traveled out through the screen door. I stepped onto the ground and twisted away from the bits of light on the deck, shifting back into the night's shadows.

"At least Tim and Rosie put us in cabin six with Loch and Eli," a different voice stated, the tone calm and indifferent.

"True, but they won't be happy either. Vic is in there too, which means we'll be stuck with the bunks." Their voices went silent for a bit, the sounds of footsteps and items shuffling taking over. "Couldn't they just shove her in with the triplets? Their cabin's a four-bed."

"With the triplets? After what just happened at chow? Yeah, because Tim and Rosie really want to explain how the girl died in her sleep the first night here." A barked laugh was quick to follow, and a hesitant chuckle joined in.

"Nah, the sisters are too cold to kill her right off. They'd play with her, and we'd finally have some decent entertainment around here. Better than hearing Jackson's latest bj or dodging his and Trig's attempts at fucking with us."

"Yeah." There was a deep sigh. "But on the real, at least we'll all be together, making those two idiots less likely to mess with our shit. Especially with Vic in there too. Another witness. They can't start too much shit if they want to get back home to their precious families."

"Fuck!" A low snarling followed the yell. "I'm just so fucking pissed about all of this. And hot. Fuck, it's hot. Are you hot?"

"Oh boy," the other, calmer voice responded.

"Don't even say it."

A chuckle. "I won't. But it certainly sounds like you're getting closer if—"

"Fuck right the hell off!"

"I'm just saying ... The cabin's gonna feel even more crowded if you're—"

"Ah, there you are, Teenie," Rosie's chipper voice spoke from behind me, almost making me jump out of my human skin. If only that would happen. It would make the transition easy enough.

But I wasn't that lucky.

I grabbed my chest and released a startled yelp just the same.

"Oh, sorry about that," she said, laying a hand on my shoulder as she moved around me. Her bubblegum pink hair sparkled in the streams of light from the cabin, and she clutched a stack of linens below her other arm. "I'm told I can be quite stealthy despite what my appearance suggests." And she was right. Her body was larger than what humans consider adequate for her height, but what most wolves consider strong and hearty ... as opposed to a small, twiggy runt like me. She was well-bred in a traditional wolf sense, possibly five-and-a-half feet tall with enough extra weight to make her appear both solid and soft. On top of that, she was bright, wearing vivid colors—her hair, her clothes. Cheerful. Loud in looks, soft in words.

"Please, call me Teagan," I uttered and tried to calm my breathing as she led us up the steps onto the deck. She used the nickname outside of the main cabin when I'd arrived, but neither she nor Tim had repeated it while giving me the general introduction information in their office.

"Oh. All rightie," Rosie said in a gentle, defeated squeak as if I'd just burst her friendship balloon. With a rotation of camp attendees, she may have been eager to make besties as quickly as possible. But I felt that would cross another camp line, like being teacher's pet or something. I wanted nothing else used against me on the first day.

I gave her a small smile just as the cabin door opened and two stern-looking guys exited through the screen door, duffel bags slung over their broad shoulders, stripped bed linens and pillows tucked under their other arms. They were Chest Number Three and Four from earlier, the ones who hadn't spoken at the main hall. They looked at me then at Rosie, their irritated expressions morphing into softer looks of concern.

"Rosie? You okay?" The lither of the two asked. He stood a good half a foot over Rosie—probably over a foot taller than me—while the other was only a few inches below him.

"Oh, yes. I'm fine, Koni. Thank you," Rosie replied, releasing my shoulder and waving her hand into the air as if to brush away his concern. Her smile was back in place as she looked between us. "Koni, Zavier, this is Teen—Teagan," she introduced, stuttering as she remembered to skip the nickname.

"Right. Teenie," the other one—Zavier—said, finishing the nickname he'd heard earlier and arching a dark blond eyebrow knowingly, the silver bar through it moving too, glinting under the cabin's small porch light. Sweat also glinted along his brow. He'd been the "hot" one during their rant. He also had to be a runt, which made the last bit of their conversation understandable. His transition had already begun. Temperature spikes and flashes of anger increased as it progressed, the process longer for runts.

Koni laughed at Zavier's use of my nickname then attempted to cover it up by coughing into his hand before tucking a few long strands of hair behind an ear.

They'd probably heard us from inside the cabin and knew I'd upset her. Well, fantastic. And the hits kept coming.

"Teagan," I corrected. Because at this point, why not? I also didn't bother to extend my free hand. They likely didn't care, and I was too conflicted to offer a polite greeting. On one end, I felt repulsed by their automatic repulsion toward me. And on the other, I found them highly attractive and wasn't sure how I'd react if we made skin-to-skin contact. That thought rattled my nerves in too many ways to explore at the moment.

Their humor died, their mocking smiles flattening as they looked back at Rosie.

She batted her lashes at them in a dramatic, non-flirtatious kind of way. "I suppose you heard already." Her eyes fluttered again, but she added a cute little frown into the mix. "I'm so sorry we had to make you switch cabins."

Ah, the batty lashes were apologetic.

"Yeah, Tim called," Zavier replied dully, shifting the arm with the trapped linens to show the two-way radio clutched within his hand. "And it's no problem. We understand."

Well, well, well, wasn't he the bullshitter. His voice was the brasher of the two, the one that had been the most irritated when they were alone in the cabin complaining about the very idea of being moved. I supposed everyone played nice to the guides here. Possibly for favor? Maybe I should have let Rosie call me Teenie after all. I was too confused and tired to think much about it. While I couldn't very well claim jet lag from a single-hour time-zone change, I'd never flown before, and it affected me more than I would have thought. The trip, the arrival ... everything else. It was all hitting me now.

"I'm so glad that you do," Rosie chirped in an airy tone. "Six is the next closest to the lake, as you know. Still has a great view, but most do anyway. And I'm certain the others are ready to welcome you in."

"I'm sure they are," Koni said with a lip twitch that almost cracked his warm and placid demeanor as if he knew the other guys' welcome wouldn't be the kind Rosie expected. The copper tone of his skin glowed in the cabin's light, and I caught myself staring a little too hard. He had to be of Native American descent. The long, wavy hair framing his angular jaw and high cheekbones highlighted that fact. He was a beautiful guy. Handsome and hot, sure, but beautiful too. As soon as I thought it, I forced myself to look away.

Zavier, however, wasn't exactly beautiful. He was rough and stoic, perfectly summed up by the multiple piercings and his mostly expressionless look. The only thing that showed a hint of emotion was that naturally pouty bottom lip, the plumpness able to strum the heartstrings—and pantie strings—of anyone graced by the view. One simple look at that lip made you want to hear him speak anything just to watch his lips move. It also made me want to bite it.

Stop, Teag. Just stop. I had to be tired. My thoughts had been taking me all over the place since I'd arrived. Hopefully, sleep was all I needed. But the shivers down my spine and that sensual tingle between my legs when I'd looked at these guys suggested I needed something else entirely. Maybe, just maybe, I needed a release. A good cry. A good orgasm. With the way these guys were looking at me, mocking me, I had a feeling the only way I'd get the latter would be the same way I'd have the former—alone in bed.

"Koni, I believe you're in tonight's study session with Tim, so you should go get settled before heading to the classroom," Rosie said to them before turning to me. "That's cabin two, beside our office. It's where most of the bookwork we do takes place. I'll tell you more in a minute." She smiled at the guys.

They nodded at her then side-eyed me before adjusting their duffels and linens and traipsing down the steps out into the night.

"Well," Rosie said, stealing my eyes from the path the guys had taken, "welcome to your new home."

3

"Boys," Rosie commented, pinching a wet towel on the floor by the bathroom and lifting it into the air, her eyes wide. She'd already dropped the clean linens onto a bed and had moved into the bathroom for a quick inspection.

I chuckled at her humor, recalling my mother having the same reaction to messes made by my two older brothers, Sebastian and Brandon, years before. I shook my head to scatter the memories as I took in the area, needing to stay in the present instead of getting lost in the past. The cabin was simple and tiny, much like the exterior suggested, the interior similar to Rosie and Tim's office cabin, with the same dark wooden planks for walls as the siding on the outside. No pictures or artwork decorated the space. There were three cushioned armchairs, a small coffee table, and an end table, all in the front half of the cabin—a sitting area on one side of the door. A tiny circle table and two dining chairs comprised the other side of the front. Four windows looked out into the night with only a thin, wispy curtain covering each. The back half of the cabin had a bathroom and sleeping room. The latter had a wide doorway with no door. Inside, two twin-sized beds with knobby bedposts aligned neatly with the planks beneath them. Both beds had a three-drawer pine dresser at their side. Across from the bedroom was the bathroom, complete with a standing shower, toilet, and a sink and cabinet combo.

I smiled at the bathroom and its door, happy to have one, to have privacy. Secretly, I'd worried this would be like a horror movie camp with community showers and was dreading the torture that would hold. I shivered just thinking about it.

"Cold, dear?" Rosie asked, her eyes sympathetic while draping the towel over her arm. She pointed at the dresser. "Extra blankets in there. It's been mild, but it'll get colder. Do you have a winter coat, something thicker than that hoodie?"

I wheeled my suitcase—the bottom and wheels now crusted with dirt—around the partition to the far bed, dropped my backpack next to the sheets she'd laid onto the mattress, then smoothed a hand down the front of my hoodie. Transitioned wolves didn't need to worry as much about the cooler weather, having a bump in body temperature that ran warmer than an average human. That was why she gave me the sympathetic eyes. I was a runt. It also could have been because she knew where I was from. While Alabama temps fell below freezing on several winter nights, it stayed fairly moderate overall. Given my runt status, I spent very little time outside anyway, which was why I didn't own or even consider bringing heavier clothing with me. The trip had also been too last minute to plan ahead. I grimaced at the flimsy hoodie then looked up at her.

My expression told her plenty. Her eyebrow quirked before she gave me an encouraging smile. "We have people enroll from all over the country. Some have left items behind, so don't fret. You can look through the collection in the office tomorrow. If nothing there suits you, I can make a trip to the store. In the meantime, keep these windows closed up tight. The heater works well enough, but you'll still want to bundle up with extra bedding as the chill tends to seep into these old cabins and linger."

I nodded, looking around again. "Thank you."

"You're more than welcome." She folded her hands in front of her as she eyed me. "Don't hesitate to come to me with any concerns. You've recently been through a lot, and being here is a big change. It is for most everyone who comes. But know that we consider everyone here family. We're here for you, whatever you need. That includes problems with others. I wasn't happy with what happened when you arrived. It's no secret that most of our kind get territorial, but those here know better than to greet someone new negatively."

"Yeah, I'm sorry for ... that too." I wouldn't lie. While I was sorry for the situation, I wasn't sorry for how I'd reacted. I felt completely justified in defending myself and had a feeling it wouldn't be the last time I'd need to.

"No longer an issue." She waved her hand, but pressed, "Now that we've gone over the basic rules with you in the office, we expect you to follow them too."

"Of course," I agreed, then added my own condition. "As long as I'm not threatened again."

One of her eyebrows raised as she tilted her ivory face, the single overhead cabin light making her skin gleam. Before she could comment or question my response, the door opened and a girl walked inside, her arms stuffed with the same standard-issue white bedding and pillow, though hers was crumpled into a mass, freshly stripped from a bed. She twisted her body and peaked around the bundle of material blocking her view.

"Ah, Keira! There you are. This is Teagan. Teagan, Keira's going to be your cabinmate," Rosie said, gaze shifting back and forth between us.

Keira dumped her duffel and bedding onto the closest chair while smiling at Rosie and me, lifting her high cheekbones even higher. "Hey. Nice to meet you."

"You too," I said, offering my own smile as I checked her out. She wasn't as purposely stripped-down as the three bitches from earlier—the triplets, as Koni and Zavier had called them—but was natural and neutral in appearance. Keira stood just as tall as them, though, and taller than Rosie. Most of her wavy black hair fell behind her back while some hung over a shoulder, nearly reaching her elbow. Shorter strands in front brushed the rich tawny skin of her chin. She was slim like me, but it better suited her height and build. Buckled calf boots covered her feet and the lower portion of her ripped black jeans. A massive green sweater swallowed her upper body.

"Well," Rosie chirped with a clap of her hands, "as we said in the office, since you haven't transitioned and won't be attending any field training, your focus will probably be study. They are individually based, so expect independent study, whether alone or with others in the room. And since you've had prior human schooling, we'll adjust courses as needed. There's also the required camp chores that everyone has, though you will have a bit more than most who have practical exercises. Your aunt mentioned a restaurant?"

"She manages my family's restaurant, yes."

"And you worked there too?" I nodded, and she continued, "Since you have experience, would you be more comfortable doing chores in the kitchen?"

"Sure," I said with a nod. Being in a kitchen would definitely make me more comfortable. My eyes shifted to Keira at the same time I agreed and immediately noticed her lips press together and her eyebrows raise in a surprised look.

"We have limited resources and workers here to maintain our small and quiet stature, so meals are usually ready-made with divided and stored weekly allotments. Most prepare their own food or appoint a cabin chef for meal times, and everyone is to clean up after themselves. There is some prep work involved and the heavier cleaning, which is handled by whoever is working the kitchen. I'll have you meet with Loch and Elijah tomorrow. They're currently in charge." Rosie tapped her chin and scrunched her eyebrows. "Hmm. What else? You already know there's no cellular or Wi-Fi service here for security reasons. You signed the enrollment paperwork earlier explaining that, the boundary restrictions, and all the other major stuff. I'll connect with your aunt periodically for updates, which she agreed to upon enrollment." She moved toward the front, where she pointed to the black speaker mounted close to the door. "Each cabin has an intercom for communication. We also use two-way radios for learning exercises outside of the camp perimeter and other activities that might keep us away from the main area for too long. They are to be checked back into the office to charge when finished. I think that's all for now. If you have questions tonight, Keira can help. She'll also show you to breakfast in the morning and maybe around the main area."

After Rosie's eyes met Keira, she replied with a genuine smile, "I can do that, sure."

"Good," Rosie said. "Have a good first night, Teagan."

"Thank you." I watched her turn and exit, pulling the thick front door closed. The rickety screen door slapped shut a second after.

When I shifted my eyes, they met Keira's stare. I was happy to find it rather calm, not unwelcoming. She looked me over and bit her lips together, sizing me up silently. In her defense, she hadn't sniffed the air to scent me. Well, at least not blatantly like the guys had earlier, or enough to make me notice.

I let out a rush of breath and kept my arms at my side despite them itching to cross at my chest. There was no need to rush to defense when she hadn't made a move yet. "This where we wait for your backup to come to give me a proper ass whoopin' welcome?"

Her thick eyebrows drew together quickly, momentarily confused. Then she threw her head back and released a tremendous laugh that startled me enough to flinch. "'Proper ass-whoopin' welcome?' Christ, that's funny."

I found myself chuckling as her laughter continued.

"There are a couple native Tennesseans here with a southern accent too, and an asshole Texan, but yours has them beat."

"It's only bad tonight because ..." I hesitated, not really sure how guarded I should be.

"I get it," she said with a soft smile. "Emotions bring out our instincts and habits, even if we've trained them to stay hidden."

"True," I agreed, returning her smile and feeling my body relax at her words. She meant more than our human nature. Not that I'd experienced all the wolf instincts, but I knew it took some effort to adjust and suppress certain things after the transition was made.

She tapped her palm onto her wadded-up bedding but hadn't moved to relocate it.

After a silent moment, I glanced into the bedroom. "Are you wanting the back bed? I can move if you'd rather ..."

"No, no. That's okay. Actually," she said, wrinkling her nose up as her gaze fell to the ground. "I'm not supposed to tell you anything. But you seem cool." Her eyes lifted again with a solemn look.

"Um, thanks. You seem cool, too, so please tell me." I let out a breath, faking a chuckle of indifference as best as I could. Whatever it was couldn't be good.

She bit her lips and moved to the window, where she pinched the edge of its curtain to sneak a peek outside. "It's kind of a rite of passage here. First-night antics, ya know? Well, since I'm assigned to stay with you, I'm supposed to be the one to take your stuff and hide it."

"My stuff?"

"Yeah, like your suitcase. While you're sleeping, the cabinmate takes it and stashes it somewhere close. That way it's not a huge deal."

I shook my head with a laugh. "Isn't everyone over eighteen here? That sounds like human summer camp shit."

She laughed lightly, the tone as smooth as her skin. "I know. It's pretty childish, but it's expected. I don't want to face a shitstorm for not doing it, but I'd also hate for you to face the repercussions too. They will do far worse if they think you're getting favored. Which, in a way, you might already be."

"What does that mean?" I couldn't contain the small spike in my tone. I hadn't been shown any favoritism ... had I?

She grimaced for a moment, then her lips evened out.

"The kitchen?" I asked, figuring it out. She had looked surprised when Rosie had mentioned it.

"Yes. That's exactly it. I have a feeling you're going to get more than the usual newbie break-in here, especially when you step foot into the kitchen for chore time."

Now it was my turn to grimace. "I can tell Rosie I'll do whatever the normal schedule is for newbies. I don't mind." And I didn't mind one bit. I'd rather bust my ass than have my ass beat. Why in the hell was I even here again? *Safety. Protection.* My aunt might be delusional if she thinks I'll be protected here.

"No, that won't work. Rosie and Tim already see you in a favorable light."

"I have no idea why. I've already made problems."

"Really?" She quirked an eyebrow as if calling me on my bullshit. But I had no bullshit, and I sure as hell wasn't lying.

"Really what?"

Her eyebrow fell and her face morphed into a pensive look as she glanced around the cabin. "Do you know anything about this place?"

"Not really, no. Just some rumors told by neighboring packs in Alabama. I didn't have time to search for more info."

"To outsiders, this place is an independent rehab that never has openings. In reality, it runs on donations. Some donors came here themselves. Mostly, though, donors are family members from well-off packs, often related to those currently here. They keep camp operating. Enrollment was cut off as soon as you came, and it's not because we're full. There's room."

"But I thought the other cabins—"

"Oh, they are busted, yeah, but they're being fixed up. Part of the chores …" she trailed off and looked around again uneasily.

"So what are you saying exactly?" She needed to spell it out because it wasn't making much sense to me.

"Your aunt dropped some mad money for you to come here and requested no one else be enrolled for a while."

"What?" I could guess why Aunt Sonya would do it. Limiting the numbers around me was smart. But … "How do you know that?"

She shrugged and let out a breath. When I simply gaped at her, she admitted, "My boyfriend Mike broke into the office earlier and saw your file. But don't get any ideas of swearing us to secrecy because I can tell you right now that everyone already knows. Everyone's always digging for info in the office. And that's why I need you to go along with the usual first-night prank for both of us, even if it is childish. You'll be better off, especially since I won't be staying here tonight. Well, any night, actually."

"Um, why? Will someone break in here too?"

She chuckled a little. "No, they won't go that far. And I'm not staying because, frankly, this place reeks of Koni and Zavier. Mike's the only one I want to smell like. And I already bunk with him in one of the busted cabins. It doesn't have a working bathroom, but the community shower is next door to it, so we use that."

"Oh," I said lamely, suddenly concerned with most everything she mentioned.

"Don't worry," she said, obviously picking up on my distress. "I heard what happened earlier and was warned by the sisters not to make nice with you. But really, I don't like them. I've always been more of a loner, until I met Mike, anyway. But you seem cool." Her eyes danced over me and narrowed on my Kate Spade backpack and my aunt's Gucci suitcase. "Even though you look a bit ..."

"Uppity?" I frowned. There was no need to explain the suitcase wasn't mine. Compared to everyone I'd met here so far, I supposed I looked preppy enough without it. My eyebrows were naturally thick and tidy, my nose was small and pert, and my lips were evenly plump with no filler. "It's not exactly what you're thinking."

She tapped a finger to her chin and gave a wan smile. She was beautiful and wasn't polished either. Her lips were chapped and her nails were nubs and bare. It didn't detract from her, though.

It made her real in the best way. She was someone not trying too hard to fit into any specific box. It was refreshing. I'd tried to please my family for years, and it all meant nothing. The only thing they wanted from me was the one thing I had no control of—transition.

Her finger stilled then lifted into the air. "You're here, so it's likely you aren't as well off as some. But you have nice clothes and things, which means your family gave you some shiny toys while they kept your runt-ass hidden."

I let out a breathy laugh. "Pretty much."

She nodded and chuckled. "Well ... the sisters, they judge because they have their own issues. No excuse, but it is what it is. Also, you're hot, so you're a threat to them."

"I'm not here to be a threat. I just want to do what needs done and leave when the time comes." I bit my lips together, wondering if I should press further. "What about the guys?"

Her eyebrows jumped upward then she gave a knowing smirk. "Oh yes. You're definitely a different kind of threat to them."

"Should I know anything about them?" When she didn't reply right away, I added, "Since everyone already knows things about me, I'd like to be a bit more prepared if I can."

"I don't think it's a good idea for me to dish all the dirt. But ..." She let the last word hang in the air, the effect as enticing as it was torturous. "The four guys you met—Loch, Elijah, Zavier, and Koni. They are hot. Not as hot as my Mike, of course." She whispered the last words, grinning conspiratorially and making me feel as if we'd been friends for years. "They're loners, like most everyone else here, but they've formed a bit of a pack themselves, which has kept others in check, especially a couple douchebags who think they run the place. Jackson and Trig. Those two are of the privileged variety, with families who have money and have donated quite a lot here. They've all fought, mostly while out training."

I considered all the information. "And do the four ... I mean ... Are they with ..."

"The sisters?" She finished for me and let out a harsh breath. "Nope. Not for the lack of trying on the sisters' part, though. They've been after those guys for the entire month they've been here. Nothing's happened as far as I know. I've only scented the douchebags on them."

"Do you think there's a reason?"

Her lips pursed, and her eyes danced around. "I'm not sure. I don't know any of them very well. But the sisters aren't very serious about this place. They're from some established pack out west, sent here right after being booted from boarding school. They messed around too much, and this is their last chance to get right or some shit. Anyway, about the guys ... They're close but not the kind of close that makes you assume they're gay. I've never seen them touching each other or anything. I honestly think they just aren't into hookups. They've also been here the longest and are seriously focused on training and school. No one's seen their files, but if the nicknames they've called each other are any hint of their past ... they don't come from money or weren't treated very well if they do."

"Nicknames?" I was being nosy, sure. Yet, I couldn't stop my curiosity.

"Runt, Stray, Bait, and Stud. I've heard them used a time or two. Rarely, though. I think they're the type of nicknames that only the closest people to you have a right to use, ya know?" Her eyes widened, and she gasped, making me jump and twist around, fearing someone was behind me. "Oh! I'm sorry that scared you. I was just shocked at how much stuff just spewed from my mouth. I hadn't planned to tell you all of that. I haven't had this long of a conversation with anyone in a while, aside from Mike."

"Ya 'bout gave me a heart attack." I inhaled deeply to calm down. "And I know what you mean. You're easy to talk to. I feel like I've known you longer than a half-hour."

At the mention of time, she lifted her wrist to view a black beaded watch there. "It's already eight. Tonight's class session should be ending soon, so I'm gonna take off. I should wait until like midnight, but I doubt anyone will be watching. Only in the morning, maybe, to see your reaction. So be sure to put on a little of a freak-out show as you walk around the cabin and find your stuff."

"Okay," I said, drawing the word out as I processed her instructions. I wanted to ask her more, about camp, about the guys ... maybe even their nicknames. But I knew I'd be pushing the new friendship too far if I did.

"You need to change into your pj's. Otherwise, everyone will know I warned you. The rest of your clothes need to be in your suitcase, so it looks like I took it all. You can keep the backpack, phone, whatever else to keep busy. It's only the semi-naked humiliation we're after."

When she blinked at me with expectant eyes, I finally followed her instructions, setting my toothbrush and hairbrush in the bathroom and changing, all the while staring at the shower I longed to take. I stuffed my other clothes into the bag and offered it to her as I exited the bathroom. She pulled it to the door, and I looked on, hoping this wasn't some horrible setup.

After peeking outside, she gave me a reassuring smile. "I'll be back at seven-thirty. You can look before I get here if you want. I'll put it behind the center bush at the back of the cabin. Night."

"Night," I replied as she carried my stuff outside. I stared at the screen door for another minute, not quite sure how to process what had happened. This was a trust fall of huge proportions. With a deep breath, I moved to close the main door. Before shutting it entirely, movement outside caught my eye. Something shifted between the cabin and the lake, barely noticeable in the dim light. Blurry. Fluffy. Fur. My eyes focused and finally locked onto the unmistakable shine of two eyes in the blackness.

Wolf. I'd seen plenty of my kind during all times of day and night, but this was the first I'd seen here. I inhaled, both comforted and worried. One person here wanted to keep tabs on me.

4

I woke with a start, gasping for breath. Nightmares of fighting alongside my family the night they died had taken over most of my sleep. For the first few wakeful moments, comprehension failed. It was as if I had really been there, trying to stop them, save them. The details of reality trickled in until the previous day's events hit me completely, forcing my eyes open. My arms and hands clutched greedily at the blankets, at the pillow beneath my face, trying to capture any form of comfort from them but only finding the evidence of misery in the pillowcase dampened by my tears. While I remained warm from sleep, my fitful body started to cool rapidly from the frigid cabin air and from dawning realization. I was at camp. Alone.

Not wanting to surrender to the cold morning yet, I stretched my limbs and shifted my face off the pillow, buried it into the mattress, and inhaled deeply. The thin sheet had done little to mask the lovely scent of maleness. I knew if I was able to smell it well, then Keira had been truthful about the cabin reeking to her. After she'd left and I'd torn my eyes from the mystery wolf in the night, I'd decided to push both twin beds together. Keira wasn't planning on being my cabinmate, so I wanted to live it up a little. And lived it up I did, at least during the moments I'd been awake. I'd instantly began to fall for the smells lingering on the beds from Koni and Zavier. There were distinct scents from each—pine and earth, and rain and soap. Those mixed in with a rich male musk that was confusing at first. At home, I never lingered near my brother's rooms because they usually stunk. But this wasn't anything like that. Not at all.

I inhaled deeply again, allowing myself to get lost in the pleasure of it. I needed to feel something, and I wouldn't let shame or awkwardness take over what felt so right, so good. I needed something good.

After a few more provocative inhales, I reached for my phone to check the time. Keira was supposed to arrive in a few minutes. I still hadn't showered, but that would have to wait until I got my clothes. I jumped from the bed and went into the bathroom, shivering while I peed, brushed my teeth, and tamed my morning hair. The heater did work, but Rosie had been right about the cabin chill. Knowing it would be far worse outside and not wanting to freeze to death while I acted out my fake outrage in my thin sleep shorts and tank top, I wrapped a blanket around myself and opened the door. Cold air caught in my throat, but it had little to do with the temperature.

The view was breathtaking.

The early morning light shone along the still water of Midnight Lake, sparkling over the soft reflection of the orange dawning sky and the scarce vibrant leaves clinging to some trees. The lake sat in a valley, peaks of the rolling mountainous terrain shooting up all around the camp like surging waves of brown and green sprinkled with color. I shivered again and gripped the blanket tighter, thinking about the show I needed to put on before I could shower and begin my first day.

Even though there was no one in view, I masked the glee I'd felt about the scenery by donning my best frown and glare. My eyes scoured the porch, then the ground, then the bushes around the front. If anyone was watching, chances were good that they were convinced. And I was actually proud of my mediocre acting skills until the moment I realized I no longer had to act. At the back of the cabin, my hands tugged and yanked one bare branch after another, on bush after bush, seeking my suitcase and finding nothing. It wasn't there.

I released a sardonic laugh that was frantic and pained. It was a wild reaction, likely appearing crazy, but it was far better than releasing the sorrowful cry that itched at my throat. I'd been played. How stupid could I have been?

"Hey!" I heard Keira's voice and turned to look at her traitorous face. As soon as she saw me, took in my crazed eyes and pursed lips, her polite smile waned. "Oh shit. What happened?" Putting two and two together rather quickly, she didn't wait for an answer as she tore around me, searching the bushes at my back as if she could magically find what had disappeared.

I scoffed at her and hugged the blanket tighter. "You think I should believe this act too?" There was no hiding the bitter tone because there would be no hiding my skepticism. "I may be country and a little naïve, but I'm not a complete idiot."

"No, wait," Keira said, standing upright before meeting my eyes and stepping closer. "I seriously had nothing to do with this. Honestly. I left your suitcase right here, dead center so you'd have no trouble this morning. I'm not lying."

Her tone was a plea, and her makeup-free face held an expression to match. I shook my head, hoping I didn't regret my gut feelings later. "So someone else stole it."

She nodded and looked around the quiet area. Several groupings of trees divided the cabin and the path leading back to the main area. There was a distant chatter but no noises in the immediate vicinity. "It likely wasn't the girls. Even after what happened last night, I doubt they'd put too much effort into messing with you. They aren't that invested in anything, except maybe dick."

A smile tugged at my lips. "I saw a wolf out front, not long after you left last night."

"Happen to catch their color?"

I rubbed my forehead absently. "They didn't come near the light. Only saw their eye reflection. Dark coloring, maybe ... I can't be certain."

"Well," she said with a huff as her eyes took in the blanket, knowing full well that I was shit out of luck. "I'm really sorry, Teagan. I didn't mean for this to happen."

My only response was a nod and a glance down at my Vans, grateful I'd kept a pair of socks on while I'd slept.

"I'm sure you'll get it back soon. In the meantime, I have a few things you can borrow, or if you want to check the office leftovers …"

While some of her things might fit, the leftovers Rosie had also mentioned had merit. Whoever wanted me stripped of my clothing likely thought that was my only option. I also didn't want to chance ruining Keira's clothes. "I have a feeling that if I borrow your stuff, my clothes might stay gone for longer."

Her mouth popped open. "Ah. You might be right. If it's the guys, it could be retaliation for the cabin. If that's the case, they probably wanna make you uncomfortable for a bit."

"Hopefully not long," I agreed with a sigh.

"Let's take a trip to the office then, see what's in there. We'll have to tell Rosie about your stuff, but I'm sure we can convince her to stay chill about it."

"Okay."

Rosie was indeed flustered by the news of my missing suitcase. She asked a lot of questions, but Keira helped to field them while I dug through the leftover clothes in the office. When Tim entered a few minutes later, Rosie relayed everything to him. Tim wasn't much taller than Rosie and nearly the same build, but that was where the visible similarities ended. He was muted in attire, with a beige T-shirt and khakis, shaggy in appearance, with long scraggly brown hair and matching beard, and plain in looks, with calm, even features. To his credit, he had at least grimaced when Rosie's emphatic and high-pitched explanation assaulted his ears. Though they both explored repercussions, they agreed with us in not making a huge deal of it. They planned to make inquiries privately with mild warnings on returning my things, and Rosie offered to pick up items from the store if I needed more than the leftovers. I was glad it wouldn't become some big production—the least amount of attention on me, the better.

Before Tim and Rosie left, Rosie explained that most others would be heading into the park for training, and I was to meet Zavier to begin my chores. He was tasked with showing me the ropes. She and Tim also issued me a couple of blank notebooks and told me they'd put together an assessment for me soon.

Keira watched them leave, then turned to me with wide eyes as she snatched the pair of guys' sweatpants from my hands. "These are ... new."

"What? No, they're not," I said, poking a finger at a tiny hole in the soft cotton material. They were most definitely worn. But they were free of stains, and the drawstring was intact. That was a win for me. I could certainly roll the top and bottoms and tie them if needed. Despite not having to want for much growing up, I'd never been one to desire too many things. I'd been camping, played in the dirt, and was taught survival tactics when I was younger. It wasn't until later that I was left alone and placated with pretty things my father thought would keep me happy enough to forget my isolation.

"No," she replied, the corner of her lips lifting. "I mean, these weren't in here the other day. These are new leftovers. In fact, a few others are new in there too. Their scent is potent even though they're clean."

"I'm not picky, and I can't smell very well anyway. So I'm taking them."

"I agree. Yes, you are taking them because I'm certain that's the reason they are there."

"What aren't you sayin'?" I asked, picking through other things in the dresser drawers. I'd already nabbed a puke-green colored parka that Rosie said had been at camp for several years and had been thoroughly used each winter. It had a few rips along the seams and two missing buttons, but the zipper still worked, and the hood was faux fur lined—a matted mess of fur, but it would block any wind that managed to cut through this wooded area.

"I'm saying that I know who these belonged to. And also that V-neck, regular T-shirt, and this other pair of dark blue sweats." She dropped the gray pair and picked through the other clothes with a wicked grin.

"And I should want to know because?"

"Because it's probably who took your suitcase."

"What? You think someone not only wanted me to be humiliated by having to wear the camp's leftover clothes, but they wanted me to wear their own too? Why do that?"

"To claim you," she said matter-of-factly as she slid her hair over her shoulder and crossed her arms over her chest.

I rolled my eyes. "It seems like too much work, let alone ridiculous, presumptuous, and a bit pervy."

"All of that, sure, but still highly possible. I'll give you four guesses."

That made me pause. She was absolutely saying it was one of The Four. I pinched the leg of the gray sweats, lifted the material under my nose, and took a whiff, my eyes still locked on her.

Her smile grew, and she waggled her eyebrows suggestively. "Now who's being pervy?"

They did have the distinct male scent. Despite my underdeveloped ability, I could tell the basic difference between female and male—a male scent was usually richer and more alluring to females. And even being a runt, I could pick up a bit more subtleties in smells than the average human could, especially pertaining to others of my kind. We all had unique scents. The broadest of which could be used to identify where we came from. This material smelled a bit like pepper and maybe cedar. My nose had gotten acquainted enough with Koni's and Zavier's mattresses to know it wasn't them. So that left two. "After what happened last night when I arrived, why would Loch or Elijah bother?"

"Nice job," she admitted. "And you're right. It does seem like too much of a hassle to bother. It really could be a coincidence that he dumped the clothes. I don't see it being a big deal either way."

"So who then?"

Her lips quirked up as she began stacking the rest of the clothes into my arms. "A hundred percent Loch's."

Chest Number One. The one who had called me feisty runt and a good girl for releasing my hold on Nima. A chill ran up my back, thinking of his voice and his intensity. If the clothes were his game, I'd play. I may be the newbie and a runt, but I'd never been one to back down when challenged. I could get feisty, all right.

5

By the time I'd gotten dressed and walked to the dining hall, all the others were gone. I'd really wanted to shower, but as my bad luck continued, the water wasn't working. And that was odd considering the towels Rosie had picked up from the floor the previous night had been wet, and the toilet and sink had worked when I'd woken up.

I'd spent only a few more minutes with Keira before Mike had collected her for the group training exercises in the woods. Mike seemed nice based on our brief greeting. He stood a few inches taller than her, his curly hair adding another two or more. There was a gleam in his dark blue eyes when he looked at her and a genuine smile on his narrow face while she spoke, but he remained mostly quiet. They both were working on their GEDs and had hooked up because of their similar childhoods in foster care in different states—she was from Ohio, and he was from Illinois. During our last bit of time, she also mentioned there were several loners on the property that occupied the upper cabins farther from the lake. They were here for rehab, struggling with addiction or simply maintaining their lives outside in the human world. She elaborated about them a little more than Rosie had in my introduction, noting that they often helped Rosie and Tim protect the area and rarely interacted with those of us here for more brief stays.

The dining hall was as old as the other cabins and even cleaner. Wooden beams. Wooden benches. Wooden tables. All of it a lighter wood than what was in the office and my cabin. Pine likely. The upkeep inside was apparent. The floor looked as if it had been sanded and refinished at least once since it was built. There were a few paintings on the wall—one of the lake, one of the woods, and the last of two gray wolves sitting together. The artist had to have stayed at some point.

My stomach rumbled as I caught a whiff of baked goods drifting from behind the closed swinging doors that led to the kitchen. I made my way back there at a quick pace, realizing that the only dinner I'd had the previous night was the small protein bar I'd stashed in my purse before leaving home.

As soon as I pushed through the doors, I halted in place, surprised by all the glinting stainless steel. The kitchen was fabulous. I wasn't expecting much for a camp setting, but the working area was larger than The Back Burner's and well equipped. If what Rosie said was true about most of the meals being premade, the equipment wasn't operating to its full potential. I skimmed my finger along the prep counter, then moved to the center island that held bowls of fruit and a stack of wrapped muffins. I snatched one of the blueberry muffins on top, careful not to let the others topple, then dug in. As I took the first bite, a door—to what I gathered was the pantry—swung wide and one of the dazzling four I'd met the previous night walked through. It was Zavier, the dirty-blond with the dual-colored eyes and a hoop through his lower pouty lip. He had other piercings, but that one was undeniably the most noticeable because of that luscious lip. Mmm.

I swallowed the bite of muffin and bit down on my own lip, eyeing him before he noticed me. Strands of his top length of hair had escaped their gelled-back containment and had fallen forward over his brows, tips skimming his lips. His focus was set on the tray of bread loaves he carried, but his eyes found mine as he moved toward the huge island counter. His brows furrowed, and he bit his lips together as if he were suppressing—

He barked a colossal laugh, his wide mouth stretching into the most gorgeous smile I'd ever laid eyes upon. *Good God almighty.* The breath in my lungs seemed to rush from my lips. I was not prepared for that. It took me too long to realize he was laughing at me. At me! I wasn't sure if this was better or worse than the angry greeting I'd received the previous night. With my eyes still locked on his smile, I decided it was better. Who cares if I was the target of his laughter when his smile was gorgeous enough to blind me? Not me. Fuck.

I swallowed again, this time trying to ease the dryness in my throat.

He dropped the tray of bread onto the island with a clank. His laughter and smile were gone, features reset to his natural resting asshole face. "Nice gear." The statement was flat, but his gravelly tone was a sound of dreams.

Gear? Oh! Oh. I looked down at the super baggy T-shirt that could have passed for an off-the-shoulder dress, then stared farther down to the worn gray sweatpants that I'd had to roll, cinch, and tie at my waist and roll again at the ankles to keep them from folding over my Vans. I frowned, then adjusted the T-shirt's stretched neck to cover my bra strap before looking back up to meet his eyes. At least it had warmed up enough outside to skip the parka.

"Yeah, thanks ... it's Zavier, right?" And Runt. That would naturally be his nickname out of the four. The others I would still need to determine.

Ignoring my question, he huffed a breath and swept a hand through his hair to contain the strays. He moved to the end of the long sink, hit the button on the dishwasher, then picked up a bottle of water and took a swig. Whatever dishes had been made at breakfast were already cleared. The area was spotless. And he wasn't. There were a few stains on his white V-neck T-shirt, though I barely noticed. I could only see the way the shirt fit, clinging to his chest almost like a second skin. It was thin enough to see his nipples easily. Regularly fitted jeans covered his lower half, with specks of paint and rips created by work, not fashion. He had on tan work boots too. There was something about boots on a guy that gave him extra sexy points.

"I know Rosie said you'd be in here for chores, but that's not happening. Loch and Eli are in charge of the kitchen. You might help in here if they're busy, but you're the camp newb, so you get to handle the unwanted and random shit."

"Uh ... okay." When he didn't reply after a few moments, I remained quiet and blinked.

"What? No argument? No demands?"

He thought I'd snap like the previous night, thought I was some spoiled brat who wouldn't be willing to get my hands dirty? They didn't want me here. That was obvious enough. Well, they were stuck with me for as long as I was stuck here.

"No," I replied simply. There wasn't much I could argue about, and I was too numb to care about stupid shit. I'd do what I needed to do. If I fought this trivial crap, things would only get worse. Plus, I had a feeling Rosie and Tim didn't micromanage or oversee all the small stuff. Why would they? We were all adults here.

One of his eyebrows drew up as he took another sip from his water bottle. "Okay then ... Teenie." I cringed at the nickname but wouldn't bother correcting him. I didn't mind enough to fight at this point. When I made no retort, he continued, "Grab a water if you want, then follow me. You've got some toilets to clean."

Ugh.

The community bathhouse cabin wasn't nearly as bad as I'd imagined, especially since I had brothers I'd often cleaned up after. *Had* ... I'd *had* brothers. I no longer had them. I shook the thoughts away and refocused. Showers, sinks, and toilets were in separated areas, six stalls of each. They even had changing stalls next to the showers so people could dress without worrying about a slippery floor or walking back to their cabin dripping wet.

I sighed as I took it all in. Zavier's eyes darted to mine. Even though he was expressionless, I knew he was curious about my noise.

"My shower isn't working so ..."

He crossed his arms over his thin shirt, but I saw a flare inside his eyes. Heat. Suddenly I understood his posture. He wasn't irritated with my admission or me in general. He was guarding himself, locking down his emotional response. But I'd seen what his eyes failed to hide. Desire. Craving. It had taken a bit of effort to control those emotions.

"Not working?" he asked, eyes maintaining our connection. It was as if he was struggling to keep them there and not let them wander down my body as he imagined what I knew he was—my showering, him watching. I never was one to blush, but my heart certainly kicked up a notch as my own imagination began to conjure thoughts of him losing that control and letting more than his eyes roam over me. I liked the idea. So much. Maybe too much. Just thinking about his hands touching, wandering, made me recall how long it had been since I'd been touched, held by a male. That sparked my own craving.

"Yeah ..." I whispered, my words faltering as I reined in control. "No, the water isn't working. The toilet and sink ran earlier, but when I went back to the cabin, nothing worked."

"Hmm." He blinked a few times and released his arms to his sides. His face was blank again, his beautiful eyes returning to their distant look. "You can't take one during chores. It'll have to be later."

"Oh yeah, that's fine. I wasn't trying to … Never mind." After looking around, I glanced back up to meet his eyes again. If someone had turned my water off, he wasn't giving any indication that he knew about it. Though, he could have been trying hard to hide it. His laughter in the kitchen after seeing my new clothes had been instant and impossible to contain, which made me think that he hadn't known what Loch had done—or hadn't done if the clothes donation happened to be coincidental. Doubtful.

When Zavier continued to stare at me without comment, I took advantage and asked, "Where are the tools kept?"

He seemed to snap out of his thoughts at the sound of my voice. "Uh. In the shed by the lake and the other near the chow. Most chore supplies are stored in them too, like paint and some cleaners. Except the bathhouse stuff. That stays here. Why?"

"I wanna take a look at my cabin's main waterline later, see if there's something I can do."

He blinked.

I blinked.

"And you're not going to tell Rosie or Tim about the issue?" It felt like his question was about more than my ability and knowledge of general home maintenance. He had to be testing my snitch limit.

"Do I need to?"

He shrugged. "They'd probably task someone to fix it. Might be the best option since you're unfamiliar with the cabins and the piping."

I let a tease of a smile lift my lips. "If it's what I think it is, I shouldn't have a problem fixing it." I'd handled my fair share of issues around the house while my dad and brothers were away on pack business.

"That so?" His lips pressed together with a nod. "Okay then. It'll have to wait until we're done."

"Of course," I agreed.

And that was it. Aside from him explaining how to do the chores, we didn't speak. The bathhouse was easy enough. Clean and restock. After his quick instruction, I could have done it myself, but he had to have been told to stay to make sure I understood because he didn't leave. And while that could have explained why I'd caught him watching me several times, given the intensity behind those different colored irises, I was positive he wasn't merely checking my mirror cleaning and tile scrubbing techniques. Usually, the idea of a guy leering at me was a turnoff. This wasn't quite the same, though. It wasn't creepy or intimidating. His gaze held a curiosity too, or maybe his stoic look had seeped into me enough to ease my concern. I was just as curious, mainly because I hadn't experienced this reaction to a guy before. The need to know him pierced through me as smooth and as sharp as a sliver of glass—the pain unnoticeable at first, then all at once with unrelenting urgency.

6

We took a break for lunch well after the others had eaten and either returned to training or retreated to their cabins. Zavier pointed out the lunch items in the kitchen—mostly sandwich fixings—then told me I had a half hour, not to make a mess, and to meet him at the laundry cabin. After eating alone, I went back to my cabin to check the water.

Unsurprisingly, it still wasn't working. And despite wanting to go search for a wrench or maybe relax with an ebook on my phone, I wound up killing the final minutes of my break attempting to find a cell or Wi-Fi signal walking along the lake's edge. It was a worthless effort, especially since there was no real reason. It wasn't as if I needed to talk to Aunt Sonya. We'd never exactly been close, and I'd seen her only twenty-four hours before. Though, I supposed I missed her a little. Missed home. That thought made me laugh out loud. It felt ridiculous to miss a place where my last name was likely loathed by the few remaining wolves in the area—those who hadn't been killed.

But the place was all I'd ever truly had.

Passing the dining hall and crossing the camp's main pathway on my way to the laundry cabin, I heard shouting. Angry and vicious. Near snarling. No one else was around. I hurried on, worried that someone had been hurt. Past the path's bend, two guys stood, hands on hips, near cabin number three. Laundry. Even in the daylight, I recognized one of them. He had gotten the blow job from Nerine near the shed the previous night. Jackson. Zavier and Koni had talked about him, about his love for bj's and for causing The Four problems. That would make the other guy Trig. Jackson's head of dirty blond hair was shaved close to his skull. Trig's haircut was practically the same, only light brown in color. Both of their backs were bare, and only gym shorts covered their lower bodies. Facing the cabin, they hadn't yet noticed me. They'd either finished their training early or had stayed after lunch.

My eyes shot to the door, hearing another scream and seeing the single rod of metal threaded through the latch outside. They'd locked Zavier inside. But why would he get so irate over this prank when he knew I'd be here for chores? His conversation with Koni the previous night came back to me. He'd been hot and angry, dealing with his transition. Sometimes the tiniest of things could set off the anger. Everyone was different in their levels of emotion and discomfort, but it was worse for runts. Supposedly, the latency amplified it all. At least that was what I'd heard. Pack members used to whisper these facts around me as I awaited my change as if amplifying my fear would help the transition come faster. Nope. I already knew what was to come. Pain. Though, that wasn't the worst part. The uncomfortable feeling of being trapped inside your own skin was said to be unbearable, like a constant crawl beneath the surface. And aside from taking hard narcotics that could withstand the burn of a wolf's system longer than simple ibuprofen, there was only one other thing that tamped down the sensation and lessened the time and intensity of each wave. Sex. Actually, the hormones and endorphins released before orgasms. Yep. That was a very valid reason for sex.

"Motherfuckers! Shit!" Zavier's shouts morphed into coughs just as pink smoke seeped from the cracks of the barred door.

They'd locked him in with a smoke bomb?! Lovely. The prank wasn't as simple as I'd assumed.

Before I even considered my actions or repercussions they could bring, I sprinted toward the small cabin. I couldn't stand by and watch it go down. After spending a few hours with Zavier, I liked him. Whether he felt the same or not didn't matter. I'd probably do the same for anyone. Well, maybe not the assholes who had just noticed me running at them.

"Uh-oh. Look what we have here." The words came from Jackson, his voice sounding more accented than during his groans of pleasure while Nerine had her mouth on his dick. Sounded southern. Maybe Texan. Oh! He was the asshole accented Texan Keira had mentioned.

"The new runt," Trig said. His tone didn't have the warmth a southern accent held and was oddly high pitched, making him sound like a runt himself. He was far from that, though. Both were. The closer my legs brought me to them, the larger they seemed. Their bodies were as intimidating as The Four, bare muscles chiseled with definition. They had power and strength I couldn't ignore. As much as I wanted to avoid them, there was no way to. I had to pass right by them to get to Zavier.

Their eyes widened then narrowed as they realized I wasn't stopping. As soon as I was within distance, their arms reached for me, hands wide to grab hold. I lunged sideways to the edge of the path, out of their grasp, and pushed myself harder toward the door.

"What's this? One runt to rescue another?" Jackson said.

Deep rumbles of laughter followed me. And for a few moments, I naively thought they'd scatter off to their cabin. I was wrong. Their footfalls pounded hard and fast behind me. I grabbed hold of the metal rod, my breaths as heavy as Zavier's coughs from inside.

"Now, now," Jackson said, and a hand wrapped around my extended arm, stopping me from removing the rod and pulling me backward.

I followed his movement without a fight, allowing my body to twist in his direction. I tucked my other arm in close as I rotated.

"Don't worry your pretty little—"

Before he could end the sentence, I swung my free arm outward and my clenched fist connected with his bony nose.

"Ah! Fuck!" His hand instantly released me and flew to cover his face. "Bitch!"

I spun around, unlatched the door, and pushed it open, not wanting to waste a single second, worried there wouldn't be another chance.

Pink smoke billowed out from the opening, and Zavier rushed out through the cloud.

I backed against the outer wall of the cabin as his large body moved past, sputtering and coughing. Trig and Jackson had retreated several steps as well, though not too far.

"Shit," Jackson mumbled into his hands. Blood leaked out between his fingers. He pulled his hands away and more coated his mouth and chin too. "You stupid bitch."

My hands remained clenched at my sides as I watched his eyes focus on me. Trig's were as well. Both of them looked positively pissed, and they weren't very far away. "Don't touch me again." It was a reminder of who was to blame and a warning in case any more dumb ideas sprouted in their heads.

The pink smoke dissolved into a haze, and Zavier's cough had stopped, but I didn't dare look away from the two guys at the corner of the cabin. They were too close for comfort.

Jackson growled and wiped more blood from under his nose. "Is that a threat? Because you can bet I won't let this shit go—"

A whistle pierced the air, drawing our attention to the pathway. Loch, Koni, and Elijah stood where Jackson and Trig had been before. Loch dropped his fingers from his mouth and tipped his chin up. Zavier had stopped coughing a few steps away. His eyes were glaring and intense, rage written all over his usually indifferent face.

I felt like a bug underneath a microscope, my limbs twitchy, muscles ready to fight or flee. Though the pink haze had thinned, the air itself was thick and charged with anticipation.

At least the others were all fully dressed. I was already struggling to keep focused. More bare-chested-guy porn was the last thing I needed at the moment.

While the others all looked serious with their jaws clenched and lips pressed, Elijah's full lips curved up into a daring smirk as if he were eager for the battle. "You thought this was a good idea? Take a shot at Z before we got back? Is this about losing the tracking exercise this morning?"

My eyes drifted to Loch, seeing his hard stare already focused on me. I instantly became more aware that his clothes covered me, like they were the cause of my body heating and not his gaze. Despite not seeing any reaction from him, simply thinking about the way his clothes felt and the possible reasons I was wearing them made a shiver run through me. It was a serious struggle, but I managed to stay still.

Those eyes swept from me to Jackson and Trig, and his brows drew lower as he said, "Leave. Before you lose more blood."

Trig blew out a breathy laugh. "Man, fuck that, and fuck you."

Shit.

Fists clenched and shoulders pulled back, The Four took a few steps forward.

"No, no," Jackson said, holding up a bloody hand to his friend as if he were going to smack him in the chest but thought better of smearing his blood on him. "Leave it, man. We'll deal later."

"Sure," Koni piped up as he reached Zavier's side. "Later, pussies." His long, wavy hair was captured in a ponytail that folded over itself at the back of his head. Without the obstruction, his narrow face and those to-die-for high cheekbones were on full display.

After a stern glare in my direction, Trig and Jackson took off up the pathway to their cabin, I supposed.

"What the fuck!" Zavier yelled, throwing his arm into the air. "I wanted to beat their asses now. Dammit!"

"No, asshole. You'll get your chance after," Koni said as both of them walked the few steps back to the others.

After ... after his transition.

"Fuck that! Now! I would have already if they hadn't been punk-asses and locked me inside." He stared down, stretching his T-shirt out in front, noticing the smoke bomb had left a thin layer of pink on his clothes. "Fuck!"

Koni chuckled but quickly covered his mouth with his hand to stifle it. Zavier punched him in the shoulder, hard enough to knock him back a step.

"You know we can't risk it. Rosie and Tim don't need that shit happening inside the cabin perimeter, disturbing all the others," Elijah said, crossing his arms.

The simple act of rubbing a palm over my sore knuckles called attention back to me, ending their discussion and my brief glimpse into their lives. Their heads whipped in my direction, and they all stared.

Shit. I ran the same palm over my bicep where Jackson had grabbed me, knowing his grip had been hard enough to bruise. It was sore too, but I'd live. All of their eyes seemed to follow the movement, so I dropped my hand and prepared to say something, anything to break the awkward silence.

When I opened my mouth to speak, Loch beat me to it. Dropping his eyes from me, he said to them, "We've gotta prep for dinner. Clean up." He nodded to Zavier's clothes.

"Right," Zavier replied. And as the others turned and started down the main path, he glanced at me one more time, his blank expression back in place, before following behind them.

7

The laundry cabin closely resembled the inside of a Pepto Bismol bottle when I'd first walked through the door. Now, though, the pink was finally gone—the four washers and dryers, walls and cabinetry, and all other appliances and cleaning products were wiped clean of the smoky coating. And if I never saw the color pink again, I would be just fine.

After the guys had taken off, I knew it was my job to clean. I couldn't bet on any of them returning, even though I had a feeling Zavier might have eventually. At one point, I'd heard someone outside, though no one entered. Still, I didn't mind, and I wasn't angry they left me to fix the assholes' mess. What else was I going to do? I was here. I had chores. I was safe. My indifference could have had to do with my numbness. Would I have protested this kind of work had I been home, had my father and brothers still been alive? I had no idea. I took care of the place more than them, anyway.

People traveled around outside, to and from the dining hall for dinner. The pathways had quieted again by the time I left the laundry cabin. It was also already dark.

"Damn. That's a fall if I've ever seen one," a female voice said as I neared the dining hall. Under the closest light, I spotted the triplets walking toward me.

Lovely.

I kept my head up but didn't reply as they passed. They looked a bit too pristine with their punk looks, each having some form of spiked accessory or jewelry. After Keira had told me about this being their last chance and coming from a wealthy pack out west, I understood their rebellion. They were bucking their family's rules, possibly playing misfit to gain leverage. But they must have done enough damage to land them here, so who was I to assume how legit their life was. I didn't know them, and they didn't know me.

"So true, Nesma. Wow, ho, you look like trash, and you stink!" another quipped, wrinkling her nose in a disgusted look.

"What the fuck are you wearing?" the last asked. Nima. She had the septum piercing and lotus neck tattoo that immediately identified her. "Wait, whose clothes are those? Are they ..."

I still didn't speak, just kept walking. Maybe it was stupid to expose my back to them, but I was tired. Too tired for their bullshit. My arms hurt from scrubbing the pink off of everything. I'd discovered that Jackson and Trig had lit and slung an entire box of smoke bombs inside the laundry cabin, after they had nailed the windows shut at some point. It had been planned, and that was why Zavier couldn't escape. He'd doused several with water, evident by the soggy cardboard tubes left inside the utility sink and on the floor. But others had rolled beneath the washers or behind cabinets. Ugh.

"Bitch, I'm talking to you. Whose shit—"

"Hey!" Keira appeared with Mike a ways up the pathway, exiting cabin two—the classroom. She leaned to the side a bit to see who was behind me, then shook her head.

I stopped in front of the dining hall's short walkway as they approached. "Hey. Haven't eaten yet." I pointed toward the wide door, ignoring the sisters. They must have given up their inquisition because I heard their footsteps disappear as Keira and Mike got closer.

"Eventful day?" she asked, and both wrinkled their noses.

Mike was carrying most of their notebooks in one hand and grasping her hand with the other, which was adorable. His curly hair stood extra high, looking as though he'd run his fingers through it ... or had yanked at it during their study session. He remained quiet, eyeing me with a look that held sympathy and maybe a bit of disgust.

My eyes dropped to see what they were seeing while I pinned my arms down, afraid my pits might be rank enough to knock them out if they caught a large whiff. Unfortunately, my deodorant had been in my stolen suitcase.

"Yeah, it was. Sorry. I really have to shower after I eat. I also need to fix the water in my cabin. But for now, food then shower."

The dining hall door opened, and The Four exited with another guy I assumed to be their cabinmate Vic. I was stunned for a moment as their stares met mine. All of their eyes seemed to narrow, the single lamplight near the entrance highlighting their scrutiny. Except for Vic, who looked to be the smallest of the group. He had blondish hair and a frat-boy look to him with khaki shorts and a white polo. Definitely more clean-cut than the others. Zavier had already showered and changed, his skin and dark blond hair no longer dusted with the bright pink now staining my clothes.

"What? Your water's out?" Mike spoke this time, drawing my attention back to them.

"Yeah. I—I have a feeling I can fix it, but I'll probably just wait until tomorrow. I'm a stinky mess and tuckered out." My body shivered as the warmth from physical work started to fade away and the evening's chill settled into my baggy clothes, which were still damp from scrubbing and cleaning.

"Tuckered out. Okay," Keira replied with a tiny laugh at my accent and choice of words, then glanced over at The Four. I could feel them still watching, though I didn't look. "Don't let the sisters get to you. And tell us if you need anything. Cabin eight, by the bathhouse."

"Right. Thanks." I nodded and finally moved for the dining entrance.

"Hey, runt girl," Elijah said in his smooth tone, glancing back as The Four walked the other pathway toward the lake cabins. "Don't get that pink shit all over the place in there."

He turned before seeing my nod and sigh combo, but Zavier saw. His head tilted as he studied me for a few more seconds, his face even more unreadable in the night shadows. He rounded the corner and disappeared with them a moment later.

I huffed a breath. What had I been expecting? A thank you? For helping him? For cleaning up the mess made by the assholes? Nah.

I knew better than to expect something like that. I'd barely gotten recognition or appreciation from my family, so receiving it from any of them seemed even more laughable. My expectation of this place and the people here was still nothing. Maybe this place was keeping me safe, maybe not. Maybe it would help my transition, maybe not. I was here for now. That was all I knew.

Most of the hanging lights in the dining hall were out except for one closest to the kitchen. It was almost eerie at night. The kitchen also had a single light on and was spotless as usual. All dishes from dinner were either drying on racks or being cleaned in the dishwasher. I poked around the refrigerator and the pantry, allowing myself to explore more than I'd been able to earlier in the day. Some sections were labeled with names and cabin numbers to show owners of prepared or leftover meals. And it was stocked with more fresh items than I'd expected after hearing about their ready-made meal reliance. It was natural that easy food was the most popular. Not many people chose to cook from scratch, especially when a quicker option was available.

Lots of meal ideas hit me as I rooted through the fresh veggies, but ultimately I took the quick and easy choice tonight too. All the scrubbing had left me feeling too drained for meal prep. I popped a frozen burrito into the microwave and downed some water while waiting. I ate in record time, barely tasting it before heading to my cabin to get my night clothes and the puke-green parka—so I wouldn't become an icicle on the walk back from the bathhouse.

Even though I held an odd fear of showering in a community bathhouse, I was too tired and smelly to succumb to it. Not seeing anyone along the path also helped ease any worry. All was quiet. I stripped off Loch's sweats and T-shirt, knowing I'd have to wash them and my night clothes the next day. Tonight, I had to wash my bra, underwear, and socks in the shower with me and let them dry overnight. There was still hope that my clothes would be returned at some point, but I doubted it'd be anytime soon. And I surely wouldn't sit around and throw a hissy fit because that was exactly what whoever took them wanted.

At least the showers had containers of free liquid soap and shampoo that I'd helped restock earlier.

I had to pry myself from the scalding water, which felt more heavenly than hellish on my skin and muscles. When I finished wringing out my socks and undergarments, I dressed in the changing area and readied myself for the chilly walk to my cabin. Before I could whip open the door of the stall, a voice halted me.

"Go the fuck away." The tone was low, menacing.

"Aw, c'mon now, Runt. You don't get to block the bathhouse." Texas voice. *Jackson*. And Runt…

"Try me. Pretty sure your nose won't survive another hit today." It was definitely Zavier's voice, but it was deep, nearly a growl.

"That anger's gonna eatcha up before the transition, Runt. Hope ya survive." Jackson's laughter trailed off.

Heavy breaths invaded the cabin, then came several loud crashes and bangs in succession. I gripped my items close and jumped from the stall, prepared to run. Instead, I stopped in my tracks.

Zavier yelled again and punched the standing cabinet two more times, its flimsy door unlatching with the force, clean towels spilling out onto the floor at his feet.

"Hey," I whispered. "Are you okay?"

His entire body stiffened, but his breaths continued loud and hard, his chest heaving. He kept his head down, only one side visible to me. "You should go."

I walked closer, freely consuming the sight of his solid frame. He'd changed again, now wearing sweats and a thin white T-shirt, likely what he wore to sleep. The shirt had bunched at his waist from his last punch, showing some skin above his low-hanging sweats, the very top of his ass cheek and the cut lines of his hipbone on full display. He wore nothing underneath. His long strands of hair fell forward with the angle of his tipped face, no product slicking it back. His lips remained parted, breaths rushing in and out between them.

"I know why you're here," I admitted. It didn't take a genius to figure it out. He knew I needed to shower out here and had been guarding me.

"Doesn't matter. You need to go."

"Thank you," I said clearly, wanting him to know how much the gesture meant, even if my logic was off, even if he didn't do it on purpose. But I had a gut feeling I wasn't wrong. "You didn't—"

He spun on me fast, and my instinct forced me to take a single step back so his body wouldn't collide with mine. Inches separated us. I tipped my face up because of the proximity, finally meeting his downcast eyes. One blue, one brown. So beautiful. I inhaled and was hit with a stronger scent than what still lingered faintly on my night clothes and my cabin mattresses. It was a scent that had evaded me all day while we'd worked together. We hadn't been this close, and I'd been curious ever since I'd woken up, wondering which bed was his, which of the scents I'd reveled in belonged to him.

Soap and rain.

Fresh and clean and enticing.

His nostrils flared as he continued to breathe heavily. "You smell like …"

I felt brave being so close to him. I also felt an urge to bury my face into his chest the way I had with his mattress. Damn, he was making me feel all kinds of things. "I smell like you and Koni. I slept in your beds last night, in these clothes."

8

A low rumble vibrated from his throat as his eyes roamed farther down my body, taking in my skimpy shorts and the tank top covering my braless chest. My boobs weren't large, but they were big enough to show their natural, weighty curves without a bra, not to mention the currently puckered nipples begging to be noticed. They had hardened at the first sight of him, but his vocal reaction to smelling his scent on me was making them so hard they ached.

"You need to leave," he said.

That anger still stormed beneath his skin, though I knew my actions, my presence had already calmed him some. After what he'd just done for me, I wanted to ease that rage even more. I wanted to touch him.

"I don't want to leave. I want to help."

"I don't need your gratitude or your pity," he replied with tight words, closing his eyes but not moving. As if speaking an afterthought, he added, "You've helped enough."

I smiled a little, accepting the small show of thanks for the earlier laundry incident. "You're welcome."

His eyes popped wide before narrowing down at me. Still, he didn't move.

"I want to touch you. Can I?" I asked, dropping my clothes to the floor and lifting an empty hand. He closed his eyes again and shook his head ever so slightly in response. "I understand why you wouldn't want me to. We barely know each other. But I only want to help, and this doesn't need to mean anything. You don't even need to talk to me if you don't want to. No strings. No promises."

"Why?" The question pushed through his clenched teeth as the muscles in his jaw flexed.

"I want to feel ... something. Anything." The truth tumbled from my thoughts onto my lips, deep and sorrowful. He didn't know me, didn't know what I'd been through. And I didn't know him. I wanted him, though, if even for a few minutes. To touch and feel and help him ease that rage within.

His eyes opened wide at my admission, and he inhaled more deeply. I leaned closer and instantly felt the poke of his erection at my stomach. That drove me on, knowing he wanted me, needed my touch as much as I needed his. I lifted one hand to his cheek, relishing the coarse scruff there, then ran my thumb over his lower, pouty lip and the hoop near the side. My other hand moved to his solid chest first before sliding downward.

He exhaled, and his eyelids fluttered closed for a few moments, taking in my touch. His muscles flexed and twitched beneath my fingers as I pushed lower, lower, until I met an exposed sliver of his warm skin. His tongue licked out across his lip, skimming my thumb. I lifted it, caressing the tip before he pulled it back into his mouth.

"Can I stroke you?" I asked, holding my hand in place along the edge of his sweats, waiting for permission. I had never completed a full hand job. I'd touched dicks before, but those encounters had led straight to sex. I'd watched enough porn to learn, though. Seeing a guy being stroked or stroking himself did fabulous things to me, helped me get off more times than anything else.

"Fuck," he growled the word, every muscle in his body still taut with the emotion he struggled to keep control. "Yes. Do it, please. Touch me."

I licked my lips with a smile. Then I dropped my hand from his face, sliding it down his back to hook and push down the edge of his sweats so I could grab the top of his bare ass. The other hand shoved the front down at the same time, freeing his cock. I wasn't the least bit surprised to find him now fully erect, hard and waiting. With the first contact of my fingers, Zavier sucked a breath through his teeth, and his cock jerked. I slid my loose grip down the length of him, feeling, memorizing. I grabbed his ass cheek firmly while my other hand tightened around his shaft and began pumping.

"Oh shit," he uttered, his eyes unfocused now, his breaths evening out. His body moved forward and turned us, backing me to the wall where he pressed a hand somewhere high against it for balance. His other hand moved first to my shoulder then slipped under my wet, limp hair to the side of my jaw, his palm and fingers cradling my face.

Seeing the way he positioned us, braced himself, shot bolts of heat through me, straight between my legs. The simple action, dominant yet surrendering, had me squeezing my thighs together, yearning for some friction while dampness pooled. I had no underwear on, and the shorts were too loose to do me any favors.

But I wasn't worried about myself as much as I was about him. He needed this release. Badly. His thumb slid over my lips as mine had done to his a minute before. I parted them, inviting him inside. His eyes flashed, then he pushed it inside. I bathed it with my tongue before closing my mouth and sucking it in.

He groaned at the sight, and I kept stroking him, his cock hot and silky. He felt so good.

Precum leaked from him, and I used it to massage his tip as I moved my other hand around front to cup his balls. His entire area was trimmed and smooth, and the manscaping turned me on even more.

"Mmm. Ahh." He panted, his eyes still locked on my mouth as I sucked and swirled my tongue around his thumb. "I want to kiss you." The words were calm and seductive. He'd relaxed into this sensation, the anger nowhere to be seen or heard.

I nodded and released his thumb. His face dipped farther, and his eyes shifted back and forth, looking deep, studying me before pressing his lips to mine. I opened for him right away, letting his tongue slip inside my mouth and lick against mine in a slow, testing way. My bare toes curled in my Vans as his mouth slanted, allowing him to dive in farther with languid sweeps. I welcomed the strong taste of peppermint inside. He was everywhere. All around me.

Inside me. The sight, the sound, the smell, the feel, the taste—it was a sensory overload in the best possible way, heightening my own emotions to levels they hadn't reached in a long time.

His hips began to thrust, needing release. "Teagan. Ah. Fuck. Faster." He spoke the rush of words against my lips, begging.

The way he grappled for words as his body chased his climax turned me on so much. Even the way he rasped my name. Fuck me, I was torn. I wanted to finish him, but I didn't want it to end. There was no telling what would happen after.

I shut that thought down, knowing what I'd promised, knowing that this could be as simple as I'd claimed. No attachments. No promises. No expectations.

I tightened my grip and quickened my pace, twisting my hand, watching his eyes clamp shut as he reached the peak moment of exquisite pleasure.

"Fuck." The single word dragged out in a long groan as his head tipped back and his cock thrust harder into my hand, bucking against my motions.

Cum spurted from him in thick strings, shooting forward against the wall at my side. Over and over, more came. His breathy moans were perfect, the sound making my clit throb with a longing to hear them again and again.

My hand slowed to a stop, and his head dropped. His eyes were closed, and his mouth was slack. I removed my hands from his body and smiled when his eyes finally cracked open and met my gaze. *Oh my.* The look on his face was mighty fine, one of the sexiest sights I'd ever seen. Sedate. Spent.

He released a long breath and blinked slowly before a corner of his lips drew up. "That was …"

"That was …" I echoed in a light tone, trying my damnedest not to let my smile grow as big as it threatened to. There was no way I'd turn into a fool in front of him. No way. I had to keep it together, show him that I meant what I'd said, even though I wouldn't mind if he let me touch him again. As ridiculous as it might sound, I was sure I enjoyed the experience as much as he had. It had certainly filled my spank bank to the point of overflow. Even if he decided never to touch me again, I would remember it all with my face buried in the mattress for as long as I stayed here.

He bit his bottom lip then licked it. "Thank you. For that … and earlier." He glanced away a moment, removing his hand from the wall and straightening as he slid his sweats up onto his hips. His brows drew down and that dreamy look disappeared. "I'm sorry I didn't say it before, but I planned to tomorrow."

I blinked and shivered, feeling the air shift between us as well as the night's frigid chill now that my arousal was waning and the shower steam was long gone. "Thank you too for letting me … help."

Zavier bent down, retrieving my stuff and handing over the parka first. As I shucked it on, he held out the wet bra and underwear, silently examining them with a brow lift.

"My only pair. My suitcase is—"

"Yo, Z!" A voice called from outside, startling us both.

Zavier's eyes went wide, the silver bar above his brow shifting and glinting under the bathhouse's overhead lamplights. His features evened out to their usual expressionless look, then he handed my things over and said, "Tomorrow." Before I could blink, he strode around the corner to the door.

"Yeah, I'm here," he replied to the voice, and the door creaked open then closed.

I didn't move. Not that I was ashamed or even worried about being spotted with him, but I'd told him it didn't need to mean anything, that he didn't even need to speak to me after. I would hold true to that. He owed me nothing. And I would continue on my path at this place, numb and with no expectations.

"Hey, man!" The voice—likely Koni—said. "I thought—Oh shit! You smell as good as Loch. Better actually. Fuck. Did you snatch some of her clothes from him or something?"

So Loch had my suitcase? And they all knew.

"No, she was in there. Jackson showed up and was …" Zavier's words drifted away.

Ugh. I glanced at the splatters of cum dripping down the wall. With that exit, I had a feeling he wouldn't want a repeat. Maybe I'd been too pushy? Maybe he'd wanted to handle the transition himself. As a runt, I understood the reasons he could have. There was a need to prove ourselves, to show we could handle the severity of it all because we weren't as weak as others thought us to be. Or maybe we morbidly wanted to take it all as punishment, even though we weren't actually to blame for the delayed change. Either way, he'd get through it fine enough, with or without me. And I had my own punishment to face eventually. Well, aside from the one I was already living. Being here. Family dead. All truly because of me.

I cleaned up the wall and fallen towels and rushed back to my cabin, listening carefully for anyone. No one was out along the paths, but someone certainly was watching.

When I was safely inside my cabin and turned to close the door, I saw a lone wolf again, watching from under the tight grouping of trees near the lake shed. The light above the shed door cast a perimeter glow bright enough to see bits of brown within its dark gray fur, and I wondered if it was the same one as before.

9

"So I can make whatever I want, right?" I asked Keira the following morning as we passed through the dining hall and stepped into the kitchen.

Several people sat in the dining hall eating, half of who I had never met. They were probably the upper cabin occupants. Four men and three women, all appearing to be in their thirties, most sitting alone. The triplets were there too, faces contorting like someone had shit in their bowls of cereal as they watched me pass. Their noses wrinkled in disgust. Though it might have very well been jealousy considering I was wearing another set of Loch's clothes from the leftover box. I'd rolled the dark blue sweats like I had the gray ones the previous day and had already given up adjusting the neckline of the T-shirt, letting it settle off my shoulder somewhere beneath the green parka.

The morning had started too rough to care about the clothes. Well before dawn, a buzzing sound had woken me. It didn't take me long to realize the source. My mini vibrator. The black bullet danced along the wooden floor just outside the bedroom of my cabin. My sleepy brain woke up super fast after remembering that

I had thrown it into the suitcase at the last minute of packing, worried that I'd be gone too long to live without it. Mortification kept me wide awake for an hour as I thought about Loch's and possibly the others' reactions to finding it in my things. Assholes. On the plus side, it wasn't the only thing they'd left. My deodorant stick and red cotton bra and pantie set were left with it. I'd stayed up even longer with thoughts of someone having entered my locked cabin. I wasn't exactly worried. If they'd wanted to hurt me, it would have already happened. Instead, I was curious as to who had brought the items. All of them had known how badly I stunk after cleaning, but only Zavier knew I'd hand-washed my underwear. And those thoughts led me to recall the details of our bathhouse encounter, which led me to reach into my sleep shorts for the second time since I'd returned to my cabin, stroking my clit as I pictured stroking him again. I finally fell asleep to the distant sounds of howling.

Keira and I breeched the kitchen door and were greeted by eight staring eyes. The Four. All of them were gathered at the center prep island. They had been picking through the wrapped pastries but had stopped mid-action as we entered.

Keira tipped her chin to them. "Morning." She continued walking to the refrigerator without slowing, raking and securing her hair into a low side ponytail.

I followed her lead while catching all of their eyes, stopping the longest on Zavier's. "Morning." I wondered if I'd see something from him. A twitch. A wink. Something. But nothing came from any of them. There weren't even quips about my clothes or the presents left in my cabin. Nope. But there was redness around Zavier's cheek, and Loch appeared to have a cut lip.

Their voices only echoed the same greeting with various degrees of wakefulness.

As much as I wanted to keep my eyes on them, I kept focused and trailed Keira. I could feel theirs burning into my back, though. Maybe my ass too, even though it was hidden by the green parka, not to mention a dress-sized T-shirt and a baggy pair of blue sweats underneath.

"So yes, you can make whatever you want. Most don't bother with full meals with loads of ingredients. If you do make something, they just want us to keep stock in mind and not be greedy or wasteful. Deliveries are Mondays. Usually, there's lots of fresh, easy-grab stuff, like apples or whatever, but also salad things."

I was grateful for the explanation since I hadn't bothered to ask before. "Great! I'm really wanting an omelet. You want one?"

"Nah. Thanks, though. I've got to get back to Mike. We've been going over geometry, and it's kicking my ass. My brain loathes formulas. A squared plus B squared equals a migraine." I laughed as she reached into the refrigerator and snatched two small milk cartons and four hard-boiled eggs. "I might see you later, okay?"

"Sounds good," I replied.

Before she stepped away, she leaned in closer and whispered into my ear. "It's faint from this distance, but your scent is definitely on them."

I nodded. She knew my suitcase was being held in their cabin, taken by at least one of them, which pretty much confirmed what I'd heard last night.

She smiled and bumped her hip with mine before walking off. That interaction warmed me in a welcomed way since I hadn't had many friendships growing up. I'd gotten along with a few girls from neighboring packs in our territory when I was younger, but like all of my other relationships, they had disappeared with age. No one wanted to associate with the runt. As if it were catching.

Pushing those thoughts away, I smiled about Keira then grabbed a couple of eggs and other ingredients from the fridge. When I turned, all the guys were staring at me. Honestly, it was the hottest thing I'd probably ever seen. It should be illegal for them to occupy the same space for too long. Their level of gorgeous masculinity within a few cubic feet might cause all bystanders to spontaneously combust—or their underwear at least, because mine were absolutely heating up.

"Omelet anyone?" I asked after a naughty-thought-clearing cough. Then, deciding to cross the line of ignorance about my suitcase and aiming to catch them off guard, I added, "Oh, and thanks for the early morning presents. I'm smelling lots better today, and that toy never fails to help me sleep."

While the others did a tremendous job in containing any possible reaction, Koni nearly choked on his pastry, releasing a laugh that he failed to cover with a cough. He regained control after a few seconds and pressed his lips tight, but his eyes still twinkled as he looked at me.

"Under the counter," Elijah said, drawing my attention to him. He stood at the edge of the island in ripped jeans and a V-neck cut low on his chest, showing off his dark olive-toned skin and a hint of hair. His head nodded toward the serving area as he dropped a muffin wrapper into the garbage can at his side. "Mixing bowls are underneath. Big and small utensils in the side drawer and the pans are over here." His long legs glided to the range. I hurried behind him, not wanting to miss any instructions, watching as he bent to the shelving alongside the stainless range. He pulled out a saute pan and placed it on the burner as he turned right into me.

He startled, dropping the pan onto the burner as our bodies collided, my free hand touching his arm. He instantly drew back. The recoil was so fast he almost hit himself in the chest.

"Oh! I'm sorry!" I'd gotten too close and hadn't expected him to turn and stand so rapidly. While clutching the ingredients to my chest, I reached out to stop the spinning pan from toppling off the burner. I caught a brief and faint whiff of citrus. There was something else there too, but my nose wasn't sorting very well.

Just as quickly, he moved around me and strode toward the kitchen door. "Don't leave a mess."

I gaped, still clutching the pan's handle as he disappeared into the dining hall. It had happened so fast, it was hard to process what I'd done to make him jump away like a frightened cat.

Movement drew my attention to the others, whose reactions were flat and unsurprised.

"Well ..." Koni's whisper sounded amused. His hair was pulled back low on his head, its wavy tail hanging past his neck. "Guess breakfast is over. Schedule says we're on traps this morning with Vic. You ready?" The back of his hand slapped to Loch's chest before he straightened up and stuffed a whole apple fritter into his mouth. When he saw me watching, he shrugged and smirked as best as he could with his cheeks puffed out.

Loch's eyes were still on me and as intense as ever. His jaw clenched before his tongue slid through his lips with a brief lick over the cut along the lower edge. Finally, he answered, "Yeah. North side first." He followed Koni to the door, lifting a single eyebrow at me before calling back to Zavier, "Later."

Knowing that Zavier was still there, I tried my best not to let the breath rush from my lungs but failed. I exhaled heavily enough to be seen and heard.

"Hey," he said softly, walking around the island.

I blinked several times at the door then glanced at him. "Hey." I didn't want it to be awkward, so I focused on the breakfast I intended to make, placing the ingredients on the counter.

Surprising me, he moved first to where Elijah had said the mixing bowls were kept and pulled one out, then grabbed a whisk, spatula, and knife before walking over.

His scent hit hard and fast, the rain and soapy smell wafting over me and making me close my eyes. My nose wasn't messing around now that it knew him.

"Omelet, huh?"

When I opened my eyes, he was scanning the ingredients. I began prepping. "Yeah. Want one?"

His lips twitched as I cracked the first egg into the bowl. "Nah. I had a muffin." When I didn't reply, he asked, "Did you cook at your restaurant?"

"How did you—" Oh. Keira had told me that most everyone would know whatever was written in my file. The Four had obviously dug through my information too. "Sometimes. I waited tables mostly." After adding the second egg, I whisked them up.

"But you know how to cook?"

"Enough," I admitted. I wasn't a chef by any means, but I'd learned and memorized plenty of basics, simple recipes, and some things we served in our place.

"How about meat? Venison?"

"I've made it in a few dishes, sure. Why?" I asked, slicing up a mushroom and a bit of ham.

He rubbed a hand over his scruffy jaw and the pink area on his cheek. I was tempted to ask, but I had a feeling I already knew what had happened after seeing his face and Loch's lip. They'd fought. Was I absurd for assuming it was about me? It could as easily have involved something else. Maybe Loch was helping him prepare for the training exercises he'd join after transitioning. Or it could have something to do with Jackson and Trig. I hadn't seen them in the dining hall.

"Hunting season is still on. When Rosie and Tim authorize it, we—they—hunt as part of the training and bring back the kill." He didn't sound upset about not being part of that yet.

"Ah. My family hunted a lot." I flipped on the burner, added a pad of butter, and waited for it to heat.

"In Alabama." It was a statement, not a question, but I nodded in response anyway. "Did you go with them?"

I knew what he meant. Had I used a gun or a bow alongside my pack? "Not while they were in wolf form, no. But I was taught as much as I could learn without the transition, including field-dressing and butchering afterward." I dropped the eggs into the pan, giving it a tilt to coat the bottom.

"Whoa," he whispered. And for the first time in a long time, I felt a sting of pride about who I was, what I knew, and for the father who taught me … the father who once cared about me rather than what I hadn't yet become.

"Did you ever learn? Or are you from a city?" I asked curiously as I added the mushroom and ham. He knew a little about me, so I wanted to learn more about him. And werewolves were everywhere. Packs or alone, we spanned the world. Though it was more common for us to live outside the concrete jungles, taking comfort in desolate areas where we could often be our other selves.

There was a distant look in his eyes before he shook his head. "No. I'm from southeast Missouri. My family's … well-off, I guess. They, uh … they didn't exactly hunt or teach me," he said, grabbing a plate and fork for me before leaning back against the counter.

"Oh." Folding the omelet in half, I waited a few moments for it to finish and for him to speak again. When he added nothing more, I turned off the burner and plated the food. He kept his eyes downcast, silently looking at his boots. A strand of hair had escaped the rest up top, falling over his cheek. My body warmed as I stared at him, recalling the previous night once again. In order to end the silence and my very naughty thoughts, I cut into the omelet with the fork and held it up to his mouth.

The movement broke whatever reverie he'd been captured in, and he eyed the food. "That's your—"

"Just a bite," I interrupted his protest. There was plenty, and I wanted to watch him eat.

His lips curved a bit then parted, waiting.

I slid the fork into his mouth and could feel my nipples hardening deep beneath the layers of clothes. At least they were hidden from view so my obvious attraction wasn't on full display. He'd taken some of my food. That might not ordinarily be a big deal, but here, for me, it was.

He closed his mouth around the fork, and I slid it out, watching him begin to chew the tiny morsel.

"Well?" I asked, cutting into the omelet again.

"Hmm." He finished with a swallow, then licked his lips with a teasing smile. "It's okay."

I rolled my eyes and slid the fork into my own mouth. "Hmm. Okay. Guess I'll keep my food to myself then."

"No, no." His voice mixed with an airy chuckle. "It was good. Please forgive me."

"Forgiven," I agreed, taking another bite and eyeing him. He glanced down again, quieting, that expressionless look settling back into place. I'd wondered if it was a mask he wore to hide his emotions, or if he was just so used to not expressing emotion that it was more unfamiliar to show them. "Can I ask you a question?"

His lips pressed together, eyes remaining on the floor. "Sure."

"How did that happen to your cheek? Did you fight with Jackson?"

His hand instinctively lifted to the pink skin of his cheekbone. It wasn't cut, and no bruise had formed yet, so it didn't seem serious. "No. Loch and I ... had some words."

"Had some words?" I prompted, wanting to know more.

"Yeah," he said, pushing off the counter. "I should, um ... I have to meet up with Tim and go out for supplies. Don't worry about the kitchen. Eli will handle the normal breakfast cleanup. But can you take care of the bathhouse and the laundry cabin for today? Shouldn't need much. I can meet you later after lunch and go over the classroom routine."

I wanted to ask more questions, to know where he was going and why Elijah had reacted the way he had. But I knew I was still an outsider, and they didn't trust easily. I needed to keep my head and expectations straight.

"Sure."

"Okay."

There was no goodbye. No smile or friendly nod. He just hurried out of the kitchen, leaving me a bit bewildered.

10

I'd done as Zavier had asked. After finishing breakfast and cleaning up the mess, I went first to clean the bathhouse, then returned to my cabin to grab my dirty clothes before heading to the laundry. While I ran them through a cycle, I'd managed to find more pink smoke bomb film in a few cabinet crevices and restocked what little had been used since the previous day. I'd also found a hammer and removed all the nails that Jackson and Trig had driven into the window frames.

My sleepwear and the first set of clothes I'd worn of Loch's weren't fully dry when I left, but there was no way I'd leave them unattended. They'd surely disappear like my suitcase had. I passed a few people during the morning, most keeping to themselves the same as me. Luckily, I didn't see Jackson, Trig, or the triplets. I ate an early lunch, grabbing a sandwich from the kitchen and not bothering to sit down in the dining area. I was on a mission to fix my cabin water. Despite my new fondness for the bathhouse and the oh-so-steamy things that had happened within, I didn't exactly care to use it again.

My suspicions about the water had been correct. I crawled between the bushes behind my cabin, locating the main pipe. But the shut-off valve wasn't simply turned off. Oh no. The turn handle had been unscrewed and removed—assholes, whoever had done it. The prank was just clever enough to be irritating, especially when added to my missing suitcase.

I found the bright red turn handle lying on the edge of the closest shelf next to its bolt and the correct ratchet and socket in the lake shed. So shady. I laughed out loud as I returned to the valve. It was back together in no time at all. After testing the water inside, I used the bathroom then double-checked my appearance before leaving to meet Zavier in the classroom cabin. Maybe there was no real reason to care about my appearance since he'd seen me looking like a drowned rat fresh out of the shower, but for the first time in weeks, I wanted to make sure I wasn't a complete mess. A few stray hairs between my thick, caterpillar eyebrows needed tweezing. And my skin could use a heavy dose of moisturizer because of the dryness that came with the winter cold and cabin heat. But other than that, I looked decent enough. Not polished, but decent. At least some of the numbness had dissipated, making me want to care a little.

Cabin number two was used as a classroom and any form of studying. The size mirrored Tim and Rosie's office cabin, though it had a more open layout with a main vaulted room and a smaller enclosed storage room at the back. No bathroom. Massive dry erase boards had been mounted on two walls, while the other walls had windows and a few rows of bookshelves in between. Six rectangular wooden desks with four wide chairs at each took up the center area.

Tim sat behind a teacher's desk close to the door, shaggy hair unbound and looking even more frazzled than I'd seen it before. His face was tipped downward, eyes shifting back and forth over a paper, a red pen suspended in his other hand.

"Hi, Tim," I said, shedding the parka and draping it over the first empty desk as a wave of heat hit me. The temperature felt higher than the other cabins, which was odd for a classroom setting. I imagined struggling to stay awake.

Tim's eyes lifted, then the rest of his face followed as recognition dawned. "Hi, Teagan."

The door opened behind me, and Zavier entered, shrugging out of a black zippered hoodie he hadn't worn in the morning and dropping it onto the desk beside the parka. "Hey."

"Hey," I replied, giving a soft smile before turning back to Tim.

"Teagan, Rosie and I will get with you soon about your wolf information and training assessment. You, like Zavier, don't require human courses since you've graduated high school and have taken some college classes. Depending on the assessment and your transition, if you're here for a while and want to re-enroll in online college courses, we can set Internet times for you in the office. Also, if you're open to helping others, we'd be grateful if you'd consider tutoring."

"Oh. Yeah. That all sounds good, thanks." I wasn't sure what else to say. While the thought of my transition and how long it might take stung enough, the idea of moving on with life also knocked some breath from me. Being here, staying here ... I hadn't thought in depth about what would happen next aside from going home. Life would continue on.

Tim's eyes returned to his desk, and he scribbled something on the page with the red pen. "I have a session in here in a little while, but you're both okay to clean up. Let me know if you need anything."

"No problem," Zavier replied. "Can we clear the boards, or do you need anything to stay?"

"It's fine to wipe it all." He looked up again. "Also, Rosie said to tell you thanks for the flowers."

Zavier walked around me, not acknowledging Tim's last words. He'd gotten flowers for Rosie? I knew she'd seemed fond of him and Koni the night I'd arrived. It made me wonder more about him, about this place. Even though outward appearances suggested most here were loners, some seemed to have bonds, and this one included Rosie and Tim. How long had he been here? How long had the rest of The Four?

Zavier went over their usual cleaning and restocking routine, including shelving and filing books. The classroom was also a library. People could check out books to take to their cabins and return when finished. There was a decent variety of fiction and non-fiction and many textbooks for various grade levels and subjects. They also had office supplies for writing and some art supplies, like sketchbooks and pencils, watercolor paints and brushes, even some stretched canvases and acrylic paint tubes. The back office stored the materials and few larger items like easels and an old projector.

"Were Rosie and Tim ever teachers?" I quietly asked Zavier as we returned the cleaning materials to the back room. Even though I knew it was good to keep my expectations in check, that knowing less about everyone was probably for the best since the length of my stay was undetermined, I was too curious not to ask.

"Tim was, yeah," he said, rinsing the sponges in the sink as I slid the spray bottles onto the counter. "High school. Biology and Chemistry, I think."

"And Rosie?"

He finished the sponges and leaned closer to me, reaching for a dry towel at my side. I didn't bother moving. For one, he didn't say "Excuse me." And judging by the way he inhaled close to my neck and his eyes closed for an extra-long blink, he didn't seem to mind the closeness.

After grabbing hold of the towel and pulling back, he said, "She was a social worker. CPS."

"Wow." Child welfare. I could see it immediately. Sweet. Kind. Caring and positive. It fit her personality. And knowing that was her background, I understood why she'd be here too.

"Yeah. It took a toll on her, so she and Tim took over this place several years ago to help adults struggling with different aspects of this life."

I nodded, glad he told me but knowing it wasn't his story to elaborate on further.

He dropped the towel onto the counter then lifted his hand close to my face, fingers catching a strand of my hair. His eyes had been focused on it for a few moments before shifting to meet my gaze. "Did you get a chance to fix your water? I can help you ..."

I inhaled as his tongue licked out along his lower lip and the hoop there. Gah. He was hot, and not only handsome hot but literally hot. It radiated from him, his body like a furnace in front of me. Mine was heating up, too, just thinking about touching him again, tasting his mouth. But what was more was the offer to help me. I wasn't sure if he was offering simply to repay me or if he wanted to be near me as much as I wanted the same. "I already fixed it. But maybe we—"

"Loch." Tim's voice said out in the main area as the cabin's door thumped closed. "How are you doing today?"

"Good. You?" Loch replied, his tone not as sharp as I'd usually heard from him.

In an instant, Zavier dropped my hair and shut his mouth, teeth snapping and jaw clenching, then he stepped around me to leave.

I blinked at the empty space where he'd been standing, feeling the heat disappear with him. A shiver swept over my skin.

"Bait," Zavier said, joining the conversation in the other room. His gravelly voice sounded rougher.

Bait? So that was Loch's nickname.

"Runt," came Loch's greeting in response.

"Do you need anything else, Tim?" Zavier asked.

"No, that should be good, thanks. Teagan's done too?"

I inhaled deeply, calming myself. Zavier's actions had to involve the transition. The heat had radiated from his body, and anger too.

But if it had something to do with me, it shouldn't matter anyway. Right? Right.

"Yep, all finished," I called out and finally stepped around the corner of the door.

"Good," Tim replied, not bothering to look up from his papers. "Pretty sure chores are finished the rest of the day. If you need anything to read, take whatever. Just remember to sign it out and bring it back."

"I'm good for now, thanks," I replied, looking at the desk closest to the exit where Loch and Zavier stood. The parka draped over the edge where I'd left it. Right between them.

Zavier's shoulders were pinned back, and his hands were clenched at his sides, one clutching his hoodie. He was tense and looked about as ready to lose it as he had the previous night. I immediately wanted to help him, possibly in the same way, though it was hardly the time to offer.

Loch seemed more relaxed. He leaned over, his hand pressing onto the desk beside a textbook and notebook. It was apparent he was here for a lesson, but he hadn't moved to sit in the chair at his side.

Zavier made a growling sound that was loud enough to draw Tim's eyes away from his work. Then he mumbled something lowly to Loch with a raspy curse.

"You okay, Zavier?" Tim asked, lifting a bushy brow and scratching at his beard. He didn't seem too concerned. He'd probably dealt with enough runts here to expect this type of behavior regularly.

"Yeah," Zavier bit out. "Gotta go." And he was gone in under a second, the door slamming behind him.

After an awkward moment, Tim shrugged and returned his attention to his work, and I moved toward Loch. Well ... the parka, I moved toward the parka, which happened to be on the desk he stood near. Though I wasn't exactly angry or sorry I'd have to get closer to him. There was a draw to do just that, similar to what I felt with Zavier. And it also wasn't simply because I'd worn his clothes for two days and had grown used to his faint scent too. His allure was also in his eyes, which were a bright hazel and clear. Despite his hardened features, I could see something else inside, as corny as that sounded. He looked at me as if he were studying me.

I had to stop myself from laughing at that thought because who was I to judge? I likely looked at him and the rest of The Four the same way. There was a need to know more about them, to help, even though I shouldn't get involved at all. And, all right, I also wanted to get close to him again so I could smell his scent in its full glory, not diluted like the washed garments covering my body.

Trying not to give myself away entirely as I stepped beside him, I picked up the parka with a long inhale. My plan was to speak immediately, to fight off a reaction and not dwell or dawdle, but when he inhaled too, deeply, closing his eyes as if he were relishing in my scent like I wanted to with his ... Well, the plan for no reaction shattered as a soft sigh escaped my lips. Because, damn. His scent did things to me too, as much as Zavier's had. It was potent, dark, and heady, with spicy pepper and smoky cedar. It was clearer than any smell had been to me. My brain and body wanted more, tempting me to lean in closer. Luckily, the rest of my senses flooded back into focus, jarring me from the trance I'd fallen into.

His eyes had shifted to the neckline of my shirt—his shirt—at the slack material draped over my exposed shoulder and at the red strap of the bra that had been returned to me. My gaze drifted downward too. Down past the jagged scars on his thick, pale neck. Down his wide chest that his T-shirt stretched against. Down the taut bulge of his bicep and the ropey veins along his forearm. Down to where his long fingers spread wide near the textbook.

His body straightened without warning, his hand quickly lifting and slapping the notebook over the textbook. But not before I read the cover.

Math Skills. Grade Five.

My eyes jumped up, meeting his exceptionally hardened stare—nostrils flared, jaw clenched.

There was nothing I could do or say at that moment. We didn't know each other, and he clearly hadn't wanted me to see the book. He was acting defensively, whether he was ashamed or not, and I was an outsider. And maybe the defensiveness also had to do with my stolen suitcase. Even if he didn't fear me speaking up about my missing clothes right here to Tim, maybe he feared retaliation by way of this. I could use this information to get even for taking my things and all but forcing me to wear his clothes. But while I generally liked the idea of getting even with people who wronged me, I'd never be that level of vindictive bitch who used people's misfortunes against them. I also wasn't a fan of pity—giving or receiving.

After a few blinks with a steeled expression, I lifted the parka over my arm—my body still too hot to need its extra warmth—and moved to leave. I didn't step around him like I probably should have. No. I needed to let him know I wasn't fazed by any of it. So despite having ample room, I brushed my body against his as I said to the room, "Have a good night."

Tim replied, "You too."

And without looking back, I could feel Loch's eyes on me as he gave a low grunt in response.

11

I went straight to my cabin after the schoolroom cleaning. And after that, I skipped dinner. At home, aside from working The Back Burner, my alone time was abundant, especially the two weeks following the deaths. Aunt Sonya had been around more than normal, but she was far too busy dealing with the aftermath to spend more than a few awkward minutes each day simply checking to see if I was breathing. So it really wasn't surprising that the amount of activity since my arrival here had grown heavy, weighing down my body and mind. Even though the numbness remained, blocking most of my feelings, there had been enough emotional surges to strip my energy. I needed time to recharge.

In order to power down my brain, I powered on my phone and read a saved ebook mindlessly for a while. That even took effort. My thoughts kept wandering home, to Aunt Sonya, the restaurant, and to the threat of Uncle Raif's return. It also roamed here too, to The Four and their appeal. I'd never been attracted to more than one guy at once, let alone be inexplicably drawn to them. I couldn't quite understand the pull. Perhaps it was knowing something sad hid inside all of them, something broken like me.

The sun had gone down by the time I'd escaped the thoughts. While the idea of showering and going to bed early was tempting, the idea of taking a short walk near the lake won out. Back home, I would sometimes travel the woods alone. This area was different, and I wanted to explore it a bit more. So despite the dropping temperature and blackness already having taken over the sky, I stepped outside my cabin for a walk.

The lake was still and silent, comforting and peaceful. Smaller nocturnal animals scurried about, unseen but heard, rustling in the dead leaves of the underbrush and along branches high in the treetops. The smell of winter's approach was thicker than I was used to, its freshness pinching inside my nose.

Two sets of boundaries comprised the camp. The outer boundary was for everyone and ran from the camp's entrance to miles within the mountains. The inner boundary, however, was where everyone stayed in human form, especially runts, of course. They didn't want those of us stuck in human form wandering too far without faster means of travel. Despite a brief urge to test the boundary, I remained relatively close to camp. Without transition, my eyes and nose weren't as sharp, making it more difficult to locate visible and scented boundary markers. I couldn't see my cabin from the water's edge—trees and the lake shed were in between—but I did have a clear view of a light from a farther cabin. Pretty sure it was cabin number six, which The Four stayed in with Vic.

I'd been staring at the water for a while when I heard footsteps crunching the ground, growing louder as they approached. Not knowing who it was, I remained silent.

"Teagan?" A male voice called quietly over the rustle of his movements, sounding as calm and pleasant as the still night. "Teagan ... it's Koni."

Koni? "Yeah?"

He appeared from behind the tree line closest to the lake shed. His dark form slowly grew closer, the soft light from the shed and from the moon above highlighting his form. There was a litheness to his body, with lean muscle on a taller frame. He wasn't as bulky as the others, but he rivaled Elijah for the tallest of their group.

"Hi," he said, stopping close enough that I could see his shadowy features.

And that meant I had to tip my head back a bit because of his height. "Hi."

He extended a hand with a small brown paper bag. "I ... We didn't see you at dinner. I thought you might at least want a sandwich. There's water in there too."

I took hold of the bag, eyeing him suspiciously. Of course I was leery. They hadn't exactly been too welcoming.

"What?" he said with a bit of a chuckle. When I lifted a brow without responding, he shook his head and added, "There's nothing wrong with it. I don't cook, but I can manage a peanut butter and jelly."

"Okay."

"You don't believe me." A statement, not a question. "All right, let me have it."

I handed the bag over. He reached in and gave me the water, showing the cap was still intact as he opened it for me. Then he unwrapped the sandwich and took a large bite, nearly a quarter of the entire thing. I gaped as he mumbled through his bite, "See? Not filled with razors or poisoned, unless you're allergic."

"Wow, am I hated that much?" The last bit tumbled out with little thought.

He flinched, then handed over the sandwich, folded the bag, and stuffed it into his back pocket. "We don't … hate you."

To prevent my smart mouth from replying to that, I took a bite from the sandwich. After a moment where he didn't elaborate further, I lifted the goods he brought and mumbled, "Thanks."

"Welcome." He sighed and looked around the lake for a minute. I took the time to stare freely, admire his long, unbound hair, the sharp cuts of his jaw, the pointed end of his nose. "Are you staring at me?"

"Yes," I admitted, my mouth full of the last bite of sandwich, a smile on my lips.

"I like looking at you too. Maybe a bit too much," he admitted, causing me to go utterly still. "I mean. It's just that … this place, our group … we're like a—"

"Family. I get it. I'm not trying to invade. I'm trying my best to stay out of the way. But …" I wasn't sure what to say. Should I lay into him about how their "family" basically were the ones to start it all by taking my stuff. I would have gladly stayed away from them after the first night. Well, maybe that wasn't entirely true. I wasn't sure I would have stayed away given how much I was attracted to them. Also, how could I respond to him admitting he enjoyed looking at me? It made me feel warm all over. But it wasn't only his words. Bringing me food was an unexpected and kind gesture. And then there was his scent. As my body warmed, the scent of him seemed to increase. Pine. It was fresher than the cabins' older smells, and earthy, like the way a good soil smelled when it was fresh and dry. "But ..." I murmured again, trying to refocus.

"But we haven't been nice," he filled in for me, fully turning to look at me and taking another step closer.

Oh God. My body grew warmer by the second. What was it about him? About them? "Why are you being nice now?"

He rolled his lips together, considering his words. He was close, close enough that I could touch those lips if I wanted. "You helped Zavier when you didn't have to. There was no real reason for you to. Also, you almost broke Jackson's nose." There was a light chuckle with the last words.

"Yeah, I guess I should really worry if *he* ever decides to make me a sandwich."

"True. I don't think he or Trig will bother you, though. At least, they better not try."

I prepared to ask him more, but we both heard a shout and saw movement in the distant light of their cabin.

"Fuck," he said.

"What is it?"

"I need to go." And he was gone, not saying goodbye or bothering to wait for the questions hanging from my lips.

As I walked toward the lake shed to return to my cabin, the shouting returned. Koni's silhouette appeared under their cabin's porch light with a few others while someone else jogged down toward the lake.

"Cool the fuck off!" A sharp, deep voice shouted from the cabin. Loch's voice. All the silhouettes disappeared inside and the door slammed.

Once again, I knew I should just mind my own business, but my feet didn't get that message. They carried me forward as I watched the person—who I knew had to be Zavier—pacing along the lake's edge.

Before I could reach him, someone else had. I stopped close to the lake shed, watching as a figure approached him.

"Hey, Zavier." A female said. It held an airy, flirty tone, like one of the triplets.

Zavier stopped moving. "What do you want?" His voice was low, coarse and irritated.

With no light source near them, it was nearly impossible to see what was happening. And while it might have been wrong to eavesdrop, I couldn't stop myself from straining my ears. I didn't want to leave without talking to him myself, checking if he was okay.

"You. You know I've been wanting you for a while," she replied.

His laugh was loud and lilting. "A while? Sure. You mean a day or so, since you noticed I'm in transition. What's wrong? Jackson and Trig not sniffing around anymore?"

"Prick!" she yelled back but made no move to leave. In fact, she only moved closer to him. He remained still, hands pinned at his sides.

She got so close that their shadowy figures almost connected. "I'll let it slide if ..."

Dammit. I couldn't hear her whispering. I took a couple of steps then stopped when he replied.

"Not happening, and don't touch me." His body backed away.

She advanced again. "You know you want some relief. I can help you. I have skills that will blow your mind. Let me."

"No," he replied, his tone nearly a growl.

Fuck. I could practically feel his anger vibrating, even from far away. I waited. She was a damned fool if she didn't leave. Sometimes the transition anger couldn't be controlled, and I was certain he was struggling to rein it in, not wanting to hurt her physically.

When she laughed and I saw the shadow of her arm and hand reach out, something in me snapped. I ran for them, my legs and feet tearing through the low brush at the water's edge, not caring about the chaotic noise I was making or if I injured myself.

She heard my approach soon enough, twisting her body to see who was barreling their way.

"He said no, bitch." As soon as I saw the lotus on her pale neck, I added, "What is with you and touching people without consent? I doubt you want that arm broken this time." I halted right in front of her, stopping before I collided with her chest. I didn't care that she was inches taller.

She backed up a step, then tried to recover by puffing out her chest and huffing. "Stay out of this, runt."

"Bless your heart for thinking I might. Now go get your dick elsewhere. This one's taken." Yep. I said it.

I heard a laugh from somewhere near the cabin, but I didn't dare look. Oh great, an audience.

Zavier merely breathed beside me, possibly with a deeper inhale but otherwise not showing any sign of being mad or amused by my claim. He was probably too busy maintaining control.

Nima laughed bitterly. "Oh, right. I'm sure he or any of them want you, Little Orphan Alabama. That's right. I didn't need any of the information Rosie and Tim are keeping secret about you being here, why this place is closed to anyone new. We know. My family has heard of yours, Teagan Wellis. Daughter of Jin Wellis, an Alpha Lead who aligned with vampires and got all of his pack and others slaughtered by Favored Reapers and wraiths."

I sucked in a shuddering breath, both hurt and embarrassed by my life and the new legacy that would be tied to my father's name and family forever.

"Aw, what's wrong? Thought nobody would find out how shitty your father was, how he wanted to force your transition by any means necessary, like using the blood of a Marked Soul—"

Instincts took over, my body attacking without thought or fear of consequence. She had no time to move. Even without much space for a proper charge, my body slammed into her, my shoulder connecting with her stomach, taking her to the ground, the force knocking the air from her lungs.

"Oof!"

I didn't bother with words. There was no need. I growled and started swinging, my fist connecting with her face only twice before my body was wrenched away. My arms flailed, aiming for anything within reach, including the captor at my back.

"Teagan, stop. Stop." The whisper barely registered beside my ear as people flooded into the area.

"Crazy psycho bitch," Nima said, holding her face as her two sisters helped her up.

The rest of The Four and Vic had appeared as well. There were others too, but they hung back near the trees, watching.

"Holy shit," someone murmured.

"Did you hear?" came another's voice.

"Christ, we were worried about Z snapping. Shit," someone else said.

I didn't hear the rest as I was dragged backward toward my cabin by arms wrapped around my middle. It was then that I realized it wasn't one captor but two, one on each side. Zavier and Koni. Zavier, though, was struggling, his body shaking.

"Rosie and Tim will hear about this, you piece of trash!" Nima yelled.

12

"Well, damn, Teagan," Koni's soft, calm voice broke through my jumbled thoughts as my breaths settled. He and Zavier had carried me away from the fight. One of them might have accomplished the feat alone ordinarily, but either my rage was terrible enough to warrant two, or Zavier needed some help in his condition and refused to hand me over completely.

"Are you all right?" Koni asked at the base of my cabin's steps.

Shame washed over me. I wasn't exactly sorry for how I'd acted. It had more to do with being exposed. I hadn't planned on explaining my life to anyone while I was here, hadn't planned on getting too close. And to have it shouted out into the air like some cheap bit of gossip ... Well, it didn't feel the greatest.

"Yeah," I finally said, not wanting to meet his eyes. I knew what I'd see there. "Thank you." My hands reached up to touch both arms anchored at my stomach. The contact with their warm skin seemed to soothe me as much as breathing.

"What about you, Z?" Koni asked, releasing his hold around my waist, his hand brushing against mine as if to reassure me, or maybe he was reluctant to break the contact.

Zavier still had his arm there, and it continued to shake. "I'm not ... I need to go."

"Don't go," I pleaded, holding his arm and peering up at the side of his face. I felt more vulnerable than I'd ever had, asking him not only because I wanted to help him but because I didn't want to be alone after what Nima had divulged. Did he care? Would he judge me too?

He dropped his gaze to meet mine briefly, and I saw the pain there as he fought his body. "I don't think I can stay. My skin is aching, and my ..." His arm tensed beneath my hold.

"Help me bring him inside," I asked Koni, shifting my arm around Zavier's back.

"Not sure that's a good idea," Koni replied. "He's close. He might need space."

I pulled Zavier, urging him up the steps. Koni helped despite his hesitation. He had to know what I planned to do, but I didn't care. They were so close to Zavier. Maybe he'd already told them what had happened in the bathhouse. Or maybe they all figured it out, had smelled me on him enough to know. At this point, I was okay with any reason. I wanted to help him, and this was the best way to do it. Even if he was on the brink, it would take some of the pain and aches away.

"Tell me no now. I want to help you, but I won't touch you if you don't want me to."

Koni eyed me curiously when we reached the top of the steps, his hand on the screen door. "You are ... you are something else, Teagan." The corner of his lips lifted as he shook his head. I wasn't quite sure if he was judging me or if he approved. I wanted to help Zavier too much to care.

A whoosh of breath left Zavier's mouth as if he'd been holding it in to combat the pain and anger. "Yes. Please, I need you."

Koni held the screen as I opened the main door. We ushered Zavier inside, and I wasted no time shrugging out of my parka then digging my hand into the front of his sweats and grabbing hold of his already hard thick cock.

"Tell me what you want," I said, grateful he'd gone commando again as I tightened my grip around him.

Koni blew out a breath beside us with a whispered, "Shit."

At the same time, Zavier groaned as I stroked him. "That. That."

I gripped him hard and walked backward, leading him through the doorless opening into the bed area.

"I'll just … go," Koni said. "But I'll be outside for a bit, in case anything happens. Don't wait, Z. You'll know when you're on the edge, if it's tonight."

His words registered, but we said nothing in return before we heard the door close out front. My legs hit the edge of the beds.

"You pushed them together?" he asked, his teeth gritted, his jaw clenched.

"Yeah." I shoved his shirt upward. He got the hint and tugged it over his head as I jerked his sweats down. "It's why I smelled like both of you, why I can't seem to get enough of your scent."

"And Koni's too then." He hummed low after the words, closing his eyes as my hand twisted and drove down his length.

"Yes," I replied, then released his dick so he could strip the rest of the way. Maybe I was greedy, but I wanted to see all of him this time.

He kicked off his shoes and socks and slid his sweats off completely.

"Oh." The word came out more like a sigh as I stared at him. He was all solid muscle and ridges, with a couple tattoos on his chest and upper arm. Geometric. Half a wolf's face and a single tree with a moon behind it. He was smooth and cut to perfection.

"Teagan," he begged, fist clenched. "I need your hands on me."

Knocked from my momentary daze, I slipped my hand around him again, and he moaned in response. "Lie down."

"I want to feel you too. Your skin. Can I?" he asked, doing as I told him. His breaths were still too fast, not settling yet.

Hesitation hit me for only a moment, knowing exactly where it would lead. I absolutely would not control myself if I were to shed my clothes unless he objected to crossing that line. But I knew I wanted it, wanted him. After a nod, I slipped my shirt over my head then kicked out of my shoes, socks, and sweats too. All that remained was the plain red bra and pantie set that had been left in my cabin earlier. I still hadn't showered and briefly worried that I stunk.

So when I got closer, and he said, "You smell so fucking good," I had a hard time containing a giggle.

"Are you sure I don't stink? I haven't showered tonight."

His long body stretched out across the bed, and I settled onto my knees at his side, leaning over a little to use both my hands to massage him this time.

He inhaled deeply then released the breath, reaching over to touch my thigh, sliding his hand up until it caressed my ass. "To me, you smell like cut grass and flowers in summer, soft and bright and … fuck." He rasped the last word out and closed his eyes as I adjusted my grip and pumped him faster.

The muscles along his stomach and thighs were still stiff, tense, the skin there taut. I stared at how large he was in my hands, feeling him throb at my touch. Though I'd never sucked a dick before, I suddenly wanted nothing more. With him spread out this way, welcoming and inviting, the idea of having him in my mouth made it all even sexier. My pussy pulsed at the very thought of his pleasure. So I licked my lips and bent over farther, jutting my ass into the air.

He groaned and some precum leaked from his tip. As soon as I was close enough, I stuck my tongue out and licked his fat crown, tasting the salty sweetness of him, then parted my lips and took him into my mouth.

His hips bucked a bit. "Ahh. That feels so good."

With a hand pressed to his thigh, I could feel his muscles loosen and relax as I moved my mouth over him. "Mmm."

"Oh. Oh, God. Wow." His fingers dug into my ass cheek hard like he couldn't control the pressure, then his palm slid over my underwear and bare skin as if to soothe the hurt he may have caused. "I want to feel you. Smell you. Taste you."

I swirled my tongue under and around before I pulled him in as far as I could and sucked. That received another long, satisfied groan.

When I didn't move, he sat upright and stroked up my back. In another moment, my bra was unclasped and my underwear slipped down over my ass. "Lift."

I did as he said, releasing my mouth's hold of him and kneeling up. He slid the underwear farther down my thighs as he looked my body over again. His breathing had slowed, and his jaw was no longer tight.

"Feeling better?"

"So much, but still not nearly enough," he uttered as I lifted my knees to remove the underwear fully. "You are fucking gorgeous. Let me taste you."

"Yes," I sighed, wanting nothing more.

Once again, another first for me. The other guys hadn't bothered. The foreplay had been barely enough to get me wet. At the time, I hadn't cared. I took whatever I could get since not many dared to even be around me.

And now ... Well, I was taking whatever I could get with him too, just in a different sense. I doubted he'd want to be around me after his transition, after what he'd just heard. I was likely to become the camp pariah. Ugh.

His body was up in a flash, switching our positions and laying me flat. "This tight body ... So firm and soft." Those large hands of his slid over my legs and parted my thighs so he could settle between them. "I wanted you as soon as you arrived. Feisty. Fiery. Sexy." His gorgeous eyes flitted over every inch of my body before he leaned over, locked with my gaze, then pressed his lips to mine.

My hands trailed up his abs as he suspended himself over me. His tongue dove inside my mouth, and his chest dipped to mine, rubbing against my nipples.

He pulled away from my mouth and kissed down my neck, biting, nipping, and licking along my skin. "You are so much more than I thought ... than we all thought."

We all? Thoughts of The Four discussing me, stealing my stuff, gave me pause. "All?" I sighed as his tongue bathed a path to one breast.

"Mmm," he hummed over my pebbled nipple as his body shifted farther down and his hands moved to grab hold of my breasts. He sucked the nipple into his mouth with a long pull, and my body arched, greedily pushing harder into him.

His lack of response made me want more information, about him, about them, about everything, but I wasn't going to ruin this for either of us with conversation. I threaded my fingers into his longer hair, pushing it back away from his face and watching him suck on me so reverently.

He moved his mouth to my other breast, giving it as much attention before he shifted farther down, lips trailing kisses over my stomach. I felt him tremble above me then he audibly exhaled, his breath caressing my pussy. "Fucking hell, you smell like honey. So fucking good, so pretty." His hands pushed my thighs wider then his fingers traveled over my small patch of hair before slipping into my lips and finding my clit.

"Ahh," I uttered as a bolt of lightning shot through my body, all my nerves spasming in response. My hands stretched out over the mattresses, reaching for some form of balance as the world tipped.

"That feels good, doesn't it?" The finger moved over my slickness and pushed inside me. "So wet. So hot. I need a taste." And then his mouth was on me, his tongue licking in the same seductive strokes he'd given my mouth. This most definitely wasn't his first time going down on a girl. It certainly didn't feel like it, and I was not complaining one bit.

"Oh. Fuck. Ah," I mumbled, fisting the sheets. "Zavier."

"Yes," he grunted against me as he pushed another finger in. "Never heard my name sound so good. I want to make you scream it."

His mouth attacked me, sucking and licking. His fingers didn't stop. When his teeth nipped at my clit, it sent me right over the edge, the climax fast and sharp like the snap of a rubber band.

"I'm ... I'm ..."

"Fuck yes. You're squeezing hard. So tight. Damn. Teagan, look at me."

My eyes shot downward to where his face remained between my legs, his mouth wet and shiny from my arousal. I let out a long breath as the aftershocks pulsed on and on.

"I want to be inside of you so much. I just can't seem to stop asking you for more, but I understand if you don't want the same." The look in his eyes was intense. Despite being on the edge of transition, on the verge of an explosion of bodily change, he would stop if I said so.

"Yes, I want you inside me too."

"Thank God. I'm losing my mind for you. I don't think I'll be able to stay away." He wasted no time crawling up my body and slamming his mouth down on mine, taking control while I seemed to be losing it. Frenzied, I wrapped my arms around his back, my fingers digging into his skin, unable to get close enough. He reached down with one hand and rubbed his tip against my clit before sliding his shaft over me, wetting it.

My breath caught as he pushed the head inside. His teeth clamped down on my lower lip, and he drove in farther, his thickness stretching me in the most delicious way.

Releasing my lip, he let out a deep, vibrating growl, and it was one of the most intoxicating sounds I'd ever heard. "Oh fuck. You're so goddamn tight. I need a second. Does it hurt?"

"No, I'm okay. Need to adjust a bit, that's all. You're … big."

He groaned at my words and stilled completely as if they alone had the power to set him off. "And you really are teenie, Teagan," he said with a breathy laugh and a smile that almost made me melt. Or it was the numbness that was melting, everything he made me feel spreading like wildfire inside. I was getting used to seeing his expressions for me, knowing he was usually so stoic.

I laughed lightly with him about my nickname but dug my fingers harder into his back, lifted myself up, and bit down on his lower lip and the ring there.

"Mmm," he hummed as I tugged him down to me.

When I released his lip ring, I tilted and lifted my hips, taking him farther inside, then said, "Move. Please, Zavier. Fuck me."

I didn't need to ask twice. He slid out slow, relishing the stroke before thrusting in a bit faster. He groaned again.

"Yes. Yes. Oh," I cried as he found a rhythm. I matched it, tipping my hips and bucking against him.

His breaths quickened with his pace, and after a little while his force grew too. He slammed into me harder and harder, his pelvis hitting like a piston. "Teagan."

I was clutching onto him, legs bending around his ass, trying to stay in place as his body moved like a machine. My toes curled as the feeling coiled inside, building higher once again. "Oh … please."

Suddenly, Zavier pushed up onto his knees, hooking my hips and diving into me at a different angle. When his thumb circled over my clit, my entire body tensed and the orgasm took hold. I moaned his name over and over, not caring how loud I was or if I sounded crazy. He had unraveled me.

"Oh fuck. Fuck," he chanted, securing his grip on my hips and speeding up until he let out his own deep moan and all but collapsed on top of me, catching his weight at the last second. His breaths were ragged, his skin slick with sweat, and he kissed me again, his tongue diving into my mouth like he was both possessed and possessive.

After a moment, he pulled out of me and disappeared from the bedroom. He returned with a wet cloth.

I gaped at him as he leaned over and started cleaning me up. The shock of it had my head spinning. Oh, he was most definitely used to fucking, but he had manners. I'd never had a guy do that either. They'd been so fast to leave, and I usually made my way to the bathroom sometime after for a shower. But this ... This was attentive and thoughtful.

And the way his gaze swept over me as his hand gently wiped the cloth between my legs, it felt like more.

He chucked the cloth into the bathroom from the doorway, then climbed into the bed beside me. "Can I stay here with you? I feel okay, but I don't know if ..." His eyes shifted around, unsure.

There was a slight risk he'd transition while in bed, but usually the pain was too great for anyone to sleep through. Plus, I knew he wanted the comfort. I couldn't deny that I wanted it too.

"Stay," I replied, reaching for one of the blankets I had on the bed before lifting his arm around me and turning onto my side.

He pulled me closer against him and settled in, his breaths blowing into my hair until my eyes drifted closed and my mind faded into nothingness.

13

"Ah! Fuck!" The scream ripped through my mind, tearing me from sleep. It was raspy and pained and ...

Zavier.

All at once, I was hit with the thoughts of the night before. His struggle. Having sex. Falling asleep with him.

My eyes popped wide, frantically searching the darkness of the cabin. My hands grappled around the bed, tugging at the blankets. When I felt nothing, no one beside me, I called out, "Zavier!" I still wasn't even sure if I'd dreamed his shouts.

A thudding noise came from outside of the room, and I lurched from the bed, not caring about my nakedness and barely feeling the cold cabin air. There was too much fear causing my heart to race, spiking my body temp.

"Zavier!"

"Te—Teagan." The reply sounded strangled.

As soon as I passed through the bedroom opening, I spotted him lying on the ground facing the door. "Oh my God." I rushed closer. While I'd been around wolves my entire life, had known enough about the transition process, I'd never actually witnessed one firsthand. My father had made sure my brothers had been isolated, not wanting any chance of injury to them or others. Their transitions also hadn't lasted very long, having experienced it early on like most others with subtle, sometimes mild warnings. The final change was also sudden, nearly as quick as all shifts that happened after. A runt took longer, the process drawn out with many painful, skin-crawling episodes before the change.

"I think I need to—" His naked body curled tighter into a fetal position. "Fuck, it hurts. My bones ..."

Dropping to my knees, I placed my hand on his shoulder, the skin there like fire. "You're close." While I wasn't sure what the usual process was here at camp, I thought being in here was better than being outside alone. "I'm going to clear the area."

He didn't respond with words, only grunts and short, heavy breaths. I moved around the cabin, shifting the table and chairs to the farthest corner. The transition was worse than any flu or fever, so I knew he wouldn't be able to keep any liquids down even if he wanted a drink. But I could ease some of the heat, even if it wouldn't take all the pain away.

Before returning to him, I slid into my tank top and sleep shorts, then wet down a towel from the bathroom. I draped it over him. A sigh escaped his lips, but his body continued to tremble.

"I'll be right back." Recalling last night, I opened the door and scanned around the dimly lit porch for Koni. He was nowhere to be seen. "Shit." I let the screen door slap but kept the main door open in case he needed to get out fast.

When I crouched beside him again, he barked, "Get back, Tea—"

And then it happened. His body seemed to explode, and I scrambled quickly away, watching him unfold in front of me, his human form stretching out before shifting in the blink of an eye. One second he was curled up, his skin golden tan, smooth, and slick with sweat, and the next ...

A howl ripped from the wolf standing mere feet from me. His fur was light gray, long, and fluffy, with white around its lower face and underbelly and black lining the tips of his ears. The howl stopped, and his face dropped low, his eyes—one blue, one brown—finding me sitting on the floor. His head tilted, seeming to study me for a moment, his nose twitching as it scented the air.

Another howl sounded outside then a couple more joined in. His head whipped toward the screen, ears perked, listening. I didn't dare speak because I didn't know what to say. He had confessed some things in the night, things that both warmed and confused me. Things like how he didn't think he could stay away and how I was better than they'd all thought. I wasn't some foolish girl, thinking and hoping there could be more when in reality I barely knew him ... them. There were doubts in my mind, even for myself, my own life. I had to keep my expectations the same. None. If this ended tonight, then it was over for good. It made sense for so many reasons. And that was why I just watched and waited.

Without another glance back to me, he darted forward, bashing the screen door open, nearly ripping it from the hinges. His body leaped from the porch and disappeared. In a rush, I jumped to my feet and ran over, catching the screen door and holding it open as I stared out toward the lake. Three other wolves stood still as he approached. I could see that they had differences, a couple darker shaded than him. Black. Dark Gray. The other looked mostly brown, though it was still difficult to tell in the dull light, with the moon hidden behind the mountain trees.

The Four. There was no doubt. They were there to greet him after transition. He continued on, sprinting past them as if he'd seen and smelled them a million times before. And perhaps he had. They were familiar. Friends. Maybe even brothers on some level. And I was... I was an outsider, possibly worse, having been injected into their life, wanted or not.

The other three held still, staring in my direction. Then one by one they turned to follow him. The last one, black as far as I could tell, stayed a few moments longer, assessing me until finally breaking away and chasing after them with a few sharp barks.

I released a long sigh as I continued to stare out into the darkness. All kinds of emotion slammed into me at once, piercing the numbness. Happiness—for Zavier finally transitioning. Fear—about when or if I'd make the change myself. Longing—with a need to have Zavier for longer than one night. Curiosity and concern—about the others and the connection and desire I felt around them too. And sadness—the despair of loss digging its claws back into me as I thought about everyone knowing the truth and spearing me with judgment.

Tears came fast after. There was no way to stave them off or wipe them away. I needed them, to feel them again. I could only hope it would be a new cleansing, one necessary to take the next step of healing. To forgive my father for what he'd done and to wash away the guilt I felt for his choice. Because he had made the decision and risked all of their lives for me. Like Nima had discovered, my father thought blood from a Marked Soul might force my transition, so he'd gotten them all killed for me.

I fell asleep long after the first tears fell.

It was still dark when a padding sound woke me. I inhaled deeply and sighed when the rich scents of rain and soap filtered through my nose. But they weren't the only smells. Damp soil and pine bark. There was even a faint tang of something bitter that had my nose wrinkling on its own accord. One side of the bed dipped, and my eyes popped open. A round, wet nose poked at mine, sniffing fervently. The rest of the massive head came into focus directly above my face. Wide and fluffy. Gray and white. Eyes, blue and brown. Just as I realized it was Zavier, he dropped down onto the bed, stretching his furry body at my side, nearly on top of me.

He came back to sleep with me … in wolf form.

Well then.

I rolled to my side, wrapping an arm over his enormous frame, digging my fingers and my nose deep into his fur. After a long, luxurious inhale, I closed my eyes with a sigh and heard him do the same.

stray

1

Heaven. It felt as if I bathed in it, slept in it. And now I was waking to it. The feel and the smell. Soft and warm and fresh. I knew what it was without having to open my eyes. Who it was. Zavier. And he was no longer a runt. I wish I could say the same for myself.

At twenty years, I still hadn't transitioned into my wolf form. Most changed in their early teen years, where puberty often hits. Those who transition late are runts. And runts are some of the rejects who came to Camp Midnight Moon near the Great Smoky Mountains in Tennessee, along with loners and those who are just plain unwanted. But being a runt wasn't the only reason I was here. Unfortunately, the other reason wasn't as simple. I came here to hide from my uncle, an outcast from my pack in Alabama, who may have found out about my family's deaths. Even though I hadn't made my transition, I still held the rightful claim of alpha for my pack. So my aunt thought it best I leave home for protection, hoping I would transition before returning home. At least then, I stood a chance at fighting him should he come to challenge me.

All those thoughts were simply too heavy for the glorious morning, though. I wanted to bask in the lightness I felt beside Zavier, allow myself to be lost in him and not think about the past or the future. I'd told him I didn't expect anything, that my helping him through his transition didn't need to mean more. Despite having sex with him the previous night and his words of longing and adoration, I needed to keep to that promise. We knew little about each other. Did he plan to stay at camp now that he'd transitioned, keep his closeness with the others who made up The Four? Or would he move on, move back with his family?

I sighed, tightening my arm around the large body of fur in front of me, trailing my fingers through his thick, soft strands, and relishing in the comfort of him. He'd been through so much the previous night. Sleep was the best thing for him. I couldn't recall how things were handled after my late brothers' had transitioned years before. I did know the times varied for the initial change back to human form, and it was never as painful as the first shift. That was a relief, at least. Even knowing Zavier for only a short time, it had been difficult to watch him endure the change. I didn't want him hurting and did everything I could to help.

That would include this morning after. I tried not to wake him as I opened my eyes and lifted my arm, preparing to roll away.

The beautiful wolf beside me stretched long onto his back and released a whine that became a low moan. His mouth opened, and his body writhed. I turned away, giving him space to move, unsure if he was dreaming or waking. He'd been out late with the others after the change, exploring the world through new eyes though his eyes remained the same—one blue, one brown. The experience was bound to be not only thrilling and joyous but overwhelming as well. He would need sleep to adjust to it all. And food too.

On that thought, I moved, planning to make him breakfast.

Only, I didn't get far. As I planted my feet onto the floor to stand, Zavier rolled over, letting out a louder yelping whine before his body curled into a tight fetal position. His next yelping bark morphed from sharp into a gravelly shout as his wolf body shifted into human. His fur disappeared. His body stretched wide, now with no hair covering its smooth skin and taut muscles.

I bit my lip, staring in awe at his glorious body. Not only had the sight of him stunned me again, but his easy shift back to human was a tremendous relief. Aside from a few scratches on his forearms and legs—likely from last night's first romp in the woods—he appeared to be unharmed.

"Teagan," he murmured, cracking his eyes open.

I smiled and moved to reach out but stopped. What I craved to do was run my fingers through the upper length of his dirty blond hair and across his pouty lower lip before pressing my mouth to his. Sure, I wanted to talk to him, to hear that he was okay, but I also wanted to *feel* that he was all right. My body longed for his to tell me through contact, show me how he felt.

Only, it wasn't my place to touch him. Our encounters up to this were mainly because of his transition, me offering myself to help ease the pain. He didn't owe me anything else, and I wouldn't assume that either.

I bit down harder on my lip, rechecking my reality, holding back the sliver of emotion digging itself into my numbness. No expectation. That was what I had here. There were no promises, no strings. And after so many people in camp had overheard what Nima had disclosed about my family—about my father getting my pack and others killed—I wondered if everyone might shun me. Even him.

"Teagan," he said again, his raspy tone rougher and more alluring from sleep and possibly from his first night of howling and barking.

"Hi," I answered tentatively, blinking at him. Even though I was holding firm to my convictions, I made no move to cover my nakedness. There was no way I'd deny or be ashamed of what we'd done. I was more than happy about it, even if there was a chance it never happened again. "How do you feel?"

With my seated body angled sideways, his hand reached up and stroked down my side, from shoulder to waist. "I'm good. How are you?"

I chuckled lightly. "You just went through the transition, and you're asking me how I am?"

He yawned, eyes closing tightly as his head tipped backward, pressing deeper into the pillow. When his focus returned to me, the very tip of his tongue ran across the edge of his upper teeth. Then his lips spread wide in the most gorgeous smile I'd ever seen from him. It was dreamy and seductive. And most of all, not pained. In the short time I'd known him, he rarely showed expression, his face usually flat and emotionless. I'd seen that crack a few times with humor but mostly with looks of pain and anger, the transition taking control.

Now, though. This ...

His shoulder shrugged as his smile fell. "Yeah, I want to know how you are after last night."

"Well, you shouldn't be worried about me. You've been through so much, I—"

"I'm fine, Teagan." His hand grabbed hold of mine and drew it to his chest. "And that's partly because of you. So yeah, I'm worried about you too. And thankful. And just ..." He lifted my hand higher, pulling it to his lips and kissing it before his eyes traveled, scanning my body. "Tell me, please. How are you? Did I hurt you at all?"

"No, you didn't hurt me. I'm all right ... was only worried about you." I bit my lip again. This time though, instead of holding back all the thoughts in my mind, I listened to the little spark in my chest telling me he wasn't running away. He was here and just as concerned for me as I was for him. So I dared to continue, "I was happy you came back to me last night. I thought maybe ..."

One corner of his lips tipped, and he kissed my knuckles another time. "Can I stay here with you? For good, I mean. I want to sleep with you every night."

The breath whooshed from my lungs in a long sigh. I shook my head, thinking I'd misheard. "Did you just—"

"Yes," he interrupted. "I want to stay with you. I know it's new, but I can't help it. I want to smell you all the time, all over me. I want to know you better." He was rambling a bit, and when I lifted my eyebrow, silently questioning his decision-making ability immediately after transition, he shook his head, knowing exactly what I was thinking. "No. I'm fine. At least as far as the transition goes. Maybe I'm losing my mind for you. I already told you I might be. Fuck. I just can't get enough of you."

He yanked my hand, drawing me down to him in one quick jerk. My body twisted and pivoted, and my other hand reached out to brace on his chest. As soon as the tips of our noses touched, his hands wrapped around my middle, squeezing me close.

I let out a harsh breath then succumbed to the feel of being pressed against his hard body. He was overwhelming in the best way—the clean soap and rainy smell of him, the feel of his warmth. "After what Nima said last night, I thought maybe ... My family ..." I couldn't bring myself to say it. If I spoke it out loud, I might break down.

"Shh," he soothed me, one hand caressing my back and the other shifting to tuck a strand of hair behind my ear. "Yes, I want you. I have a deep need for you. Your past, your family, where you come from ... none of that matters." His lips fluttered against mine with the words, then he sighed and closed his eyes. "Tell me I can stay. I want to talk more, but I'm still so tired. I just need a bit longer ..."

I pushed my lips to his gently, receiving the tiniest of kisses in return before his hands fell away from my neck and back. "Yes, you can stay."

His breaths slowed, and his body went completely limp, sleep retaking him. I leaned down and pulled one of the covers over him before standing. Looking down at his body, seeing how relaxed he was after having professed all of that to me ... Well, as much as I wanted to deny all that he'd said, chalk it up to some kind of post-transition delirium, I nearly melted. I couldn't explain his sincerity away. What was happening between us wasn't some simple one-nighter.

Wanting to let him rest, I showered, dressed in the clean set of clothes, then left for the dining hall to make the breakfast I knew he needed.

2

The dining hall cabin was empty when I arrived. Benches and tables cleared and cleaned. And while I was excited that I hadn't run into anyone since I'd gotten a late start to the morning, I knew my luck wouldn't last.

I pushed the door to the kitchen open and was greeted immediately by Rosie turning in my direction along with three sets of staring eyes at the island behind her. *Super.*

"Morning," I said so softly I could barely hear myself.

"Teagan! Just who I was looking for," Rosie chirped. She wore a bright pink T-shirt that matched her hair and a simple pair of black leggings. It was her usual camp-guide-casual style, from what I'd learned so far, and it suited her so well. Her hands twisted together anxiously.

At her back, Loch, Koni, and Elijah stood—the rest of The Four. Their hulking presences continued to both intimidate and enchant me. While Loch and Elijah had their arms crossed over their chests, Koni was chowing down on what looked like a breakfast burrito. Their stares seemed to soften a bit, and I couldn't tell if it was because they were softening up to me or they were simply tired.

They had been out late celebrating Zavier's transition, too, no doubt. Their faces were drawn a bit, lax, with bloodshot, hooded eyes and stubble along their jaws. Their bodies even swayed enough for me to notice. Yeah, they were exhausted. They must have run Zavier ragged. No wonder he passed back out.

"Hi," I said, mustering all the courage I could to face Rosie. She had to have heard about the fight. I shook out my hands, the slight soreness in my knuckles suddenly demanding attention.

"So, I hear something happened last night." Her eyebrows shot up with a questioning look, and she pressed her thin pink lips together.

"Yeah." The word was a sigh. "I know I shouldn't have, but I hit Nima."

"Hit? More like bombed." Koni released a monstrous laugh and doubled over to exaggerate it, his loose long hair flying forward with the momentum.

Elijah smirked with a chuckle, and Loch's lips twitched upward too. Holy fuck! Those two actually reacted to something involving me. Color me surprised.

"Boys!" Rosie chided, twisting around to point her finger at them before spinning back toward me. "Yes, well ... She did have to visit us for some minor injuries."

"Meh. Mostly fake injuries, Rosie. C'mon now," Koni said, winking at me. "Nima was being a bitch, trying to get up on Z without—what's the word?"

"Consent," Elijah said, his smirk now totally gone.

"That's right," Koni agreed, lifting his finger to point at Elijah in agreement. "Consent."

Rosie's mouth turned down. She glanced back at Elijah for a moment with a soft nod, then turned back to me but spoke to Koni. "Right. As you've already explained. But I want to hear Teagan's side, if you don't mind. Should I take her to the office to do that, or will you keep your commentary to yourselves since you've already said your piece?"

They agreed by giving soft grunts.

While I may have asked to speak to Rosie alone before, not wanting an audience, I got the distinct feeling that because I had been on Zavier's side of this fight, they were on my side as well. That set me a little at ease.

"So yeah, I'm sorry if I hurt her …"

Koni grunted, louder this time. "You shouldn't apol—"

"Koni," Rosie admonished, throwing her hand up without looking back at him. He shut himself up by shoving the last of his burrito into his mouth and smiling at me.

I pressed my lips together, not wanting to smile in return. It was difficult. I glanced at Loch, which helped me refrain easily enough. His square face was set into its usual hardened state—intense eyes boring into me, barely blinking, solid jaw clenching tight. Elijah, however, held an inquisitive look, his eyes roaming over me not exactly in a sexual way, more like a curious assessment. He scrubbed fingers through his thick wave of top hair as he leaned onto the island with his opposite hand.

I cleared my throat. "I am sorry that I struck her first. I lost my temper over something she said, but I know that's not a great excuse for getting physical. I never want to hurt anyone unless it's in self-defense. So, if you need me to apologize to her ..." My teeth snapped together, stopping the previous night's anger from bubbling up. "I will if you want me to."

Rosie smiled and folded her hands in front of her with a shake of her head. "Thank you for owning up to that, but I don't need or want you to apologize to her. It won't do any good for either of you, I'm sure. But understand that she also won't be apologizing for what she said to make you angry. I know what it was and have already dealt with her for it. We attempted to keep your information private, but some have discovered things on their own. And while Tim and I have already discouraged the others from repeating what they've heard, we have no real way of stopping it from spreading further. I will be in touch with your aunt today to inform her of this. I suppose it's up to you and her to decide whether you will remain here as planned. Would you like to speak to her later?"

"Only if she wants to talk to me," I replied. Even though I wanted to talk to her, I didn't enjoy the thought of having another conversation about our family, this time over the phone. I didn't see any reason for me to leave at this point. At home, I was less concealed, and there was no other option. This place might have been a last resort when Aunt Sonya had chosen it, but she knew it would be the best choice if I transitioned. Better than being alone with no guidance, or worse, a spot too close to humans. Plus, there was Zavier now and ...

I glanced at Koni, Loch, and Elijah, then back to Rosie. "I'd rather not leave."

All the guys' eyebrows lifted at the same time. Shocked. Had they expected me to bail? Or had they wanted me to?

"Okay then," Rosie said with a nod. "I'll let her know what you said and radio you if she wants to talk. How's Zavier this morning?"

My body heated with that direct question. She obviously knew what had happened and where he had stayed last night. I swallowed down the lump of embarrassment in my throat. Koni's eyes caught mine from behind Rosie. He waggled his brows, and I couldn't stop the smile this time. "He's good. Tired but good."

"He should be," Koni offered with a smile and nod. "We ran him out last night." He smacked the back of his hand to Loch's bicep.

To my surprise, Loch and Elijah both smirked, and Loch replied, "We did. And he's going out again later."

"He has our camp assessment first," Rosie said, turning her body sideways to better see us all. "But he needs to recoup some energy and to eat."

"I'm gonna make him some breakfast now. Probably a loaded omelet and some toast," I said, adding the last bit to myself, thinking it over.

She smiled brightly at that. "Well, now. That's really sweet of you. I'm sure it'll help him recover from the night."

"I'm sure it will," Koni added. "Lucky son of a—"

"Koni," Rosie warned with a laugh.

"What? I'm just saying. He was in a cabin for his transition. Had us to meet him after. Getting breakfast made the next day by someone who's taking care of him. Not to mention having something sweet as honey beforehand." The last bit was a soft murmur, but I still heard it.

If I were a blusher, that would have lit my cheeks ablaze. The "honey" was definitely me. Yeah, they all knew I'd slept with him for sure.

"Well, he is lucky he's here at camp," Rosie agreed, choosing not to pick apart the details. Thank God.

"Yeah, lucky he's not alone in the middle of a cornfield," Koni added, his smile fading and taking my embarrassment right along with it.

"Or in a dark basement," Elijah uttered, his eyes staring blankly at the island.

As shocked as I was by their admissions, I hadn't expected to see the same faraway look on Loch's face. But then I nearly gasped when he spoke too. "Or chained to a pole."

I couldn't stop my mouth from falling open. Christ. What had happened to them? My chest pounded as if it were cleaving wide open at their words, at their wounds. Oh, my heart.

"Yes," Rosie said softly, her eyebrows drawing down as she glanced at all of them. "We are glad for him. We've all had struggles, but we've survived, and we learn to rise above them."

At her words, they snapped out of their own heads and straightened up again. I avoided their eyes and caught Rosie's when she turned and walked to me.

"Thank you for taking care of him, Teagan," she said, laying a hand on my arm and rubbing it gently. "I know it isn't easy for anyone to give so generously, especially when we're so used to being alone or being treated poorly." I nodded, a little shocked by her words. Though, I had a feeling that I had been right about how close she and Tim were to those they helped care for here. Specifically, The Four. In fact, Rosie behaved more like a mom. And maybe she was as close to one as they'd ever had.

When I didn't reply, she continued, "Nima and her sisters were told to stay away from you. I expect you to do the same. You can keep caring for Zavier, though I'm sure he'll be his normal self by the end of the day, with plenty of food, of course." She winked. "You're still on for chores, but don't stress over them. And I'll let you know how the call goes with your Aunt."

"Okay," I said, giving her a tiny smile.

"Don't keep Zavier out too late again, boys," she called over her shoulder to them as she passed me.

"Sure thing!" Koni replied as she pushed through the door and disappeared into the dining hall.

I turned from where Rosie had exited and found all the guys staring at me again. There was an itch inside, pushing me to cross my arms, but I kept them firmly pinned at my side, fingering the pockets of the parka instead. Since it was getting awkward, I chose to set about my breakfast task and moved to the refrigerator for the ingredients.

"So our boy is okay this morning?" Koni said while my head was in the fridge.

"Yeah. He changed back a little while ago, then fell asleep again before I left." I sorted through some ingredients but settled with mushroom and ham since I knew Zavier liked what I'd made the previous day. As soon as I popped my head out with the food, I asked, "I take it everything went well ... out with you guys."

Elijah moved around the kitchen, grabbing the items I'd need to make the food. He didn't reply. Neither did Loch, who remained by the island, staring stiffly like usual. They didn't care to share info, obviously.

Koni exhaled a breath and pushed away from the island, moving toward me. "Yeah. He did fine. Gonna take a little while to get used to his legs, but that's normal. What about you? How are you feeling?"

The question stunned me a bit, and I eyed him suspiciously. He had been nice the night before, yet I couldn't help my reaction since we weren't alone. "I'm ... okay. Thanks."

"You sure? I mean, have you seen someone transition before? Is that why you were okay with him coming inside?" He bit his lips together with a slight smile as if he were about to make a sex joke but thought better of it.

I heard Loch let out a huff of air behind me, but I didn't turn.

Elijah placed the cooking materials next to the griddle near the ovens and burners. "Did you want to use this instead of the range?

It might be easier if you're making more than one." He tapped the counter beside the flat surface, his long fingers skimming the front edge. My eyes roamed upward over his tight forearms and their deep skin tone that looked as if he'd stepped off a yacht in the Mediterranean. Like the other day, he wore a V-neck that showed a peek of chest hair. And his face, well ... those sultry brown eyes were staring at me now, waiting for my reply but also studying me more intently than they had before.

I tore my gaze from him and glanced at the griddle. It looked practically new, with very few burn spots or scrapes. It was tempting, though I didn't think it was necessary to use. "I'm only making two. Unless any of you want one?" I asked, glancing around to catch Koni's and Loch's eyes as well.

Koni lifted the ingredients from my arms to help put them on the cutting board and counter. "We already ate."

"And we have things to do," Loch added.

Elijah nodded. "Use what you need, just—"

"Clean up," I interrupted, beaming a smile at him. He sure was predictable in his love of cleanliness. It was a little adorable and a lot hot, actually. Big Italian who takes care of the kitchen? Oh yeah. I pictured him making food with only an apron and felt my body flash with warmth. I inhaled, smelling Koni at the counter behind me—earthy—and then a hint of leather and maybe fresh citrus. Elijah's scent.

He blinked at me, several in rapid succession as if my smile had surprised him. The muscle in his jaw flexed. "Yeah."

I nodded with a bite on my lower lip, then turned and started prepping.

Koni slid an empty mixing bowl over to me as Loch and Elijah moved toward the door. I watched them stop behind Koni, waiting.

"Look, Teagan. I—we just wanted to say thanks for helping Z. You, uh, you're—"

Loch didn't wait for Koni to finish. He shoved through the door into the dining hall, Elijah on his heels.

Koni whipped his head back around after the interruption. "Don't mind them. They're typically cranky. Like Z. Though, I have a feeling Z's not gonna be so cranky anymore." He chuckled then left quickly, jogging after the guys. I knew he meant more than Zavier's transition, and that implication had me giggling while I started to cook.

3

"I brought you an omelet," I announced to the closed bathroom door.

When I returned to my cabin, Zavier was already showering. He'd also changed the sheets since his paws had tracked ground soil into the bed with us the previous night. I was grateful he switched them because I'd planned to do it myself before working in the laundry cabin.

The bathroom door opened, and he exited, his skin mostly dried as he tucked a towel around his waist. "You made me this? Toast too? Oh yes, I'm starving. Thank you." The words barely had time to escape as he took hold of his plate with one hand and shoved a piece of toast into his mouth with the other.

I laughed, watching his eyes animate his pleasure as he chewed, crossing and rolling and clenching shut. Wanting to dig in, too, I set my plate and the orange juice cartons on the coffee table.

As I moved to sit, he dropped his plate down in a rush, then grabbed hold of me, pulling my body against his. "Thank you." One arm cinched around my waist, and the other hand slipped around the back of my neck, drawing my mouth to his. His lips teased mine, barely touching. "I'm starving for you too."

I opened with a sigh at his words, letting him dive in to taste what he wanted. My tongue curled and twisted with his, the sensation causing shivers to scatter all over my skin. My body trembled in response.

"Oh, yeah, that's the feeling," he said, speaking over my lips again while his fingers dug into my skin greedily. "I want more."

"Eat first," I whispered, having to tear my own hands from him. I wanted him just as badly. Especially now after his transition, when he seemed more alert, aware, alive. But most important of all, not pained.

He released a sigh, pressing his forehead to mine before pulling away completely. "I don't want to sound ungrateful, but I think you're gonna taste better." I chuckled and shoved his body into one of the armchairs. He laughed too, then added, "Honey is also delicious for dessert."

"Stop," I said as my laugh faded, forking my eggs. "You sure have a lot of energy. I thought I'd be walking back in here to more snoring."

His eyebrows raised as he chomped down a massive bite of his omelet. "Do I really snore? The guys never said anything."

"Joking. But I wouldn't care if you did. I enjoyed sleeping with you. Even the hairy version."

"I wasn't sure how you were going to handle me last night when I came back. I couldn't quite make myself change yet, but I needed to be beside you again."

That admission made my heart swell a bit and threatened to rip the numbness away. I didn't fight it, though. I welcomed it—this, being with him, near him. "I know what you mean," I admitted, then tore into my toast and sipped my juice.

After a few silent moments filled with only chewing and easy stares between us, he gulped down his juice in one go then said, "So, you are okay with me staying?"

"Yeah, I told you I was. I want you here with me."

"Sorry, I was in a haze this morning. I remember it all just wanted to make sure I wasn't dreaming." His plate was empty. The extra-large omelet, two slices of toast, and a banana were all gone. Devoured.

"I'm glad it wasn't a dream either. Also that it went well last night for you. I saw the guys and Rosie this morning."

"Oh yeah? You aren't in trouble, are you?"

"No."

"Good. The guys and I communicated some last night ... so weird, by the way, understanding words and intent through different types of language. Barks. Body movement. I can't wait for you to feel it too. It's unreal and so ... potent. I'm not sure how to explain it. Anyway, they changed when we got back and mentioned talking to Rosie. So everything's okay?"

I blinked at his words, taking all of him in, how vocal he had become compared to the last couple of days. Maybe it was the transition, or he was more comfortable with me, trusting of me. "Yeah, I think it's okay. Nima and her sisters were told to stay away from me, and I'm to do the same. Rosie is hoping that word about my family won't travel any further because ... I came here to hide after what my father did, after what happened. Rosie's going to talk to my aunt today. I told her I didn't want to leave."

He licked his lips and shifted forward in his chair, his knees turning and touching mine. "I was worried you would, that after last night you might choose to bail. But I still don't understand why you came here to hide."

"Since my family is dead, I have alpha claim for the pack territory but can't take it until after transition. My Aunt Sonya—Dad's sister—was chosen to be interim alpha by the supernatural council in our area—reapers, vampires, and what's left of the wolves. She was worried that my late mom's brother, Uncle Raif—who was outcasted years ago—might return to challenge me, claim the spot, and take my house and the family restaurant. If he were to find me before my transition, it would be far easier to deal with me."

"He won't get near you," Zavier said, his gravelly voice low. He snapped his teeth together. The sudden protectiveness had my lips tugging into a small, sad smile as I thought about him getting involved in my drama.

"I'm glad you told me," he continued. "I wasn't sure what might happen, not really knowing you but feeling close. I ... I guess I was worried you might not stay. I don't want you to leave. That's why I told you so much last night, told you how much I want you." He pushed his plate forward and grabbed mine from my lap, setting it out of the way so he could stand and pull me up to my feet. His palms cradled my face, and he inched in closer. "I hope this doesn't make me sound too needy. I mean, I know I was needy enough with the transition, but I want you to know that I didn't only need you for that. I want you. More than here, maybe." He bit his bottom lip, and I was pretty sure pink tinged his cheeks, color that wasn't there before, given that the small mark from his fight with Loch had already disappeared.

"You ... want me after here?" I asked, wondering if I'd heard him correctly.

His eyes closed briefly. After a deep inhale, he said, "I know it might sound stupid. Maybe it's too early. I know we don't know each other very well, but ... The things you've done for me in such little time, how you make me feel ... you've claimed me. I've never thought I'd say these things, ever. I never thought I'd be so ... struck. I've seen it before in some others—my family when I was young—but I've never felt this way. Please tell me I'm not an idiot for saying all of this. I might have kept it to myself, but I feel like I'd lose you if I didn't tell you right away. And I don't think I can handle that. Well, I obviously could if you aren't feeling the same ... I would have to."

I reached my hands up to his neck, pulled his face down at the same time I pushed onto my toes, and slammed my mouth to his. He didn't need to say anything else. It was as if he had crawled into my head and professed my own thoughts.

He moaned, happily giving up on words in exchange for the feeling of my tongue.

I broke away, and his face dipped farther, kissing down the side of my neck. "I feel the same. I want you. But I also want to know more about you. Tell me." My voice was soft, the feel of him making me breathless.

His roaming hands slid over my sides and down to my ass, palming my cheeks over the sweats then grasping them hard. Between kisses, he spoke. "I have no home. My family cared for me in a financial sense only. Kept me home for schooling, especially after I showed no signs of transition." His hands gripped harder, then scooped me into the air.

My legs locked around his waist, which knocked his towel from his hips, dropping it to the floor. "My father was the same," I admitted.

With my legs secured around him, he lifted the hem of Loch's shirt and tugged it up over my head, glancing at it as it fell to the floor. "I'll get you your clothes back. Or you can wear some of mine." His face dipped, kissing along my chest as I let my head fall backward, speaking against my skin. "Where was I? Oh, yeah … They kicked me out at eighteen. They decided my older brother was more than enough for them to be proud of. They tossed me some money and told me goodbye."

I sniffled, feeling the hurt he must have felt, the same kind I'd felt too.

"No, Teagan, it's not a sad story. I'm here now, with you," he whispered, his kisses stopping on my collarbone and his breath caressing my skin. He walked us back to the bedroom and crawled us onto the bed.

I reached up and captured the loose hair hanging down, pushing it back so I could better see his eyes. "I know, but it's like what I went through, so I felt it, felt how you must have then."

His lips pressed gently to mine, and one of his hands skimmed over the white lace bra covering my breast. "After that, I roamed some, spent most of the money on places to stay, heading east with no life plan. Eventually, I found this place. I've been here about a year. Still don't have any solid plans. I've taken some extra classes but was too focused on my transition and not what came after. I guess I've gotten comfortable here." He chuckled before dipping his face down, licking and kissing his way to my breast. "Got comfortable with everyone here, too, with the other guys."

I ran my fingers through his hair again, enjoying the way the silky strands slid between them. "They've become your family. Rosie, Tim, and the others."

"Yes," he agreed, slipping my bra cups down and under, freeing my breasts. His tongue licked around a nipple, bathing it lovingly. "I think of them as family. That's why ..." He groaned and sucked me into his mouth.

"Why what?" I prompted, my body beginning to writhe beneath him.

"Why when you first got here, smelling like a runt like me but also like a fucking gorgeous summer day, all flowery and bright, and feisty ... We agreed that night we couldn't mess with you. You had to be off-limits because you would derail us, fuck us up, maybe rip us apart. We knew it."

I gasped with a laugh. "What?! You guys looked like you were two seconds from tossing me in the lake and letting me drown. You were worried I'd come between you?"

He chuckled, the sound all husky and sexy as his lips trailed over to the other nipple, licking and sucking between words. "We smelled you, saw how you handled Nima and the sisters—who we can't stand—and were instantly hard. Well, I was. And Koni, too, because he told me he was. We were pissed about it, but, oh yeah, we knew we were fucked." He sucked me in, and I moaned at the feeling of his tongue. Then he lifted higher and dropped his pelvis down to mine, his hard dick pressing against my pussy, my underwear and Loch's sweats the only barrier between us.

I sighed, watching his eyes roam over me. "So after our time in the bathhouse ..."

"Loch and I threw fists. We all planned to stay away from you, but after you stood up to Jackson outside of the laundry and fuck ..." He groaned and shifted over me, sliding his cock over the sweats, grinding against me. "I couldn't stay away when you offered to touch me, to help me. And Loch's stunt with your clothes was a power play, a reminder to us that you were off-limits. It's also why he donated his own for you to use. But I don't think—actually, I know that's not the only reason."

"Not the only reason, huh? Does he hate me as much as it seems?"

"Oh, baby ... He doesn't hate you. He hates that he wants you too."

4

Zavier dropped that knowledge bomb then didn't wait a single second more before stripping my clothes off.

"What?" I asked breathlessly, so turned on by how he was handling me I could barely breathe, let alone speak. "He stares at me as if he loathes me. I guess he has a reason if I'm going to tear your friendships apart." I'd been doubtful of it, but I knew deep down I'd felt something from Loch too. Something from all of them. At least I knew I wasn't going completely insane, that the numbness hadn't driven me into delusions.

His hands tossed the sweats and underwear onto the floor, and then he leaned over me. His breaths were as heavy as his cock looked while his eyes traveled my naked body, taking in all the dips and swells. I was more sticky than curvy, but I could tell by the look in his brilliant eyes and the way he licked his lips that he liked everything he saw more clearly in the daylight.

"God, Teagan. You are gorgeous. So fucking sexy." Those rough hands slipped up my legs as he lowered himself closer. "Loch, Eli, Koni ... they want you too. I know they do. I can feel it from them. See it. And they aren't sure what to do now that I crossed this line."

"Aren't you worried?" I asked, gripping the sheets as his lips kissed my inner thigh.

His eyes kept locked onto mine. "About them?" When I nodded, he added, "I don't want to give them up. Our bond is like a brotherhood. But now that I've had you"—another open-mouthed wet kiss graced my thigh—"I don't want to give you up either."

"I don't want to come between you. Ruin the family you've made—"

"You won't. We'll work it out. I know it will happen. I feel like … you belong with us. Do you feel that too? Do you like them?"

Us. Them. "I … I …" his mouth slammed down onto my pussy, his tongue licking from my opening to my clit in a long, languid stroke. "Ah!" My body bucked from the bed, but his hands clamped down onto my thighs, pinning me back down while his tongue started circling my most sensitive spot. "Ah. Ah. I like them, yes. I think. I don't know them very well either, but I feel something like a pull for all of you. I'm not sure how to explain it—ah!"

"Mmm," he hummed into me as his tongue pushed inside, penetrating and tasting me. "I can't get enough of your taste. Like honey and summer. Fucking delicious." His lips and tongue moved up and began assaulting my clit fervently, sucking, biting, and then he slipped a finger inside me. I rocked against his mouth and hand, and he moaned. "Yes. I don't think I'll ever get enough of you. And I'll let them know. I'll talk to Koni first. He and I are closer. He's the most easygoing, so I know he'll accept us … this … possibly more. Fuck. Mmm."

"Ahh," I repeatedly said as he finished talking and went to work on me again. My brain stopped thinking. I could only breathe and feel him all over me.

Another finger joined and curled inside, hitting the spot that sent my body into convulsions and made me see stars behind my eyelids.

"I'm coming. Oh, yes," I screamed, wracked with the intensity of the orgasm. With aftershocks still coursing through the muscles, my body wanting to milk his finger of all the pleasure, I felt another finger circling the rim of my tight hole, wetting it. "Oh."

"I want you back here. Have you ever had anal?"

"No. Never, but ... oh ..." It felt good. His fingers slid around me, probing the area while his others kept pumping into my pussy. I felt it everywhere, the tingles of desire spreading all the way down to my toes. They curled in response.

"That feels good, huh?" With little effort, the finger slid inside my ass. The pressure there was ... exquisite. I found myself rolling my hips with his movements, wanting more of it. "Yes. Look at you. You are liking this. Fuck, I'm gonna come just watching you. Mmm."

Without warning, he leaped away from the bed and disappeared for a moment before returning with a small bottle. He shook it for me to see, then climbed back between my legs. "Lube. Had it hidden under the sink for better showers. Forgot it when I moved. Thank fuck I did." His smile was so devilish that it made me giggle.

I stared down at his cock, his large, very solid cock, its head thick and a deep shade of pink that made his arousal look almost painful. "I'm not sure you'll, um …"

"I'm going to take my time, don't worry. This stuff will help and make it so much better." Suddenly that smile vanished, and his face grew serious, as emotionless as I'd often seen it before. "Tell me to stop, okay? If you don't want this. I'll take anything you want to give me. But this … you being even willing to try this with me … that alone has me wanting to fall to my knees to eat you all day long."

There was no stopping the spurt of laughter that escaped me. It was nearly an ugly laugh, almost with accompanying tears. "Eat me all day, huh?"

"Oh, fuck yeah. I will be on my knees for you forever just to taste you. I know I've probably lost my mind. I've never …" He closed his eyes and shook his head, his longer blond strands falling over his forehead. "I just want you so damn bad. All of you. Fuck, please don't think I'm crazy."

"I don't. I want all of you too," I sat up, reaching down to stroke him while pushing my lips to his for a kiss. He thrust into my hand with a moan. "Be gentle with me."

He broke the kiss and pulled his dick from my grasp, devilish smile back in place, taking my permission and not wanting to waste a single moment. I watched him drizzle lube onto his dick. He stroked himself, his eyes focused on me as I watched, biting my lip. Seeing his fingers slide around his thickness, twisting and gripping hard, made me want to jump on him. Before I could make a choice, though, he released himself and shifted down, his face diving back to my pussy.

His tongue licked my clit, teasing and flicking as his fingers slid to my entrance and then my ass. I swiveled my hips, feeling them inside each place. He moved them at an easy pace, pushing in and out in a slow, seductive rhythm. Then the pressure returned, another finger joining in, stretching my tight hole.

"Oh," I said on a sigh, gripping the blankets at my side.

"That's right, baby. Oh fuck. You are doing so good. This must feel amazing." His lips sealed around my clit and sucked hard. I whined and bucked, and he quickly backed off with slower tongue flicks, knowing that he'd almost brought me to orgasm again. "Not yet. I want inside you first."

More pressure came, and his hard breaths puffed against my clit. He was getting so worked up I could hear and feel him panting.

"Fuck. Oh, Zavier. Oh, yes," I whined, losing my damn mind. My body was climbing its way back toward a climax.

"God, you're so relaxed for me. You're ready. You're so ready." He lifted onto his knees and stroked his cock again, watching me. Then he leaned in and pressed his tip to my ass. "Tell me if it hurts. Oh fuck, that is so hot. You are taking me. Feel that?"

And I did. There was enough pressure to be nearly painful, but it also felt so damn good. His tip popped inside, and he let his head fall back as he moaned to the ceiling. His muscles were all taut, straining for control and for release. I couldn't keep my eyes from him, turned on and ready to orgasm just from seeing his reaction to me.

When his head leveled and his gaze met mine, he slipped his fingers over my clit and rolled them around, spiking my pleasure. He pushed in farther, my hole stretching around his thickness. "Oh yes. Are you okay?"

"Yes. Yes. I'm okay. It hurts some but feels good too."

"You're so good. God, I might explode." He grabbed the bottle again and dripped more lube onto himself before massaging the area.

I was full, so fucking full of him. He was everywhere, and I loved it—the smell of him in my nose, the weight of him between my legs, and his hardness buried inside. It was like a sensation buffet. My body and mind wanted to take everything and more.

With one last push, he was seated flush against me. We both groaned and gazed at each other, watching and enjoying the reaction and the feeling.

"I'm gonna move. Tell me if I'm hurting you." He slid himself out nice and slow before pushing back in at the same speed. "Oh damn. You feel incredible. So fucking tight here too." After a few strokes, he fell forward, letting his chest press against me before dipping his head to take my mouth with his. He moved his hips, setting a faster tempo while his tongue mimicked the movements. His lips left mine, kissing down my neck as his pace sped up.

The feeling was indescribable. I'd thought it would hurt, but that wasn't entirely right. The bit of pain I'd felt at first had morphed into the strangest kind of pleasure, different from the normal but so good in its own way. And the way Zavier moved also deserved credit. His endurance, his control, and his attentiveness to my needs blew my mind in every way. He started pistoning me, tipping my ass higher to drive himself inside. His grunts and moans filled the room, a euphoric melody that made my body blaze hotter.

"Zavier. Zavier. Oh my God," I murmured, as his hips slapped against me and his cock buried harder and faster.

He pushed up onto his knees, grabbing my hip with one hand while his other fingers returned to my clit, circling mercilessly. When his thumb pushed inside my pussy at the same time and curled against my inner wall, I was launched over the orgasm edge. My body bucked against him, my muscles convulsing without control.

"Zavier! Ah!" I screamed his name, pressing my head into the mattress and arching my back.

"Fuck. Yes," he said through rasped breaths, pounding my ass over and over, faster and faster. And then he released a loud growl as he spilled inside me. His thrusts slowed then suddenly stopped as his body arched over and his forehead dropped between my breasts. Long breaths rushed out over my sweaty skin, cooling and caressing.

I lifted my hands to the back of his head, massaging his scalp with the tips of my fingers. After a deep inhale, I said, "My ... that was ..."

"So fucking good, baby. What have I done to deserve that?" he asked, the last part more to himself, I supposed.

But I still answered. "Everything."

His laugh was breathy. He finally lifted his head and looked right into my eyes. "It seems strange to thank someone after sex, but I can't help it. Thank you. For trusting me. Letting me have you. I've never had anyone give me so much. Ever. And I'm not just talking about—"

"I know," I said, smiling. Because I did. I knew exactly what he meant. It was more than me giving him my body. It was apparent that I'd been there for him in ways no one else ever had, except for maybe his closest friends here. "Thank you too." I said the words because I felt the same, and I just inherently knew he would be there for me too.

The corners of his mouth tugged up, and his lips parted, revealing the broadest, most dazzling smile. His teeth gleamed, and his eyes beamed.

I sighed and shoved his shoulder. "You keep smiling like that, you'll have to explain to Rosie why I skipped chores."

He laughed before sitting back onto his knees and pulling out of me. The loss of him tugged at me beyond the simple physical aspect. And that was an odd sensation, like separating part of me. How could I feel so connected to him? Was it possible that I had bonded with him? Was this what a coupling was? The rumors about this place said not many bonded here, but ... Keira and Mike seemed to have. Maybe it was true. If so, what would we do? It all felt so quick. But my mother had told me when I was young that her and father's bonding had happened suddenly.

Zavier flashed me another smile before disappearing into the bathroom. "Do you want a shower?"

"No, took one earlier," I replied absently, my thoughts churning. The sink turned on, and I imagined he was also skipping a shower since he'd just taken one before breakfast.

He came back a minute later, holding a wet washcloth and bending to clean me up.

"Oh, I was about to get up—"

"Let me," he insisted, wiping it over me. "I can clean most of you, but you'll probably—"

"Yo!" A voice called into the cabin after a swift knock on the front door. Somebody had walked in.

Before we could even reply, Koni's face appeared in the open doorway. "Hey. Oh!"

"Koni, fuck!" Zavier shouted over his shoulder but was laughing as he attempted to hide my naked body with his own. The effort was almost nonexistent, though. Aside from his hand and the cloth covering my pussy, I was pretty sure Koni had seen all of me and Zavier's ass too.

Koni's laughter rang out as he disappeared back into the front area. "Sorry!"

"No, you aren't, Stray. Always wandering..."

Stray. That was another one of their nicknames that Keira had mentioned. Somehow I knew Koni had gotten the nickname for reasons beyond walking in on people after sex.

Shaking his head, Zavier helped me to my feet. After gathering my clothes, he slipped into his sweats and watched me dress. "If I can't get your stuff back, I'll give you some of my things to wear too."

I lifted an eyebrow with a smirk. "Yeah? You don't think that'll stir the pot?"

He huffed a breath, and Koni laughed out front, overhearing our talk. When we walked out there to meet him, he said, "Forget stirring. The pot's already been flipped the fuck over."

5

"Shut up," Zavier said, shoving Koni's chest playfully.

"Just stating the obvious. There's no turning back now," Koni replied, running his fingers through his long, wavy hair while eyeing both of us. He grinned and waggled his brows. "The smells in here ... Mmm. Hot like fire."

Zavier wrapped an arm over my shoulder and pulled me against his bare chest while letting out an amusing little growl. "Is there a reason you're here?"

Koni chuckled. "I came to check how you're doing and let you know Tim and Rosie want to see you in the office. They need to take you out for your first assessment."

"Ah. Okay. They mentioned it before, knowing I'd transition soon. Guess I'm the lucky one who has an excuse to get out of chores," he quipped, his head inclining toward me.

"Ha, ha," I said with a smile up at him. "Don't worry about me. I'll be just fine by myself."

"Yeah, she'll be fine but not by herself. She has me to help," Koni said, winking.

"Oh really?" Zavier asked, raising his eyebrows as he released his hold of me. He started glancing around the cabin for his shirt, lifting the throw pillows on the chairs then moving to the bathroom.

"Yeah, I—we thought it was probably a good idea that someone hangs with her—you," he said, correcting himself while looking at me, then continuing, "after what happened last night."

I scrunched my lips. "You mean with Nima? Rosie said they were told to stay away."

"That doesn't matter," he replied, shaking his head. "We respect Tim and Rosie and listen to what they tell us, but that doesn't mean anyone else here gives a shit. Despite threats from their families, most still have places to go home to even if they fuck up. That means they can't be trusted to follow rules. Plus, we wouldn't trust them, anyway."

"I don't either," Zavier added, pulling his T-shirt over his head as he returned to my side. "So, yeah, I'd feel better if you stuck with Koni today too."

I rolled my eyes. "Have my recent actions not proven that I can take care of myself?"

They exchanged glances as Zavier ran a hand over my ass, the touch so familiar and content it made me want to sigh. "We know you can. But that line has been crossed. If anything happens now, it probably won't be a fair fight. I wouldn't put it past them to pull something like Jackson and Trig did to me in the laundry."

"True," Koni agreed, placing a hand on my shoulder and staring right into my eyes. His large amber irises were mesmerizing and seemed to penetrate me the same way as Zavier's and Loch's even had. He nodded and winked. "Safety in numbers. More fun too, usually."

"Yeah, yeah," Zavier said. He was joking, but he didn't seem bothered by Koni touching me or even looking at me the way he was. With Koni's hand still on my shoulder, Zavier leaned closer into my side and kissed me. He made no move to force Koni's hand away. And it wasn't a quick kiss either. He deepened it, sweeping his tongue inside to meet mine, his hand grasping my ass while Koni's slid slowly from my shoulder down my arm, the touch gentle and exploring.

Oh. That stirred something else inside. The feel and smell of them both so close to me, touching me at the same time. My body flushed with heat and shivered in response.

"Mmm," Zavier hummed into my mouth. He let out a grunt when he finally pulled away.

"Looks like torture," Koni said with a chuckle.

I eyed him dubiously as Zavier joked, "You have no idea. I guess I better go. I'll take the dishes to the kitchen before I meet with Tim and Rosie. See you later." His hand patted my ass before he gathered up the plates from breakfast and moved to the door.

"Later," Koni said while I smiled with a nod.

"Give me a minute." I retreated to the bathroom to clean up a bit more. Then, knowing it was best to get them done right away, I scooped up the bedsheets and we exited the cabin.

As soon as we started walking, he shoved his hands into his jeans and asked, "Laundry first?"

"I guess. But I could drop these off and move onto the bathhouse. I doubt anyone will mess with sheets."

"True, no one will. Everybody's busy. Loch and Eli are scrubbing the kitchen and running perimeter tests. Pretty much everyone else is working on one of the upper cabins. It got a roof leak or something. One of the older residents lives in it. Ford. He's been here half a year or so. Anyway, they'll probably break for lunch soon, but I think there's a good amount of work to do on that cabin, so we shouldn't need to worry about them."

"Remind me why you need to be with me then?" I shot him a side-eye glare and grinned.

He chuckled and ran a hand through his long locks, pulling it back into a low ponytail with an elastic he'd had around his wrist. "Because I'm so nice and personable. I make excellent company. You must have felt that at the lake last night."

Oh, yes, I certainly had. He'd admitted to staring at me too much after he'd caught me doing the same. "Yes, you make excellent company. Thank you."

He reached over and took the bundle of sheets from my arms. "So Alabama, huh?"

"Yeah. I'm a 'Bama girl."

"I like that twang in your voice when you say certain words. 'Bama," he repeated, trying to mimic the sound. I laughed as we turned up the path toward the laundry cabin. "Your restaurant is there too? What kinds of food did y'all make? I got that right, right? Y'all." He chuckled to himself. "Y'all."

"Oh my God! You're adorable."

"No, you're adorable," he said back to me, imitating my accent again with another laugh. "I'm too manly to be adorable. Or at least too tall. Not fun-sized like you."

I pushed his arm, charmed easily by his humor. "Fun-sized? Oh dear lord."

"Oh dear lord." His voice dipped and lilted exactly like mine had.

"Would you stop!" I was laughing so hard, I could barely get the words out. And I couldn't stop. Just as we reached the laundry, I snorted. His eyes widened in mock horror, and he gasped, poking fun of me some more. I slugged his arm and covered my mouth as tears leaked from my eyes. Pains ran through my stomach. I hadn't laughed so hard in … in ages. It felt good. Better than good. It felt fantastic.

"Okay, okay, I'll stop if you tell me what your place served for food."

"Deal," I agreed, holding the door open as he moved inside with the bundle of sheets tucked under an arm. I went about setting the washing machines I needed to use for the sheets, then loaded them. "We make several things. A fair amount of seafood, like catfish and crawfish and whatever is in season. Also shrimp, lots of ways, but usually like a shrimp boil. Of course, we often do N'awlins gumbo or jambalaya." When Koni merely stared at me as he leaned back against a dryer, I clarified, "New Orleans style. And then, let's see, fried green tomatoes and fried chicken, and I won't get into the desserts."

"Wait, back up. Fried chicken?"

"Uh, yeah," I said, scrunching my eyebrows. "Of course! It's a staple in The Back Burner. Like grits."

"And you make it too?" His tongue popped out of his mouth and proceeded to lick between his lips as if he were starved.

Gah. Why did that look so hot? Why did it always look so damn sexy when he did it, or Zavier or Loch? I think I'd even seen Elijah do it once. Fuck. Now I was thinking about all of them licking their lips. Mostly Zavier, though, after he'd gone down on me. I clamped my thighs together, feeling the soreness there after having him invade my asshole so thoroughly and ... enjoyably. *Sigh.*

After catching Koni's eyebrow lift at my very pregnant pause, I coughed. "Well, sure, I can make that in my sleep. Some other things I'd need the recipes because I didn't cook them often enough to memorize them."

"Fried chicken, though?"

"Yes," I let the word drag out as I finished stuffing the sheets into the washer and closing the lid. "Would you like some for dinner tonight?"

His eyes bugged right out of his head, almost like a cartoon. "What?! Are you offering to make me fried chicken?"

I laughed before turning toward the cabinets to grab cleaning supplies. There wasn't a ton of work to do in here, but it was a good idea to get started since we'd still need to check the bathhouse and the classroom. I eyed him over my shoulder. "Yeah, sure. I'll make it for you and Zavier. Maybe the other guys too, if they want."

As soon as I refocused on the cabinet, preparing to pull out a spray bottle, Koni had rushed up on me. His arms wrapped at my waist, and he lifted me into the air, my back firmly pressed to his chest, squeezing me in a massive bear hug.

"Oof!" I squeaked, kicking my feet for a second, then going totally limp when I realized he was hugging me from behind.

His face pressed into the parka between my shoulders, and he spoke several muffled words I couldn't understand.

"What?" I managed to breathe out, the air leaving me in a rush.

His arms eased a little but not enough to drop my feet to the floor. "Thank you! Fried chicken is my favorite." His words were clear after he'd unburied his face from the parka.

I chuckled, tickled by his exaggerated gratitude. When he felt me vibrating, he finally let me down back onto my own feet. I turned around, seeing the sincerity in his amber eyes, so big and honest. He wasn't laughing. "Oh ... you aren't kidding around, are you?"

"No way would I joke about that," he said, licking his lips again.

Stray. The nickname sprung to mind again, and I felt that could be why he was so serious about food. Fucking hell, that hit me right in the chest. But I fought back that quick stab of emotion and blinked up at him. "It's been a while since you've had it?"

"Yes, too long. I mean, Rosie made it for me a while back, but it's been months."

"Well, shit. That settles dinner then," I said, smiling brightly. "We'll have to make sure we have the ingredients, though. Oh wait, and what sides?"

"Sides?! Fuck me. I don't even know. Mac and cheese?"

"Mmm. Yes, that sounds good. If we have the stuff, I can do baked mac."

His hand covered his heart dramatically.

This time, I smacked his bicep lightly, seeing the playfulness. "And here I originally thought you were the calm, relaxed one of the group."

"Hey, I am," he said, reaching behind me for a few cleaning rags stacked in the cabinet. "I'm the most cheerful too, though. The most fun to be around."

"Hmm," I mused, tapping my chin. "I can't agree with that yet since I don't exactly know all of you very well."

"Oh, you will soon enough. I have a feeling."

"Do you now?"

"Yes, I do," he said with a wink. And it wasn't a creepy admission. It was as if it were a fact, and it didn't matter if I knew yet or not. It would happen.

Maybe because he had seemed to accept me so quickly and more freely, which may have been easier since Zavier had already crossed the line, making Koni feel comfortable enough to dive headfirst over it. I almost laughed to myself at that thought because it was so accurate. He had bounded at me like a happy puppy and practically acted like one too. Playful and cheerful, and lovey even. His personality was welcoming and wanting. It likely had to do with his past, which I was curious about. There was a need to know him the same as Zavier, and if he was telling the truth about getting to know them, then he was more than willing to open up and let me in.

6

"You missed a spot," Koni said, pointing to a smudge on one of the drains inside the bathhouse.

It was late afternoon. We'd finished up the laundry cabin and the classroom, not speaking too much while we worked. He was a hummer, humming away while we scrubbed and wiped and restocked. But he also kept an eye out, staying closer to the exits as if he were waiting for an attack. Those working on the cabin with the leaky roof had already eaten lunch, taking breaks at different times. We'd heard them travel along the paths or saw them when we'd moved to the next place to clean.

"Pretty sure *you* missed that spot," I said, eyeing the polishing rag dangling from his hand. He'd been cleaning and buffing the shiny surfaces and fixtures.

"Oh. Whoops," he replied with a shrug. He had been focused most of the time, but now and then his attention would stray. Stray …

"So," I said, choosing to voice my musings. I really wanted to know, and I couldn't help but ask. "Stray, huh?"

"Ah," he said with a breathy laugh as he bent to polish the spot he'd mentioned. He wiped the rag over the plated grating without looking up at me. "You caught that, huh?" When I didn't reply, he continued, "I don't know my family. Like, at all. I was ditched around my earliest memory, which actually was of my name."

I didn't dare speak, though my heart beat so hard learning the beginning of his story. He'd been abandoned?

"They found me wandering near Choctaw Nation, a reservation. I was four, I think. When the police inquired about my family, no one claimed me. Someone had called me Koni, which I didn't find out until later meant skunk. From what I pieced together, after jumping around different social workers and foster houses, they assumed I'd been dumped. No one at the initial place wanted or knew me, so the police thought I might have been born by a trafficked woman. I guess the person who dumped me thought anyone near the reservation might take me in. They probably had a guilty conscience or something. I don't know. They could have been my father and where I got my wolf gene, which was likely the main reason no one wanted to keep me. They could sense my difference, knew I was a mix of something. I must have smelled bad for them to call me skunk."

"Oh, I'm so sorry. That must have been a hard way to grow up." I recalled his comment in the kitchen about transitioning in the middle of a cornfield alone.

"It had its bad and good," he replied calmly. His words were nonchalant, but I knew he was covering, concealing the pain of it. That was his personality. My first impression of him had been so calm, yet he was easygoing and fun. Full of life. I supposed he had adopted that mentality through all the struggles. Maybe it was when he settled here, where he could finally relax and just live.

"How'd ya get here?" I asked.

He looked up at me then, the pointy nose scrunching before he smiled. "Well, I got sick of foster care pretty early and wandered east from Oklahoma. Landed jobs that paid under the table wherever I could. Stayed off the grid. I came across another wolf at one point who mentioned this place. I didn't think much about it at first, at odds with learning more about who I am—who we are. But then, about a year ago, I decided why not? I got here about a month after Zavier."

Why not? Oh, Koni. I knew he was probably like me too, didn't want to get or give pity. So I simply said, "I'm glad you did."

"I am too," he replied, nodding. A loud rumbling sounded from somewhere inside him, and his eyes widened.

"What the hell was that?" I joked, even though I already knew. We'd blown through lunch, and his body was not happy about it.

"It's the beast inside." He grabbed the hem of his T-shirt and lifted it upward as he looked down at himself. His stomach flexed, the ripples of his abs on full display. His other hand rubbed along his copper-hued skin slowly. "I'm sorry I've neglected you."

His last words barely registered as I watched his hand stroke down his skin. Fuck. It was as if I were watching in slow motion, my body heating as the sexy sight played out in front of me. The day had warmed up enough that I'd shed the parka during the cleaning session, but now I was hot and ready to shed my T-shirt too.

He coughed, and I blinked before looking up, knowing full well I'd been caught. "You're staring at me again." Though his words playfully recalled our exchange at the lake, they were deep and husky, as if he were turned on by my watching.

"I am," I admitted, choosing not to deny it. Was I being crazy for acting and feeling this way? I had just been with Zavier, and while he seemed adamant about not wanting to lose his friends or me, about needing to figure something out, I highly doubted he meant what was going through my mind. And really, what *was* going through my mind? I knew I was attracted to them. All of them. I'd be a fool if I didn't admit that to myself. But having some kind of relationship with someone else at the same time as Zavier? Did that make me a cheater? Unworthy? Was I a fool for thinking about it at all? Was I willing to jeopardize what had just started with him by flirting with one of his closest friends? Or was I a fool for getting involved with any of them, knowing that while being here had already helped me, changed me, I still planned to go home? And where would that leave him? Them?

"Good," he said, letting his shirt fall down and coming over to where I was squeegeeing the tiled walls. He lifted a hand to my face, trailing a single finger beneath my eye. "I like your beautiful eyes on me. Light gray, like the sky on a rainy summer day. I bet your coat will be this color. So pretty."

I tipped my face back as he stepped in closer. My lips parted, wanting to speak, but nothing came out. Thoughts escaped me at that moment. His finger moved down, his eyes following the progress as it slid over my cheek and then to my open mouth, the pad sliding over my lower lip.

He inhaled deep and closed his eyes. "You smell so good."

"So do you," I replied, finally finding my voice. "And you have beautiful eyes too. Is your coat amber colored?" I knew it wasn't always the case, but with brown eyes and gray eyes, the fur usually matched eye color. And blue eyes were more often gray wolves.

"Kind of," he breathed, and a tiny smile appeared on his lips as his hand dropped from my face.

My body felt a jolt as if my mind was slapping the sense back into me. I'd just let him touch me so intimately. While I didn't want to feel dirty about it, it still didn't feel right to do behind Zavier's back. I couldn't upset him that way.

I pulled away quickly, picking up the rags I'd been using.

Koni cleared his throat, possibly jarred by my sudden reaction. "My coat is a mix. Browns, amber, copper. I'm pretty too." He joked with a soft laugh.

I nodded as I passed by him to deposit the rags into the dirty bin. As soon as I tossed them and set the squeegee down, his hand wrapped gently around my forearm. "You're afraid to touch me?"

Well, I supposed we were going to come right out and talk about it. "Um. Well, I don't think it's a good idea."

"You don't want to hurt Zavier," he stated, staring into my eyes as he dropped his hold on my arm. "You can't ignore what is happening. I know I can't."

I closed my eyes, knowing that I didn't exactly want to ignore any feelings I was having lately. From him. Zavier. Even the mixed-up feelings I was having about Loch and Elijah. I enjoyed it all after being so numb. "I ... No, I don't. I know it's new, but I really like him. And I ..."

His thick eyebrows furrowed but evened out as an easy smile formed on his lips. His voice was calm as he said, "And if it wouldn't hurt him?"

I blinked up at him. He wasn't nearly as close as he had been before, but I still had to tip my head to see his face. Fuck. Had he just suggested that Zavier wouldn't mind sharing? I swallowed with a gulp, and he smiled bigger. "I, uh ..."

"We'll talk to him. Unless you want to talk to him alone?" Before I could even consider all that he was suggesting, his stomach grumbled again, and he groaned. "Teagan, I need to eat. I was going to save this hunger for that fried chicken, but I can't last," he joked, moving to help put away our cleaning supplies. "I have to get a small snack before dinner."

I shook my head, snapping myself back into reality. I'd think more about his words later. "Okay. I can check for ingredients and maybe start prepping for dinner since it's close."

"Good," he agreed.

We sorted and stacked the rest of the materials, then made our way to the dining hall. I was surprised to see Keira, Mike, and another guy in the kitchen when we entered.

"Hey, girl," Keira said as Koni and I walked in. "You look ... well, a little better than I saw you last."

I laughed, glancing down at the same pair of sweats and T-shirt I'd been in the other night. "At least the pink came out, eh?"

She laughed, then grabbed my wrist and pulled me back toward the pantry as Koni strode to the fridge while talking to Mike and the other guy.

Keira released my hand and looked straight into my curious eyes. "Spill it."

"Spill what?"

"Man, I've never really had a best friend, so you need to indulge me here. The tea. The secrets." She giggled quietly and raised her eyebrows. "You and Zavier, huh? I heard you claimed him last night and tossed some punches at Nima. She has a shiner, by the way. Not bothering to cover it up with makeup. She's wearing it like an accessory so she can feel badass or something. But that's not the point. She's definitely worse off than you. I overheard her saying she got a punch in, but your face looks fine. What a liar. And she's also spouting some ugly things …"

"Ugh." I groaned and looked at Keira for any signs of disgust or hate over what she may have heard. Honestly, she'd said so much so fast, I was trying to replay it all too. "She's not supposed to talk about my family."

"She mentioned that in her bitch-fest during cabin work, believe me. She said something about not retaliating but not promising to keep quiet. Some shit like that. But I wouldn't worry about it. We all have pasts, most being tragic in one way or another, so I doubt anyone cares for any reason aside from curiosity."

Except for the fact that most don't know I'm hiding here because of my shitty family, I thought bitterly. I groaned again.

"I am sorry for your loss. It seemed like you weren't very close to them, but I know it still is family you've lost."

"Thank you," I said with a sigh.

She reached her hand up again to squeeze my shoulder and stayed silent. I shifted my stance, the awkwardness creeping in. As if she realized the same, she said, "So tell me more. Zavier, huh? I honestly thought it'd be Loch after his move to get you in his clothes."

I glanced down again at the clothes on my body and the parka hanging from my arm. "Yeah, I just … I don't know. I felt this pull to him. And I wanted to help him."

"Oh, I bet you did," she teased. "But it is so good that it happened that way. I'm sure he's feeling higher than a kite today, changing and snatchin' you up at the same time. But also, in case you weren't aware, Koni is looking at you like he wants to devour you as thoroughly as the cinnamon roll he just took down in two bites."

I laughed out loud, not bothering to look in the same direction as her brief glance. "He's something else."

She popped her mouth wide open as if a thought had physically struck her. "Oh, shit."

"What? No," I said quickly and moved away from her to set the parka onto the counter.

"Oh, yes," she urged, following me through the swinging pantry door. As I rummaged through what I would need to make fried chicken, she openly stared at me. "No judgment here. Honest. I had a feeling that there might be a package deal with them."

"What? No." I scoffed half-heartedly because I'd had the same feeling, though it was so strange to think about it being true ... It didn't seem natural to even consider it. But after all the mentions with Zavier, and what Koni had just said in the bathhouse ...

"You're repeating yourself. I don't know you very well, but usually people who are super quick to deny things and repeat phrases are often guilty."

"Wh—" I almost repeated it again, and she started giggling.

"Fuck, I don't really know," she said as I laughed with her. "But seriously ... I'm not judging. I'm only glad things might be looking better for you here. Now, you just need to get your clothes back."

I nodded, letting a whoosh of air pass through my lips before plucking a box of macaroni and a container of flour from the shelf. "I'm hoping dinner might help with that. Koni requested fried chicken and mac and cheese. But if the real perpetrator isn't as swayed by food, Zavier told me he'd give me some of his clothes too."

"Oh, that sounds like a decent plan. And that dinner sounds good, too."

"You want some?"

"No, actually Rosie is letting Mike and I use her minivan to escape camp for a little while tonight. We're hitting some steak place in town to celebrate passing several practice exams."

"Oh! That's great! I hope you have a good night."

"Thanks! So ... you're going to leave it up to the food, huh? You won't just give in and ask Loch for your stuff?" She prompted, too inquisitive to let it go.

"Probably not, no. I can be stubborn too." My skin heated at the thought, like a rush of fire all over. Odd. Sure, I was a little pissed about not having my things, but I hadn't exactly been angry about it since finding my suitcase gone that first morning. Right now, though, my blood boiled as if I were about to rage war on Loch over it.

She took some of the ingredients from my arms and helped me carry them out. As soon as we settled the stuff onto the prep counter, she turned to glance at Koni, who was looking at me despite conversing with Mike.

"Well, you have a good night, too," she said, bopping her head and its long wavy locks from side to side and giving me one last cheeky know-it-all, I-told-you-so grin. "Let's go get ready, Mike!"

7

After everyone else disappeared from the kitchen, I grabbed a water from the fridge and drank half of it before returning to the pantry for the other ingredients needed to make dinner. My body temperature continued to climb despite the cool water I'd gulped down. I also got flustered as I looked at all the items in the pantry.

What else did I need? What else?! My mind blanked.

I gripped the edge of a shelf, hoping to relieve the tension building inside. With a scowl aimed at the bottle of vegetable oil, I sorted through the small list in my head. *Chicken, flour, salt, garlic powder, onion powder, pepper, paprika, buttermilk or milk. And what for the mac and cheese? Fuck! Think, Teagan. I'm so pissed off right now! Macaroni, milk, butter, cheddar, parmesan...*

I growled to the ceiling as my insides churned beneath my skin. What the hell was happening? The sensation burned but also made me anxious and uncomfortable.

"Teagan?" Koni's voice called to me before the pantry door swung inward. He glanced at me from the doorway. "You okay? I heard—Shit!" He rushed over to me, and I held up a hand to stop him.

"I'm fine. I'm just ..." I pushed the words through my teeth. They tasted bitter and sounded as angry as I felt.

"Oh shit," he murmured.

"What?!" I lifted my head to see him more clearly and wiped my brow. I was sweating. "It's hot in here, right? God. I'm just trying to figure out what I need to make dinner! What the hell!" I shifted from one foot to the other, my legs and arms shaky. My insides felt like a spring, the coil tightening then loosening, compressing then extending, over and over.

"Teagan," Koni said again, stepping close enough to put a hand on my bare shoulder where the stretched neck of Loch's T-shirt had settled. I hadn't bothered to even adjust the shirts anymore. There was no point, and it only made me more frustrated!

"Yes?" I asked, closing my eyes at the simple feel of his soft palm and fingers resting against my skin. It was as if all the energy in my body had switched focus to that contact, latching onto the only pleasant sensation as if it would be the last I'd ever have.

"It's starting for you. The transition. I heard you growl in here. You're having an anger flare, right? Have you been getting hot flashes before now?"

My limbs shook, and his hand traveled down my arm, easing me. I fought off the pain and recalled the past few days. There had been times I had shed the parka, using it less and less. In the classroom the other night ... "Maybe. But I thought it was because

I was cleaning or just being around ..." Around all of them. Being aroused.

"Yeah," he said, already knowing.

I growled again, huffing hard and fast breaths and taking hold of the counter. "Fuck! It's intense." I had known it would be bad, had been warned, had even seen how Zavier had reacted, and yet ... there had been no way to know how it truly felt.

"Dammit," Koni said before rushing to the door and looking out into the kitchen. After a grunt and another curse, he let the pantry door close us in. "I can help you ... let me help you."

"Huh?" I asked, gripping the shelf so hard I felt it might break off the wall.

"I want to help you," he said, stepping closer to my side and putting his hand on my shoulder again. When I lifted my eyes and met his, he added, "Like you helped Zavier."

Oh! Oh. I swallowed thickly, unsure about everything—processing the fact that I was finally starting my transition, wondering how long it might take, uncertain about letting Koni help me. My body responded to his touch, focusing on how good his skin felt against mine again. Cool, soft, and calm compared to my heated writhing flesh.

"Let me, Teagan." His voice was coaxing. He had dipped his face close to my neck, speaking gently, his breath a flutter of blissful seduction over my skin. "It's fine if you don't want to, but if you're worried only about Zavier ... I can tell you right now that he'd be glad I was here to help you. But if he is angry in any way, I will take all the blame for this. Every bit. He won't be mad at you. I promise. I've known him long enough to know."

My jaw strained as my teeth ground together. My bones began to ache. I moaned and growled again, angry at myself, angry at the stupid bottle of oil I was staring at. I didn't want to wait the flare out. Was there any good reason to endure it? From his calm words, I knew I could trust what he was saying. So and inhaled deeply and relented. "Please. Yes, please, help." I knew then exactly what Zavier had felt when I asked to help him in the bathhouse. He'd tried to stay away from me since The Four had made an agreement, but the transition was too much to handle.

"Good," Koni said, not bothering with any more words. His hands worked quickly, lifting my shirt up over my head and pulling down the cups of my bra, exposing my breasts enough for access. He dipped his head down, and his lips and tongue took over, licking and kissing the swells before traveling over a hard nipple and sucking it inside his mouth.

"Oh!" My hands grabbed hold of his head, fingers slipping into his soft, thick hair.

One hand played with a breast while his other moved down my stomach and slipped beneath my sweats. There was nothing slow about this. He knew what I needed and was not taking his time. His fingers slid into my underwear, pushing down over my trimmed mound before finding my slick pussy.

I moaned and arched my back at the sensation. He echoed a moan, deep and throaty, with my nipple in his mouth, the vibration adding more feeling. His finger trailed over my wetness then pressed against my clit before stroking it. My body curved as he bent me backward, nearly supporting all of my weight.

He released my nipple and stood straighter before slamming his mouth down onto mine, his tongue diving inside at the same time his finger entered my pussy. I cried out into his mouth, and his finger started pumping into me. Another joined, pushing in and out and curling.

My body still felt as if it were on fire, only now the tension and the anger were slipping away as the pleasure took the front seat to it all. It radiated through me, dulling the aches, letting me feel every part of him. His touch. His kiss. His muscles flexing beneath my hands as I clutched his body to me. And fuck! The smell of him was driving me mad—thick and heady, earthy and woodsy pine.

"Oh, yes. Lift your leg, sexy." His free hand reached down and guided my leg on his hip before snaking around to my lower back and pulling me closer. He drove his fingers into me faster and faster, his thumb working my clit with the same punishing rhythm.

The new position had me grinding on his hand, matching his movements, chasing release. "Ah, ah …"

"Does that feel good? C'mon Teagan. Give it to me. Come on my hand. Fucking hell. This is so fucking hot. Watching you. Smelling you." His low and seductive voice spoke close to my ear as he pressed kisses along my neck and jaw.

His mouth met mine again, and he licked inside, swirling his tongue with mine. I felt his hardness above my thigh, felt him rubbing against me, and I knew his motion was mimicking what he wanted, imagining his cock thrusting into me instead of his fingers.

The pleasure climbed, the sensation spiking, building and building. "Koni. Ah, yes!" I panted, digging my fingertips into his back and pulling his ponytail as the tension cracked wide open, the orgasm hitting sharp and heavy, splintering through my body. My muscles spasmed, my legs and arms quivering uncontrollably.

"Oh fuck," Koni breathed into my ear, his fingers slowing inside me while his other arm eased its grip around me.

My body quieted, and my leg fell to the floor as he slid his hand out from my sweats. His fingers were coated with my arousal. He stared down at them then closed his eyes with a deep inhale.

"Are you all right?" he asked after a moment, his eyes opening again and finding mine.

My breaths slowed, and I settled my breasts back into my bra cups. "Uh ... yes, I am. I feel so much better." And I did. Relief seemed to permeate every part of my body. Orgasms definitely had healing power for transitions. But as far as being all right with what had happened between us? It wasn't exactly awkward, but I almost felt bad, like I'd used him. "Thank you for that. I'm sorry ... I—"

"Oh, no," he said, dipping down to grab my shirt for me with this other hand then extending it to me. "Don't be sorry for anything. Fuck. That had to be the hottest thing I've ever seen. Goddamn. I mean, I've had sex with girls before, but ... That's not something I need to tell you. I just ... Shit. Yeah. I should be thanking you. Damn."

I started chuckling at his rambling while pulling my shirt on. It was adorable. There was a tinge of pink beneath the copper tone of his cheeks. I looked down at the erection in his jeans and bit my lip. "Are you okay?"

He glanced down too and laughed lightly through a grimace as he grabbed hold of his massive bulge and adjusted its position. "Uh, yeah. Totally fine." His lips tugged into a shy smile as he locked eyes with me again. "I have a feeling it might stay that way if I'm helping you cook, and not just because I'm wanting to eat your fried chicken."

I licked my lips and smiled too. Well, then. I still wasn't sure what to do about everything. About him. About Zavier. I let out a breath, worry washing over me.

Seeing my sobering expressions, he ran a finger beneath my chin and tipped my face up. Those amber eyes stared at me so intently, I thought I'd melt. "I won't push you into anything, okay? I'll keep my distance until you tell me otherwise. I don't want to make you uncomfortable."

"Okay," I replied, a little breathless. Because really, the fact that he was considering my feelings over it all, knowing that I was uneasy, meant so much. My own family had never been so thoughtful, so concerned.

He bit down on his lip, and his eyes dropped to mine. "I only have one request. Can I have one more kiss before we leave this room? I'd hate to think it'll be the last ... but just in case it is, a guy's gotta shoot his shot."

I shook my head at his honesty but chuckled since I knew I'd tell him yes. How could I deny him, especially after what he'd just done for me? I licked my lips with a nod.

He was quick to respond, apparently not wanting to chance me changing my mind. He slipped his clean fingers around the back of my neck and bent down, slanting his mouth over mine. There was no rush as soon as our lips and tongues met again. He was both gentle and firm, showing me the urgency and the longing. He flicked then sucked my tongue, tasting me thoroughly, acting as if it might just be the last taste he'd get. The thought made me ache in a way I didn't think possible. It was a conflict I hadn't thought about. I knew I wanted Zavier. Badly. I felt like I wanted to keep him forever. But now, Koni … God, my body and heart were stirring the same way for him too, the pull only growing more fierce with more contact.

His teeth nipped at my upper lip, then the bottom, before his lips pressed to mine two more times. He released his hold on me and took a step back.

I was in a daze from his touch, his smell. A part of me didn't want it to end either. I blinked at him, seeing he held the same dazed look. After a soft laugh, I tried to speak but failed.

He cleared his throat and was the first to break through the haze. "All right. I'll be your kitchen assistant. Tell me what you need me to do, and I'll do it. I'll do anything."

With the twinkle in his eye, I had a feeling the last part meant so much more than cooking dinner.

8

"All right. The baked mac is almost done. You sure you don't want another side? Vegetable maybe?" I asked Koni as I removed the next batch of chicken pieces from the skillet.

"Nah, this is plenty. I doubt there'll be any leftovers, though," he replied, rolling the last of the chicken into the flour mixture and setting it aside for me.

He'd been completely honest about giving me space after that last kiss. He'd helped me with dinner, following all of my instructions with barely any awkwardness at all, except for a few times I caught him staring at me, giving me bedroom eyes. And, wow, was that hard to ignore. The looks were fiery, making my body so hot I almost thought I was having another transition flare.

"Okay, if you think it'll be enough. I know they'll probably be starving." Especially Zavier. I hadn't seen him since the morning. He had to have had lunch at some point, but I was willing to bet his stomach would be near empty after shifting again and doing his assessment with Tim and Rosie.

"We're always starving." The grunt that followed his words made me shiver. He was definitely thinking about more than food.

God. Knowing what was on his mind made me hot all over again. I stole a glance at him and was not disappointed by what I saw.

His eyes raked up my body, and his hand splayed over his stomach, rubbing a slow circle. I don't think he meant for me to even notice, but I did, and the view was so sexy, I had to bite my lip to focus on dinner and not picture him doing the same thing in a bed.

"Hey!" Zavier's voice broke through all my thoughts, and we both looked over to see him striding through the door.

"Hey!" Koni and I both replied as Loch and Elijah entered also.

"How's it going?" Koni asked them, coating the last piece of chicken and dropping the tongs into the bowl. He didn't bother moving away from me.

Zavier's T-shirt and jeans were smudged with dirt, as were Elijah's and Loch's. They looked like they'd been playing in the woods in human form too.

"Good," Zavier moved right for me, not stopping or hesitating even though the others were watching. "Fun. These guys are relentless." His body pressed to my back while I placed the last of the chicken into the skillet.

I kept on my task, not wanting to call more attention to us by turning and kissing him like I really wanted to. I would play it cool. Despite what we'd been through in a few short days, it was still very new, and I wasn't a fool. The Four's relationships meant a lot to each of them. They had a bond, and it was solid. I didn't want to rock that boat.

But …

Zavier leaned against me, dipping his face into the crook of my neck, wrapping his hands around my stomach, and inhaling long and deep. "Mmm. This smells so good." And with a low whisper, he added, "You smell even better. And ... Hmm." His face lifted away from my hair, and I saw out of the corner of my eye that he'd looked right at Koni, who was still at the counter beside us.

He knew! He scented him on me.

Shit! So much for telling him myself later. I should have thought more about that, should have known. I clutched the set of tongs in my hand, expecting some kind of fallout.

Zavier tightened his grip around my belly and pushed his face back to my neck, kissing me there.

Koni cleared his throat, possibly waiting for either of us to say something.

"I, uh, started. I had a flare," I admitted, keeping my eyes on the skillet.

"I know," Zavier replied in a whisper. "I'm just sorry I wasn't here to help you."

Oh God. More heat flashed through me at his words. He was calm, but I still couldn't tell if it upset him. He hadn't growled or anything, so I took that as promising. To what outcome, though, I wasn't sure. Would this be the end? Now I was getting flustered. *Concentrate. Relax.* I had to focus on what I was at camp for, remember that there was no promise beyond the here and now.

"Did you make this for all of us?" Zavier asked, straightening up and moving away from my body.

"Yeah," I replied a bit too quickly.

The oven timer went off. Koni moved to go get it, but Elijah beat him there, opening the door and removing the casserole dish with potholders. "Homemade mac?" he asked, staring at it before looking over at me. The rich, soulful eyes were wide, and his full lips parted. The dimple in his manly chin appeared to twitch.

"Oh no! You aren't lactose intolerant, are you?" I asked as I flipped the last pieces of chicken in the pan, cursing myself for not making something else. I really should have questioned Koni to make sure.

Koni burst into a fit of laughter at my other side, which set Zavier into a laugh too, and I turned and scowled at the instigator. "What the fuck? You didn't tell me—"

"He's not, Teagan," Koni managed to force the words out through his laughter. "Shit. You're just so fucking cute. With your accent. And being all thoughtful."

I heard a grumble somewhere behind me. And even though I didn't want to look, I did, seeing Loch over by the refrigerator, eyeing us as he grabbed a bottle of water. I was tempted to glare at him but refrained.

Zavier patted my hand then brushed some escaped hair back over his head. "Eli's just—"

"I fucking love baked mac and cheese," Elijah cut in, shocking me. His eyes returned to the dish, staring longingly at it.

I laughed and turned my focus back to the chicken, not wanting it to burn. "Well, good. Y'all can start eatin'. This last bit's almost done."

Koni moved the dirty bowls to the double sink and started washing while Eli and Zavier followed to wash their hands on the other side. They spoke of the last times they'd eaten a full homemade meal—Rosie over a month ago—smiling happily and shoving each other at the sink. Even Elijah smiled. Though it was faint, and obviously not directed right at me, it soothed me to my very bones. I'd seen his sarcastic smile when I'd first arrived, when I'd bumped into The Four and hadn't known the turn my life was taking. But seeing them act this way together, so easy and almost carefree … I felt something lift from me, like more of the numbness was crumbling and falling away.

"You gonna eat some?" Zavier asked. I didn't have to look to know the question was for Loch.

"Nah, man. Gonna catch some sleep before going out tonight," he replied. I saw him move to the kitchen door in my peripheral vision, and I turned to look. His shoulders were slumped, and he clutched the water bottle and a wrapped sandwich in his hand. Although his features were relaxed and not sporting his usual scowl at me, all the angles in his strong square face still looked fierce. Those hard eyes flitted toward me before jumping back to Zavier. "Don't be late, or your shitty nose won't be able to track me."

Nods were exchanged, then Loch left. The guys remained silent for a few minutes, busy getting prepared to eat.

"Teagan, you want something to drink?" Zavier asked, eyeing me from the fridge.

"Water, please," I said as I placed the last portions of chicken onto the transfer plate with paper towels to soak up extra oil.

"This looks amazing. Thanks for making it," Koni said, choosing a couple pieces of chicken and adding them to his plate, which already had a mountain of mac and cheese.

"Thanks for helping," I replied, smiling at him. "It felt good to cook for you guys."

"Don't say that, or we'll be hitting you up all the time." Zavier stepped beside me, set the water bottles on the counter, then leaned down and planted a kiss on my temple.

Whoa. I didn't know what to expect after the night together, but him showing so much affection hadn't crossed my mind. Maybe I was just so used to being ignored most of the time that I hadn't considered how he would treat me when we weren't alone. The sadness of that thought was quickly doused by excitement, though, as the meaning of his actions took root. He made me feel wanted, maybe even needed.

Even if making food was all they needed me for, it would still feel good.

I blinked, tugging hard internally to calm the sudden emotional spike. My chest thumped as I looked around at them. "I wouldn't mind," I replied honestly. "I like to cook."

"Well, damn," Koni said with a chuckle. "I will definitely take you up on that offer."

"You would," Zavier teased.

As I moved to grab a plate, Elijah held one up beside the mac and cheese. "I got you. How much do you want?"

"Oh! Thanks. Yeah, that's fine," I said, walking to him as he dropped a scoop onto the plate.

He hadn't plated anything for himself yet. He'd waited for me, which was so thoughtful. Standing beside him, I reached out to take the plate and my fingers touched his. He inhaled sharply but made no move otherwise. I remembered how he'd recoiled when we'd touched the other day. While it may have been a knee-jerk reaction to the physical contact with me, deep down I knew the reason wasn't so simple. But I was relieved it wasn't as severe this time around.

"Thank you," I said as he let the plate go. Despite my curiosity, I didn't ask him about it. Maybe I would one day.

After a brief pause, he nodded. "Thank you for cooking. This looks really good."

We didn't bother moving out into the dining hall. We all stood at the island to eat, the guys chowing down appreciatively, making grunts and groans as they did.

I couldn't help but giggle. They—well, Koni and Zavier—were being dramatic with their appreciation. Elijah smirked a few times but otherwise remained focused on eating.

When I couldn't eat another bite, I rinsed my plate and loaded it into the dishwasher. They were nearly done too, so I moved to begin clearing.

"Stop," Elijah said, drawing our attention. He scooped up the last bite of mac and cheese then chewed it down as he dumped his chicken bones into the trash.

Not knowing if he was talking to me, I looked over the destruction. "You sure y'all don't want any more? There's only like a single serving left of each, not really enough for leftovers."

"I said stop," Elijah repeated, walking to me and taking the spatula from my hand.

"Oh, sorry. Did you want—"

"We're clearing and cleaning. You cooked," he said, turning to the dish and scooping the remnants onto a clean plate.

"Right," Zavier agreed after dumping his trash too. "We got this."

"It's house rules, what we usually do for Rosie when she cooks for all of us," Koni added before scraping his plate and stuffing the last heap of macaroni into his mouth.

"Oh. Okay," I said, nodding and wringing my fingers together. "I guess I'll—"

Right then, the kitchen door opened, and Jackson and Trig entered. They shot us glares as they moved to the pantry and the fridge. I caught a glimpse of Jackson's nose for the first time since I'd hit him. It wasn't red anymore, but there was a faint amount of purple under one eye. *Good. Asshole.*

Zavier was at my side in a few quick steps. He grabbed the two pieces of chicken left and dumped them onto the plate Elijah extended that held the rest of the macaroni. Silently, they cleared. Koni stepped up to the double sinks and began washing.

I stood quietly, feeling awkward for not doing anything, so I finally moved to dry the dishes Koni washed and Zavier rinsed.

"So you got yourselves a kitchen bitch, huh?" Trig said from behind us.

Jackson laughed with him, then added in his southern drawl, "What's the payment? Oh, wait ... Must be the dick you claimed.

You only worth fried chicken, Runt? I admit that's better than a sandwich." More laughs. "Darlin', if I gave you what I got, you'd be makin' an eight-course meal."

I rolled my eyes and gritted my teeth, trying hard to hold my tongue. Zavier tensed up at my side, and I touched his arm as he rinsed the last dish.

I saw Koni and Elijah leaning back against the counters, their eyes trained on the assholes on the other side of the kitchen.

"I heard about your family. Shame." Jackson's voice lowered as if he were about to offer condolences instead of spitting more vileness. "You know, some of us actually can commiserate with that kind of loss. Those of us with families who care enough about us to risk death. You were worth something to them, more than making fried chicken for this pack of scrubs, anyway. You can always change your mind about who might be good for your future. Of course, I'd have to have a test drive before I considered taking you home to Texas."

"Fuck off," I said, turning to face the asshole and his shit-eating grin.

"Dammit," Zavier muttered at the same time Koni let out a harsh breath.

I cast Zavier a sidelong glare, daring him to say something. I'd be damned if someone told me to shut up. But they didn't say one word. Smart.

"Ooh," Jackson said like a hoot. "Did I ruffle your little feathers? I think I would enjoy taking a spitfire like you home to liven things up a bit."

"The only spitfire you'll be taking home is your STD-infested dick." The guys all laughed. Even Elijah let a burst out. "I have a home. My own home. I don't need anyone else's."

"Okay then, sweetheart. I just thought you had nothing left there, is all. Since they're dead. Except the one aunt, right? You never know, though. Maybe someone else'll be there waiting on ya, to help run things."

What?

"You sure are takin' whatever you can get here," he continued as he and Trig moved toward the kitchen door. "Gettin' your fill before you leave. Think you'd opt for something better, but, hey, to each their own." He smiled brightly and pushed the door open to leave.

I took a step forward, his previous comment niggling at me. "Did you just threaten me? My home?"

Zavier's arm wrapped around my waist, stopping me.

Jackson let out a sardonic laugh as he disappeared into the dining hall then called out, "No, doll. I don't bother with threats."

9

"I want to fuck him up," Zavier spat as soon as we got back to my cabin—our cabin. He'd brought his things over before he came to dinner with the others and was currently unpacking his duffel and angrily shoving stuff into the dresser drawers.

After Trig and Jackson had left the kitchen, the silence had been deafening. All three guys seemed to stew, breathing hard and just attempting to remain in control so they didn't chase after him and kick his ass. I would have been right with them if they had. Instead, we finished cleaning up then went our separate way from Elijah. He took the last of the dinner with him, stating that he'd offer it up to Loch again. I didn't mind. Hopefully, Loch would eat it and not be so damn stubborn.

Koni came back to the cabin with us and was now pacing near the bedroom doorway. He barked out a laugh without warning, drawing our attention. "You basically said his dick spit fire because of STDs. Which is fucking hilarious even though we can't contract them."

I scrunched my nose up at him and exhaled a sharp breath. "Yeah, not my finest comeback."

"I thought it was pretty good," he replied with a shrug.

"Same," Zavier said at my side, drawing his arm around my waist and pulling me closer. "I thought you were gonna go for him."

"I was tempted," I admitted. "That one comment really made me uneasy. He said someone would be waiting for me back home, like he was threatening it."

"Yeah, I heard that too. I wouldn't worry about it right now. He's not going anywhere. Unless he fucks up. His family has paid a good amount to keep him here."

Koni nodded. "Don't listen to his bullshit about family either. Money's the only thing his has sacrificed for him."

That statement struck me. Were they worried about what he'd said? About him trying to sway me away from them? As if I'd even consider it. "I know what he was doing. I don't believe anything from his mouth, and I doubt he'd understand loyalty if it hit him in the face. Now, you guys on the other hand … Sometimes we make our own families who actually mean the world and would sacrifice it too."

"True," Koni agreed, but when his amber eyes lifted to mine, there was something off, as if he didn't fully believe.

"You shouldn't listen to him either. You four are close. It seems like you've made your own family here with Tim and Rosie. And you obviously have protected that."

Zavier cleared his throat and released his hold on me to push his long hair away from his forehead. "I may have fucked up by getting too close to you. But I don't regret it … even if you're leaving soon. Going back to your home."

Oh. Shit. "Well ... I ..." He'd already admitted how strong his feelings were. He'd been open and honest and vulnerable with me, said he might want more after camp. But we hadn't discussed it further. We hadn't talked about what would come later, even though he knew what I had back home. Did he not want me to leave? Or did he want to come with me?

"This is some heavy shit to be worrying about right now. We know you came from somewhere. Have a home." Koni dove right into the thick of it, his words seeming less for me and more for Zavier, a reminder. Though he hadn't been with us earlier in the morning during our talk.

We hadn't known each other long, but I felt what Zavier felt. And though the conflict remained, it was shadowed by the pull and connection with him, with them. There was no other way to describe it and no good reason to fight it. I've seen and felt enough to know their hearts were true. Shouldn't that be enough?

"I meant what I said earlier." Reaching out, I touched Zavier, sliding my fingers along his smooth, tight forearm. "I want the same as you—something after this. But I'm not sure what that should be. There's a lot involved, a lot more we need to talk about. I had always planned to go back home, to fight for what's mine there ... and I also don't want to lose you or break up your brotherhood. I just ... I'm conflicted too. I could stay, or maybe you could come with me. But I wouldn't ask that of you unless both of you wanted to, or even all of you. And I doubt that would happen ..." I stopped for a breath, catching both of their eyes. They looked as if they were processing it all too.

Not knowing what else to do, I continued on. "You both heard what Nima said last night. And I told Zavier this morning more about it. Most everyone in my family is gone. My father got them killed when he chose to work with vampires and go after a Marked Soul protected by reapers. He assumed her blood would help force my transition, which was his sacrifice and now my guilt. But what's worse is worrying that my outcast uncle might return to challenge me for my alpha spot and for my family house and restaurant. It's why I'm here, hidden. And so that's why I had always planned to go home. Everything that's left is there. Except now there's here, and now there's you guys. I'm confused about it all."

"That is a lot to think about. But we understand," Koni commented, reaching from my hand and grabbing hold while my other one remained on Zavier's arm.

"Yeah, we understand. And I'm sorry I got irritated about what Jackson had said. You told me it all already. I knew. I just hadn't thought about it, being so busy all day. So when he brought it up, the idea of you leaving hit me harder than I expected." Zavier lifted my arm from his and slipped it around his neck before gathering my body closer. His scent enveloped me, inviting me in more.

"Don't be sorry," I said. "It all hit me too. And I should thank you both for having my back."

"You don't need to apologize either. He's a dick. And we're here with you." Zavier dipped his head down and kissed my lips chastely. When he backed away again, he stared at Koni and added, "We both are, right?"

"Absolutely." Koni's hand squeezed mine, not letting go even as Zavier practically wrapped himself around me.

"Maybe this was why you both should have stayed away from me, huh?" I teased, trying to shake off the rest of the worry.

Zavier's hand slid down to my ass and pulled me flush against his solid body. His lips moved to the side of my face, his breath carrying over my cheek and making me shiver. "Not a chance. You are worth the confusion and everything else that comes along."

A sound almost like a purr came from Koni. He released his grip and trailed his fingers along the inside of my palm. "I'm thinking it's a good time to talk about what happened in the pantry."

Oh! Yes, he was probably right. We'd already had so much happen, but it was better to get out now than later. My body heated at the thought, hit with a mix of even stronger emotions. Apprehension. Concern. Desire. Anticipation. I took a deep breath, recalling what Zavier had mentioned in the morning about being so close to them. There was a chance that he wouldn't be upset.

"Tell me," Zavier said, pulling away from me slightly to glance at Koni before tipping his face down to see my eyes.

I looked back and forth between his brown and blue eyes, seeing only calmness. "My transition started. I hadn't really noticed the flares before because I thought … I just thought I was aroused, I guess." I smiled at my admission and was rewarded with a small smile from Zavier too. "So, yeah, it happened in the pantry as I was getting stuff to make dinner. I got so hot and then mad. I was seriously pissed off at the ingredients."

Koni chuckled, and Zavier held his own laughter back and said, "Aw, baby. It sucks, huh? Was it really bad?"

"You guys know. I wasn't myself, and yes, it sucked. My bones and my skin ... nothing anyone tells you can prepare you for what happens."

They both nodded, knowing, having been through it all.

"So Koni helped you?" Zavier got to the point. He'd already smelled it in the kitchen, he'd known Koni was all over me and vice versa.

"Yeah. Liked I helped you in the bathhouse."

Koni whistled lowly. "Bet that night was fun."

Zavier laughed lightly, eyeing him. "Well, you got to see the aftermath of me crossing that line."

"Sure did," he replied, sticking his tongue out and shooting a wink at me. "Glad Eli and I tore you and Loch apart before you did any actual damage to your pretty faces."

"Shut up," Zavier said to him before peering down at me again.

I lifted my eyebrows, not sure what to think about it all or how to proceed. "So ..."

"So," Zavier licked his lower lip and the ring there. "Did he do as good of a job as you did?"

Well ... I glanced at Koni, watching his grin widen. "Yes, he did. He made me feel a lot better. So much."

"Good," Zavier replied, and the hand on my ass squeezed roughly. "I told you what I thought this morning. I knew he liked you too. Eli and Loch, well ... I know it's the same even though they have their own issues to work out. But I'm not worried about them right now. I'm focusing on you and us."

You and us. Me and them. "Does this ... are you saying that ..." When he'd talked about it earlier, he'd been eating my pussy. I had barely been able to think, so while he'd mentioned all of them liking me, I was convinced my mind had mixed everything up.

"I want you too," Koni piped in, leaving no room for doubt as he pushed closer. His hand lifted from mine and moved to my face, sweeping my hair back from my cheek to palm me there, commanding my attention.

"And, you ..." Words failed me as I grappled with what was happening.

"And I don't mind sharing." Zavier answered what I'd failed to ask properly.

Holy fuck. I blinked at him, then at Koni.

When I didn't reply, he added, "I never thought I'd want to share someone, but you are ... you are fucking special, Teagan. And they are special to me too. Like chosen brothers. I told you I don't want to give you up or them up. I want it all. I know you're perfect for us. You're true and real, and feisty and brave. In the short time you've been here, I have no doubts about your loyalty. Aside from what Rosie and Tim have done for us, I don't think any of us have had someone so ready to accept and defend us."

"I know I haven't," Koni confirmed, his fingers toying with my hair and tucking it behind my ear. "Look at you. It's no wonder we want you. Sexy Alabama girl. And that pull we feel between us ... I'm feeling it, and there's no way I'm ignoring it either."

Oh. Heat rippled through me at their words, at the confirmation that what I had felt for them, they felt for me. I wasn't crazy for wanting them the way I did, for being attracted to them both, to them all.

"It may not be normal, but fuck normal! I've never been normal and don't give a shit about normal. I care about what we need. And that's you," Zavier said, dipping down to kiss my neck. "So now that you know we're both wanting to be with you, wanting to share you, now it's up to you. Do you want both of us too?"

I looked at Koni, watching his amber eyes take me in as Zavier kissed along my neck. His lips parted, and his breaths sped up while his fingers trailed down the other side of my neck, waiting not so patiently for my reply.

"Yes," I breathed out, giving in to what I already knew I wanted, what I needed.

10

"Fuck yes," Koni replied to my admission, and Zavier chuckled against my neck, his hand cupping and rubbing my ass over my sweats.

I smiled at Koni, thinking I should have replied exactly the same way because, damn. Seriously, damn. I was so out of my element with this, wanting to be with two guys, but it felt more natural than I would have imagined. And though I was concerned with how it would all work out, what would happen after, I pushed the thoughts away for now. We already knew we didn't have all the answers.

Koni moved in and tilted my face toward him. "I'm so glad that kiss wasn't the last." And then he leaned down, pressing his lips to mine. I opened for him, and his tongue slipped inside, gently tasting me again, unhurried with his strokes. He was exploring me, learning my movements and reactions to his.

Zavier's body shifted, stepping around to my back. His hands crept under my shirt, brushing along my skin. They traveled higher, grabbing hold of my breasts over my bra, kneading them before pinching my nipples. Seconds later, they fell down, grabbed the hem of my shirt, and lifted.

My hands shot up automatically, wanting to shed the layer, craving the skin-to-skin contact between all of us.

Koni's lips broke away from mine long enough for Zavier to remove my shirt, then crashed back down again, this time with more urgency, more demand.

I sighed into his mouth, and his hands joined Zavier's on my body, roaming, the rough calluses stimulating even more sensation.

A knock at the door made us all pause. "Z, it's time, man," Elijah called from outside.

"Fuck," Zavier said, kissing my shoulder once before tearing himself away. "I've gotta go."

"Yeah," Koni mumbled over my mouth, not willing to surrender his attention to what was happening around us.

"That looks so hot. Dammit," Zavier said with a grunt, keeping his eyes on us as he moved to the door. "Take care of our girl. I'll be back later."

Koni smiled against my lips, grabbed my hips, and started walking me backward toward the bedroom as Zavier opened the front door.

"Good, you're here. Loch sent me because—" Elijah stopped speaking when he looked inside.

Shit. My eyes locked with his through the screen door. My shirt was off, and Koni had his arms wrapped around me as he continued to move us toward the bedroom. Well ... Elijah definitely saw what was happening. There was no hiding it. But was I worried? Not really. Especially when the shock disappeared from his eyes and morphed into a heated curiosity as they surveyed my body.

I smiled and bit down on Koni's bottom lip.

Koni chuckled then mumbled, "See ya later," over his shoulder while walking us through the doorway.

We heard Zavier say "Fuck" right after the front door slammed shut.

"Oh, I want you so bad. I want to do so many things to you." He groaned into my mouth with another kiss, his hands spreading wide over my back, feeling my skin slowly, reverently. "I want to taste you. In the pantry, I wanted to bury my face in you, wanted to lick my fingers clean after you came on them. But I thought you might think I was gross or insane."

"No," I said, panting now, as he unhooked my bra. I helped tug it off, and then his hands were on my front.

His body dipped lower, and his mouth followed, trailing down my neck, over my chest, kissing and licking until he reached a nipple. He sucked me in, and my hands instantly went to his head, my fingers working into his hair before freeing the long strands from their ponytail.

Koni nibbled at me, then licked his way to the other breast. "I was going to lose my mind if I couldn't touch you again. That last kiss wouldn't have been enough."

The backs of my knees hit the bed. Emboldened, I dropped my hands down to his jeans and began working to undo the button and zipper while I turned our bodies.

"I felt the same, wanting to repay you for the pantry. I want to now," I said, my breath heavy and my tone so sultry, it was almost unrecognizable in my own ears.

He chuckled, lifting his shirt up while I worked his pants down. "You don't owe me anything, Teagan. That was completely my pleasure."

Dropping to my knees, I watched as he hiked his shirt over his head before finally noticing my position. His eyes popped wide open with his mouth. "And this is my pleasure too." When I yanked down his boxer briefs, his dick bobbed up, pointing straight and hard. The skin there was a deeper shade of brown but had a pinkish color along his shaft too. He was large and cut, possibly longer than Zavier though maybe not as wide. He had a beautiful, sexy dick. I smiled, thinking that his dick matched his beautiful face and body too.

He stepped out of his jeans and underwear, kicking them away while I remained kneeling in front of him. With a groan, he grabbed hold of himself as if he couldn't control his own movements or wait for me to touch him. His palm slid down his shaft, and my pussy clenched from the sight.

With a sigh, I licked my lips, mesmerized by his taut arm and the tense grip he had on his cock. His eyes were on me, feasting on the view of me at his feet as well.

Unable to contain myself for a moment longer, I crawled my hands up his thighs and pushed him to the bed. Not fighting the movement, he released his grip and fell backward onto his elbows. I spread his thighs apart, kneeling between, and took hold of him, feeling the weight in my palm before wrapping my fingers around. His cock jumped at the contact, and he hissed a pleasured breath through his teeth, letting his head fall back onto his neck.

I pumped him slow, sliding down in a long stroke before pulling upward. He grew harder in my hold and let out a groan. His head lifted again, and his hooded eyes watched as I opened wide and swirled my tongue around his tip.

"Fuck, Teagan. Ah yes."

I bathed his shaft next, licking the underside while I grasped his base and cupped his balls with my other hand. His eyes flashed, the amber color all but disappearing as his pupils dilated with his arousal.

"You made me feel so good earlier. Does this feel good to you?" I asked before filling my mouth with him.

"Oh, fuck. It feels amazing, better than you can imagine."

I opened wide, took him in farther, and sucked hard. After I heard another moan, I started to move, bouncing my head over him and twisting my hand at his base. He was so long. I couldn't take him fully into my mouth and throat. I hadn't been able to with Zavier either.

His fingers threaded into my hair, drawing it away from my face and tugging. By the sounds of his grunts and sighs, I knew he was struggling for control. "Get up here, babe. Fuck. I want to eat you." He jerked on my hair more firmly, urging me to release his dick. Then he leaned down and kissed me hard before crawling backward onto the bed and stretching out. "Come here. Sit on my face."

"I want to touch you too," I said, reaching for him again. Hearing and seeing and feeling his reactions while I sucked him was too good to give up. That alone had me so wet. I should have been embarrassed, but I'd had no control over how hot it was making me.

"Turn around," he instructed, helping me lean over his body while he pulled my ass and legs toward his head.

"Oh!" I said, realizing we'd assumed a sixty-nine position. I giggled as he spread me over his face.

"Oh, yes. Sweet honey. I smelled you in the pantry. I even smelled you on Zavier before. Mmm." His hands wrapped over my ass, and he pulled my pelvis down to him.

I grabbed hold of his cock and took him into my mouth at the same time his tongue licked a long stroke over my pussy. "Ah!" I yelled out, my mouth too full to make more noise than a garbled cry. So I moaned and arched my back and hips. He speared me with his tongue, pushing it in and out while his fingers dug into my ass cheeks, holding me down on his face.

"Oh fuck," he said, his hips bucking upward, his cock shoving farther into my mouth and hitting the back of my throat.

I choked out a breath, my gag reflex kicking in. He eased back down, but I kept moving on him, sucking and licking and stroking with my hand.

His tongue hit my clit, flicking and circling, making my body climb higher, building me up, the pleasure coiling tighter and tighter.

"Hold on. Ah. Teagan. I want inside you, babe. Fuck. I need to be inside this sweet pussy when I come."

"Yes, yes, I need that too."

He lifted me effortlessly and without another word. Before I could blink, I was turned and flipped beneath him. His mouth crashed down on mine, and I could taste my own salty sweetness as his tongue dove deep. He was ravenous. Wildly hungry. Keira had been right in the kitchen—Koni wanted to devour me like the cinnamon roll. Thoroughly and completely. Though I was lasting longer than two bites at least.

His body settled between mine, and his cock rubbed between my lower lips, sliding through my slickness. "So hot, so wet." He kissed me hard as he angled his hips. The tip of him nestled at my entrance, blunt and ready. Slowly, he pushed.

I sucked in a breath and spread my legs wider as he sunk into me inch by incredible inch.

"You okay?" he asked, unsure. His wavy hair curtained the sides of his face, the ends tickling my cheeks as his eyes blinked down at me, eyebrows knitted with concern.

"Yes, oh yes. Good. You feel so good. More," I begged, needing him to push in all the way.

"Yes," he said, dragging the word out as he eased inside, little by little. "Fuck. Fuck. You feel so good. So damn good."

"You too. I'm so full. Feels incredible. Oh." I writhed under him, adjusting to the stretch from his cock as my hands roamed over his chest and then around his back, digging my fingers into his firm, flexed muscles.

He moaned, tipping his head as he braced himself higher above me. His pelvis shifted away, withdrawing with mind-numbing slowness. It ignited every part of my body with craving. I wanted more—more of his earthy smell, more of his wet kisses, more of his hardness filling me.

I tilted my hips and tightened my legs around him, chasing his retreat, demanding he come back inside. "Koni. Please."

He released a breathy kind of chuckle that made my body only tingle more. "You are so fucking sweet, Teagan. You want more? You're too feisty for slow, aren't you?"

"Right now, yes. I need more. Oh," I whispered as his hips tipped, angling the head of his cock into my front wall, the mind-blowing feeling making my eyes roll into my skull.

"It can be good to take your time. I needed to really feel you first," he said, the words pushing through his gritted teeth as he buried himself inside me again. He was fighting hard to maintain control. He wanted more, too, but was holding back.

"Yes," I agreed as he slid out another slow and torturous time. "But not now. I want you harder. Please, fuck me harder."

"That's the hottest damn thing I've ever heard." He growled, and it was as if I'd thrown water onto a grease fire. Dropping closer, he crashed his mouth to mine at the same time he plunged forcefully into me, just how I'd wanted.

"Ah!" I screamed into his mouth, the intensity of that single hit causing my body to seize up momentarily.

Then he was off, hips thrusting and retreating, in and out, in and out, his cock driving in at a fast and punishing rhythm. "Yes. Fuck. Oh. You like this better?"

"Oh, oh, oh," I managed to squeak out with every slap of his pelvis against me.

"Am I calm now?" he asked, smirking while his brows scrunched in concentration. His breaths sped up too, quick, carnal pants escaping him while his lower body worked at maintaining his pace.

I smiled at his question. It was what I had assumed about him early on, calmer than the others, not as hyper or outgoing as I'd seen in recent hours. And surely not the same as how he was behaving sexually. Fuck no. "No, oh no. Nothing wrong with calm, but this is so hot."

"Yeah, it is," he agreed, dipping his head down to bite and lick at my nipple before kneeling up. His hands gripped my hips, digging in and lifting my lower body higher to him. "Yes." He groaned at the change in angle, at how deep he was fucking me.

"Oh, oh, oh. I'm so close, Koni. Ah." My words were a mess of mumbled whimpers while all of my muscles flexed in anticipation.

"So fucking tight. Fuck. Your pussy is the best thing I've ever felt. Goddamn."

That pushed me right to the edge, and when he flicked a finger over my clit, I completely unraveled. "Ah!" I cried out, my back and neck arching into the mattress, my pussy clenching as the orgasm wracked me.

He growled as he let himself fall, his hips pushing harder, faster, his body pounding against mine. With a roar, he came, spilling into me thrust after thrust, not stopping until he had given me everything.

His lips pressed to my cheek then to my mouth, his breaths heavy over my skin. With our chests together, I could feel his heart beating as wildly as my own.

"I want to do that again. As soon as possible," he uttered before kissing me and swallowing my responding giggle. "I mean it. I'd probably be ready in ten minutes, but last night was long and today was ... incredible and overwhelming in a good way because of you. So I think I need a quick nap. But after ... oh, I want to explore every inch of you if you'll let me."

I sighed as a feeling of contentment washed over me, and it wasn't simply from post-coital bliss. Even though I hadn't been looking for anything here at camp, I seemed to have found so much. Affection. Reverence. Protection. All of it had broken down barriers around my heart, had seeped through the numbness and had overtaken it. The void that had lived within me for far longer than my family's deaths wasn't so large anymore. The cracks inside were mending, and that void was filling.

11

A squawking noise woke me. Apparently, after I'd done a quick post-sex wipe down in the bathroom, I'd drifted off with Koni too. Having such a good meal and then a thorough fucking, I had been equally exhausted, even at seven o'clock.

With his limbs draped over me, his soft, sleepy breaths tickled my ear. The position was so natural, as if it were an everyday thing for us. Normal. It had felt the same with Zavier, too. Though he had been in wolf form at the time, all fluffy and cuddly. While both human and wolf forms had made me feel protected and comforted, sleeping with Koni's solid body curled around mine added even more salve to my heart, building a sense of belonging and being needed.

The squawking noise sounded again, and an airy, cheerful voice followed, though it was broken up and scratchy, like a busted drive-through speaker.

I eased out of Koni's embrace, lifting his arm, settling it onto my pillow, and scooting out from under his leg before scurrying around for my clothes. Another moment later, I heard the sound again and realized where it had come from. It was Rosie's voice coming from the intercom near the door.

Blinking as my eyes adjusted to the cabin's main light, I pushed the button marked with a tiny microphone and said, "Hello? Hello?"

As soon as I released it, she replied, "Oh, Teagan! Great! I was starting to worry and was about to come down there."

I glanced toward the darkened bedroom and was kinda glad she hadn't. She knew about Zavier and me, but what would she think about me being with Koni too? I supposed it wouldn't be hidden for long either way. Everybody had a better nose than me, could tell whose scents I'd have attached to me from now on. I sighed. We were consenting adults. Even if other people didn't understand or wouldn't accept anything beyond a normal wolf coupling, I couldn't let different opinions affect my relationship with them. In my heart I felt it was good, something stronger than I'd ever known.

"Yes, sorry," I said into the mic. "Fell asleep."

"Oh gosh. Sorry for disturbing you, but I wanted to let you know that I spoke to your aunt."

"No, that's great! Thank you for telling me." That was an enormous relief, especially after what the asshole Jackson had said earlier. His odd, vague threat had worried me.

The speaker crackled some, making me flinch as she spoke again. "Can you come to the office for a bit? I realize that it's getting late, but I'd rather talk in person, maybe go over some items with you, like what Tim had mentioned about tutoring."

"Oh. Yeah, I can come. I'll be there in a minute."

"Great."

While Koni had stayed with me all day as some kind of protection, I hadn't really thought it necessary. Not that I minded the company or anything. It just felt over the top, given how Rosie had already discussed things with Nima and her sisters. And right now, I was more concerned with hearing about my aunt and home than worrying about having someone with me. I could only hope that she was continuing to handle everything okay with little help. Managing the restaurant, the extra house, and all the deaths with virtually no support was a burden bound to grow heavier as time went on.

After using the bathroom, I finished dressing, slid into the parka, and left for the office. I didn't bother writing a note for Koni. He was dead to the world, not even hearing the intercom or the flush of the toilet. I'd be back before he knew I was gone.

"Ah, there you are!" Rosie greeted me. Her thick bubblegum pink hair was clipped into a low tail, the length not quite long enough to be called a pony. She's stripped her face clean of the light makeup she regularly wore, and she'd donned comfy nightclothes, looking ready to tuck into bed herself.

"Here I am," I said back with a smile. I couldn't help but absorb her energy. Her upbeat personality had become harder to shy away from the longer I stayed. And after learning that she was practically a surrogate mother to The Four, I was growing to like her even more. "How's my aunt?"

She sniffed the air, her pert nose wrinkling a little before her eyes popped wide. It was so quick that I wouldn't have see it if I had blinked. But, yeah, she smelled Koni on me. If she wanted to say anything, she decided against it and continued the convo. "She sounds fine. A bit stressed still. Says things are fairly slow at the restaurant, but it's been picking up. Despite the other wolves who turned their noses away, there's been an uptick in human diners. Guess they aren't getting as heavy of an off-putting feeling when they eat there."

"Yeah, makes sense with less of us there," I admitted. "Did she mention anything else? My uncle?"

"She said she hasn't seen him or heard any talk about him yet."

I sighed long and hard, the relief a tangible thing, like a weight falling from my shoulders. "Good."

"She agreed with your choice to stay. I mentioned too that you're showing signs of transitioning. I hope that wasn't overstepping, but I did agree to keep her informed when she enrolled you."

"No, I understand. She has a right to know. She's taking care of so much there ... I don't want her feeling that I'll be away too long."

Rosie's head tilted, and her usually happy features took on a sour look, her lips and eyebrows dropping downward. "Do you think you will leave right away then, after your transition and maybe passing a basic wolf assessment?"

Taken aback by the question and its possible reason, I had to pause a moment. "I'm sure that whatever she's agreed with for payment, she'll follow through with no matter how long I'm here."

Rosie's cheeks reddened, and she chewed on her lower lip. "Oh, it's not that I'm worried about, dear. I'm—Well, I don't want to overstep more than I already have … I've just seen a difference in them." When I didn't reply, she added quickly, "The boys. I know it's not my business, and I'm happy about what you've done for them, but I've seen and felt a shift here in the last few days since you've arrived. They've been through a lot, and I … I don't know what I'm saying." She shook her head and clenched her eyes closed for a long blink. "Please ignore my ramblings. You're doing great, and I'm sure everything will work out just fine." She reached out a hand and placed it on my shoulder.

This was more than her being grateful that I'd helped Zavier. She was worried for them, and maybe for me too.

"You care a lot about them. I know what you mean, and I don't want to hurt them. I … We have some things to work out together, I think." I shuffled my feet nervously.

"I'm sure you'll work it out," she said in a soft, assuring tone before clearing her throat and dropping her hand from my shoulder. "So, about the school tutoring. Tim and I went over your records. We think you'd be perfect to help. Obviously, it won't be all the time. It'll be remedial lessons for someone farther behind with school, so you won't be teaching calculus or anything. Just helping to guide someone who does well alone but needs a little help."

Ah. It sounded like she was referring to a single person, and I was pretty sure I knew who it was. "And if this someone doesn't want me to help them?" There was no doubt in my mind that Loch wouldn't agree to my help. He'd looked as if he wanted to burn the classroom down just because I'd seen his textbook.

"Oh, he'll accept the help, whether he likes it or not," she said, with a knowing smirk. "He recognizes what's good for him in, knows he still has a lot of work to cover and he can't accomplish it all without help. He also won't let something petty like pride stop him from achieving the goals he's set for himself. He's intelligent and highly driven."

I lifted my eyebrows with a smile. She knew them well and acted so much like an actual mother. It made me wish I'd known my own better, wished she'd lived longer for me to have. She might have kept my father in check, might have stopped him from making his horrible choice … But those were thoughts I didn't want to have. What ifs didn't matter. What mattered was the here and now.

"Okay, I'll help. I can't promise that I'll be as patient as you or any other teacher."

"Good. And a lack of patience can often be a positive thing when battling stubbornness."

"I'll keep that in mind," I said with a smile. "Was there a day you want me to start?"

"Nothing set yet. I'll keep you posted. We'll also have your chores covered either way."

"All right."

"And if there's any concern on your end, be sure to let me know. I realize that you are starting into your transition. So if you are having any flares and need to step away from any situation, that'll be completely fine. We all understand how temperamental we can get and how challenging the whole process can be."

I nodded and tried my best to stifle a yawn that had crept up on me. I didn't want to seem rude. "I'm sorry."

"No, no," she said, lifting a hand and waving me off. "Don't be. It's getting later. You must be tired. I was a little on the late side for my transition and remember being extremely tired during the days it took. I won't keep you longer. You have a good night."

Her words were kind, and they also reminded me of how being a runt drew the transition process out longer. Each of us was different, of course. I'd likely had been having heat flares since I'd arrived, yet only once had I'd dealt with a full flare, with anger and bone aches. I was certain there would be more.

I pondered that fact as I stepped outside the office cabin and began the walk back to mine. It also made me wonder how long the full transition had lasted for Zavier, how many flares he'd had. I'd helped him through a few, counting the final change. Thoughts of relieving him in the bathhouse, so hard in my hand with his heavily dazed eyes on me as he shot cum over the wall, made my body heat up. The memory of that would be in my mind forever, along with visions of him in my bed. And now Koni too.

The thought of having two hot men fuck me within a day's time gave me all kinds of feelings, though, at the moment, most paled in comparison to my arousal to it all. *Fucking sexy.*

My body was on autopilot as my thoughts drifted around between The Four, camp, home, and also how cold the night had turned, so I barely registered the sounds rushing up on me until it was too late to react with even a scream.

12

Something slammed into me, knocking me off my feet and onto my back. I hit the ground hard, and air rushed from my mouth and turned into a cloud of smoke. I stared up at the night sky that was half blocked by trees. The only word repeating in my mind was "breathe," yet my body refused to listen. My chest felt as if it had collapsed, my lungs too stunned by the impact to inhale the breath I wanted so desperately.

"How does that feel, you little bitch?" A female voice invaded my ears, but I had a hard time focusing on anything but the dark night.

More blackness seeped into the edges of my vision, making me feel as if I'd fallen into a hole, and the tree branches above were the only exit. Tiny flecks of white filled the sky, streaking through my narrowed view. One landed on my cheek, another on my nose, their touch cold and wet. Snow. I'd never seen snow before.

"Shit, I think you knocked her out. She's not even blinking, but her eyes are open." A male voice this time. Not familiar. "That's fucking creepy."

"It doesn't look like she's breathing." A different female said.

Some rustling and footsteps moved closer to my ears.

As if my body had restarted, my lungs expanded and drew in the most painful, ragged breath I'd ever taken. Pins and needles and razor blades seemed to attack the inside of my chest, the pain pricking and slicing as my airway kicked into action.

"Shit. I thought you might have killed her with that tackle, Nima. Damn." This third female voice was nearly a whisper.

Nima's face came into view as I gasped and sputtered up toward the sky, the black hole fading away. "You hoped I'd let what you did go? Pff. Not a fucking chance, runt." A bruise lined the underside of her eye from where I'd hit her, dark enough that at least one layer of makeup couldn't hide it. "Better stand up before you get kicked." A brown work boot lifted above my head and twisted for me to see.

I pushed upward onto my elbows, breathing in low and slow, my lungs still protesting. The world tipped and turned a bit, and my brain thudded in response. "Ah." I winced, fighting for focus.

Laughter came from behind me. "Come on now. I don't have all night."

"To kick my ass?" I wheezed the words out and managed a scoff. Fuck, the hit had hurt more than I cared to admit. I hadn't been ready for it.

More laughter followed. This was a deeper timbre. A guy.

"Yes, to kick your ass. You think I'd let you get away with hitting me? You can't really be that stupid."

"Nope, not that stupid. Just wondering what else you have to do tonight that's more important. Why do I need to hurry?" Of course, I knew why. She assumed she'd get a few licks in and get out of here before getting caught. I wasn't planning to scream for help, but I wouldn't make things easy for her either.

"Because I said so, bitch. Now, get the fuck up or ... Nah, never mind." That boot appeared again, lifting above me, prepared to stomp downward.

I'd expected a straight soccer-style kick to my side or head, mentally preparing to roll away since my body felt sluggish. So when she had lifted that boot, I changed my plan and shot my arm out to grasp her other foot. I pulled hard right as she stomped, knocking her off balance. She lurched forward awkwardly with a small yelp. Her foot still landed on my stomach, just not with the intended amount of force. I clenched my belly and took the hit while she toppled over, her hands landing on the other side of my body.

I shimmied from beneath her, grabbing her foot so she couldn't stand before me. Then, knowing I was outnumbered and the time I had to strike was running out, I leaned back and swung a leg in the same kick she should have taken in the first place. My sneaker collided with her side, and she let out a pained puff of air.

"Fuck!" One of her sisters said, and I dropped Nima's leg, preparing for the attack for everyone else.

I wasn't prepared enough.

The first blow struck me on the cheek. Blood instantly coated the inside of my mouth, bitter and metallic, and my eyes watered.

Blinking the tears back, I focused as quickly as I could and glanced around the area. We were on the path to the lake and my cabin, far enough away from the main camp area and the path-end lamposts to be shadowed in darkness. Snowflakes fell harder, dropping onto the group that had ambushed me, speckling heads of hair and shoulders, and leaving a wispy coating of white along the dirt.

Nima, her two sisters, and two guys were the attackers. I didn't know the guys. Both had brown hair, one with shaved sides and the other with longer, loose strands to his ears. They hung back while one of Nima's sisters was shaking her hand out from the punch she'd landed on my cheek. All wore jeans and T-shirts, seemingly unaffected by the cold and snow.

I worked my jaw open and closed, trying my hardest to fight through the pain radiating through my head. It wasn't easy.

"How's that feel, skank?" The sister asked, probably to mask her own pain while she shook her hand again. Was she Nerine or Nesma? It didn't really matter. They looked even more alike now that my head was dazed.

"Skank is right," Nima spat, moving closer as the two guys started circling. She made a show of sniffing the air. "So you're not only fucking Zavier but Koni too? Wow, you know how to spread 'em, don't you?"

I laughed, keeping my eyes on her but still aware of the others walking around me. *Fuck.* While I didn't enjoy the idea of screaming, my body and head weren't crazy about taking more punishment. "Man, I thought that septum piercing was an ugly look on you, but slut-shaming and plain ole jealousy make you look even worse."

That did it. She launched for me, ponytail whipping behind her. Her sisters didn't wait either. They bounded forward, all ready to take their shots.

I dropped into a duck before they reached me, then sprang upward, fist clenched and aimed at the sister who had hit me. I landed a single hit to her eye before I was struck square in the back. It felt like a boot, every bone and muscle in my body rattling in response.

My body stumbled forward, but I was able to stay on my feet long enough to collide with the third triplet. She wasn't quite sure what to do. Her hands and arms popped outward, shoving at me in a disoriented way. I swung on her, but my fist didn't connect. Someone had grabbed hold of my arm from behind. As soon as they had a grip, I tried to thrash, only to have a hand wrap around my other arm, pinning them together at my back.

"Got you," one of the guys said, his face pressing close to my neck over the bunched hood of my parka, his breath reaching my cheek.

Nima was in front of me again, her sisters behind her, Nerine—or Nesma—clutching the eye I'd struck. The other guy was nowhere I could see.

The snow fell heavier, but it didn't bring the peace it should. On any other day, at any other time, I would have felt happiness from watching it fall, enjoying a sight my eyes had never seen. Not tonight, though. Now, I'd be lucky if I saw the aftermath. My eyelids would swell closed soon enough, one side of my face already throbbing with the threat.

I refocused on the moment, promising myself any tears would be from pain alone, no emotions.

Nima rubbed her hands together, looking as menacing as she wished to daily.

Before she reached me, I spat to the ground, the blood from my mouth staining some of the snowflakes red as they melted. "So I guess this kind of fight makes you feel pretty badass, huh? Couldn't take care of me yourself so—"

Her fist crashed into my face, and my head whipped to the side. The guy at my back held fast, gripping my arms harder to keep me in place.

"I'm done listening to you talk. Who wants next hit?" she asked, turning to her sisters.

"I do," an eerily calm voice said from somewhere behind me. A low snarl followed. Koni.

"Hey man, I—" the other guy sputtered before a loud crack and a pained grunt cut off his words.

The guy at my back shifted, spinning us to the sound. My knees went weak, seeing the other guy bent over as he held his face with Koni standing next to him. He was still beautiful, even though his typically sincere face was set in a fierce scowl. As his eyes traveled over my face in assessment, his jaw clenched tighter. Then he lifted his spread fingertips to his lips and whistled loud and clear into the snowy night.

Different hands took control of my wrists, allowing the guy at my back to sweep around to my front and take a wide defensive stance.

"Luke," Koni said, then tsked and shook his head before glancing over to the other guy. "Ryan. I'm surprised you both got involved with this shitty idea."

"I don't give a fuck what you think," Luke replied, casting a nervous look over to Ryan, who wiped a smear of blood from under his nose where Koni had hit him.

"He's stalling for the others," Nima said close to my head, grasping my hair harder and yanking me backward, obviously fed up with the discussion.

My body tipped and my feet scrabbled, but I couldn't keep my balance. As I fell, I saw Koni launch forward toward Luke. All three sisters were on me within seconds, no longer holding back. I lifted my arms to cover my head as their boots and fists started raining down on me.

I kicked my legs out and thrashed my body, keeping my head protected as much as possible. There was no reason for quiet now. This had become something far bigger than a simple fight. I shouted as a boot slammed into my thigh and something else struck my arm.

A scream broke through the shuffling and grunts. At first, I thought it was me who had released it, but when another rang out, pitched high with terror, I realized the hits to my body had ceased.

I peeked out from my arms and saw Nima on the ground, clutching her arm while the other sisters stood utterly still. Nima's lotus neck tattoo was stretched longer as her head tipped backward, her eyes pinned to the light gray wolf standing behind her with its lips pulled back as it snarled within inches of her face.

I'd recognize Zavier in wolf form anywhere now after having slept snuggled up with him. He was glorious, though also truly frightening as anger and malice poured from him, easily seen in his raised hackles and exposed teeth.

Fuck.

More scuffled footfalls and swift movements drew my attention to my other side. Loch had arrived at some point. He and Koni were swinging punches at Ryan and Luke, who were doing their best to fend off the punishing attack, but it was evident they weren't as skilled in fighting. After only a few punches, they were on the ground, knocked cold.

"You fucking bit her!" The sister I'd hit cried, falling to the ground beside Nima. "You are so done!" I winced, knowing that this gave them cause to report him. I hadn't paid much attention to the paperwork when I'd arrived. Truthfully, I'd been in such a fog when I'd signed the rules, I hadn't cared, especially about the rules more focused on wolf behaviors. Why bother when I hadn't even transitioned yet? But now, I wondered how bad it was for him to bite someone while they were in human form. It couldn't be good.

Zavier's jaws snapped the air threateningly, but he made no other move in response to the sister as she helped support Nima's forearm.

Another wolf approached, this one a medium gray with flecks of brown along its shoulders from what I could see in the dim light. Elijah? Both wolves had snowflakes clinging to their fur.

"You okay?" Koni asked as he and Loch walked to me. While Loch crossed his arms over his chest, Koni's slipped under mine to help me to my feet.

"Yeah. Fine now. Thanks," I uttered, keeping my eyes on Nima.

"Take me to Rosie," Nima said to her sisters, still holding her arm. She looked at us and squirmed away from Zavier. "All of you are finished. You think you can get away with everything. I'm telling Rosie what—"

"No need," Rosie's pitched voice boomed from the main pathway, and all of our heads whipped in her direction. Still in her nightclothes, she also had on a bulky pink duster that hung almost to the ground. Her hands were clutched in front of her, and her eyes were narrowed.

"Rosie!" The sister I'd hit said, getting to her feet and immediately covering the injured eye. She started toward Rosie but stopped when Rosie held up a hand. "They just—"

"Defended someone who was being attacked, Nerine," Rosie filled in, the pitch of her voice dropping lower than I'd ever heard.

"But Zavier bit—"

"I saw," Rosie confirmed while Nima sniffled from the ground. "And while it is against the rules, I feel his actions were warranted in this situation."

"What?!" Nima's sniffles died with Rosie's words, her anger taking over. "You can't be serious! You let them—"

"If the roles had been reversed and one of you was held against your will and ganged up on, they would be at fault." Rosie's voice had become a near growl.

Tim exited their office cabin behind her, watching and listening. Nima laughed bitterly and shook her head.

Rosie shook her head. "You agreed not to engage in any form of retaliation. You broke the rules. You're done."

"But—" Nesma squeaked out, trying to argue and plead.

But Rosie continued. "Nesma, Nerine, Luke, and Ryan, you are all in breach as well for planning an attack on someone enrolled here and harming them. Go pack. You will sign paperwork and leave in the morning. All of your families will be notified immediately. Nima, go shift at the boundary to heal. If you are still in need of medical treatment after, come see me. The rest of you, go to bed. We'll talk tomorrow."

They all followed her to the office, except for Nima, who shot us an angry glare before she ran off path and passed into the darkness behind the dining hall.

Koni lifted my arm over his shoulder, supporting me while Loch stood motionless in front of us.

"I'm okay. I can walk," I said, trying to shrug Koni off and instantly feeling the aches and pains from the hits and kicks to my body. I winced, but I knew I could walk myself.

"No," he said, refusing to retract his gentle hold. "Don't be stubborn." Before I could reply or argue, he asked Loch, "You mind getting some ice?"

Loch dropped his arms as his eyes shifted to me. "Sure." He walked off, though with his usual stride, it looked more like an angered stalk. Perhaps it was that way whenever I was around.

Tonight, maybe he was mad at having to get involved at all. Koni had whistled for them to help me. That much was true.

The gray-brown wolf sauntered closer and tilted his head before following Loch. Zavier, however, moved in close and nudged against my side.

"Yeah, we're going," Koni responded to his push. "Let's get her to bed."

13

"Why weren't you with her?" Zavier growled after shifting back to human form. The clothes he'd worn earlier were still intact. Like all other times the shift occurred, clothes became part of the process. Even though the transformation into wolf was mostly physical, that supernatural aspect added many levels to what we were. It was also why wolves could sense—see, feel, hear, taste, smell—so much more than any human, and could interact with other supernatural beings, like reapers, witches, and vampires. I'd learned all about it early in life but hadn't experienced all the effects yet. That came with transition.

"I was here with her. I ... we ... and then, well, I fell asleep," Koni said, his face getting a bit pink. "I didn't know she left."

"Please don't talk about me like I'm not here and part of this." I rolled my eyes and immediately regretting as my head pounded in response to the rotation. "It was my fault."

"Why did you leave?" Zavier stripped the parka off me, tossing it onto the coffee table, then lifting my shirt to inspect my stomach.

Despite the urge to pull away, I knew my body would protest the sudden movements more than his inspection. Plus, it was nice that he was concerned. "Rosie called on the intercom. She asked to talk about my aunt and some other stuff. I didn't want to wake Koni."

Koni huffed and paced beside us, eyeing me with his eyebrows drawn. He was concerned too. "You should have." He grumbled the words.

"I didn't think it would be an issue. They were told not to mess with me and weren't around all day, so ..." There was no reason to finish. They understood. "Guess I don't need to worry anymore now, huh?"

Both grunted.

The triplets, Luke, and Ryan were getting the boot. I could only sigh in relief.

A knock at the door sounded, but Zavier continued his inspection, lifting my T-shirt fully from my head, leaving only my thin lace bra to cover my boobs. He didn't seem fazed about partially undressing me, only focused on his clinical examination. His beautiful eyes scanned my skin meticulously.

But his eyes weren't the only set on me.

Glancing up, I saw the door had already opened and closed again, with Loch inside now beside Koni. Loch held a metal ice bucket, and Koni was refastening his topknot. Both stared at my body.

Oh, my stars.

Loch's hard stare seemed to bore into me. Even though the flicker of heat in Koni's eyes told me he was both concerned and aroused, Loch still looked plain angry, that usual scowl back in place with his lowered brows and clamped, square jaw. A flex in that jaw was the only evidence I could see of him possibly being affected by me. Still, even then I couldn't tell if he was enticed by my state of nakedness, mad about my injuries, or simply pissed about having to come help me—out there with the fight and in here with the damage. Being pissed about helping me seemed the most obvious choice.

"Shit," Koni said, stepping closer. His hand reached out to skim a finger over my stomach as Zavier moved around behind me. "This whole red area might bruise. Is it hurting?"

I blinked at him, but my eyes wandered to Loch. "Yes, a bit. I'm … I'm sorry you all had to get involved. Really."

"Baby," Zavier said at my back, his fingers moving up my neck, lifting my choppy blond strands away from my skin and making me shiver. My nipples pebbled from the chill and from the contact. "It's fine. Don't worry. I'm just glad we got there. Anything else hurt here?"

"No. I mean, someone kicked me, I think." Grunts and growls came from them, possibly even from Loch. I kept on talking. "It's sore but not bad. Y'all don't need to fuss." Even with Koni shielding some of my front, there was a fleeting urge to cover up. As soon as I saw Loch's eyes drift downward, though, taking me in more thoroughly than they had the day in the classroom, I resisted. His face seemed to relax during his unhurried perusal.

I wasn't quite sure how to feel about it and was still processing as Zavier spoke again, snapping me from my thoughts and tearing Loch's eyes from my body.

"We need to get ice on you," Zavier said, and Koni agreed with a nod. "It sucks you can't shift yet because this would heal in no time."

Loch took the few steps to us and handed the bucket over to Koni. Without saying a word, he turned and left.

Fuck.

"I'm so sorry," I said as he was pulling the door closed. When the door paused for a single moment before closing, I knew he'd heard. I could only hope he might not hold all of this against me.

"You don't need to be sorry," Koni assured me. "This might hurt a bit, but it'll keep the areas from swelling. He put water in here too. Want some?" He handed off a refillable ice compress to Zavier while he lifted another to my cheek.

"No, I'm fine right now." I hissed a breath as both touched my skin.

"Come on. Let's get you in bed," Zavier said as his other hand helped guide me to the room.

They had me sit down and took places beside me. Tears started flowing before I even realized it. *Dammit.* I'd done a good job of holding it in, but now that my body was calming and my mind was churning, all control disappeared.

"Oh, baby," Zavier said, lifting his hand to the uninjured cheek and wiping away some tears. His efforts were worthless as more continued to fall. "Don't cry. It's fine. You'll be fine."

"I'm just ... fuck ... I'm sorry that you had to bite her. I hope you don't get into trouble because of it, because of me. I don't want you to lose your home here because of me. Christ. I never meant for any of this to happen. I didn't plan to get involved with anyone here, didn't plan to feel so strongly for you, for you both. And now—"

"Now nothing," Koni said, slipping an arm around my back, above where Zavier held one pack. "You heard Rosie. She won't punish Zavier or any of us. She already knows what you mean to us. And besides that, we were doing what we were supposed to do, which is protecting this place. We're like the enforcers here, making sure everyone stays in line, and those fucking sisters crossed a big one tonight. It's one thing to fuck around with pranks or work each other over when we shift and train. But that never goes beyond a fair fight. Equal numbers."

"Mm-hmm," Zavier agreed, his hand slipping down from my cheek to caress my neck. "So don't worry about it. They leave tomorrow, and we don't have to worry about them anymore. We just need to make sure you heal."

"I'll be fine. I'm just a little tender." I moved their ice packs away, needing the break from the cold, and stretched my limbs and twisted my torso, assessing the damage from my seated position.

"You're feeling okay right now, but you might be worse off tomorrow," Koni said. "You should get some sleep. Your body will heal faster."

"True," Zavier said, and both of them stood to leave.

"Don't leave," I said, reaching out. "I ..." I bit down on my lip, worried that I was maybe assuming too much. "Will you stay with me?"

"Oh, I'm staying. I haven't changed my mind about being here with you," Zavier replied with a grin. "You still wanting both of us?"

Koni lifted a brow as if he were unsure what my answer might be. Had he thought I'd planned to kick him out?

"Yes. I want you both here with me. You want that too, right?"

"Absolutely," Koni replied as he let out a deep breath. "I'm gonna grab the ice bucket."

When Koni left the bedroom, Zavier stripped his shirt off then stood me up. "Let's get all of this off of you. It'll be more comfortable while you sleep."

"Will it?" I asked, lifting an eyebrow as he bent to slip off Loch's sweats and my underwear.

He peered up at me, and his lips curved into a mischievous smirk. Even though the bedroom was mostly dark, I could see the amusement glinting in his eyes. "As much as I want to be inside you, I don't want to hurt you."

"You won't," I replied as I lifted my feet, allowing him to remove the clothes completely.

Still crouched in front of me, he placed his hands on my bare thighs and kissed my skin with a groan that made me clench my pussy tight. "Oh, baby, don't tempt me."

Koni walked back into the room, dropped the bucket by the bed, and placed the packs inside, his eyes glued to us as if he didn't want to peel them from what was happening.

"Then lay down with me at least." Because I needed them close, needed the feel of them, the safety and comfort from them after what had happened. I knew I was safe, but I wanted to know they were okay too. "I want to feel you both."

Koni's dreamy eyes met mine. With no thought or question, he lifted his arms and tugged the shirt from his body. They both kicked out of their boots and pants but kept their underwear on in what I assumed was an effort to maintain restraint. After helping me onto the bed, each took a side and wrapped themselves around me protectively. I faced Zavier, tucking my head against his chest while his hand threaded into my hair. Koni lay lower at my back with his face pushed between my shoulder blades and his bent leg settled between my thighs.

I sighed, feeling utterly blissful by the heat of their bodies and the sound of their heartbeats and breathing. The contentment seeped through me. And while I should have felt happy, I was hit with a sudden sadness as my mind wandered back to the fight. It flickered quickly to the chance of them getting hurt and then shifted to the death of my family. Tears leaked from my eyes, and I sniffled as silently as I could, not wanting to worry them more. I knew the tears flowed because of my comfort with them, my subconscious allowing me to release everything I'd held inside so fiercely because I finally felt at ease.

"We have you," Zavier whispered, and both of their grips on me shifted. They knew there was another cause for this round of tears.

After that, sleep came fast and without warning.

Sometime in the night, I woke, my hands roaming and rooting, one reaching over Zavier's back while the other—the one pinned between us—pushed against his underwear and clutched his dick.

The movement had been accidental to start, but in the hazy moments between sleep and wakefulness, I'd grabbed and held on.

Zavier exhaled roughly at my touch. His hand clenched my hair as his hips shifted forward, pushing his hardness into my hand.

My thighs tightened against the leg between them, and I felt Koni's body respond behind me, his hand traveling around my waist, splaying wide over my stomach.

"Baby," Zavier whispered. "Are you awake?"

I was starting to love how he called me baby and Koni called me babe. I'd never thought I'd be anything other than Teagan or Teenie to anyone, have somebody close enough to call me something meaningful and endearing. And now I was his ... theirs.

"Yes," I sighed and gripped him harder.

"Mmm. We shouldn't ... we don't want to hurt you." His raspy tone was grittier, from sleep and from a struggle for control.

"So don't be too rough," I said, my tone almost pleading, but I wasn't the least ashamed.

Koni released a long breath against my back, a hot caress. Then his lips were there, pressing tiny kisses to my skin. "I can be gentle."

I gave another sigh, knowing that I'd won the weak battle. I was so grateful for how much they cared, but I was too horny to worry about my wellbeing.

The hand Zavier had in my hair tugged gently, tipping my head back, and then his mouth was on mine, his tongue pushing between my lips and licking with a moan.

Koni lifted his thigh higher between mine, pushing it against my pussy while his hand traveled from my stomach down to the same area. His fingers found me already wet, one sliding the length of me, slipping between my lips. His teeth took tiny nips at the skin of my back.

"Ah," I said inside Zavier's mouth and stroked my hand down his length before he pulled away from my reach. His mouth left mine and traveled farther down to my breasts. The scruff of his jaw scratched the path, and his tongue and lips kissed and licked and soothed right behind.

My body began to writhe as Koni's finger circled my clit.

"Teagan," Koni whispered against my back. "Fuck, babe. I'm ready to come right now just thinking of being inside you again."

Zavier latched onto my nipple, making a noise that blended a chuckle and a moan, agreeing with Koni. My hands went to his head, fingers gripping at the longer strands, needing to touch something.

"Fuck," Koni murmured, then his body disappeared from behind me. A moment later, I was eased onto my back, and my legs were spread wide. "Stay as still as you can. We'll be good to you." Koni knelt at the edge of the bed and leaned in, burying his face between my legs.

"Ah!" I cried out. Zavier sucking and licking my nipple, massaging my breasts, and Koni's mouth attacking my pussy—the sensations made my entire body shake.

"Damn, baby. I can smell how sweet you are from here. Mmm," Zavier murmured over my breast.

I could see his body rocking against the bed, and I tugged his hair harder to lift his face. He chuckled and pulled away from me, his piercings sparkling like his eyes in the dim light. "Tell me what you want."

"To suck you," I said.

He groaned. "Damn, I can't refuse that. Stay there." After sliding off the bed, he positioned himself on his knees by my head and adjusted the pillow to support my neck and prop me high enough. "You okay?"

"Yes," I replied, gripping him and pumping a couple of times before urging him closer. His eyes stared intently as I took his wide cock between my lips.

He moaned, and Koni did the same, the sound vibrating my pussy.

"Fuck," Koni said, slipping a finger inside me. "That is so hot. I've never done this. Shared. Watched."

It was my turn to moan, knowing he was watching Zavier sink deeper inside. Although I was fine to move my head some, able to work him myself, it was sexy as hell to release control and let him fuck my mouth. His hips pulled back and forth, easing in and out, being very careful not to hurt me.

I was so turned on by the feelings and also by how careful they were that tears pricked my eyes. These guys were mine. They were mine.

"Neither have I. It is so fucking hot, watching you eat her pussy. Come on his mouth, baby," Zavier said, urging me on as Koni sucked on my clit and curled his fingers inside me.

All the feeling and dirty talk spiraled me out of control, and I screamed out around Zavier's cock.

"Oh fuck, that felt good," he said.

"Yes, babe." Koni kissed up my stomach then hooked my legs around him as he lifted onto his knees. "I need inside. Tell me if I'm hurting you."

I mumbled a yes and twisted my grip around Zavier. He jerked and groaned to the ceiling before looking down at me and sweeping some hair from my face. "You are so beautiful. And those lips around me … Ahh."

Koni's cock slid along my pussy, wetting himself before pushing inside. All of my muscles tensed up at the euphoric feeling of his thrust. Because of that, sharp pains shot through me from the places I'd been hit earlier, but it wasn't enough to overpower the ecstasy or make me stop. He found an easy pace as Zavier tore himself from my mouth.

"I'm so close to coming," he admitted.

"Do it. Come in my mouth. I want to taste you," I whispered.

Both of them groaned at that admission. Zavier leaned down for a kiss, then slid his tongue in slow and deep.

Koni's rhythm picked up below, jostling me a bit, but my need for them still outweighed the pain. They felt too damn good. "Fucking hell, I'm close too. Come again, Teagan." His fingers slipped along my clit, flicking and pinching it.

"Ah, yes!" I cried as Zavier leaned back up and pushed his dick to my mouth again.

"Take me, baby. I'll warn you," he said with a groan as I sucked him as far in as I could. "Ohh. Yes."

After another circle of Koni's finger and harder thrusts inside, I mumbled a cry around Zavier, my body jolting as another orgasm hit.

"Fuck. Fuck. Fuck. You're gripping me so tight. So tight. I'm coming," Koni shouted.

Zavier grunted several times as he shoved inside my mouth, almost losing control of how hard he was pushing. "Coming too."

I felt them both jerking and twitching, and it was the most erotic thing I'd ever experienced. Koni rocked into me, his thrusts slowing as Zavier's hot cum spilled into the back of my mouth and throat. He was salty and a bit sweet too, and I didn't mind swallowing him down.

"Damn," Zavier murmured, pulling away from my mouth and leaning over to kiss my lips.

Koni did the same to my stomach, so gentle and loving. "That was incredible, Teagan. You aren't hurting, are you?"

"A bit, but nothing worse than before," I replied honestly. "Please don't worry. Okay?"

"For now," Zavier agreed, scooping the hair back from his face. "Let's clean you up before more sleep."

They both disappeared and returned a couple moments later. Koni held a wet towel and wiped me down while Zavier grabbed water bottles from the ice bucket.

He handed one to me with a couple of pills. When I eyed him, he said, "Ibuprofen. Loch put a bottle in the bucket. Probably won't last long, but it'll give you a couple pain-free hours to sleep at least."

I took the pills and nuzzled into bed, inhaling their scents, now so much stronger in the clean sheets and blankets. They settled against me again, and I sighed loudly. When they both chuckled in response, I couldn't help but do the same. We were sated, spent, and happy. And though I was moments from sleep, my mind shifted again, this time thinking about the future, about my transition and what would happen after ... after I returned home and left camp behind.

bait

1

Three days had passed since I was attacked at Camp Midnight Moon and nearly a week since I'd arrived. The temperature had dropped lower in this valley at the edge of the Great Smoky Mountains, bringing along more snow after the first fall on the night Nima and her crew had jumped me. But I hadn't exactly experienced much of the weather.

Koni and Zavier had been babying me, outright refusing to let me do anything. Including them. Well, not entirely anyway. The day following the attack, my body was in pain, with bruising from all the various hits. Face. Back. Stomach. I also had random marks from minor hits, including the grip used to restrain my arms. So, yeah, the guys barely wanted to touch me.

I sat up in bed and looked myself over. Though the bruises had been purple and blue to start, the worst had already faded into a light yellow color, and the rest had vanished altogether. Wolf genes were decent for that reason. Even though I still hadn't transitioned and couldn't shift to speed up the process, our bodies naturally healed fast.

During the past three days—that I'd been babied and held captive inside the cabin—I'd also endured a couple of transition flares. Regardless of the guys keeping their distance to avoid the temptation of full-on sex, they couldn't refuse helping me through the flares. I clenched my thighs together, recalling the two times it had happened. Koni and Zavier had each handled me well alone, making me orgasm to relieve the anger and body pains.

I sighed, wanting them again so badly.

Koni had moved his things to the cabin the day after the attack, declaring it as his place too. It was comforting to have both of them with me. They'd also brought another bed but separated all of them to avoid temptation and any accidental harm during the night. They kept close enough that I could feel their heat and hear them breathe, though. And while that was incredibly soothing, it also stirred up thoughts of going home, making me incredibly sad.

We hadn't discussed the future again. Deep down, we all knew we needed to talk about it, needed to figure out a plan. Yet we avoided it because the worst-case scenario was too painful to consider—them staying and me leaving, us ending.

This place had been their home for some time, and Rosie and Tim like parents. I didn't feel right asking them to go home with me, given their bond with Loch and Elijah too. The Four were close, like brothers. Admittedly, I was reluctant to leave them as well. My heart belonged to Koni and Zavier, sure, but part of me felt tied to Loch and Elijah. The pull was there, and from what Zavier had said, they also felt something. We just hadn't gotten as friendly ... yet.

I'd seen Loch and Elijah only twice over the last few days. The two times I'd escaped Koni and Zavier's lockdown and ventured to the kitchen for my own food, Loch and Elijah had been there. Their eyes were on me, yet we barely spoke. It wasn't so much weird as it was frustrating. I felt something simmering below the surface that I couldn't break through. They were still guarded, and I was sure it had to do with the future too. That was why they all had originally agreed to stay away from me. They feared I would tear them apart, and I feared they might be right.

Koni and Zavier had left early, not bothering to wake me when they went off to handle whatever duties assigned to them for the day. They'd obviously deemed me well enough to fetch my own breakfast. I was thrilled and more than ready to fly the coop.

After a quick shower, I towel-dried my hair and threw on a pair of Zavier's sweats and a long-sleeved shirt of Koni's. They'd told me to use whatever I'd needed of theirs since Loch still hadn't returned my suitcase. I was growing tired of waiting for him to fess up and hand it over. He was stubborn. That much was clear. Even more so than Zavier, possibly more than me too. I was at my breaking point. The Alabama clothes I'd brought with me weren't exactly the best for the wintery temps in Tennessee, but at least I wouldn't have to roll the guys' sweats or worry about my boobs being exposed when I bent over wearing their V-necked shirts.

As soon as I opened the cabin door, snow fell inside. It had to have been gathering on the small porch for hours. The indents of Koni's and Zavier's boot prints had even filled in since they'd left.

For a few moments, I breathed in the crisp air and allowed myself to admire the white stuff that I'd never experienced before coming here. The lake area looked like a painting, with snow clinging to the banks and the surrounding trees' branches. I sighed, enjoying the peacefulness, pushing all worries away, especially knowing the triplets and the guys who had helped them attack me were no longer here. They'd left the next day as Rosie had instructed. And now, the only other headaches remaining were Jackson and Trig. Thankfully, I hadn't seen them in a while.

My stomach grumbled, reminding me it was time for breakfast. I moved to step outside, lifting my foot over the mound of snow and eyeing my Vans. "Shit." The walk would be interesting.

I'd learned from Koni and Zavier that there was a big difference in types of snow. Wet and heavy, dry and powdery. I'd thought little about their explanation until I began walking. The dense, wet snow slipped into the sides of the shoes, soaking through them and the bottoms of Zavier's sweats as I trudged the path leading to the main camp area.

My body temp was no match either. The parka kept me warm up top with my hands shoved into the pockets, but my feet felt numb by the time I reached the dining hall.

Everyone had already come and gone for breakfast. Tracks from footprints pressed into the snow, pointing to and from the doors. I wiped my wet shoes on the entry rug and stepped cautiously to the kitchen, where I heard Rosie speaking before I entered.

"Now, stop. You know I'm going to buy you something for your birthday anyway, so it might as well be something you want. Tell me," Rosie's pitchy voice scolded someone in her motherly way. It made my heart warm, even though I had no idea who she was talking to.

Birthday? I shook my head. It was something I hadn't even thought about. Zavier, Koni, and I had talked a good amount over the past few days. We discussed more about the camp, about Rosie and Tim, about how they'd arrived within a month of each other the previous year. I'd told them a little about my house in Alabama, about The Back Burner restaurant, and about my relatively dull life leading up to my arrival at camp. We'd brought up movies, music, books, and about some of our favorite things—other than sex and Koni's love of fried chicken. But we hadn't discussed birthdays. I supposed since we knew we were around the same age, there had been no drive to know.

The male grumbled low as if he had argued enough and was prep to her insistence. I stifled my chuckle at that, practically feeling his frustration. "Fine. I'd like a new book or something." Loch. I could tell from the sharp tone it was him, though it was always softer with her.

"Just one?" she asked. And after a long pause, where I assumed he had shot her an incredulous look, she added, "Okay, okay. Any preference?"

"Non-fiction, fiction, anything about space, the solar system."

My teeth nearly started to chatter, and I knew I could no longer eavesdrop by the door. I needed to grab food and get back to the cabin before I got frostbite on my toes.

"What about a cake?" Rosie asked just as I pushed the kitchen door open. "Hi, Teagan! Oh, good God!" she said as he head of bubble gum pink hair dropped forward, her eyes falling from my face down to my feet. "You don't have any boots!"

Her snow boots looked comfortable. Padded. Thick. Warm. Aside from that, she was dressed normally in a pair of orange leggings, an oversized black sweatshirt with a winged cat flying over a rainbow, and no jacket.

Loch stood against the center island, his hip propped to the countertop. He wore his usual—V-neck T-shirt a bit snug to his chest, black jeans, work boots. No jacket either. His lips pressed tight together as soon as I'd entered and stayed that way while Rosie had assessed me. But his mouth popped open when she turned back to him with a scowling face.

"All right. I wasn't going to step in here, but I'm gonna. Go get her suitcase. We all know you have it. Her scent is on you. And honestly, I thought you would have pulled your head out of your ass before I had to get involved."

His eyes darted from her to me and back again. "Fine."

When he made to move to go, she propped her hands on her wide hips dramatically. "Now, Lochlan."

Lochlan? *Oh. Wow.* She really used her foster mama voice and, from what I could guess, his full first name.

He licked his lips and had the decency to drop his eyes from her scolding. Which ... God. My legs and feet weren't cold enough to keep the heat from spreading through my body at the sight of him. Something about the vulnerableness he just expressed made me want to both comfort him and fuck him at the same time. He was always so hardened and angry. This was a crack in his exterior, and I wondered how thick his outer wall was and how long it took to break into. I wanted it, to be inside with him, to see the realness there because I knew there was so much more to him that I hadn't seen.

"You need boots," Rosie said, turning back to me while Loch stalked past. His eyes dropped down to the wet lower parts of my body, taking in my current problems.

My teeth chattered as the door swung closed with his departure. "I think I do, yes. I hadn't thought about it."

"I'm so sorry," Rosie said. "I did think about it before, but it completely slipped my mind. And now ... well, now we're officially in the snow season where you will need them. I'm going shopping today anyway. I need to grab some things, so I'll pick up a sturdy pair and maybe some extra cold weather stuff for you."

"You don't have to get more than the boots."

"Nonsense. I owe you. If not for anything else then for how long it took me to get on him about your stuff. I swear ..." She tsked, and her eyes wandered around the kitchen for a moment as if she were deep in thought. "So stubborn."

I wanted to laugh at that, but the stinging in my thawing feet kept the humor at bay. "You've said." Her eyes found mine again, knowing I was referring to the other night when we'd discussed my tutoring that stubborn student. When she simply pressed her lips together in a quaint smile, I added, "And it's his birthday soon?"

"Today, actually. December fifteenth. I hate that I almost forgot that too. I should know better than anyone … Well, I won't get into his business. But even though he's stubborn, he's good, kind, and appreciative. Hardworking and dedicated. So yeah, I feel like garbage for only remembering this morning. That's the main reason I need to shop. I was going to …" She looked around the kitchen again. "I was going to make him a meal and maybe a cake. But his favorite food is pizza, so I think I'll just get a pick up from the local place that he likes."

"I'll do the cake," I blurted without much thought. *Shit. Really, Teagan?* Should I really do something nice for him after he held my clothes hostage for so long?

One of Rosie's eyebrows lifted as she pinned me with a stare. She was obviously thinking the same thing I was.

I let out a breath with a smile. "It's not a revenge plot if that's what you're expecting. I'll bake it while you're out. It's my thanks for the boots. So do you know his favorite type? And do we have what I would need to make it?"

Her face seemed to relax, seeing that I was serious and not preparing for some childish prank. "You're going to have to ask him his favorite. I don't recall if he even has one. We should have most ingredients for anything plain vanilla or chocolate. If anything special is needed, then I can grab it while I'm out." She lifted her finger in front of her. "And … I just remembered that I have an older pair of boots you can use today while I shop for your new ones. Stay here. I'll go grab them for you."

"Okay," I replied, biting on the edge of my lip as I figured out how to spring the cake question on Loch. It made me nervous. I hadn't thought that I would need to ask or disclose that I'd planned to make his birthday cake. I figured I just would make it and not have to see him when he found out. But that was dumb. Why shouldn't I be proud to make it for him? Be the bigger person, right? It was better than trying to ride out his stubbornness like with the suitcase. Face him head-on. Be as direct as Rosie. But, as soon as I ask him, he might disappear for the rest of the day anyway, refuse to see me or eat the cake. Ugh … I'd have to ask right away when he brought the clothes.

2

After making a cup of coffee and scarfing down a muffin, I'd went through the pantry and found just about everything needed to make a simple vanilla cake and icing, but they didn't have the cocoa powder required for chocolate. They had candles, though. Striped little sticks of wax, like pastel-colored candy canes. I had my doubts about Loch wanting candles to wish on. I almost laughed at the thought. Maybe I did want to witness him seeing the cake. The judgment was out on whether he'd smile for getting one or if he'd simply scowl at it, then grumble angrily as he took a bite and chewed it down with his powerful jaw.

"Here ya go, Teagan," Rosie said, sweeping into the kitchen with a brown pair of scuffed and faded snow boots. "These should work for today, even if they're too big."

When she handed them over, I checked them out and laughed. "Yeah, they might feel like clown boots. No offense."

She giggled. "None taken. What size are you, Teenie?"

"Touché." I smirked at her. "Six."

"Yep. Those are definitely a clown size ten. It's essential to up-size with thick socks. I'll buy a six and a half for you. And some thick socks. We need to take care of our human feet out here. No good getting frostbite."

"I can tell," I said, shuffling my wet ones around in an attempt to warm them.

"Oh, gosh. I should have told you to take them off before I left. It's fine to do in here. I'll grab you an old wash rag to dry them. Hang on."

I dropped to the floor beside the center island and peeled my Vans and socks off, trying my best to ignore how cold and wet Zavier's sweats were against my legs. My feet had already wrinkled like old prunes.

"Here," Rosie said, walking to me with a frayed hand towel. She glanced over her shoulder, looking toward the kitchen door. "You should probably get back to your cabin to change. Don't dawdle while you're wet and cold, okay?"

Hmm. I wasn't sure why she thought I would. "I just ate so … Yeah, I guess I'm done. Do you think he—"

The door opened before I could finish voicing my question on whether Loch might take my stuff to the cabin. He strolled in casually, his demeanor looking less scorned and more confidently controlled again.

One of his hands clutched a pair of jeans, presumably mine. The other held a pair of my socks—the fuzzy ones with the pizza slices, which I loved to lounge in more than wear with shoes. "I dropped the suitcase at your cabin. Thought you'd want to change as soon as possible." His voice was flat as he moved closer to me. He placed the jeans on the island and leaned down to hand over the socks. Amusement flickered in his eyes as I took hold of them.

"Thanks," I murmured, unsure how to read that sliver of expression. Rosie had said his favorite food was pizza. I supposed that was why he had chosen to bring them.

He straightened up and looked at Rosie, who had been watching us intently. Was she expecting an argument? Or maybe she was waiting to see what kind of magnetic reaction we'd have—attraction or repulsion. I was still uncertain myself.

"Good! That was kind of you, Loch. All right, I should get going. Teagan, if there's anything else you need, stop by the office or radio it to us. If I'm gone, Tim will message me."

"Okay." I slipped the socks over my pruned feet with a sigh. They'd dried and thawed a little with the kitchen's temperature, but I couldn't deny that the fuzzy material instantly made them feel better. It also didn't hurt that Loch's hand had warmed the socks first.

"Space books," she noted with a wink to Loch. "Ooh! Also, I'm getting you pizza from Charlie's. So don't eat too late in the afternoon. And … since Tim will be working with Elijah later on some office stuff and I'll be out, I need Teagan to help you in the classroom today before dinner. Teagan, you'll have time, right?"

I nearly choked on my spit. Shit. Why hadn't she brought this up before? Oh. She was such a sly fox. There was no way this was a case of forgetfulness. This was a sabotage situation, throwing us into the fire without warning. I almost expected her to ask him about the cake while she was at it. Air it all out. But, nope. She was letting me handle that because I'd been dumb enough to volunteer.

"Um, yeah. I can do that." If I managed to peel myself out from under the bus she'd hit me with.

"Good. He'll fill you in on the curriculum. See you both later." She sauntered out, a crooked smirk on her lips.

With that, the day had gotten exponentially more complicated. Knowing I'd now need to make the cake before the study session, I had to ask fast. Like a Band-Aid. Just rip that fucker off.

He turned like he was about ready to bolt, which was totally understandable after the bomb Rosie had dropped. But I couldn't let him leave. Nope. It was his birthday. I had to ask.

"What's your favorite cake?" I blurted in a much too high pitch. *Well, shit.*

His body spun slowly back around, and that hardened stare fell to the ground, where I was still sitting.

Crap. I had the socks on, but I didn't want the sweats to saturate them. When he didn't respond, I tugged the bottom rolls up over my calves and jumped to my feet. "Hold that thought. Let me get the jeans on. Don't leave."

I didn't look at him while I rushed into the pantry, shed the sweats, and yanked on the jeans he'd brought. I sighed at their snugness. Usually, sweatpants would rank better than anything on the comfort list, but the guys' were too baggy and cumbersome to compare to a well-fitted pair of jeans.

There was a sound from the kitchen, almost like my sigh had been echoed. I ignored what it could mean and rushed back out.

Loch looked me up and down, his features remaining as hard as ever. *Geez*. It seemed impossible for him to relax.

"Happy birthday," I said, giving him a hint of a smile. "I'm ... uh ... Well, I'm going to make you a cake, so I wanted to know your favorite kind in case Rosie needs to grab extra ingredients."

He stood silent for a moment, only blinking at me as if I hadn't spoken. What the fuck? Is this where we were? I thought maybe things would be different, especially since he'd seen me half naked after the attack. A million thoughts bounced inside my head, reasons why he might hate me so much. Because honestly, even after feeling that pull to him, thinking that he had felt it too, and hearing Zavier basically say the same ... at that moment, with his silence, I highly doubted all of it. He seemed to loathe my very existence. He didn't want me to make him a cake. He didn't want me to help him with schoolwork. He didn't want me fucking Zavier and Koni. He probably didn't want me breathing the same air in this same space.

I sighed and let my eyes drift to the floor where I'd left Rosie's boots. I would not cry about this. Whatever the reason, it wasn't my business to know. I had veered way off my course and had started feeling so much these past days, so many emotions. Maybe I had been fooling myself with it all. Maybe I was naïve and needed this reality check to keep my head on straight. No expectations, right? No one had to like me or to care. They knew I had plans to leave. That could very well be the reason he hated me, and I couldn't fault him for that. It was a valid reason, but it still hurt. I couldn't lie to myself.

After slipping into the comically large boots, I stuffed the laces inside without tying them, hoping I wouldn't trip on the way back to the cabin. I wouldn't leave without speaking again, though. I had some things to say, whether or not he wanted to hear them.

"Look, I already told Rosie I would make you the cake. I don't want to disappoint her any more than I already have. So if you don't have a preference, I'll make a simple vanilla cake with whipped icing. No big deal. And as for the school stuff, I'll come because I said I would. If you don't want my help, that's fine." I was preparing to leave, gripping Zavier's sweats tight in my arm, hooking the heels of my wet Vans in one hand and stuffing my wet socks inside, but I realized there was more I needed to unload.

"I get that you don't like me, and that's fine, even though we've barely said boo to each other." My arm waved out a bit dramatically, and I had to straighten my spine to reel in my southern attitude. "But what I just don't understand is why take my stuff? Was it simply to use your clothes as a marker so they wouldn't get near me? I guess that could have made sense if you didn't trust them enough." And now I was rambling and talking myself into a circle. "Christ. Never mind. It doesn't really matter." I was ready to toss the towel. Why did I need an explanation from him? I shouldn't. I didn't.

Now feeling utterly stupid, I gripped my things and took a few hurried steps to move past him. Only, he took one large side step and blocked me with his massive chest. Literally. I smacked right into him, too slow to react and stop myself. Flush with his body, feeling his heat and even the beat of his heart against that big ole solid chest, I tipped my head back to stare up at him. His face angled down, his hazel eyes locking with mine. They arrested me, the light brown center with speckled green borders simply too captivating to look away from. And his scent ... God. It was all-encompassing, that smoky cedar and peppery smell curling around me like an embrace.

"It does matter," he said in the softest tone I'd ever heard from him. His breath wafted down to me, minty and fresh.

"Why?" I replied in whisper automatically, mimicking the softness of his tone.

His eyes closed for a couple of moments, and he inhaled deeply. When they opened again, his pupils had dilated, leaving little color to be seen. "It matters because ... you matter ... more than you should ... more than you were supposed to."

Oh. Well. The admission hit me hard. I blinked up at him, unsure what to say, afraid if I even spoke, the slight crack I'd just found in his wall would fill back up and shut me out again.

When I didn't reply, his tongue peeked out from his mouth and licked his lower lip. It was as if he was stunned by his own words too.

I had a feeling he was battling something inside, unsure of what to do with himself, with me. It made me wonder if Zavier and Koni had even talked to him about me, if they'd discussed my openness with him. Being with multiple partners seemed unnatural on the surface, to people and wolves, to even me before coming here. His hesitation and reluctance could also involve that complication.

Maybe he was conflicted about it all. Maybe he didn't want to share me or anything.

There was really only one way to find out for sure. He'd taken the first step, literally stopping me from leaving. Maybe I needed to take the next?

I licked my lips then dropped everything I held to the floor. The only reaction I saw was a slight flicker in his eyes before I reached my hands up his body, over his broad shoulders, and up his scarred neck to draw his face down closer. He let me, allowed me to touch him, to pull him to me. If he hadn't wanted it, I was sure he would have jerked away, so I was silently screaming with joy inside.

I pushed up onto the tiptoes of the oversized boots, leaning against Loch to find stability. Palming the sides of his wide jaw, I pressed my lips to his with a soft sigh. At first, he didn't move, didn't flinch. It was chaste and awkward for a couple of seconds. Then I licked along his closed mouth, begging him to open for me. In a flash, he did, and I slipped my tongue inside. His arms finally moved, snaking around my back to support me, tugging me even closer. I felt his tongue flick mine in a shy, tentative way. The minty taste of his mouth was addictive, the flavor sweet spearmint, not a strong peppermint like Zavier's preferred kind. Craving more, I sucked on his tongue.

A groan vibrated in his throat, and his arms tightened, pulling our lower halves together and pressing his hardness high against my stomach. Solid and forceful. There was no doubting his enjoyment, his pleasure. I sighed inside his mouth and went a little weak in his arms, relishing this new experience with him, the fact that he was opening up to me. The assumption of his possible dominance flitted into my mind. With how hardened his usual demeanor was, the strength and toughness that always radiated from him, I'd pictured his kissing to be aggressive and reckless and rough. But this was nothing like that. I was surprised but nowhere near disappointed. Honestly, I was more turned on by the gentleness and not simply because it was unexpected. It felt as if it meant so much more, as if he were opening that wall and letting me in further. And that was fucking hot.

I moved my hands over the shaved sides of his hair, enjoying the feel against my palms. His hands slid down my waist, squeezing and digging in, then farther, dipping up under the bulky parka to feel the top of my ass.

Suddenly, he removed his lips from mine and pulled back. As he tore his body away, I was left with my lips parted and my hands still suspended in the air.

Confused, I uttered, "I ... Are you ... Was that ..."

He wiped a hand over his mouth, simply staring at me, a look of wonder and bewilderment in his eyes. "I'm not sure."

I blinked at him and dropped my arms awkwardly to my sides, my body already missing the feel of him, the heat of him. "Not sure about what?"

He glanced around the kitchen, seeming to refocus on where we were. "Cake. I'm not sure what my favorite is. I haven't had ... I've really only had the snack kinds. I like chocolate, I guess."

Only had the snack kind? Oh. Christ, that made me want to cry.

"Okay. Chocolate."

He didn't smile or do anything to suggest that he'd enjoyed the mouth sex we'd just had in the kitchen. Well, aside from the thick bulge straining against his jeans.

"I'll ... I'll see you later," he said, turning and striding from the kitchen.

At least he wasn't scowling.

3

My head was foggy after the super sexy kiss I'd had with Loch in the kitchen. I didn't know what happened. One second, we were on fire, and the next ... snuffed. While I was ecstatic that he'd crossed over whatever line he'd created for me and had let me kiss him, I was also worried he regretted it, despite the undeniable enjoyment displayed by his body.

My mind wandered through random explanations as I physically wandered the kitchen for a recipe book. I couldn't recall exact ingredients or measurements for cake baking, and I wouldn't chance getting it wrong. After finding a recipe and making a mental list to pass to Rosie, I gathered my things and a few items for lunch to take back to my cabin. I had no plans to return to the kitchen until after everyone else had taken their midday meal. That way, I could make his cake then meet up with him in the schoolhouse prior to dinner.

Not wanting to chance seeing Rosie in person for fear she'd read the kiss all over my face and smell him all over me, I'd skipped going to the office and used the cabin's radio to message her what I'd need for the cake. Even though she hadn't planned to return until dinner, she assured me either she or Tim would make an earlier trip and have the ingredients in the kitchen after lunch.

"Thanks, Rosie," I said before releasing the intercom button.

The cabin door opened, and Zavier, Koni, and Elijah walked inside, removing jackets and stomping their feet to shake excess snow onto the front carpet where I'd previously kicked off Rosie's clown boots.

"And thank you too, Teagan," Rosie's voice spoke through the speaker, prompting the guys to stop and go silent. "Can't wait to have some of the cake later. And please remember to be in the classroom at four. I forgot to mention the time earlier. I hope that gives you enough time to bake."

I pressed the button again as I eyed the guys' curious expressions. "It'll be fine, yes. I'll be there. Bye."

Zavier kicked off his boots and walked to me with an eyebrow quirked. "There's so much to discuss, I'm not sure where to start," he said, not stopping until he was flush against me and wrapping me in his arms. My hands slid around his back automatically, and I inhaled his fresh, comforting scent. He buried his nose into the hair at the top of my head and breathed deeply. His entire body tensed up. A second later, he leaned down and pressed his lips to mine softly before backing away and lifting my shirt to inspect the faded bruises over my stomach.

"I know where to start," Koni said, kicking off his own boots and lifting his arms over his head to fix his topknot while he eyed the doorway to the bedroom. My suitcase was there. I hadn't even noticed yet. "Guess you finally got your stuff back, huh?"

Elijah stayed close to the door and kept his black utility jacket and work boots on. He shoved his hands into the front pockets of his jeans and chuckled a little before his eyes returned to Zavier and me, watching Zavier's inspection ... and maybe the parts of my skin Zavier was exposing.

Wow. It was nice to see him so relaxed and not so tense around me. His amusement by the suitcase was a bonus, and so was his possible interest in my body. He hadn't looked away, at least.

"Yeah," I admitted to Koni, batting Zavier's hands away as he made to unfasten my jeans. He flashed me a sheepish grin, realizing what he'd been about to do in front of Elijah. Both Elijah and Loch had seen my upper body in only a bra during different circumstances, but that didn't mean I was comfortable dropping my pants in front of either just yet.

Zavier took a seat on the closest armchair, legs spread open in that manly way, watching as I continued, "I went for a late breakfast, and Rosie told Loch to give it back."

"No shit?!" Koni said, nodding with a snicker.

Elijah whistled. Those full lips of his forming a luscious pout to emit the sound. *Damn. Those lips.* "Bet that went over well."

I breathed out a laugh. "She saw that my Vans and sweats were soaked, so she gave me an old pair of boots to use today while she buys me new ones. He was okay. It was fine."

"Like your ass in those jeans," Zavier said, patting his thigh for me to sit. I lifted a teasing brow before obliging him, settling onto his lap sideways. His hand stroked down my back to the very ass he was admiring. "So, I distinctly heard Rosie say cake."

I nodded. "Did y'all know it's Loch's birthday? I told Rosie I'd make a cake, and she's picking up pizza." When they all remained silent, I glanced between them. "What?"

"Well," Koni started, looking around. "It's his chosen birthday. It's actually the day he arrived here, but yeah, chosen."

"Chosen?" I asked, not fully understanding.

After more glances between themselves, Koni was the one to answer. He leaned his hip against the bedroom doorway. "You know how I told you I was dropped off and found around age four? So I don't know my actual birthday. They gave me a fake one in foster care, which I decided not to keep. Now my birthday is October thirty-first because I picked it. Rosie helped with that, to make it legal and all. Loch's like me. He doesn't know his actual birthday, so he chose the date when he and Elijah got here two years ago."

"Oh," I breathed the word out, trying my best to control the air so it didn't rush from my lungs in an emotional burst.

Still standing in front of the door, Elijah nodded, while at my side, Zavier's face dipped down a bit.

"Well, I'm glad that he chose a good date," I said honestly. Inside, my heart was hurting over his past … all of their pasts.

"Yeah," Koni replied, his tone somber.

"And you picked Halloween?" I asked, seeing their discomfort speaking about Loch's personal business and steering the conversation away. "Why?"

"Uh, because it's badass," he replied, shooting me an incredulous look as if my question was the stupidest in the world.

I giggled and giggled some more as my body vibrated on Zavier's lap, then I snorted most unattractively.

"Ha! There it is!" Koni yelled, pointing at me. "Told you she snorts."

"What?" I looked around, trying to reign in my laughter. "You told them?"

Zavier's body shook under me. He was laughing too. Then a laugh escaped Elijah, deep and throaty. My mouth gaped as I studied the enormous smile on his face.

"You did snort. That's funny." Elijah said, his laugh dying off more quickly than the others. The smile lingered, though, those full lips drawn upward, pressing his cheeks higher. The sight was so stunning and sexy it made me shiver.

"It's fucking adorable," Zavier said, squeezing the top of my ass firmly as his other palm stroked higher up my thigh. He bounced his leg, and my body jiggled in his lap.

I gave him a side-eye glance with a smirk. "Sure it is." Then I glared at Koni playfully, teasing him for disclosing my snorting incident while we'd worked chores together. After a few moments of silence, I asked, "So how old are you, Halloween?"

Koni shrugged. "Twenty."

"Me too," I admitted with a small smile.

"So when's your birthday, then?" he asked.

"Not as cool as yours. September fifth."

"Shit, that's close to yours, Eli," Zavier said to Elijah before squeezing my thigh harder and speaking to me. "And I knew yours had to be in the summer since you smell so much like it."

I grinned at him, my body heating at his words. My eyes shifted to Elijah. "When's yours then?"

Elijah straightened his arms, shoving his fists farther into his pockets. He rocked onto the soles of his boots lightly. "September seventh, and I'm twenty-one."

"And you?" I asked Zavier, turning my body a little more on his thigh.

Those different colored eyes stared up at me, dazzling me with the way they seemed to sparkle every time they looked at me. "June twenty-sixth. And twenty, like you and Koni."

"So Elijah's the oldest. Well, unless … How old is Loch then?"

"Nineteen." Elijah was the one who answered, his eyes down on his boots. "That's what he thinks, anyway."

"Ah." I pondered that bit of information. They'd arrived two years ago, which meant Loch had been seventeen. Underage. I supposed Rosie and Tim had made an exception to their adult camp rule. I was glad they had. Not wanting to focus on Loch again, I said, "So that makes you the oldest."

"Yeah," Elijah confirmed with a shrug. His mood had taken a turn with the conversation, and I was suddenly regretting it.

"Rosie said she's getting pizza for dinner?" Koni asked, pushing off the bedroom doorway and coming to sit in the seat next to Zavier.

I laughed. "Yes. Charlie's, I think."

"Oh damn! I'm so glad Loch didn't refuse that or your cake. Gonna be good eating tonight between boundary shifts." He smacked his lips together. "We should get some lunch soon, too, before we get back out there."

"What do you guys have to do?" I asked curiously. They'd been out all morning, and from the sound of it would be for the rest of the day too.

"Bear season is still active in certain zones near us. Hunting is mostly illegal inside the park, but some hunters wander. So our boundary needs to be checked for traps and also for breaches."

"Whoa. Are they a threat?" I asked, unnerved by what they were dealing with. While hunting was common in our area back home, we'd had plenty of wolves in our pack to monitor things. As alpha, my father handled all of that. I supposed now I'd need to when I returned.

"We've had some hunters spot us occasionally," Koni answered. "Most aren't used to seeing wolves, and they usually won't bother reporting because that would only incriminate them for being where they aren't supposed to be." He laughed at that fact, and Elijah chuckled with him.

"And other times?" I asked, scared to know but wanting to anyway.

"Well, we've had a couple of hunters try to go for us. We're hard to resist, ya know?" Koni quipped.

My gut twisted, and I felt sick. I'd known of it happening in the south too. I just hadn't been privy to as much information in recent years. My father had taught me standard wolf lessons early on, but he'd left most of the in-depth stuff to teach after I'd made my transition … which never happened.

"Oh, baby, your face just went pale. It's fine. There's no need to worry about it, okay?" Zavier said, stroking my thigh and back.

Koni reached over from his chair and smoothed the back of his knuckles over my cheek before adding, "Yeah, even Zavier has enough skill to handle them if he needed to." Zavier reached out to backhand him, and Koni leaned back into his chair with a jolt, narrowly avoiding the hit to the chest.

They both laughed.

"So when are you making Loch's cake?" Zavier changed the subject.

"Oh. Well, I planned to hang here for a bit, eat the sandwich I brought, then head to the kitchen after everyone's finished with lunch. After that, I need to help Loch in the classroom since Rosie will be out, and she said Tim's busy with Elijah around the same time."

Koni blew out an audible breath. "Does Loch know that?"

"Yeah." I let out my own breath with a chuckle. "Rosie told both of us earlier, so …"

"Right," he said with a grimace. "Maybe we'll talk to him after lunch then, in case—"

"No, no. It's fine." I cut off his words. "He, uh … He seemed all right with it. It'll be okay."

Elijah rocked onto his heels before backing up the two steps to the door. "I do have some things to do with Tim later, so I better grab some food. I'll see you all at dinner."

"Yeah," Zavier said.

"Yep," Koni replied too. "Later."

When Elijah's eyes landed on me, I lifted my hand stupidly in a small wave. "See you."

As soon as he was out the door, Zavier gripped my thigh and back tighter. "You sure I don't need to talk to him? He needs to get over his shit and stop being an ass to you."

I smiled and looked down at his large hand, watching it grasp my thigh so possessively. "I think he has, in a way. We ... well, I kissed him." I bit my lower lip, hoping that hadn't been a bad decision, hoping I hadn't made an even worse decision by telling Zavier and Koni about it. Maybe that was betraying his trust? But if I hadn't told them then maybe I would be betraying their trust. Was I damning myself either way?

"What?!" Koni asked, sitting upright again and scooting to the edge of his seat so his lower legs were touching mine.

Both of their eyes were wide. Zavier scrunched his lips together. "I thought I smelled him on you. I know his scent is on the suitcase and the jeans you put back on, but ..." He leaned up closer to my body and inhaled. "Yeah, it is clearer up top."

My body warmed, thinking about the kiss again and the way Koni and Zavier were looking at me. They didn't seem mad, only intrigued. "I didn't pin him down or anything." My breath rushed out, worried that they were considering the worst.

Zavier tilted his head curiously, a few longer strands of hair falling out of his pushed-back pompadour.

"Do you not believe me? I would never take advantage of someone like—"

"No, babe," Koni said, grasping my knees. "It's not that. We know you wouldn't, especially after the whole Nima thing with Z here."

"Then what?" I asked with a huff.

"It's shocking," Zavier admitted. "And it's not because of you. We're shocked because we didn't think he'd ever give in. We've known he's as crazy about you as we are. I told you that. But he's been so against the idea of you, we thought it would either take a long time or he wouldn't break at all."

"Well, I don't want him to break in any way."

"You know that's not what I meant," Zavier admonished me. "I only mean his resolve."

"Yeah, he's fucking stubborn," Koni added and blew out a breath. "The most out of all of us. When he's set on something, he rarely changes his mind. He might be the youngest, but he's a fighter and hardheaded enough to lead in a lot of situations, especially out there."

"Oh. Okay. Well, yeah, he is stubborn. And honestly, I was shocked too. I feel like his wall cracked a little for me."

"Oh, yes, you cracked it all right. You're going to crack it wide open and make him feel things he's never felt," Koni said with a little laugh.

Zavier scrunched his lips and drew his brows together as he glared at him. "Really? Not cool." After Koni shrugged and gave a wry smile, Zavier looked back at me and pressed on despite my obvious confusion about their exchange. Why was that comment not cool? "I told you, you're good for us. With us. I'm glad he let you kiss him. He needs you too, baby."

I wasn't as sure as him, especially not knowing what the future held, but I agreed about the kiss. I was glad it happened, and I hoped any affection for him might help, even if the last thing he takes from me is a birthday cake.

"And I think I speak for both of us when I say, we need you now." Koni's voice was low and seductive, making me bite my lip.

"Aren't you guys tired? Don't you have work to do after lunch?" I asked with a giggle. Because the way they were looking at me made fire lick across my body.

"Baby, we have so much pent-up energy to use on you now that you're feeling better." Zavier's raspy tone sent another rush of heat through me, this time right between my legs.

Koni stood and grabbed my hands to pull me to my feet. "I'll be fine having you for lunch."

4

"You cannot just eat me for lunch," I said with a giggle, then gasped when Koni immediately lifted me to my feet and stripped my shirt over my head.

"You're probably right. I could eat you all day and not be full. But I am not worried about food right now." Koni's hands smoothed over my arms as he stared into my eyes. "You interested in having us right now?"

Was I? Was that even a question? I hadn't had them in a few days. Well, I'd had their mouths and their hands, but not their dicks, and I wanted them badly. "I'm starving for you both."

In an instant, Koni had his shirt off and his hands on my bra-covered breasts. With a pantie-melting smile, he leaned in and kissed my mouth, driving his tongue inside as soon as I opened.

Zavier's solid body pressed against my back, his hands snaking around to my front where his fingers made quick work of unfastening my jeans and pulling them down. His rough palms smoothed down my thighs as he slipped the underwear down next, then lifted each foot to remove the clothing. They returned to my legs, and his mouth joined them, kissing and nipping bites along my flesh, up to my ass cheeks.

I whimpered into Koni's mouth as his tongue lavished mine, and his hands worked to unclasp my bra.

"Fuck, Teagan, you are just too good to be true," Zavier said between his bites and kisses. "Let's move this back to the bedroom."

Koni pulled away from my mouth and discarded my bra, leaving me completely naked. "Yes. I'm so ready to push those beds together now that there's a third. So much more room for activities."

I laughed as he awkwardly walked backward, not wanting to take his eyes or hand off me. They were both still in their jeans, but I reached behind me and rubbed my hand over Zavier's bulge.

"Baby," he said with a grunt. "I want to fuck you so hard. I don't want to be gentle."

"I don't want gentle either," I admitted.

"Good, because I don't think I can after fucking my fist these last few days. Don't get me wrong, it was such a turn-on to jerk myself while I ate you. But there's nothing like being inside you. In your mouth. In your pussy. In your ass." His hands rubbed over my ass as we walked.

Oh, his dirty mouth did things to me, made my body writhe in response.

"Wait, what? You fucked her ass?" Koni sputtered and looked over my head to Zavier. "Why did neither of you tell me this?"

"It didn't come up," Zavier said, then spun me around and crashed his lips to mine as soon as we reached the bed.

I giggled into his mouth. These two were so bad, and I loved it. My fingers scrambled to unfasten Zavier's jeans. I pushed the edge down and did the same to his soft boxer-briefs before pulling his cock out and grabbing hold. A pleasure groan sounded in his throat as he sucked my tongue into his mouth.

"I want your ass too. Damn, Teagan. Babe. That's so hot." I heard Koni jostling around behind me. The wooden bedposts vibrated as he slid the three beds together. Then I felt his hands roaming my ass before something stiff and smooth pressed between my cheeks, rubbing up and down. "I'm so fucking hard. Goddamn. Will you let me back here too?"

I broke away from Zavier's mouth, panting, and he moved his mouth down my neck, sucking and licking. "Yes. But I don't think I can handle it rough back there. I've only done it once. It felt good but hurt a bit too." I used my free hand to reach back for Koni. He laid his cock in my hand, and I squeezed him, then stroked down to his base.

"Ah, yes," he said with a hiss. "Mmm. Maybe not now, then? Later. Soon."

"Mm-hmm."

Zavier's fingers pinched and tweaked my nipples before he leaned down and sucked one into his mouth. He flicked his tongue over the stiff peak then bit down, drawing a cry from me. In the next second, he was upright and guiding my body to the bed. He sat on the edge of the first one and laid back all the way. "Come here. Sit on my face, baby."

I let go of Koni and crawled onto the bed. Zavier guided my leg over his head, settling my knees outside his shoulders. His hands braced my ass from behind. I looked down at his face, and he licked his lips.

"This is one of my favorite views. Your wet, pretty pussy." He licked his lips. "Spread those thighs more and sit on me."

I bit my lip with a smile, glancing over my shoulder to see him stroking himself. Oh, fuck. It was so hot when he did that.

Koni moved around us and positioned himself in front of me, cock in hand too. My eyes were on that while I sank down onto Zavier's face and moaned when his mouth instantly started to devour me. His scruffy jaw rubbed the outside of my lower lips while his tongue licked up and down my slit. His hands helped move me, encouraging me to ride his face.

Koni leaned in and kissed my mouth and grabbed hold of my breasts, kneading the soft flesh and pinching my nipples.

The stimulation was so intense I was coming within a minute. I broke away from Koni's mouth and screamed to the ceiling, rolling my hips over Zavier as he moaned below me. He sucked my clit, shooting me into climax. My pussy clenched as he thrust his tongue inside, over and over, continuing on through my orgasm's waves. He lapped at me slowly, taking in my juices.

"So sexy," Koni murmured as I fell forward onto my hands.

Zavier lifted my ass and kissed the inside of my thighs before sliding out from between my legs. The next second, he was kneeling behind me. "Fuck, yes, she is. The sexiest woman. So soft and strong. Teagan, baby, suck him. I'm gonna fuck you from behind."

I looked up as Koni slid down onto his ass and spread his legs around me, bringing his cock closer. "Mmm. Yes," I said, almost purring from the excitement. What had I turned into? A cat? I was starved for them. I wanted it all with them. I'd fallen for them in every fucking way in such a short time that I thought I was losing my mind. And I knew they felt the same, professed the same, hoping I didn't think they were crazy. Maybe we all were crazy. Maybe we felt it even more since we didn't know what our future held. How much longer would I have them?

Koni reached out and gathered my hair as I leaned over and grabbed his cock. He was so solid in my hand. I pumped him a few times, looking up through my lashes to see his eyes roll back, then I trailed my tongue over his crown, swirling it around his tip, tasting the precum as it leaked out. He groaned. And as soon as I slipped him inside my mouth, I felt Zavier's tip at my entrance. With one hard thrust, he shoved his cock fully inside.

The motion pushed my body forward, making me deep throat Koni's cock at the same time. I screamed out, which also made me gag and swallow reflexively. The combination of it all made Koni buck his hips up and groan loud with pleasure.

"Oh fuck," Zavier said, feeling my pussy clench him tighter with my cough and gag. He paused, holding utterly still.

After pulling Koni's dick from my throat, I sputtered out a laugh, half amused and half turned on by the forcefulness. Their chuckles joined me but quickly died as soon as my mouth was back on Koni, sucking him and twisting my grip at his base.

Zavier eased himself out of me, then hooked his hands on my hips and thrust inside at full force again. "You feel fucking amazing. You're so tight. So wet. Fuck."

I moaned and sucked Koni deeper as Zavier picked up speed, crashing his pelvis against my ass. My entire body shook after each ram of his dick, the hits and their sensation almost too good to handle—my pussy stretching around him, my breasts jolting forward each time he thrust inside.

Koni tensed beneath me, then he pulled himself from my mouth. "Oh, Teagan. Mmm. I was close, babe. Shit. This is too much. You're too much."

"Yeah, she is," Zavier said, his rhythm picking up, slamming harder and faster into me.

"Ah, ah, ah, ah, ah," I chanted with each hit. The feel of him sliding in and out, his wideness hitting the sensitive spot along my front wall differently from this position. It felt phenomenal.

"Yes, baby. Fuck," Zavier said, rutting into me relentlessly, frantically, powerfully.

"Oh, oh, Zavier. I'm ... I'm coming."

"Go, baby. Ah," he said, grunting from his exertion as he continued at such a punishing pace. "I feel that. You're gripping me so tight. Oh, fuck."

Unable to hold myself up, I collapsed onto the bed. Koni moved slightly so I didn't jar my neck by landing on his leg. With my body flat on the bed, Zavier straddled my ass and continued to dive into me from above. It didn't take him long to come.

With a roar, he let go, shooting deep inside. "Fuck. Oh fuck. That was so good, baby."

My eyes locked on Koni as he stroked himself, watching us climax. I almost felt bad, but I knew he hadn't wanted to cum in my mouth. At least, not this time.

"Koni, do you want my ass?" I asked, biting my lip.

"Fuck, babe. Just asking that makes me want to come right now. Shit."

"I'll get the lube." Zavier's body disappeared from behind me in an instant, and I wondered if this was some kind of bro-code situation. *If ass is offered, do what's in your power to get your friend inside.*

I giggled at the thought and shook my head, planting my face into the mattress.

"You're a damn treasure, Teagan," Koni said, his hands threading through my hair. "So sexy."

"Okay." Zavier returned and flopped onto the bed at my side. "I'm going to help you feel good while he does you. So lay on top of me."

"You're so bossy," Koni told him with a laugh.

I laughed too but followed Zavier's direction, climbing over his body. He handed off the lube and positioned his legs where Koni directed him to as he settled behind me. Zavier's hand slipped down to my pussy and began stroking my clit softly. I could feel his cum leaking out of me, but he obviously didn't care one bit. With his other hand at the back of my head, he guided my lips to his and began kissing me languidly. My body moved with him, rolling over his hand.

"Oh, look at this pretty ass," Koni said, the lube bottle lid popping closed. His fingers moved around back farther than Zavier's, one pushing inside my pussy while another teased and prodded my tight hole.

"Oh, God. Yes. That feels so good." I said, breaking from Zavier's mouth for a moment.

"You like this, huh? You are so beautiful." Koni's finger shoved inside, stretching me. Another joined, and soon I was rocking against him. "Fuck yes. Oh, babe."

"Is she ready? She was so receptive her first time. Her muscles relaxed and wanted more," Zavier whispered.

"Yes, that's it. It's happening now. Fuck. I think you're ready for me, babe." Koni shifted behind us, and Zavier's fingers kept circling my clit. After a moment, Koni's thick tip was pushing against me. It burned some, my hole yielding to the pressure.

"Ahh. Ahh. Easy. Ahh." I sighed, hearing him put more lube on. The slickness helped, and in a few moments, his tip popped inside.

"Fuhhhhck." Koni's voice almost sounded pained as he entered farther. "So hot. So tight. Ahh. Damn. This feels so good. "

"Yeah, it does," Zavier agreed with a groan, knowing exactly how it felt. His dick hardened beneath me, the experience so erotic that he was aroused again already. His fingers moved faster as Koni pushed farther in, making me moan. Then his finger curled inside my pussy.

I squealed, and Zavier grabbed my head and pulled my mouth down on his again, eating my delighted sounds.

"Fuck. I gotta move. I'm so close already." Koni leaned in, his cock shoving in entirely before he backed out with a groan. And then he started moving, thrusting forward and retreating again. Over and over, harder and faster. Fucking my ass. He was drilling into me as roughly as Zavier had. I hadn't thought it would feel so damn good, but it did. It was dominant and exhilarating and had my body shaking.

I came on Zavier's hand and whimpered inside his mouth, so spent from three orgasms. It was all I could do to keep myself from going totally limp and collapsing again.

Koni slammed against my ass two more times, practically holding my hips upward as he yelled my name and came inside me.

5

Koni's mouth slanted over mine. He licked against my tongue so tenderly as his fingers ran through my hair. So gentle. He was so loving and sweet.

After resting a few minutes together in bed following our epic sexcapade, it was time for us to go our separate ways again. They'd eat a quick lunch before going back out into the park to check the camp's boundaries and rid them of any set traps and wandering hunters. And I had to eat that sandwich I'd brought to the cabin then head to the kitchen to make Loch's cake.

Zavier bounced on his feet, and he yanked on his jeans behind Koni. We'd all skipped showers, opting for more time to revel in a post-orgasm haze together before having a quick cleanup with soapy wet towels and a rushed tangle of sheet changing.

"Don't do the sheets. You have enough to do. I'll do them tomorrow," Zavier said as he pulled on his T-shirt.

I hummed against Koni's mouth in acknowledgment, still fully engrossed by Koni's touches and too smitten to pull away. His hands cradled my head as he made love to my mouth. I think that was the best way to describe it, really. His movements were both possessive and adoring. If I were a swooner, I would have.

"Koni, man. Come on. Get dressed."

I giggled, feeling Koni's erection against my covered stomach. Stiff and ready again. I was already dressed, but Koni was still very much naked. His taut, tall body pushed into me more as if he couldn't bear the separation.

He finally pulled away the slightest amount and replied to Zavier between chaste kisses against my lips and jaw. "I. Can't. Get. Enough. I. Don't. Think. I. Can. Leave. Her."

His body was forcibly wrenched away, and I let out a full laugh as he landed haphazardly on the bed, his legs flying up, his arms flailing back, and his solid cock slapping against his stomach.

"My turn for a see-you-later kiss," Zavier said, stepping up and wrapping me in his arms. He tipped his head down and simply stared into my eyes, silently connecting with me on a deeper, more intense level. He was speaking to me without saying a single word, professing so many things in the silent stare. I felt it. His tongue licked out over his piercing. "Promise to tell me if he says or does anything shitty. I don't care how close we are. I will fuck him up if he's too stubborn to see you, to let you in."

He was obviously speaking about Loch. "You don't have to worry. Promise. I honestly think I chipped his barrier this morning." I let out a breathy laugh, still so uncertain. "I'm not sure I deserve it. I'm not sure I deserve you guys."

"Don't say that. It's more the other way around, baby," he whispered.

"True," Koni agreed as he shuffled into his clothes somewhere behind me.

"Well ..." I wasn't sure what else to say to that. It would be difficult for them to change my mind. They had become the very best thing to happen to me in a very long time. I inhaled deeply, holding off the emotion threatening to burst out.

Without another word, Zavier pressed his lips to mine. We both opened, and our tongues slowly met. The kiss was just as evocative as Koni's had been, teeming with emotion and tenderness, telling me even more than his eyes had. His mouth worshiped mine, and his hands held me close, showing me how much I meant.

I hope I relayed the same through my touch, my kiss. I cherished him, all of them, and I needed him to know that.

Koni sighed neared the doorway. "Okay, we better go before I change my mind. I mean, do we really need to go out there again? Does Loch really need a birthday cake?" He groaned. It was followed by a soft thud, which I realized had been his head hitting the doorframe as soon as Zavier and I parted.

"Yeah," Zavier replied. "We most definitely will pick this back up later."

I laughed and shook my head as I followed them to the front door. "I might be tired later. Or maybe have a headache."

"Oh, woman, please don't tease," Koni said, biting his lip. "I know for a fact that sex is the best medicine for a headache."

"And if I'm tired?"

"I'm not opposed to sleepy, lazy sex," Koni replied with a laugh as Zavier shoved him out the door.

"See you later, baby." Zavier ran a hand over his hair before pulling the door closed.

I ate the sandwich slowly and waited a little longer before making my way to the dining hall. Thankfully, since our sex session had lasted well into lunchtime as it was, the massive cabin was empty by the time I trudged there through the new snow. The white stuff continued to fall, though it had tapered enough during the day that footprints from the morning hadn't filled.

As soon as I entered the kitchen, I saw the ingredients Rosie had gotten for me to make Loch's cake. I pulled out the book I'd found earlier and flipped to the recipe—triple chocolate cake. If Loch liked chocolate, he was getting a lot of it. I used two ten-inch round pans, knowing it was better to have more than not enough. It would cover everyone living here, regardless if they showed ... or if Loch decided he didn't want cake after all.

Time flew by as I baked, but I kept watching the clock, not wanting to be late to meet with Loch in the classroom. When I finished whipping the last of the icing and started frosting the cake, Keira and Mike entered the kitchen.

"Hey!" Keira greeted me. She walked to the counter and gave me a side-hug, her head lopping over mine and her wavy, long hair draping onto the side of my face.

"Hey," I replied with a giggle and a stiff exhale to blow the hair away.

"Oh! Sorry!" she said, pulling back.

"Hey to you too, Mike," I called over my shoulder, watching him disappear behind the refrigerator door.

"Hey," he replied, waving a hand in the air, not bothering to look our way.

"Ignore him. He's moody because our GED tests aren't until Monday, like five days will kill us," she whisper-shouted the last bit and rolled her eyes. "So? How are you feeling?" Her arm squeezed around me one last time before she stepped away, looking over my body as if she had X-ray vision to view the bruising beneath my clothes. She'd visited the cabin the day after I'd been jumped, seeing the aftermath firsthand.

"Better. Almost fully healed. Thankful nothing was broken."

She nodded. "They're lucky they only got kicked out. Well, and whatever their families are doing to them too. Pretty sure the triplets' only punishment at home will be normalcy. Not nearly enough."

"Meh." I shrugged, spreading the chocolate icing over the bottom piece of cake. "I've already forgotten them. They don't matter."

"That's the spirit," she agreed, sniffing the air. "Plus, you have plenty of other things on your mind ... and in your bed." She elbowed me playfully.

I giggled and shook my head. She'd get no argument from me. "True."

She grabbed a small spoon and dipped the tip into the icing. Before I could object, she scooped a tiny bit and shoved it into her mouth. Her eyes closed, and she released a comically loud moan. "Oh my God, that is fantastic! This is for Loch, right?"

"What's for Loch?" The southern accent entered the kitchen before Jackson's body appeared.

Great. Not someone I wanted to see again, ever.

I remained quiet, and Keira did the same, keeping to ourselves at the far end prep counter as Trig and another guy entered the kitchen too. Mike stepped beside us, handing a can of Coke to Keira and shooting an irritated glance Jackson's way.

"Well, fine. I was only asking a question. Just trying to be cordial on this fine day," he said. "We're doing just peachy, thanks for asking. Aren't we, Trig? Ford? How about you, Teagan Wellis? Recovered well enough to be let out of your cage, I see."

Why did he use my full name? Was he just being extra annoying and haughty?

I really didn't want to be near him when the guys weren't here with me. I knew I could handle myself, but that was part of the problem. They might be more inclined to hold me back if I snapped on the asshole. I wasn't sure Keira or Tim would.

I didn't meet his stare, but I could see it well enough out of the corner of my eye while I continued spreading the icing and set the second cake layer in place. His nose seemed fine again, the evidence of my punch long gone. He had a smirk that was as smug as ever. Sidekick Trig took his usual hype-man stance, staying close to his friend for immoral support. And the other guy? Ford? Well, I wasn't sure who he was, except that he'd had the leaky cabin roof most of the others had helped fix a few days ago. He wore black jeans, a dark blue sweatshirt, and a baseball cap holding a collection of snowflakes melting in the warm kitchen air. Trig and Jackson looked their usual douche-baggy selves in coordinated workout shorts and shirts, as if it weren't twenty degrees outside.

Trig moved to the fridge and grabbed them all waters. It made me wonder if they'd been working out somewhere and had just run into Ford. But really, I didn't care.

"Wellis, huh?" an unfamiliar voice spoke, the curious tone and the question making me shiver. I didn't need to look to know it was Ford. I still cast a swift glance over my shoulder, sizing him up. His body was large but not unfit, like a man in his mid-thirties. His eyes were thin with wrinkles at their edges, and his face was scruffy with an unkempt beard and permanently tanned skin as if he'd spent many summers in the south despite his voice having no noticeable accent. Hmm. An uneasy feeling churned in my stomach.

When I didn't answer and merely went back to my task, he added, "Jin Wellis?"

My body stiffened even though I fought the reaction. He didn't need the confirmation, but now he'd gotten it.

"Ah," Jackson said, his tone catlike. "That was her father. Did you know him?"

"Nah. Not exactly. A friend knew him. Shame what happened there." It sounded sincere, but I still wouldn't play into the conversation. I knew nothing about him and surely didn't trust who he may or may not have known. It made me even more uneasy, having someone older here familiar with my family.

"Yeah. Not exactly a fun subject to discuss, so if you don't mind, she needs to get back to this," Keira said, stepping closer as if to guard me.

"All right, all right," Jackson drawled like a knockoff Matthew McConaughey. "We just needed something to drink. We'll be on our way. Don't get into any trouble now, Teagan. Would hate to see what would happen to your boys."

I gritted my teeth with a snap, nearly biting my tongue to keep from speaking.

As soon as they left, I let out a huge breath.

"Hey," Keira said softly at my side. "You okay?"

"Yeah, just …" I shook my head. "He has a way of rattling me."

"Try not to let him get under your skin. They're probably extra pissed that their sex toys got the boot from here. Must be blow job withdrawal."

I laughed at that, though my heart wasn't entirely in it. My gut was still churning, something not sitting right. "Do you know anything else about Ford? Like where he's from?"

She shook her head and cast a look to Mike, who shrugged with a frown. "We learned a little more because of the leak. We had to help the others when they worked on his roof. Pretty sure he got here six months ago or so. Rehabbing. Is an alcoholic, I think. Not sure how much longer he'll stay. Are you worried about him knowing your family?"

"Maybe. I don't know. It's the way he sounded about it, like he wasn't exactly genuine." I shook my head and continued the cake's top frosting. "It felt … off. I'm probably being paranoid."

"Nah. I'll see if I can find out anything else. And you should talk to Rosie about it. She might know more."

"Right," I agreed. But I wasn't sure I would. She could know more, but why would she share personal information about someone here just because I had a bad feeling?

"Well, I guess we'll see you at dinner. Can't wait to taste this and to see how someone reacts to it." She waggled her eyebrows with a grin before tugging Mike toward the door.

"See you," I replied, smiling before they disappeared into the dining hall. My smile fell as soon as the door closed. While I was excited for the rest of the day, my mind was still heavy with thoughts about Jackson's threats and Ford's cryptic comments about my family. Was it connected? Or was I reading too much into things because of my Jackson hate?

I exhaled deeply as I finished the cake, then stored it inside a cake stand before checking the time. Four o'clock.

6

"Sorry I'm late," I said, rushing through the classroom doorway, not even bothering to look around as I shucked off my parka. When I finally did, my eyes landed on Loch's back as he sat at the first table. His shaved head was hunched over the books in front of him, but he stiffened at my voice, straightening his body and revealing the top of his head and its longer mass of dark black hair.

When he didn't reply, I moved around the table to the chair opposite him and hung my parka over the back. "I ... well, I just finished your cake. It took a little longer than I thought."

"You shouldn't have bothered," he replied, his tone flat as he continued to stare down at the book in front of him.

It was opened somewhere in the middle, with shapes and colors popping from the stark white pages. He also had a notebook open, his fingers tapping a pencil to a blank page. By the looks of it, he hadn't gotten any work started in the two minutes I'd missed.

"To make the cake or to come here?" I asked, not really knowing which he meant. When he remained silent, I whispered more to myself than to him, "Both, maybe." I shifted in my chair, feeling that in the few hours since our kitchen kiss, we'd regressed two steps. Not as distant as my first day, but definitely not as comfortable as the sweet and sexy tongue embrace we'd exchanged.

Or maybe he'd meant I shouldn't have bothered with the kiss.

I pushed that thought away, not wanting another punch to my already unstable gut.

"It wasn't that it was difficult to make," I said, choosing to believe his statement had only meant the cake. "I got a little sidetracked while making it. I was hoping to have an empty kitchen, and it was for most of it, but then Keira and Mike came in and started talking. Which would have been fine, but then Jackson, Trig, and Ford showed up …"

His eyes snapped up to meet mine for the first time, the hardness looking even more prominent with how narrow they were. "And?"

I blinked, a little taken aback by his reaction. Was it just annoyance about them, or did that trigger something like protectiveness?

When I didn't reply fast enough, he scowled. "What did they do? Did they fuck with you?"

Protectiveness. That was most definitely protectiveness. Wow. His shoulders flexed, and he straightened fully in his chair. Honestly, I had no idea how the legs of the chair didn't buckle beneath him. They were certainly constructed with sturdy wood, but his muscled body was massive enough for me to question their durability.

"Not exactly. Just talked … It wasn't a big deal. He likes to get under my skin, I guess."

"It's because you almost broke his nose," he stated matter-of-factly.

"Ha." I chuckled. "That, and Keira seems to think he's bitter because he's going through blow job withdrawal since the sisters got booted."

The tension in his eyebrows eased, lifting them up a fraction and opening his narrowed eyes more. His shoulders also relaxed, the muscles there and in his arms no longer straining tight.

After another silent moment where he didn't react to the joke, I said, "Honestly, I liked making it for you, and I hope you enjoy it later. I'm also happy to help with your studies. I might not be the best teacher, but I can try. What are you working on? Decimals?"

He inhaled deeply and let out a long breath, resigning to my intrusion. "Yeah. Multiplication and division. Percentages too."

"Do you want me to help go over the lesson, or is there something specific?"

He tapped the pencil a little aggressively, and I felt a vibration on the floor too. His leg was bouncing beneath the table. I waited, not wanting to push him. An entire minute passed before he answered. "Tim went through the lesson. There was a trick … a way to shift the decimal that isn't in this book." His voice was softer.

I stared at his bowed head, at the shaved hair at the sides and the mass at the top. It was long enough to brush fingers through, and I so badly wanted to do that, especially now. He seemed even more vulnerable than he had in the kitchen, letting me see this insecure side of him. I shook my thoughts off, knowing that I needed to snap out of it and help him. I didn't want him to mistake my delay as judgment.

"Okay, yeah. I think I know what you mean. Um …" I went to grab the book but stopped. With the size of the table, being across from him was not conducive. I stood abruptly, moved to his side, and pulled a chair closer. Grabbing a different pencil, I tapped the notebook. "Can I?"

"Sure. Yeah," he replied, shifting in his chair and letting me turn the notebook a little my way.

"So … Let's take this first problem. Okay, so stack them up to multiply, right? Then forget the decimals for now. Do the problem. Carry up. Let's see …" I worked the problem to demonstrate. "After you add them together for the full answers, you shift the decimals over and count the spaces. Then count them in from the right side for their final placement."

He pulled the notebook back and did the next one without speaking. I took the time to openly stare at him. His hazel eyes focused on the book, then on the problem. The muscle in his jaw clenched with concentration. His thick, long fingers cradled the pencil, gliding it swiftly over the page.

I watched the nostrils on his wide nose flare with an inhale as he considered the last steps. When I glanced at the page, I ran through the problem and saw it was correct.

"Nice."

His responding grunt was barely audible. He did the next couple of problems with no issues. Rosie had been right about his determination, and I'd never doubted that. His stubbornness was a dead giveaway for the work ethic he had. I could tell he was intelligent, but he'd obviously had little education to start with.

I remained quiet, watching and admiring him as he continued on. Time passed quickly. I'd offer any insight I had whenever he'd pause and seem to struggle with something. Mostly, though, he understood the lesson well enough to move on. After a while, I lifted my arms over my head and inhaled deeply, needing to stretch but also wanting an excuse to overindulge in his smoky peppered scent. I wanted to bathe in it and lay in bed with it, like Koni's and Zavier's.

His head tipped to the side, his gaze sweeping from my breasts up to my eyes.

"Sorry," I said, dropping my arms and biting my lower lip. I didn't want to be a distraction, but I also didn't mind that his heated gaze raked over my body.

He closed his eyes, and his lashes touched his cheeks in a glorious fan. His prominent Adam's apple bobbed with a swallow, which drew my eyes to his thick neck and all the jagged scars there, translucent pink lines embedded in his pale skin. They varied in width and length and included many puncture holes. They had to be bites. Bait. Hadn't Zavier called him that when we'd been in here cleaning? That was his nickname of The Four. The list that Keira had told me was Runt, Stray, Bait, and Stud. So he was Bait, which made Elijah Stud. Hmm. I flinched at the thoughts that conjured, including Loch's admission of being chained to a pole when he'd transitioned. I wanted to murder whoever treated him so poorly. Had it been his mother? His father? All of it made me sick.

"I didn't go to school when I was younger." His voice almost startled me as much as the statement. It was a mild version of his deep tone, like he'd had in the kitchen. His eyes opened again, focusing on me. I didn't reply, wanting him to continue. And he did, shifting a little in his chair and stretching his neck as if he had to prepare himself first. "It's why I'm so far behind. Elijah and I got here two years ago. I'd never sat inside a classroom before that, never formally learned to read or do math."

"Oh. Wow," I said, twisting my fingers together on the table, wanting so badly to touch him but refraining. "You've been working really hard."

A humored breath escaped his lips, and his shoulders rolled back. "Yeah."

"I hope you're proud of yourself then. You deserve to be." Unable to stop myself, I dropped my hand beneath the table and placed it on his thigh.

He didn't move, only replied, "I'm not sure about that, but I'm working on it."

Oh God, I was melting with a need to hold him, hug him. Wanting to comfort someone so large and strong ... It was an odd notion, really, but I was getting used to feeling it with The Four. And Loch ... well, he was harder and tougher than anyone I'd ever met.

"Good," I admitted. "I know Rosie is proud of you. And the guys admire you. Look up to you." His eyes widened almost imperceptibly. "It's true. And that says a lot since you're the youngest, from what I hear."

He let out a breath, tossed his pencil onto the notebook, and glanced at the ceiling for a moment. "I don't really know for sure."

"Know what? That they admire you?"

"No," he shook his head and licked his lower lip. "I'm not sure of my actual age. Did the guys tell you that today's my chosen birthday?"

"They mentioned that with your age but didn't tell me anything else." I needed him to know they hadn't betrayed him by telling me anything more.

He nodded. "I never knew the real date. When I transitioned, it was early. I overheard my ... pack mother say that twelve years was early to transition. It was winter at the time. Snowing. So that was the only reference I had to keep track through the years before I left there, met Elijah, and we found this place together."

The breath whooshed from my lungs as if something had hit me in the chest. Fuck. I felt sad and furious for him, but I didn't want to show him that. I knew he hadn't wanted pity. So, I turned more to face him and squeezed his thigh, giving him reassurance.

"I'm glad you chose the day you got here as your birthday," I said, clearing my throat lightly to fight off the emotion building there. "And just so you know, you're younger than me too. I'm twenty. Anyone might assume the opposite because of our sizes."

His lips twitched a little, threatening a smile, but he didn't reply.

"Maybe it won't mean much, given that I haven't known you long, but you should know that I'm proud of you too. And happy to have made your birthday cake, even if you didn't want me to make it."

He looked down to where my hand remained on his thigh. "It's not that I didn't want you to make it. It's that I didn't want to celebrate. I didn't last year."

"But you're giving in this year for Rosie," I said, understanding. "She's pretty damn persuasive."

"Yeah. I owe her a lot." He lifted his eyes to me again. "And you are ..."

"And I am ..." I echoed the open statement with a smirk. "Annoying and maybe as stubborn as you. So you better eat my cake after your birthday pizza." Oh, that sounded dirty. Heat rushed through my body as I noticed something flicker behind his eyes.

He smiled then, and I inhaled a sharp breath. The smile was a tiny one, one to mimic the one I'd given him surely, with only the very corners of his lips lifting. No teeth showed, but beggars can't be choosers. He had smiled at me, for me.

7

"You shouldn't do that, you know. Smile at me. Especially if you'd rather I leave you alone." My tone was easy and teasing, but in a way, I was serious. It was too much to take. Being around him and possibly not having him ... it made me a little weak. I'd thought he seemed interested in the kitchen, with the kiss and the look and feel of his erection. But maybe that had only been a reaction to the closeness. Maybe I'd read into the kiss, or he had changed his mind. He could just be tolerating me since I was sleeping with his friends.

His smile fell, and my stomach plummeted with regret.

Worried I'd been too brash, I prepared to explain. "I—"

"It's not that." He exhaled, and I could smell his sweet minty breath. "I'm not used to this, letting anyone else ... I guess it was easy for Z and Koni, getting close to you so quick, but I ..."

I tightened my hand on his thigh again and closed my eyes. Shit. I knew exactly what he meant. This big, tough guy was hesitant to get close, possibly for fear of losing someone he might get attached to. "I know what you're saying. I'm worried too. We—they and I—agreed that we didn't need to be anything more. We barely know each other. But they feel the same way I do, feel this strong pull between us. And we don't know what'll happen in the future. I've been honest about who I am and that I plan to go home to Alabama, but I'm not sure if anything'll change while I'm here. It's hard to make that choice, to give in without knowing. So I understand if you don't feel the same or if you choose differently."

"I feel it," he admitted. "I've felt it since that first night, since I stole your suitcase and couldn't get your scent out of my head."

I smiled. "Jerk."

He huffed a breath. "I had my reasons."

"Oh, I know. And me wearing your clothes was a reminder for them to keep away."

His chin dropped to his chest, and he licked his lips with another glorious smile. "Yeah. It was that, but also more."

"Oh yeah? You liked seeing me in your baggy clothes and liked creeping through my things. Were you sniffing my panties or something? I know y'all surely had a good joke about my mini-vibe when you found it the suitcase." I was surprised that Koni and Zavier hadn't brought that up again. Though I hadn't needed to use it recently, that was for sure.

Pink flashed on his pale cheeks while his eyes remained pinned down to the desk. He was blushing! *Whoa.* And then a thought occurred to me suddenly. He was younger. Could he be a virgin? I stared at him, gaping a little, wondering if it was possible. Koni and Zavier sure hadn't been. They'd likely gotten laid a fair amount before coming here. But maybe Loch hadn't. And Koni had joked earlier about me making Loch feel things he had never felt before. Oh ...

"Did you sniff my panties, Lochlan?" I pressed, using his full name, wanting to explore this more, tease him.

"I, uh ... I slept with your clothes. That's why Rosie and everyone knew I'd taken your stuff."

"I gathered that. And for the record, I love your scent too," I replied, squeezing his thigh another time and moving my hand up a little higher. Wanting, no, needing to know how he felt, I asked, "Do you want to kiss me again? Because I want to. I want to do more with you."

He sucked in a breath and cut his eyes to me but said nothing.

"I won't touch you anymore if you don't want it. If you don't want to get closer to me because I plan to leave, I understand. But you need to tell me." I wasn't sure how to act with him. His hardened exterior had hidden so much inside. It was an act, a barrier, a way to keep others away. And it was a convincing one. I'd never imagined he'd be this way on the first night I'd arrived. He was gentle and shy and unsure. But he was so guarded. If I wanted more to happen, I had to be the one to initiate, to push him outside his box.

"Or if you don't want anything to do with me because I'm with Koni and Zavier, I understand that too. It's not exactly normal." I chuckled nervously, then tucked a strand of hair behind my ear before trailing my fingers over my lower lip. "But we've talked about it, and ... I don't know. We just feel like it's normal for us, if that makes sense. It feels right to us even if it seems weird to others."

When he didn't reply right away, I moved to lift my hand from his thigh only to feel his large palm settle on top of it. His hand completely engulfed mine. My eyes shifted there first before looking up to meet his intense hazel stare.

"It's not weird. I get it, just by seeing their connection to you," he said. "And yes, I want to. I want to kiss you again."

"Thank God," I admitted, turning more, lifting my hands to his chiseled square jaw, and pulling him closer. Seated, he was still so tall. I leaned up in the chair and crushed my lips to his with a sigh. As before, he didn't open for me right away. I licked along his lips with a whimper, begging him. After a delayed reaction, he opened, and I thrust my tongue into his mouth, craving that minty goodness mixed with his very own taste. He was delicious. I commanded the kiss, seeking his tongue with long licks of my own. As much as I loved our first gentle kiss in the kitchen, I wanted to show him how much I wanted him, show him what I needed.

I felt his body shift his chair, giving us more space, giving me more access. When I locked onto his tongue and sucked it into my mouth, a small moan vibrated in his throat. It urged me on. I climbed onto him, pushing him back and straddling his parted legs, grateful that the chairs were armless with short backs. My fingers skimmed over the sides of his shaved head before climbing into the thick strands up top. I grasped them and pulled as I thrust my tongue in deeper.

His hands decided to join the party. I almost chuckled about him having another delayed reaction, but I didn't dare, knowing that I was to blame, overwhelming him in the best way. He made up for the delay quickly, rubbing his hands all over my back, digging his fingers in, then moving them down around the curve of my ass.

I wanted to grind down on top of the erection I could feel growing below, but I held still. If I did that, I would be tempted to ride him in the classroom, which wasn't the smartest thing to do out in the open. Although, other things were possible.

I moaned into his mouth before pulling back and nipping little bites on his lips. "Oh, you feel so good, Loch."

He let out a long breath when I shifted my mouth along his jaw and then down to his neck. I felt him stiffen then, and I realized it was reflexive, possibly because of the trauma he had to have endured. But I didn't dare stop. I needed to show him this was something good. So I licked over his scars and trailed my fingertips on the opposite side as my other hand smoothed down his shoulder and chest.

"Teagan." My name was a breath. "This feels …"

"Yes," I agreed, taking a tiny nip at his prominent Adam's apple as he tilted his head back farther for me, giving me more access to his neck. My heart squeezed at his trust, at his offer. I eased my hand farther down his body, enjoying how his muscles tightened then relaxed for me. I wanted his skin, to feel his warmth. When my lips reached the edge of his shirt's neckline, I grunted. No skin left. Getting fully naked was not an option.

His splayed hands clenched at my ass cheeks, and I whimpered, feeling the dampness between my legs, wanting so badly to rub myself against him. But this was more for him than me. I wanted to show him he could trust me, that I would make him feel amazing.

"Can I touch you more? Can I touch your dick?"

His eyes snapped wide and seemed to pierce right through me. Then his mouth parted on a pant, and his eyes hooded. Oh, it was such a sexy look on him. Eager and seductive. He nodded with a barely audible "Yes."

I slipped my hands down between us, unfastening his jeans and sliding my fingers into the edging of his boxers. As I pushed inside, he sucked in a heavy breath. His cock was long and felt as solid as a steel rod in my palm. I smiled as my hand slid down his length, and he let out a moan. "Do you like that?"

"Yes," he admitted, closing his eyes briefly, taking in the sensation while I gripped him harder.

There wasn't enough room. I wanted to do so much more. "No one comes here when you study, right? No one will interrupt us?"

"No, no one should," he said, his eyes opening wide with panic. They settled into their heady gaze again with another stroke of my hand. I felt some sticky precum leak from him, so I swirled it around his tip using a finger when I wanted to use my tongue.

Maybe I should have worried more about an interruption, but really it was part of the thrill. With Rosie and Tim occupied, chances were slim anyway. Full-on sex wasn't the best idea, but I wanted to give him more.

"I want to suck you." I released his cock and hooked the edge of his jeans and boxers, needing more space.

His hands dropped away as I slipped more and more down his body until I was between his legs with my knees on the floor. He watched me, mesmerized by my actions. There was no smile or arrogant glance, no notion of him expecting it or knowing what was to come of this. He was unassuming and awed.

"Lift a bit," I instructed, and he did, reclining even more as I tugged his pants down past his ass to give his cock the room it needed. It whipped hard and proud against his stomach when I pulled him full out. "Fuck, you are big," I said, eyeing him with a soft smile before kneeling up to take him in my hands again.

He hissed a breath, still voiceless as he watched me control him. He had a bit more hair there than Koni and Zavier, but it was trimmed. I didn't need to go on a wilderness exploration to find him, at least. Though, I knew I would have without complaint, anyway. Because, damn!

My hands were not nearly large enough to hold him, my fingertips not touching when they wrapped around. He was huge, as muscled and veiny as the rest of his body implied. I twisted my grip and began to pump him, first only watching his eyes take it all in. He writhed a bit in his seat, and I couldn't help but clench my thighs together in response. He was losing control, and I loved it.

Not willing to wait longer, I moved my mouth over him and pressed a soft kiss to his tip. Eyeing him through my lashes, I let my tongue dart out and lick a swirl over his crown, fluttering around its edge.

His body jerked, unable to hold his movements. "Ah," he rasped apologetically as I bathed the underside of his shaft with my tongue. "I ... Ohhh." His whole body tensed and relaxed, and his head fell backward.

Gripping his base with one hand, I cupped his balls with the other and opened wide to take him into my mouth.

The moan that escaped his lips was extraordinarily erotic, as good as the sounds Koni and Zavier made. My panties were so drenched, I worried briefly that my jeans would be too. I took him in farther, sucking hard. There was no way I'd fit him all the way in. He was too big. But I tried my best to go as far as possible, hitting the back of my throat and making myself gag, my throat closing reflexively.

"Fuck!" The word was sharp and was followed by heavy panting.

I drew him back out then slid him back in, swirling my tongue, tasting the saltiness of him. With a long hum, I began to bob. In and out, faster and faster, twisting my grip at his base and massaging his balls.

"Oh. Oh. Fuck. Teagan," he rasped out through ragged breaths. His hands found my head, and he gripped my hair.

He was losing it. I pulled away and quickly said, "It's okay. Finish in my mouth."

His eyes flashed as he stared down at me. Before he could object, I took him back in and sucked harder, moved faster.

"Fuck. Argh." His body tensed then his hips thrust rhythmically with the pulse of his cock. He released a guttural groan as thick cum shot to the back of my mouth and slid down my throat.

I hummed, stroking him as I slowed, milking him for all he had. His body went limp, his legs falling open more and his arms dropping to his side. I stopped pumping and licked around him, cleaning him. His taste was saltier than Koni or Zavier, but I still loved it. That, mixed with the pepper, smoke, and the male musk of him, had me curling my toes. I wanted badly to touch myself, but it could wait until later.

His head lifted while I settled him back inside his boxers, his hazel eyes peering downward, dazed and appreciative.

"Happy chosen birthday," I said, licking and biting my lower lip.

8

"Loch, are you smiling?" A guy's voice traveled to us from the neighboring pathway to the dining hall.

It was five o'clock. Loch and I had just left the classroom cabin and were making our way to the dining hall since Rosie was due back with the pizzas at five sharp. She'd told Loch it would be an early dinner because she refused to risk going later and getting stuck in town with tourist drivers and heavy snow. So we'd had very little time after the blow job to collect ourselves before we'd noticed the time.

The lampposts along the pathways had just kicked on, the darkness slowly starting to overtake the day. As soon as I looked around Loch's wall of a body beside me, I saw his cabinmate Vic emerge from another offshoot path, one I guessed led directly to their and Elijah's place.

Loch choked out a nervous cough. He hadn't expected anyone to catch him off-guard, smiling as he walked with me. Blow jobs. They're magic.

Since he chose to remain silent or possibly couldn't find the right words, I said, "It's his birthday, and he's getting pizza and cake."

"I heard that, yeah," Vic replied, jogging a few steps to catch up with us. He had a light gray sweater on with dark jeans and boots. They looked high-end, nice and clean, as preppy as his khaki and polo combo the first time I'd seen him. He fell in step with Loch and gave him a soft slug to the arm before running his hand through his short length of dirty blond hair. "Hi, Teagan. Glad you're feeling better."

"Hi, Vic. Thanks." I supposed everyone had known about the attack.

"So pizza from Charlie's and cake too? Lucky guy. I only got a book a few months back."

"What can I say? I'm special," Loch said, his stern, snappy tone returned. "I asked for a book too."

I chuckled at that, which drew a look from Vic around Loch as we reached the door to the dining hall.

"Your laugh is cute, Teagan."

A growl rumbled from deep inside Loch's body, making my eyes bulge wide and shoot up to his. But he was not looking at me, oh no. His stare was set on Vic.

Vic swung open the dining hall's door with a shit-eating grin. He cast a look over his shoulder to Loch and chuckled. "Down, boy. Just complimenting the lady."

Oh, that had definitely been a test. And now he knew that Loch had staked a claim. Living in the same cabin meant that he had been privy to Loch's antics with my suitcase. So he probably knew it was only a matter of time.

I grinned at his back, then I lifted an eyebrow at Loch while he held the door for me to enter.

No one was in the main area. We followed Vic and moved back toward the kitchen. As soon as he pulled the door open, I noticed the large circle of people behind the center island. Not wanting to take away from birthday wishes, I swiveled behind Loch.

When Loch's muscles tensed up and no one had uttered a word, I looked around his body. Most everyone stared at the floor, their mouths drawn down.

I stepped beside Loch to see what everyone was staring at and gasped when my eyes locked on the mess splattered across the floor. Chocolate cake.

"We don't know who did it." Koni's voice was the first I heard, and I looked up to see him standing across from us, along with Rosie, Zavier, Elijah, Keira, and Mike.

"No one does," Rosie added, tsking under her breath.

Tim was leaning against the center island, his arms crossed over his chest. He inhaled deeply. "Sorry, Loch. Teagan. No one is fessing up to doing it or seeing it. But if we do find any information, they will be punished accordingly."

Fat chance. I only needed one guess to know who had done it, and he was standing near the refrigerator, sporting a Stetson, too-tight jeans, and a bored look. Though bestie Trig struggled with his poker face, his eyes darting around the room, looking anywhere else to avoid my glare.

My shoulders slumped. But I resigned myself to let it go. There was nothing I could do to fix it except to make a new one, which I had every intention of doing. I just wouldn't be stupid enough to leave it unattended again.

Before any of these thoughts could process, I heard a warning uttered from the other side of the cake mess. "Don't do it." *Zavier's voice.* I glanced up, assuming he was talking to me and worried that I would fly off the handle. But his eyes weren't on mine at all. With pressed lips and a sharp shake of his head, he was staring at Loch.

There was no time to react. A grunt sounded at my side, giving the slightest sign of what was about to happen. Loch bolted away, ripping through anyone in the way, barreling toward Jackson.

Someone screamed. It may have been Rosie yelling at Loch to stop. But with the way his massive body moved so swiftly through the others, I had my doubts he could even stop himself. His fist slammed into Jackson's mouth, emitting a loud crack. Jackson's attempt to dodge the strike was weak. He recovered quickly enough from the hit to throw his own. Loch blocked it but didn't see the other blow coming from his side. Trig had helped his friend without hesitation, landing a punch to Loch's ear.

People scattered from the kitchen, most of the upper cabin residents not wanting to be involved. Who could blame them? It had turned from silent to chaotic within a second. Keira and Mike came to my side while Zavier, Koni, and Elijah tried to help Rosie and Tim break up the fight. After Ford and another random guy joined in with Jackson and Trig, the scuffle grew.

Koni was launched backward. He slammed into a counter, knocking over the stack of pizza boxes, spilling a couple of them onto the floor. Fists and arms swung, and bodies crashed together.

Grunts and groans of both exertion and pain sounded through the space, making me cringe.

While all the others kept fighting around them, Loch had managed to get Jackson pinned and was landing blow after blow. And then I watched in horror as Jackson shifted in the middle of it all, knowing the beating he was taking from Loch was one he could not escape any other way.

His wolf emerged, causing the others to back away for a moment. His jaws snapped at Loch, clamping down hard on Loch's forearm. Loch growled as the wolf thrashed, ripping at Loch's skin.

"No," I uttered, feeling fucking helpless and useless. I wanted to attack Jackson. I wanted to rip his goddamn head off for hurting Loch.

Keira's hand tugged at my arm, pulling me back from the melee. I had taken a few steps forward, drawn toward the fight without realizing it.

"Enough!" Rosie yelled as she and Tim attempted to pry the bodies apart.

But it was no use, especially when Loch's body shifted too, his wolf form unfurling, deathly angry. The mass of muscle and black fur snapped right back at his gray opponent, teeth bared and ears pinned.

Fucking hell.

"Outside now!" Rosie said, knowing there was no hope to control it all.

Others also changed in the blink of an eye, adding more violence to the already fearsome brawl. This included Tim. Though, his shaggy brown form had taken to the rear, working to corral them out through the door.

Keira and Mike moved to the door, too, watching the fight's progress. Chairs and tables clunked and scraped out in the dining area, the noises joining the vicious growls and jaw snaps until there was nothing left but silence.

"Fuck," Keira breathed.

"Yeah," Mike agreed, passing out the door. "I'm gonna go try to help Rosie and Tim."

"Okay. I'll stay and clean up." Her voice had softened.

I hadn't been watching, only looking down at the mess of chocolate cake streaked across the floor, wondering what to think of it all. It was my fault. And that made me feel like complete shit. Ever since I'd arrived at camp and gotten involved with The Four, I'd only caused problems, chaos.

"Hey," she said to me, drawing my eyes from the mess. She was bent over by the fallen pizzas, lifting the pieces that had escaped and tossing them into an open box. "You okay?"

"Yeah," I replied with a nod before moving to the lower counter shelves for trash bags.

When I added nothing else, she said, "Loch was fucking pissed. Holy shit. I don't think I've ever seen him so mad. I was beginning to think he was all bark, with that everyday hard glare of his. But, damn. I mean, he really tears up the wolf sparring exercises when we have them, usually beating everyone in fighting techniques without breaking a sweat. But in human form? To lose his shit like that …"

"My fault," I murmured to myself.

"Nope. Don't even with that. Whoever pokes the bear—or in our case, wolf—is who's at fault. That Texan has a death wish. Besides, shit's been brewing between all of them for a while. You're more like the little straw that broke the back. Or insert a better idiom here. My brain's too fried from study to be clever."

I laughed at her, thankful for her levity. "Christ. What a fucking mess. Obviously, I don't just mean the cake."

"Hmm," she hummed in agreement as she closed the two boxes of dirty pizza. Standing, she hurled them into the large trash bin alongside the counter then moved to wash her hands. After drying them up, she gathered the salvageable pizzas that had stayed on the countertop. "They really have claimed you. And Loch … I knew it as soon as the clothes thing happened. I can't say I'm surprised about it being all of them. You've all just clicked. You're not regretting it, are you?"

"Oh, no," I admitted without thought. It was messy, sure. The entire situation was unconventional and probably a bit odd. But regret it? No way. I could honestly say I felt closer to them than anyone, even the closest members of my family. I was grateful for my upbringing. At least I'd had stability and a safe place to live. But all the younger years of the hesitant love and teachings that I'd received still didn't outweigh the emotional neglect and coldness I'd had to endure for well over four years. My father, my brothers—I barely knew them when they died.

I scooped the rest of the cake inside the bag, tossed it into the larger bin, then went to get the mop. "I've … bonded with them."

Keira gasped. "Yeah?"

"There's no other way to explain it. It was hard and fast and completely unplanned ... but yeah, I've bonded with them in a way I can't ignore, a way I don't think I'll be able to walk away from." I lifted the bucket to fill in the sink and added cleaner.

"Wow," she said with a nod, picking one of the slices of pizza from the box and taking a bite. "Mmm. I know what you mean. It's why I'm with Mike. There's just this connection. It's so strong." After a silent moment, she laughed around another bite. "I know it's usually called coupling, but what would you guys be called exactly? Not throupling or quadrupling. Quintupling?"

I chuckled with her while I mopped the pizza mess first, then moved on to the cake cleanup.

"Honestly, though, I'm happy for you. I hope it works out, whether you leave or stay."

Leave or stay. That was the real messy part, the biggest question. Was my bond with them strong enough to let go of what waited for me at home?

9

"Teagan?" Zavier's voice traveled through the cabin. "You here?"

"Yeah, bathroom! Give me a minute."

No one had returned to the kitchen while Keira and I cleaned, or for the next hour and a half. Everyone had disappeared from the main camp area. After Keira left, I chose to make Loch another cake. There weren't enough ingredients for the same size I'd made before, so I made a mini cake. I'd had time to let it cool and apply the frosting, and still, no one had returned.

When I emerged from the bathroom in my taco sleep set, four sets of eyes welcomed me, all hooded and tired looking. But, oh, what a sight. Their bodies crowded just inside the front door, engulfing the entire area. They hadn't removed their boots.

"Are you all okay?" I asked, surveying them as I approached. Zavier's lip was cut near his lip ring. Koni had a swollen cheek and a few scrapes on his exposed forearm. Elijah didn't seem to have any injuries. But Loch ... his arm was bloody with scratches and bites. "Is there a first aid kit somewhere?" I hadn't seen one in the cabin, so I was prepared to go to the office if needed, even if they protested.

"Brought it," Zavier said. Standing behind him, Elijah held up a white box for me to see.

"I love tacos," Koni murmured, his eyes fixated on my silky nightclothes. They were skimpy, the way I preferred my pajamas, giving a barely-there feel. I hadn't bothered with a bra. And that's where Koni's eyes were focused. The shirt came down to my midriff and wasn't too tight, but the thin material outlined my breasts well enough. Plus, my nipples had hardened the very second I saw all of them, demanding their attention.

I smiled coyly at him, making no move to cover up. I enjoyed their eyes on me this way.

Elijah cleared his throat like he needed a subject change. He found one when his eyes fell on the cake on the small circular table. "You made another cake?"

Loch's eyes shifted back and forth, too, his eyebrows raised in question.

I took the last steps to them all. "Yeah. No one came back, and I was too pissed off to take off right away. I only had enough for a small one, and there was no way I'd leave it in the kitchen. I'm just sorry the other got ruined, Loch."

"It wasn't your fault," he replied to me. "You didn't need to make another one."

"I know I didn't. I wanted to. You did promise to eat it, so ..."

He smirked a bit while Zavier and Koni, who were closest to me, eyed us both.

"Do you want me to clean this up for you?" I asked, turning my attention to Zavier first, trailing my finger over his lower lip, close to the cut.

"Nah, I'm fine. It's a scratch, so it'll heal after I shift again." He kissed the pad of my finger before leaning down and kissing my lips. That lower lip pushed under mine seductively despite the kiss being quick.

"And you?" I asked Koni when Zavier released me, lifting his arm to inspect it.

He huffed a breath. "I'm all right. Same as Z. Nothing deep," he replied, dipping down low to kiss my neck below my ear, purposely giving me shivers.

"Did you get any of the saved pizza?" Elijah asked me. He remained closest to the door.

I eyed them all, noticing that they still hadn't moved. "I had a slice. Did you guys? Is that why you all look ready to dart outta here? Hunger pains?"

"Nah, not that," Koni offered with a laugh. "Well, actually, yeah, we ate. But, no, it's not the reason we need to leave again. We're still on boundary duty until later, so we need to go back out."

"Especially since the fight lasted so long. We'll have to cover more ground tonight, checking for traps mainly," Zavier said.

"And also to see if Jackson and Trig return," Elijah added.

Loch remained quiet and kept eerily still. It was almost as if he were uncomfortable in this space, unsure what to do or say.

Wanting to be near him, I stepped in front of his imposing body and eyed his arm where Jackson had bitten him. Tentatively, I took hold of his hand and higher up his forearm to lift it closer. He let me, silently regarding my inspection. "So they left then?"

Zavier coughed lightly. The subtle tone of amusement held within told me he was watching my interaction with Loch. He and Koni had probably realized something had happened between us as soon as Loch pounced on Jackson in the kitchen, possibly sooner. But now, they were studying us attentively, more aware with the fight adrenaline gone. They wanted more info. They knew this next connection affected us all, wrapped us all tighter together, maybe even moved us toward an answer for the future.

"Yeah, they left," Koni said, breaking the small gap of silence. "The others gave in and got their asses handed to them from Rosie and Tim. We got in trouble for fighting again, but it's mostly added chores."

"And what about Jackson and Trig? Will they be allowed back if they took off?" I asked, still eyeing Loch's arm. Most of the dried blood coated newly healed scratches. There were a couple of deeper holes and gashes, though.

"No." Loch's deep voice held no sharpness. It was almost warm, and it most definitely warmed me. "They aren't allowed to stay."

"Rosie and Tim will let them get their shit as long as they come in human form," Koni said with a huffed breath. "But we're all to be on the lookout in case they try to sneak in and retaliate or something."

"Oh," I said, releasing the top part of Loch's arm but keeping hold of his hand. The whole thing made me a little uneasy. "You think they will?"

"They'll probably come to their senses later tonight. Rosie or Tim will be waiting for them. They put the rest of us on a rotational watch as backup."

"I wish y'all didn't have to go out again, but I get it. I'm just glad you're all okay. I was worried." I looked pointedly at Loch. "Do you want to share your cake or eat it alone?"

Oh boy, the cake talk sounded dirty again. Heat rushed through me in a wave, and I giggled nervously.

Koni and Zavier huffed breathy laughs, catching on to the double entendre. My perverts.

"They can have some if they want," Loch said flatly, his fingers twisting with mine.

Koni moved to the table to dive in, but I grabbed his arm and tsked. "Loch gets first bite and most of it."

Zavier and Elijah chuckled, and Koni let out a little playful whine. I gave him a side-eye glare and dropped my hold on everyone so I could grab the mini cake. I handed Loch the single fork I'd brought and held the cake plate between us.

"Happy birthday," I said, and the others echoed the same.

Loch eyed the cake before dipping the fork tines into the double layers and scooping a bite. He shoved it into his mouth without preamble, removed the fork as quickly, then passed it to Koni.

Koni didn't bother to wait for Loch's reaction, but my eyes stayed fixed on Loch as he chewed and swallowed it down, his thick Adam's apple bobbing in his sexy throat. He licked his lips, and I had to fight the urge to squeeze my thighs together at the sight of it all. *Damn*. But then he made me wet when he let out a low hum and uttered, "Fuck. That's good."

I beamed at him, both delighted and turned on.

"Fuck yes, it is!" Koni said, adding an exaggerated, high-pitched moan that made me laugh and bounce onto my toes.

Zavier took a huge bite and handed the fork over to Elijah. I stepped closer between them so Elijah could reach the plate for his own taste. Loch let me lean in against him, not backing away at all even though there was space for him to.

Zavier licked at his lips and let out his own little moan. "Baby, that is so delicious. I wish there was more. Fuck. I'm really pissed off now. We could have smeared some of it—"

"Stop, man. Shit," Koni said, glaring at Zavier. "You can't be putting that in my head right before we have to leave."

I laughed at their banter, knowing full well that I would have enjoyed smearing leftover cake on them too.

"It is really good. Thanks," Elijah said, handing the fork back to me. "Thanks for cleaning up the kitchen, too. I appreciate that."

"No problem. Keira helped me."

He nodded and ran a hand through his thick poof of wavy brown hair. He licked his luscious lips, seeming to search for more chocolate like the others had. "I'll be sure to thank her too. We should probably go, guys." He smacked his hand to Koni's shoulder.

I glanced down at the cake. After all their heaping bites, only half remained. "Do you want me to save this for you here?" With my body still pressing against Loch, I tilted my head a little sideways and tipped it back so I could see his face.

His hazel eyes blinked down at me silently.

A response came from Zavier instead. "He's not leaving. He has the night off. Ya know, being his birthday and all." He chuckled, then leaned in to steal a quick kiss on my cheek. When he righted himself, he said to Loch, "Have a good night. Take care of her."

Despite the chuckles from him and Koni, Loch didn't bother replying.

Koni dipped down and kissed my lips softly. "He better give you a bite at least."

Elijah handed off the first aid kit to Loch then said, "Later." The door closed behind them, cutting off Zavier's and Koni's grumbled complaints of having to go and leaving Loch and me in silence.

I kept still against Loch, holding the cake and staring at the door. Heat curled inside my body, and I wondered if it was because of my proximity to him or simply the warmth radiating from his body. Tilting and tipping my head again, I glanced up and found his eyes already on me.

"Hi," I said with a tiny smile.

"Hi," he replied simply, unmoving.

Hmm. "If you don't want to stay …"

"Do you want me to?"

"Yes," I admitted. I wanted much more. "You still have the rest of this cake to eat if you want."

"I do want. And I want you to eat it with me."

"Okay. Let's sit." I finally stepped away from him and placed the cake on the table. The two dinette chairs in the cabin seemed smaller than those in the dining hall and the classroom, and Loch's body proved it. I almost worried it would buckle, but it held him well enough. I sat beside him and forked a piece of cake, taking it in my mouth. The next second, I was forking another and offering it up to him. "Mmm. That did turn out good. Open."

His stare had been fixed on my mouth until the fork cut into his line of sight. He did as I asked, his eyes piercing mine. After he chewed it, he took hold of the fork and proceeded to feed me. My body flashed with heat again, this time my bones aching too.

I licked my lips and closed my eyes, hoping that I only imagined the flare. But then anger started to build up. I groaned at the sensation and the curling beneath my skin.

"No. Why now?" I grumbled through my gritted teeth as I stared down at the table. There was still cake left. "Hasn't enough happened tonight?"

"Teagan?" Loch said my name, unsure what I was rambling about.

"Dammit!" I yelled, standing up quickly and stalking toward the bathroom. My skin was on fire. Already?! I'd just had a flare yesterday morning!

"Teagan! What's wrong—Oh. Shit. It's the transition, isn't it?" He moved around me as I stalled in the bathroom doorway, grabbing a towel and wetting it in the sink.

"Yeah. I'll be okay, I think. You want to grab that first aid kit and bring it in so I can check your arm."

"My arm's fine."

"It doesn't look it!" I yelled at him, splashing water onto the towel, sighing as the coolness spilled over my hands.

"It's fine." His tone returned to its usual hard and sharp glory. He threw in a growl, too, as if he were reflecting my anger.

"Fine! I just ..." I leaned onto the sink and glanced in the mirror. My face had paled, but my eyes were wide and wild. I met Loch's gaze in the reflection, his hazel stare almost as wide as mine as his hulking body heaved heavy breaths at my back. Lifting the towel against my forehead, I groaned at the twisting inside my body, at the heat, the anger, the aches ... "I think I need help."

10

As soon as I sagged against the sink, Loch swept his arms beneath my body, lifted me as if I were a rag doll, and walked me to the bedroom. "I went through this fast. I don't really remember much of the pain. It wasn't as bad as ..." He trailed off, not wanting to go farther into his truth. The admission was meant for me, but it sounded as if he were telling himself too, trying to recall that point in his life.

I barely cared about anything. The pain was so intense this time, coursing through my body and not relenting. Sweat leaked from my pores, my skin fighting to cool itself and finding little reprieve even from the cold towel slung over my face.

My body was laid onto the bed, and I grunted as I gripped the sheets and blankets. Twisting my head around, the towel slipped off, and I couldn't bring myself to care enough to replace it. I stared at Loch as he paced back and forth beside the bed. Worry and concern were written in his taut expression, making him appear his nineteen years for the first time despite his very hulk-sized body.

"Fuck." His voice strained as he wrapped his hands around the back of his head, jutting his elbows outward. "What do you need, Teagan. What can I do?"

Only one thing helped calm a transition flare. I had to orgasm. My hands finally started moving, drawing themselves over my body, needing touch to calm the ache. With one hand, I lifted my shirt, exposing my braless breasts and stroking them. The other, I slid down between my legs, pushing my silky sleep shorts and underwear away. My fingers slipped over my pussy, and I sighed at the contact.

"Touch me if you want. If not, leave me, please," I grunted, clenching my teeth at the pain threatening to break me. I wasn't sure if he was ready to do anything else sexually. I'd given him head hours ago, sure, but he had limited experience. It was obvious enough. And while that wasn't a bad thing, I didn't want him to feel pushed to do more if he wasn't ready.

"I won't leave you like this. I ... Fuck. It's just that I ... I haven't ..."

"I know. It's okay. I can tell you what feels good," I said, opening my eyes to him, the sight of him easing me more than my touch alone. I started dragging my shirt up. "Help me."

He helped me sit upright to remove my shirt. His rough hands lifted my lower legs and slid the shorts and underwear completely off of me. I sighed when he laid my legs back onto the bed, happy to be free of the restrictions.

My body cooled a little from the chilly caress of the cabin air. I writhed and grabbed hold of my breasts, massaging them and pinching my nipples. Lifting my eyes, they instantly found Loch's in the dim light. He had stayed at the foot of the bed, his stare fiery as he watched me touch myself. It made me feel better, knowing that he was enjoying the view. Bending my legs up, I let my knees spread wide and pushed one hand down to my pussy again. I moaned, sliding the pad of my finger over my clit and circling. Loch's gaze moved there. Biting down on his lower lip, he grunted and adjusted the bulge growing at the front of his jeans.

Using two fingers, I parted my lower lips for him to see, then trailed a finger back and forth over my slickness before shoving it inside.

"Ahh," I said in a breathy whimper. The sensation dampened the aches and coiling beneath my skin for a moment, pleasure overruling all the pain receptors. "Loch. Lay with me. Touch me."

He moved to the side of the bed, shoved his arms under my body again, and positioned me in the middle of the three mated beds. With his clothes still on, he lay at my side, bracing a forearm near my head.

I groaned, feeling his heat, smelling his breath, aching for him. He made no move, still unsure. I reached up to his head and tugged him down, pulling his lips to mine. His mouth opened right away, his tongue licking fiercely, as needy as my own. Without too much of a delay, his hand touched my bare stomach and moved north. His cool, rough skin was mind-blowing, covering and soothing so much area. I sighed when he covered my breast, his tentativeness disappearing as he grasped my tender flesh more roughly.

A throaty moan escaped him, and he swirled his tongue around mine then thrust it deeper. Using his fingers, he pinched my nipple, sending delicious spikes of pleasure down to my pussy. I rocked against my own fingers there, pushing two inside myself with a cry.

As he pulled his mouth away and trailed his lips over my jaw, I whispered with a strained voice, "Yes. Touch me, please." My body still hurt—bones aching with a constant throbbing, muscles stretching beneath the surface.

He kissed and licked his way down my neck, taking tiny nips with his teeth like I'd done to him in the classroom. His hand skimmed along my skin, over my belly, down, down, down, until it touched mine. When he stalled, I grabbed his hand, guiding him. His breaths came fast and heavy over my breast. He was panting, and the sound was so damn erotic. Finally, he bathed and flicked my nipple with his tongue, then opened wide and sucked me in.

I moaned, arching my back, pushing myself into his mouth, chasing the feeling. It dulled the aches even more. My hand covered his, my fingers using his to slip over my lower lips, coating them in my wetness before swirling them over my clit. His fingers were so big and thick. Unable to wait, I pushed them down farther and guided one inside me.

"Ah!" My excited response elicited a moan from him while he continued to suck and lick on my nipple. I ran my other hand over his head, crushing him closer, threading my fingers through his hair.

He added another finger and began to work them in and out.

"Curl them," I told him while I moved his thumb to my clit, showing him how to stimulate it at the same time. When he followed exactly what I was doing, I started to pant too.

"Oh, oh, oh. I'm so close, Loch. Yes, I'm going to come. Oh!" My body let go, shooting into the climax.

My pussy clenched around his fingers as he slowed their movements.

His mouth drew away from my breast, and he whispered, "Fuck, you are gorgeous."

I had my eyes closed, my body wound so tight that I struggled with handling the release. But as the orgasm washed over me, easing all the tension, everything relaxed, and I opened my eyes.

He had lifted his head and was gazing at me almost reverently, with his swollen lips parted and his hazel eyes soft and affectionate.

"Thank you," I said, letting out a relieved breath. "For the compliment and for the orgasm. My body feels so much better."

"Good," he admitted with a sigh, still looking enamored. "I was worried. I've never felt that way about anyone else."

"Yeah?"

"Yeah. I wasn't sure what to do because my own transition had been so fast. I know everyone says it's worse for runts, so I was afraid for you and didn't know if I'd be able to help."

"You're just a big softie, aren't you?" I teased, smiling as I licked my lips.

"Funny," he replied, lifting his eyebrows with a smirk. His eyes flickered between mine, his face still so close.

I shifted my body more against his. "That was the worst it's been. More painful. Probably getting closer to the finale." I let out a wry, breathy laugh. "But I'm glad I didn't scare you away. I wasn't sure you'd want to do any of that."

"That's a joke, right?"

"No. I wanted to be certain."

"Oh, I understand. It's just ... I doubt any guy would pass up the chance to help you this way. Fuck. Your body is beautiful. Your skin tastes like heaven. And your scent ..." He dipped his face closer to mine for a moment and inhaled deeply. "I can't get enough of it."

"Really? Well, I couldn't really tell that when I first saw you in here earlier. You looked scared, like you weren't sure you made the right choice to come into the cabin."

"I was processing," he said simply. His fingers trailed over my stomach, scattering chills across my flesh.

"Processing?" I echoed, closing my eyes for longer than a blink as I soaked up the feeling of his feathered touches and the settling of my turbulent body.

"Having your suitcase, then having you on top of me in the classroom—the smell of you is strong and incredible. Sweet and bright, like sunshine. But as soon as I walked into this place, I got hit hard. Your scent is so potent in here. Zavier's and Koni's are too, but they're male, and we've lived in the same space before. This cabin is filled to the brim of you, though, and it stunned me and turned me on instantly, the same as the night you were attacked. It's why I haven't been over since."

"Oh."

"Yeah. Oh." He chuckled, and I found myself grinning like a fool as I eyed him. Those heavy eyebrows arched up again. "What?"

I licked my lips. "So you've been hard this entire time?"

He huffed a breath and groaned.

"You can leave. Or you can stay." I pinched the shirt covering his solid chest. "You can take all of this off and lay with me, maybe sleep. Or … we could do more together if you want." I wanted more. I was greedy now, asking for every bit of him, but it had to be his choice.

His reply was to ease himself from the bed. My heart sank right along with my smile as I realized he was deciding to leave. So when he stood upright and tugged his shirt from his body, my mouth parted, and my relief escaped with a whoosh of air. I let my eyes roam over him, watching the muscles in his chest and arms flex as he unfastened his jeans. He had scars all over, their thin skin shining in the dim light casting in from the front of the cabin. He slid his jeans and boxers from his lower body. When he straightened back up, he was fully naked. His body was like a sculpted marble statue, massive and wondrous, dips and sharp angles shadowed, plains and peaks of muscle highlighted. That huge cock was still very much hard and curving upward toward the ceiling.

My mouth watered. "You are beyond gorgeous, Loch. Wow."

I watched his Adam's apple bob with a hard swallow before he climbed back into bed with me.

11

My body practically hummed, rippling with delight as Loch eased himself against me, leaning up onto a forearm as he had before. My hands were on him in under a second, feeling his skin the way I'd craved to do inside the classroom.

The first thing I explored was his massive chest. Even though all of them were fit, he had a fair amount more muscle than Koni and Zavier. Zavier was the closest to his bulky size, both of them not as slender as Koni ... or Elijah, as far as I could tell.

"So strong," I mused.

His entire body flinched back a bit, and his eyes slammed closed.

"Sorry." I yanked my hands away as quickly as I could. "Did you not want me to—"

"No," he replied, his voice strained. But as he opened his eyes to mine, he took my hand, placed it back on his chest, and kept it held there. "I want you to. The words ... they just triggered a bad memory."

"Oh." Oh, God. Oh no. The possibilities of what happened in his past hit me like an avalanche, stealing my breath. What horrors had he endured? "I'm so sorry."

"Don't be." His eyes pierced mine, genuine and a little sad. "Certain phrases take me back sometimes. Not as often as they used to."

"Okay," I said, watching as he inhaled deeply. His hand released mine and settled on my side. My fingers explored his chest again, trailing over the ridges there. "You are beautiful. I love how you feel. And your scent too," I admitted and curled closer to him to mimic the way he'd smelled me minutes before. "Smoky cedar and black pepper. I think I loved it as soon as I picked your donated clothes from the office."

He sighed and closed his eyes, absorbing my words and my touches. When he opened them again, the sadness had disappeared, an intense desire burning in its place.

I took that as a green light to keep touching, to move farther. Leaning in, I kissed his chin and skimmed my hand down over his abs and the deep indent of the sexy V cut past his hip. His breaths sped up, and his hand snaked around my back, digging his fingers in. I licked my tongue out along his jaw and felt the muscle there flex as he clamped down. My hand brushed over his cock, and it jerked in response. I grabbed hold and stroked to the base, feeling him grow even harder.

He lifted his hand to the back of my head, using the grip to angle my face closer. His lips crashed against mine fervently, opening wide and thrusting his tongue inside my mouth in a wild charge. I stroked him faster, matching his excitement. A guttural groan of approval made my entire body quiver, and I whimpered into his mouth.

He broke away with a grunt. "Fuck. I want you. I want to be inside you." He shook his head, inhaled heavily, then more words followed in a rush. "You probably guessed by now, but I didn't get all the words out before ... I've never done it. I've seen others a couple of times, talked about it with the guys, but I haven't had sex. I don't know if I'll do it right."

My chest squeezed at his admission, and my hand stilled. For a split second, I wondered if I was doing the wrong thing. Was I selfish for wanting him, for wanting all of them, despite the uncertainty of our future together? Should I have him when he could find someone else, someone he might not have to share?

I couldn't ignore that, not in good conscience, even if this wasn't like my own experiences with the high school dude or the pack visitors wanting to brave a quick lay with the runt. I wouldn't immediately walk away from him. "Are you sure you want it to be with me? We don't have to do more. You might want someone different, someone else in the future."

"No," he said firmly. "I want you. Only you."

"Even though you have to share me?" I asked hesitantly.

He shook his head. "I don't care about that. I know what it means, know that this—we—are different. It doesn't matter."

"Okay." My lips met his in a brief kiss, then my teeth nipped and tugged at his bottom lip. I stroked him again, relishing his pleasured sigh before releasing my hold and pushing against his stomach. "Lay back."

He did as I asked, settling onto the bed, eyes focusing on me as I looked over his glorious body.

Waiting no longer, I lifted a leg over him, straddling his hips. I leaned over and slanted my mouth over his for one more kiss the pushed up to a seated position. "This is my first time being on top, so I hope I don't mess it up." Finding his cock laying hard and ready on his stomach, I spread myself over him and rocked back and forth, wetting his length between my lips.

"Fuck," he said with a grunt, easing his palms onto my thighs.

"Mmm. That feels so good." I licked my lips and inhaled as his hands traveled up my sides to my breasts. He grasped and squeezed them, then rolled my nipples between his fingers, completely enraptured. "Are you ready?"

"Yes." It was a breathy word, one I barely heard.

I lifted a leg, needing more room, then reached between us to grab hold of his cock. After positioning him upright, I lined his tip up with my entrance and sank slowly onto him, my pussy stretching to accommodate his wideness.

"Oh fuck," Loch said, dragging the words out in a long breath.

I kept going, easing my leg back down onto my knee. "Is this okay?" I asked, watching in utter delight as his usually hardened facial features went through an array of movements. His heavy eyebrows scrunched and lifted, his eyes closed tight, his nostrils flared wide, and he clenched his jaw so tightly I thought he might break a tooth.

"Yeah. Yes. Fuck. Fuck. Yes. This is more than okay. You. Are. So fucking tight."

Despite the blow job I'd given him earlier, he was likely on the verge of coming hard and fast if I didn't take things slow. So I held still and bit my lip to keep from screaming out in ecstasy. The sound could push him over the edge too, and I was not ready for that yet. Because damn ... he felt phenomenal. So large. So filling. And I wanted more.

When his panting eased and his eyes reopened, I sank lower, letting my body dip down little by little until I was fully seated on his hips and he was buried all the way inside. "Ohh." I let myself breathe the contented sigh.

His hands roamed over my breasts as if his mind and body had rebooted and started working again. "You feel so good. Too good."

"So do you. So big and deep in me. I'm gonna start moving." When he grunted his response, I leaned forward, letting his cock slide almost entirely out before pushing back down onto him. We both moaned, our eyes remaining locked. "Oh yes." I did it again and again, watching him for cues, studying him. "Do you like this?"

"Yes. So much."

"Me too. When I grind down this way"—I rocked my hips while he was completely in—"the base of you rubs over my clit, and it's driving me wild."

He watched me do that several times, transfixed. Then I shifted forward, wanting to go harder and faster. I propped one hand on his stomach and moved the other to my clit, needing to feel more. His eyes took it all in, watching my fingers circle there as I adjusted myself on top of him.

I started to bounce, lifting and falling onto him more aggressively, riding him. Sweat gathered on my skin, and tingles built deep inside my belly and my spine.

"Teagan, ah. Yes. Damn." His hands dropped to my waist and held on tightly.

"Yes. Yes. Yes," I chanted, picking the pace up even more.

"I'm going to come. I can't ..." His eyes went wide, and he clamped his jaw together again.

"Go, go. I'm coming," I cried out, flicking my clit as my orgasm exploded, shooting shocks all through me and contracting my pussy tighter around him.

Loch dug his fingers into my side and bucked his hips upward, matching my bounces as he growled and grunted. Those deep throaty sounds excited me even more. His eyebrows pinched together, but he kept his eyes on me as he thrust forcefully from below, over and over, hips ramming against my ass as he came.

His thrusts were so forceful, I nearly fell off him. Unable to contain it, I giggled and tipped forward, catching myself by slapping my hands down onto his chest.

"Ahh. Ahh." The pleased sounds expelled in long sighs as he dropped his hips the final time and looked up at me. Every single one of his muscles had been taut and active, and I watched in awe as his powerful body relaxed beneath me.

Wow. If that last bit was any indication of how he would perform when he got the hang of things, I was a really happy girl. I bit my lip and moaned, my body already anticipating a second round as I thought about him driving into me from different positions.

"Was that ... okay?" His words sounded hesitant, shy even.

I grinned and smoothed my hands over his chest before leaning down to press my skin totally against his. Lying on top of his strong body felt exquisite. Feeling his warmth, his breaths, his heart. "Oh, it was beyond okay for me. What about you?"

With my hands propped under my chin, I peeked through my lashes at him. Still connected at the hips with our height difference, our faces were nowhere near close enough to kiss. And my pussy was not quite ready to release his softening cock.

"Was it not obvious how much I enjoyed it?"

"Yes, it was. I just wanted to make sure you weren't having any regrets."

"Regrets?" he asked, his mouth popping wide open. "I may be behind in schooling, but I'm not a fucking idiot."

12

A laugh burst from me at his reaction. He'd made a joke! My body shook violently, and I buried my face into his chest, feeling so relaxed and connected with him. His hands clamped tighter around me. When I peered up at him again, he had the biggest, most adorable smile on his face. I stilled, awed by the sight, by how sexy he looked with such a broad, pleased grin. "You're so handsome." My voice sounded more like a purr. He lifted one of his stern eyebrows in response, and I pushed against him, preparing to dismount.

"Where you going?" he asked, reluctantly loosening his hold around my back, a worried look erasing his smile in a blink.

"To clean up before we leak on the sheets. Also, to use the bathroom. Give me a minute first, okay?"

He nodded and let his arms fall away from my body.

I slid off of him, clenched my thighs together, and shimmied to the bathroom. After shutting the door, I peed and wiped up. He was standing at the door when I opened it, naked and gorgeous, taking up most of the doorway. I swallowed thickly, then handed him a wet washcloth while I used another, grabbing hold of his arm. I hadn't been able to clean the dried blood from him when my flare had happened.

"It's not bad," he said, placing the towel he'd cleaned himself with on the side of the sink.

"Yeah, not as bad as it looked before," I agreed. It would likely heal with his next shift like the others had mentioned too. "Did you want to shower? I have some of your clothes that I might let you have back."

He smiled down at me. "Nah. Can we just go back to bed?"

"Eager, are we?" I teased and lifted a brow. It wasn't like I'd deny a second round, that was for sure.

He smirked down at me. "Yes, I am. But that's not what I was thinking for now."

"Oh. Yeah, all right." Curiosity had me trailing behind him as he took hold of my hand and walked to the bedroom.

I crawled into the bed, and he followed, situating our bodies so we faced each other. One of his arms stretched above his head while the other wrapped around my waist and pulled me close. He kissed my lips softly, and my fingers trailed over his jaw and up into his hair.

"Do you want a blanket?" he asked, feeling me shiver in reaction to his hand gliding over my back and ass.

"No. You're plenty warm enough." And he was. I wanted to soak up every bit of him.

His eyes closed as my fingertips massaged his scalp. "That feels incredible."

"Good. I love the feeling of someone else's fingers in my hair too. There's something so relaxing about it. It's almost better than hugging."

At that, his arm tightened around me as if to test my comparison, which made me smile. "I'm not so sure about that. They're both so good. I don't think I've ever felt anything like it."

"This?" I asked, scratching my fingernails a little more.

"All of it," he admitted. "I've never had …" He let out a long breath. After a minute of silence, he continued. "I grew up in northern Pennsylvania, near the New York border and the Allegany National Forest. I didn't know my family. The pack who had me told me I'd been traded to them. They were a fighting and hunting pack. I know you heard Zavier call me Bait the other day … That's what they used me for, for hunting and fighting. I was a bait dog."

I kept my fingers working through his hair even though I wanted to stop, wanted to hug him even closer. Christ, what had he been through? Hell it sounded like. But I knew he needed to tell me this, and I was honored he felt comfortable enough to. So I remained quiet, fought off my emotion, and let him continue.

"They hadn't expected me to transition so quickly. But that didn't matter much. I was still used, just watched more and chained better. I lasted longer than others, when there were others. Some died while I was there, from fight wounds or being bound and gagged in freezing weather. So I only had myself. The pack rarely talked to me. Most interactions were because of meals or changes to where they kept me. They moved pretty often so the human police or other supernaturals wouldn't catch on to the underground fighting.

"The alpha was down a fighter once and needed me to fill in for a match. It was the first time I could fight back, and I won. The other wolf was giant, but I ended it fast. After that, the alpha entered me into more fights, no longer using me as bait. I was a moneymaker. That lasted a few months.

"Until he got drunk one night, didn't chain me right. I'd been waiting for it to happen, seeing him get more sloppy as the money piled up. So I took my chance. Ended him and took off. I met Eli a day or so later in the forest, found out he'd escaped his home over the border in New York. He knew how to read and write better than me, so I gave him all the locations, and we secretly dropped that information off at the nearest police station."

"Do you know if they found them?" I asked.

"Yeah. We laid low for a few days and saw it on the news at a rest stop. Several were arrested. We left after that. Eli had heard about this place. We looked it up and came."

"Wow. I'm glad you got out of there. I can't even imagine how horrible that was for you. I'm so sorry."

He let out a sigh, sounding contented or relieved. "We all have our own history. We have to learn and grow from it, no matter the circumstance."

I pressed a light kiss to his lips. It was obvious he'd grown a lot in his time at Midnight Moon, learned so much from Rosie and Tim, and the other guys. My chest felt tight, worried once again about what my interference may have done to their dynamic and if I'd be able to leave them behind.

"I know about your family too. I'm sorry you lost them."

"Thank you." I inhaled deeply, needing to share more with him since he'd trusted me with his past. "I lost them long before they died. My father was a proud alpha, one who couldn't handle the fact that his youngest child and only daughter was a runt. He and my brothers, and all the packs connected to ours, had barely spoken to me in four years. I mean, he fed and clothed me, let me stay in our house, and let me work in our restaurant. But other than that, I was alone. The only person who paid me any attention was my Aunt Rosie. My dad's sister. She manages the restaurant but is a loner outside of work. Never coupled. Never had kids. She's taking care of everything while I'm here. All of it is mine when I return, though." If I return. The thought flashed to mind, and I shook it away. "She made me come here, for transition and for a place to hide from my mother's brother, Uncle Raif. He was outcasted when I was younger, around the time my mom died. But he knows he has alpha claim there if something happens to me."

I felt his body stiffen. "Is he there?"

"No, he left years ago. We don't know where he is, but my aunt didn't want to risk him finding me before my transition. At least after, I'll have a better chance to defend myself. Aside from my aunt and me and a few other loners, the pack is gone. There's no real risk of any others challenging me there after what my father did. My uncle, though, he would have more to gain with the house and restaurant added in."

A low growl worked up Loch's throat, and I smiled and moved my fingers through his hair. "It's okay. He probably made a family somewhere else in the world."

"But there's a chance."

"Sure. He could have found out what happened …" It was my turn to stiffen at that thought. But also about Jackson's threats and Ford's unknown connection to my family.

"What?" he asked, jerking his head back to look directly into my eyes.

"It's just that … Jackson said something before, like a threat, about someone waiting for me at home. I kinda brushed it off. But when I was making your cake, that other guy Ford knew my dad's name from a mutual friend and said that it was a shame what had happened. Jackson seemed to lead him into our conversation. It just had me a little concerned. I should have used a different name here, maybe. Small world, and all."

Loch's throat made another deep rumble. "I'm regretting that fight even more now. He's vindictive, and … Well, if he tries anything else from here, he won't like the outcome."

I shivered, not at his threat but at the idea of Jackson seeking revenge. Would he do something?

Loud bangs pierced through the silent night, and we both jolted.

"What was that?" I asked, my body stilling, listening for the sound again.

Loch untangled himself from me and was off the bed in a second flat. "Gunshots. A rifle."

"That sounded really close."

"Yeah, look ..." he said, yanking on his jeans. "Stay here, okay? I need to check it out, make sure it's under control."

"And if it's not?" I asked, fear tearing through me. Fuck. I knew my father and brothers had dealt with random outsiders hunting in our area, but it didn't make it less frightening to think about the harm it could cause. What if someone had been shot?

The thought had obviously made me pale because Loch leaned over and touched my face after his shirt was on. "It's going to be fine. Stay here. I'll be right back." His lips kissed mine in a quick rush before he disappeared from the room. Inside another minute, he'd wrestled on his boots out in the front area and was out the door, closing it so quietly I barely heard it click.

I worried my lip, then wrung my fingers. My breaths had become short, desperate pants. The fear was all-consuming. My ears pounded as blood raced through my veins. The cabin's silence was amplified by my straining to hear anything else. I jumped from the bed, jerking on my nightclothes and scurrying to the front door. I listened hard, cracking the door open the tiniest amount. The night was pitch black and snow white. The moon was absent, leaving only a soft glow from the cabin's porch light and the other mounted near the shed. They only sharpened the contrast, brightening the snow and darkening the lake and sky.

Without much thought, I slipped into the parka and stepped into Rosie's boots. Quietly, I exited as Loch had, following his large boot prints down the cabin steps and out toward the shed. Just beyond the shed's light, the boot prints changed into paw prints and disappeared.

Fuck. I gripped the edges of the parka and pulled it tighter against my body, not fighting the cold but the fear.

A howling sounded not far away, and then a clamor of activity rushed into the area along the lake. Wolves appeared, running toward me. They shifted just before the edge of the light I hovered near. Elijah, Loch, Zavier, Koni, Vic, Keira, Mike, Tim, and a few others I didn't know stopped for a moment and stretched their bodies.

"Get him to Rosie," Tim ordered, running a hand over his shaggy hair then rolling his neck in a stretch.

That's when I noticed that Koni hadn't stood upright again but had crouched into the snow.

"Oh my God," I whispered and darted toward him, pushing through the others.

"I'm fine, babe," Koni said as soon as I dropped to my knees beside him. Overall, he looked okay, but he was holding his hip.

"He got shot in the ass," Vic said with a laugh. Before I could give him a glare, a few others had started laughing also. Zavier, Mike, and Keira.

"He'll be fine, Teagan," Tim confirmed. "Rosie will clean his *upper thigh,*"—he stressed the last words and lifted an eyebrow at Vic—"and when he shifts again, he'll be good as new. Don't worry."

"See, babe? Don't worry," Koni said as Zavier and Elijah helped him up.

"Come on. Get back inside before you freeze." Loch lifted me onto my feet.

While the others went off in different directions, I walked with Loch to the cabin. My eyes stayed on Koni as he limped along the darkened path toward the office, using Elijah's shoulder as a crutch and laughing with Zavier.

When we stopped at the base of the cabin's steps, movement close to the shed caught my eye. Through the stacks of snow-covered equipment behind the shed, I noticed a set of shining eyes.

"He'll be fine," Loch reiterated, grabbing hold of my hand to coax me inside. My eyes flitted to him for a moment before going back to the spot where the eyes had been. Only, they were gone.

"Did you see …"

"What?" Loch's body turned, and he was instantly at my side, staring off to where I was focused.

"I thought there was someone behind the shed. Another wolf. Was anyone else with you all?"

"Yeah. Almost everyone. It's normal practice when we find out aggressive hunters are involved, like all hands on deck kind of thing. Everyone here knows to respond because more numbers ensure they won't fight and won't return either."

"Oh," I replied simply, shoving my worry away despite the churning in my gut.

13

It had only been a half-hour since Koni had gone to see Rosie about his bullet wound, but it felt like an eternity as Loch and I waited in the cabin. He'd tried to convince me to relax and go to bed. Needless to say, that didn't happen. I had too much adrenaline and worry banging around inside, so I paced the cabin instead.

"Finally!" I said as Koni limped through the door, running and slamming myself into him.

"He's fine," Zavier said with a hint of amusement beside us, removing his boots and shaking his head.

"Rosie bandaged it up, babe. The bullet clipped me, went about a half-inch in and right through. It's already healing," Koni explained as I pulled away to assess him, tugging down the side of his sweats, baring his ass cheek and thigh, needing to see it for myself. He stumbled a bit, attempting to kick out of his boots while I accosted him.

"You got lucky, idiot." Elijah huffed, closing the front door and crossing his arms. "What in the hell were you thinking when you charged that fucker before we got closer?"

"What?!" I gasped out, releasing my hold of him. I scowled at his cute face, then smacked his arm. "You fucking charged a hunter who had a rifle?"

"Ow!" He rubbed his arm playfully with a laugh. When he noticed my seriousness hadn't shifted with his humor, he frowned. "I saw him taking aim. I didn't want to risk him firing on someone else. Babe, it's fine. I'm sorry, okay?"

Before I knew what was happening, fat tears were streaming from my eyes, and I started sobbing. Any emotion I'd been holding back rushed forward and took total control. "You could have been …" My knees went completely weak, but before I could collapse, arms wrapped around my body, steadying me.

Koni pulled me hard against his chest, keeping me on my feet. "Shh. I'm fine. It's okay. It's okay."

"It's not. It's not okay. It's not. I can't lose you. I can't lose any of you." I wailed the stream of garbled words as I buried my face into his chest, my heart and mind seeming to break with the realization. They meant more than anyone else ever had. The connection I felt to them was beyond anything I'd ever experienced. It didn't matter the length of time we'd spent together. I knew I needed them all. Forever. Whatever that took. I couldn't lose anyone else.

"You won't, baby," Zavier said from behind me. Another hand slid my hair from my neck, and lips pressed to my skin. "We know. We feel the same."

"I'll stay. I'll stay here if y'all want me to. I just can't even think of losing you. The house, the restaurant … it means nothing."

"Shh, beautiful." Loch's voice soothed from behind me too, and then I felt another hand on my head, thick fingertips threading through my hair to massage my scalp. "Don't worry about it right now. We'll figure it out."

I sniffled a few times, loving the way they were surrounding me, protecting me. I couldn't help the way I felt for them, the strength of our bonds. There was no way to deny any of it, and now I knew there would be no separating us.

After a few silent moments, Koni cleared his throat. "So Rosie said I need to heal a bit in human form, keep things clean before I shift again. She ordered me to go to bed and stay there a while. Think I can have company?"

"Christ." Zavier's body shook at my back as he let out a chuckle.

"What?!" Koni asked, his tone lilting and cheerful.

My head vibrated against Koni's chest as he laughed with Zavier. One-track mind. My goofy pervert.

I peeled my body away from his, wiping my eyes as I looked around to meet theirs. "I'm sorry. I'm not sure why that happened."

"You don't have to be sorry for your reaction. We understand," Zavier said.

Even though I knew it was the truth, I still felt like an idiot for losing control of myself that way. As I glanced at him, I worried my lip then chuckled. "I shouldn't have lost it like that. I'm not the one who got shot."

Loch's eyes narrowed at my lame self-deprecation. "It's all right to let go. We know it. Feel it." The admission from him was a whole lot deeper. He understood. It had taken him a while to let go and open up to me, so I knew his words were more than simply thoughtful and comforting. They were also introspective.

"I've gotta piss. Meet me in bed, Nurse Teagan. You can get a better look at my ass in there and get started on my physical therapy," Koni said, taking hold of my face and bending down to kiss my lips before walking away.

"Oh my God," I said, shaking my head with a giggle as I stared down at my feet. He sure had a way to lighten the mood.

Loch and Zavier chuckled from behind me. When I lifted my eyes to the door, my gaze met Elijah's. With his hands shoved deep into his jean pockets and his pouty lips parted, he shifted his stance.

"I'm going to hit the dining hall for a quick bite before I meet Tim back out there," he said. "Anyone need anything?"

"Nah," Zavier said. Loch echoed the same.

My gut twisted again, and I tried my best to keep my voice level and my emotions in check. "I thought the hunter was gone. You have to go back out there?" I glanced over at Loch and Zavier, who shook their heads.

"Yeah, there were two of them, but they're gone. And it's just me going. Normal boundary checks with Tim. Nothing to worry about," Elijah said with a nod.

"Okay." I absently touched my fingers to my lips and took a step forward but stopped myself from moving farther. It had been a while since I'd been near him, and I really longed to hug him too. In the times that we'd been close, though, he'd been hesitant about physical contact. He'd been nice, and I felt as if he wanted to be near me too, but I still couldn't tell for sure.

As soon as I halted, I grasped my fingers and wrung them together. "Be careful, okay?"

He didn't move right away, merely stared, his soulful brown eyes thoughtful. They flickered the tiniest amount before he pressed his full lips tight. And then he stunned me. Instead of turning to open the front door, he crossed the few steps to me and engulfed my body, pulling me flush to him. I inhaled against his chest, momentarily overwhelmed by the action and by his scent, a heady mix of leather and citrus. I sighed and gently snaked my hands around his lower back.

His lips touched the top of my head, and he murmured, "I will."

The bathroom door opened, and it was like a switch had been flipped. Elijah released me and was out the door within a few seconds.

"Holy fuck," Koni whispered in the complete silence that followed.

"Yeah," Zavier agreed.

I took a deep breath before I turned to face them. Given my previous encounters with Elijah and by the guys' reactions, the fact that he'd hugged me was momentous. All three sets of eyes were on me. Loch's hardened gaze was soft. Zavier had a twinkle in his eye and a tiny smile tugging his pouty lip.

And Koni ... well, he was completely naked, except for the bandage secured just below his right hip.

I giggled then snorted. *Ugh.*

Loch's eyes went wide, then both he and Zavier looked behind themselves to see what I'd giggled about.

"Oh, for fuck's sake, Stray," Zavier said, laughing.

"What? Rosie told me to get comfortable as soon as possible. I got comfortable. Now I want my nurse to put me to bed." Koni winked at me, freeing his long hair from its topknot.

"Did you just snort?" Loch asked, ignoring Koni and his birthday suit. His eyes were back on me with an inquisitive stare as I covered my mouth with my hands and continued to giggle. My emotions were all over the place.

"Yeah, she snorts," Zavier said, eyeing Loch at his side. Loch's lips curled into a wide grin at the news. "And apparently, you can smile. Who knew?"

"What?" Koni said with a gasp. "Loch smiles? I know what that means. Teagan gave you that smile. Oh yeah. Come on, babe. Come here. I want a smile like Loch's too. Give me one. Or two."

"Shut up," I said, shaking my head but grinning like a lunatic as I walked past Loch and Zavier to him, touching his bandage with a finger. "Maybe you need to chill out. You don't want to make this worse."

"It won't get worse. I just need you to kiss me better, please. Then we can cuddle."

I moved to smack his arm, but he blocked the hit, grabbing hold of my wrist, pulling me to him, and slamming his mouth over mine.

"You're my medicine," he murmured over my lips.

Heat spread throughout my body.

"Loch? You sleeping here with us? You all good with this?" Zavier asked, clearly wanting to be sure before anything got started.

"Yeah," Loch murmured the reply. It sounded unsure.

I detached myself from Koni and looked at Loch. "If you don't—"

"I do," Loch replied, not letting me finish and running his tongue over his lips.

"Okay," I said, lifting a hand out to him, my legs quivering at the prospect of having all three together.

When he grabbed hold, I led the way into the bedroom.

"Clearly, we will need to add another bed in here," Koni said, crawling onto the far side and spreading out, his dark hair fanning out over the pillow behind him.

"Damn, it smells so good in here," Zavier said, tugging his shirt over his head. "Baby, I've been dying to eat you. Loch, did you taste her yet?"

I grabbed the hem of Loch's shirt and lifted it up. He helped from the top, yanking it off fully.

Since he hadn't answered Zavier, I replied for him as I ran my hands over his tight chest. "No, that's something we didn't do."

"Oh shit," Koni said. "I was about to call first dibs on that since I got shot and all. But if Loch hasn't tasted you yet, I think he should. You agree, Z?"

"Yes," Zavier replied, stripping out of his jeans then moving to me quickly to do the same with my sleep shorts and underwear. "That cake was awesome tonight, man, but her pussy is so much better. Fuck. I'm hard already."

I unfastened Loch's jeans and shoved them down. As he stepped out of them, he lifted my sleep shirt, trailing his hands slowly up my skin.

As soon as the shirt was off, Zavier said, "Lay down, baby. Let him taste you."

There was no way I'd argue with that. I settled onto the bed, and Koni crawled to my side, leaning over to kiss my mouth.

"Oh fuck, look at you, so wet already," Zavier said, and I felt hands spread my legs wider apart.

"Beautiful," Loch said, and the bed dipped under his weight as he moved front and center.

I broke contact with Koni's mouth, needing to see. Loch's eyes met mine from between my thighs, his big hands digging into them. I sighed as his face sunk closer and his tongue licked a long stroke over me. He closed his eyes with a moan.

"Like honey, right?" Zavier asked, crawling onto the bed near my side. He knelt up and started stroking his cock as Loch gave an agreed murmur against my pussy, sucking on me. "Fuck, that's so hot."

"Ah!" I panted, my body climbing at the feeling and at the sight of them all naked in bed with me, their solid, taut bodies clenched and aroused, all of them stroking themselves. Even Loch had his cock fisted at the end of the bed. I could see his angled arm jerking beneath him. As Loch explored me with his tongue, lips, and teeth, Koni licked down my neck and over a breast, latching onto the nipple and swirling his tongue around.

"That's it. Yeah. Slip a finger in and curl it. She loves that. And flick your tongue over her clit at the top. Yes. Fuck," Zavier said, coaching Loch. "Baby, I need you to suck me."

"Yes," I replied to him, reaching out as he came closer. Before I could grab him, he instructed. "Flip over and take us both."

Loch got the message, too, letting me turn and get onto all fours. Koni and Zavier knelt in front of me, their cocks hard, long, and ready for my attention. Loch started eating me from behind, gripping and spreading my ass cheeks. Bracing myself on one hand, I grabbed hold of Koni with the other and opened wide for Zavier. He threaded fingers through my hair and rocked into my mouth with a satisfied groan. Koni grunted as I squeezed him and began pumping.

After a minute, I switched between them, letting Koni fuck my mouth while I stroked Zavier. The cabin was filled with sounds of pleasure and Loch's wet kisses and licks. He trailed his tongue over my asshole, making me squeal onto Zavier's dick as my toes curled.

"Fuck yes," Zavier said inside a moan. "Teagan, you are so good to us. So fucking sexy."

I felt Loch's face move, then his body pressed behind me. "Is this okay, beautiful? Can I take you like this?"

I glanced over my should at him, at his hulk of a body settling behind me, his cock sliding between my thighs and rubbing along my entrance. "Yes. Yes, please."

He wasted no time, pressing his tip into my pussy then easing himself inside. A deep rumble came from him as I took Koni back into my mouth and moaned my own pleasure onto him.

"Damn. I don't think I can hold, babe. It's all too much. So much," Koni uttered as I drew him farther into my mouth. "Where do you want it?" I looked up at him and blinked. "Yeah? Okay."

He hit the back of my throat as Loch pushed in fully. I writhed my body and bucked my hips, needing the movement. Koni's breaths picked up while he took hold of my head and thrust in and out of my mouth. I was getting it from both ends while working Zavier in my hand, and it was the most erotic experience of my life. Koni tipped his head back and let out a thunderous moan before shoving deeper. His hot cum shot into my throat as Loch continued to pound into me from behind.

Koni grunted as he finished. "Oh, babe." After pulling out, he slid his hands under my body, massaging my breasts while they swayed from Loch's powerful thrusts.

"Ah. Oh," I cried out, feeling closer and closer to the edge. My body was both coiled and pliant, accepting it all and ready for release. Leaning over, I took Zavier between my lips while I continued pumping his shaft.

"Give it to him, baby," Zavier murmured, rocking his cock into my mouth faster. "Come on his dick."

Loch was close too. His grip tightened as he drove into me, his hips hitting my ass cheeks with a smack at every thrust. My spine and center tingled, and then an orgasm ripped through me. I screamed out a garbled cry around Zavier's dick, and he shoved himself deeper into my throat.

With a roar, Loch came inside me. His movements slowed, then he grunted lowly and leaned over to kiss my spine. He eased out of me a moment later.

"I'm close, but I want in too," Zavier said, leaning down to kiss my lips before rolling me onto my back and settling between my legs. "Hold on to her."

Koni and Loch were at each side, their hands on my breasts and arms, massaging while Zavier lined his cock up and pushed into me with one hard thrust.

He stayed on his knees, his fingers hooked on my hips, and he pumped into me without restraint. "Fuck. You have to come again." His fingers found my sensitive clit, and he attacked it without mercy, flicking and circling while he continued his pace. I was there immediately, screaming out his name. He was right with me, grunting, heaving, as he spilled himself inside.

"Damn," Koni said as Zavier practically fell on top of me, a sweaty pile of limp muscle.

Loch chuckled. "I second that." I turned my face to him, watching as his eyes shifted down to mine, a smile brightening his face.

"Third," Zavier muttered into the crook of my neck before kissing my skin.

"Fourth," I said, agreeing with them. "I feel thoroughly fucked."

Koni laughed, then jumped from the bed and called from the bathroom, "We're running out of clean towels."

After using the bathroom and cleaning up, all of us fell into the bed. The guys had words for a minute, fighting over who would lie next to me. In the end, Zavier opted to let Koni and Loch sleep at my sides while he took an outside spot. He was going to attempt to sleep at the head, but the beds simply weren't that accommodating, and we were all too exhausted to figure out a better option. The day had been too long and tiresome.

Loch wrapped around my back, his face pushed into the top of my hair. Koni pressed to my front, his arm at my waist and knee between my thighs. I reached over him to Zavier, stroking down his side before relaxing with a deep, contented sigh.

This was my new life. Them. They were mine. And I knew now I wouldn't be able to leave them behind.

stud

1

It had been two days since the hunters had traveled close to camp, Koni had been shot, and I realized that I truly loved The Four and could not lose them.

In the hours since, thoughts of leaving and staying consumed me, and worse than that, thoughts of them dying. Koni and the others had shaken the occurrence off fairly easily, stating that it hadn't been too big of a deal to encounter eager hunters. They'd also chalked Koni's wound up to a bad judgment call and that he'd learned his lesson well enough. But I wasn't buying their indifference. It felt as if they were hiding something they didn't want me to know or controlling their reactions in order to protect me. Either way, I couldn't shake the twisting in my gut, that intuitive warning that something worse might happen.

My life had changed as soon as I'd arrived at Camp Midnight Moon. I'd been so numb following the death of my family, so detached from myself to know what might happen here. My Aunt Sonya had convinced me to come, hoping to force my transition and hoping to hide me from the threat of my outcasted Uncle Raif, who could challenge me for the alpha spot of my family's pack now that all the rest were gone. I never thought I'd find any form of love or support in this place, let alone more love and support than I'd ever encountered. I'd thought The Four would have only been headaches during my time, and now they'd become my entire world, shifting my life completely. The only headache I had from them now was of my own making, worrying about our future together and where that could be. I either had to give up my family's house and restaurant and ask Rosie and Tim if I could stay here or ask The Four to leave their home. This is where they'd started their new lives, where they'd formed a bond together. The choice seemed impossible.

"Thank you so much again for the boots and the sweaters, Rosie," I said, staring down at the comfortable black boots she'd given me the previous morning.

Thursday—the day following the shooting—had been business as usual, everyone returning to their routine tasks, chores, and lessons. The only real change was longer hours for the guys on boundary patrol. They kept watch for the hunters' return and for Jackson and Trig. Apparently, Ford and the others involved in the fight apologized and were given a warning by Tim and Rosie. Any new infractions and their cabin leases would end. There had been no signs of Trig and Jackson. They hadn't even come back to collect their things. No one seemed concerned by that, knowing they'd likely returned to their prominent pack families, who Rosie had already contacted about the fight.

"You're very welcome," she replied, stopping along the path to her office. "How are the boys today? Is Koni feeling better?"

"Oh, yes." I shook my head with a laugh. "He's fine today. I saw him this morning before cleaning the bathhouse. Don't tell him I told you but he was fine yesterday too. He just used the time to get more attention, sleep, and food, of course." Had he ever. I knew he was full of shit after he'd shifted and his wound had disappeared, but I babied him anyway, doing anything he wanted, mostly because the fear of losing him, or any of them, had embedded itself so strongly I ached at the thought. And doting on him had been nothing like a chore, especially because it had been reciprocal. He'd doted on me too. All over me. Buried himself deep inside me repeatedly. He also ate every bit of food I'd made for him ... then ate every bit of me in appreciation.

Rosie chuckled at my response. "I'm sure he enjoyed all the attention."

You have no idea. I contained a sigh at the memory. But he wasn't the only one I'd pampered. Zavier and Loch had returned to the cabin whenever they had a chance, all of us taking and giving as much pleasure as we could, feeling the need to be together, the relief of having one another, and also fearing the threat of loss. It combined into a massive longing to be even closer and to give even more. Elijah had stopped by too, mainly coming to get the others for their watch shifts. He hadn't touched me again, but he'd watched me, his soulful brown eyes holding a conflicted look of what I could only see as desire mixed with hesitation. The guys had urged him to move in with us, feeling bad that they had left him alone to share a cabin with Vic, even more so when Loch had moved his bed out and brought it to our place. As far as I could tell, Elijah had ignored the invitation. I didn't know what held him back, but I knew I couldn't push him like I had with Zavier or approach him in the slow yet assertive way I had with Loch. He was altogether different. They all were.

"How is everything else going for you?" she asked curiously, slipping her hands into the front kangaroo pocket of her neon yellow hoodie.

"All right, I suppose." I bit my lip, several thoughts turning up. "Have you heard from my Aunt Rosie at all?"

"No, not since I'd spoken to her about the situation with the sisters. Why?"

"Well, I'm just concerned after some things Jackson said before his fight with Loch. He knows about my family, so … I want to make sure she's okay, I guess."

"I can certainly try to reach her from our landline. Or if you'd prefer to call her yourself, you can come by the office."

"No, I think maybe you should call," I said, knowing that if I talked to her it would only make the decision to stay here with The Four an even bigger struggle. Those thoughts tumbled into the next set of concerns.

She nodded, and the little pink ponytail at the back of her head bobbed a bit. "I'll call and let you know after."

"Okay." I smiled weakly. When she returned the gesture and moved to leave, I called out, "Wait. Rosie … My flares are coming faster. I think I'm really close to transitioning …"

When I grasped for the words I wanted but froze, she replied, "That's great, Teagan. I'm sure the guys will help you in any way they can to make it easier for you."

"I ... They will, I know. I just ... I wanted to ask you something else." With a deep inhale, I pressed on, needing the information from her. The guys and I hadn't even talked seriously about it, but I needed to find out our options. "Is there any way I could stay here? After I transition? I know it wasn't the plan, and my aunt probably paid for me to stay until then, but I'm not sure I want to leave ... them."

"Ahh, I see," Rosie said with a long exhale. She studied me for a moment, her curious eyes roaming my face then darting to the cloud-covered sky. "Your aunt is expecting your return soon."

"I know she is. It's why I can't talk to her yet. I want to make sure she's okay, but I'm afraid she'll be upset if I stayed away longer, and I understand why she would. She's taking care of so much for me already, dealing with everything while I'm here, even though the house and the restaurant are mine and I'm old enough to handle it myself."

"Are you sure you're not more concerned that she won't accept the circumstances with you and the boys?"

"Oh, no. I'm not worried about that," I replied quickly. "I care about them, and I really don't care what anyone else thinks at this point."

She smiled a lopsided smile and squinted her eyes. "Good. That's good. I didn't doubt the way you felt for them. But I did worry someone else's opinion might be too strong to ignore."

"I care so deeply for them. No one can change that. That's why I wanted to know about staying."

"Yes. Well ..." She nodded. "Tim and I would have no problem with you staying here longer. But I want to be honest with you. There is a time limit for your stay. And that's not only for you. It's tied to them too. See, they've been here for a long time, well past most. That's because Tim and I have grown to love them like our own, have wanted to help them learn and grow since they've needed more help than others. But they know their time has to end here, too. We need the space and the opportunity to help more wolves. And they need to stand on their own, or together, or with you ... whatever the case may be when the time comes. I know it can be anytime now because all of them are ready, ready to be part of a pack and maybe lead one. So even though I'm saying yes to you staying longer, I need you to understand that there is an end to that time ... and it's closer than any of us might want."

"I understand. It makes sense." And it did, though it only made my head swim with more information to sort through.

"I suggest you talk with them about all of this soon. You all need to decide what's best, especially since your choice of going home might also come with a time limit. Your aunt's filling in for you, and she may not be able to handle all of it for very long."

"You're right. I know she's doing a lot." When I only stared at my boots, losing myself to all the thoughts, Rosie reached out and patted the bulky parka covering my shoulder.

"My opinion is obvious, I think. Stay together. Take them with you. Pretty sure they'll follow you anywhere anyway, especially if there's a restaurant involved."

I laughed at that and met her kind eyes. "True."

"Before I let you go, would you mind asking the guys if they tracked down the missing two-way radios? Two weren't returned yesterday, probably just misplaced since everyone's been scattered and tired. I'm hoping someone has found them."

"I haven't seen any extras. But, yeah, the guys were gone most of yesterday and today. I'll ask when I see them."

"All right. Thanks, Teagan. I let you know if I get ahold of your aunt."

With that, she headed toward her office cabin, tramping through the foot trail already created in the pillowy ground. Despite the hovering clouds overhead, no more snow had fallen in over a day. The area remained magical, though, the ground, trees, and roofs all coated in sparkling white. But I couldn't shake the gloominess that hovered like the clouds. It was that gut feeling. After speaking with Rosie, the only thing that might settle it was to talk to the guys. We needed to discuss everything. I just hoped it wouldn't wreck us.

2

"Hey! What are you doing in here?" I asked as soon as I stepped into the kitchen.

Activity had been scarce around camp all morning. All was back to normal, but there were fewer people now. The sisters had been kicked out with a couple of others. Then Jackson and Trig had left. And the loners from the higher cabins rarely showed their faces as it was. So camp was looking even more desolate. This was especially true between meals and why I liked eating at abnormal times.

Elijah stood in the kitchen by himself. In jeans ripped at the knees, loosely laced work boots, and a fitted white T-shirt, he looked like he'd rolled out of bed and sleepwalked to the dining hall. His thick mass of hair wasn't styled as it usually was, and pieces poked in all different directions. A stack of clean dishes sat on the counter in front of him. His downward stare hadn't wavered when I spoke. It was as if he'd removed the plates from the washer, stacked them, then had fallen asleep on his feet.

"Hey," I repeated, easing closer to him. "I thought the guys said you had off most of today to rest."

With his head still down, eyes on the basic white dinner plates, his tongue licked out over his full lips. "I couldn't sleep. I … I come here when that happens. Clean up. Organize."

"Oh." I glanced around at the spotless kitchen. He kept it so clean, I wondered how often he couldn't sleep. Was it worse now that the guys had moved out of their cabin and in with me? Feeling a rush of guilt, I wrung my fingers together. "Here, let me help." I stepped closer, grabbed half of the plates, and carried them to their cupboard near the refrigerator.

He let me, without protesting, without even flinching, and I knew he had to be exhausted. He usually took charge of most everything inside the kitchen.

After I took the rest and put them away, I stepped close again. Aside from leaning over a bit and bracing his hands on the edge of the stainless steel counter, he still hadn't moved. His eyes remained where the dishes had been.

"Is it because the guys aren't in the cabin anymore? I'm sorry if you feel like I've taken them away or something. Maybe someone would be willing to—"

"What?" he asked, his eyes blinking faster than they had a moment before.

"Uh … you aren't sleeping. Is it because they guys have been staying with me? I'm sorry if so."

"No." The word was drawn out in his smooth, rich tone. I shivered, thinking about how sleepy and sexy it sounded. He blinked a few more times and shook his head. "It's not that. Not the entire reason anyway."

"You haven't stayed out tracking longer than the others, have you?"

"I have, but only because I wanted to. I've needed the extra activity lately."

"Oh," I whispered, my thoughts wandering again. Maybe I'd read into the hug the other night. It could have been a simple way for him to show his support for my relationship with the other guys, to show that he had accepted us. He might want nothing to do with me. That thought hurt worse than anything. Even with Rosie saying all of our time here was limited, would Elijah choose not to leave with us if the guys came with me? I hated that I could be the reason to split them up, especially him and Loch. They had come here together, had obviously endured a lot in their pasts. I wasn't sure how I could handle causing their separation.

"I'm just going to grab something to eat, then I'll be out of your way." I had no idea if I was the reason he needed more activity, but I wouldn't ask him. He seemed exhausted and unfocused. Avoiding any discussion that could bring up my future with the guys or with him was best. Even though he'd always been calm and rational, I didn't want to risk upsetting him and ruining a chance to get to know him better.

I opted to keep lunch even more simple, snagging an apple from the fruit bowl on the counter and a bottled sweet tea from the fridge.

"Is that all you're eating," he asked, his body turning as I moved to leave. He leaned his high and tight ass back against the counter and crossed his thick arms over his chest. I almost felt jealous of the thin T-shirt stretching over his torso, hugging him so closely. I wanted to hug him again, too. The way his body and scent had wrapped around me the other night had instantly made me crave more of him.

I held up the apple with a smile and stopped before I reached the door to leave. "Yeah. It's close enough to dinner anyway. I'm gonna take this and maybe a nap too." I obviously hadn't been on the long patrols they had been doing, but I had been just as exhausted physically. With how much the guys had been working me in the bedroom, all of my muscles ached. Not that I was complaining. I loved the lingering soreness from sex, especially between my legs. My thighs clenched instinctively, and I sighed. I would never tire of them and their appetites.

He nodded and licked his lips again. There was a look in his eye that held me in place, seeing he wanted to say something else. When a few moments passed, and he hadn't spoken, I resigned to being wrong and took a step. His long arm snapped out but didn't touch me. It was an immediate physical reaction to get me to stay, his movements coming before any possible words.

Words still didn't follow, so I made a move, taking two steps closer to him as his arm dropped and his hand hooked onto the counter's edge beside his hip. "Do you wanna talk about it?" Lifting the apple, I took a large bite, the crisp snap like a shot inside the silent kitchen.

He watched, eyeing my mouth as I chewed. When he reached out for the apple, I held it up for him. His eyes never left mine as his hand wrapped over my grip. Instead of lifting my arm, he leaned down and bit into the fruit.

I didn't want to think it was sexual. I mean, he was simply taking a bite of my apple while I held it. But there was no denying that it held some significance to him because his stare had gone from sleepy to intense, his dilated pupils overtaking his irises in a flash.

Nothing could have taken my eyes away while his large lips spread over the apple flesh and his teeth sunk in. Not even when he drew back and chewed his bite slowly could I have pried my eyes from him. He was beyond attractive, with lustrous olive skin and soul-stealing brown eyes. He could have been on a billboard in Times Square on New Year's Eve, modeling the latest and greatest. That's how good-looking he was. Classically handsome, with a face and body that completely shut down a person's mind while their eyes soaked him in. Without witnessing him walk along a busy street or enter a random coffee shop, I knew he'd have every eye on him, every breath in the area hitched, and a wad of number-scrawled napkins in his pocket as proof.

I lifted my eyebrows at him as he finished chewing, the apple clutched in my hand now hanging limply at my side. "Was that your way of making me get something else to eat?"

The dimple in his chin seemed to twitch at the same time the corners of his lips did. "Nah. Well, maybe that too. But really, it was my curiosity again. About your generosity."

My eyebrows quirked another time. "A test? And did I pass?"

He licked his lips, and I had to blink a few times to keep from thinking about those lips in other places ...

"You've only ever passed. You're much more than I ever expected … more than any of us thought you'd be."

"Ah," I said with a soft chuckle. "I've heard something like this before. Y'all assumed I'd be some monster, right?"

His head shook the slightest bit. "It was a normal expectation of another chick coming here for a couple weeks or a month to get straightened out or whatever. Usually with giant attitudes, self-centered and uncaring, looking for a hookup or someone with a powerful family to support them so they could leave their own."

"Oh. Nope. But I am just another cliché, lost girl, numbed by her past … with a big attitude." I laughed at the last part, and he surprised me by chuckling too.

"Maybe. But your attitude had everything to do with self-preservation and nothing to do with selfishness."

With a hum, I pondered his meaning. "I suppose. I'd planned to keep to myself. Think I should have?"

"No," he said without hesitating. "I know we kinda made that impossible. Actually, I might have left you alone … But I'm glad that the others didn't. You've been good for them. How selfless you are …"

"But not for you?" I asked, unable to ignore the way he'd said "them."

"Well … that's another reason I've been keeping busy."

I wanted badly to ask, but I held my tongue, waiting for him to explain.

He inhaled, glanced around the kitchen, then at his feet for a moment. "I don't usually sleep well. And lately, I've been sleeping better, actually. I think ... no, I'm sure it has to do with you and your scent. Your smell calms me, and I've been fighting that realization."

"Why?" I wondered out loud. The word had slipped out on a breath, and as much as I regretted it, it relieved me. I wanted to know.

He crossed his arms and smacked his lips together with a gentle nod as if he were debating the truth. Finally, he looked at me and tilted his head a little. "I didn't want to like you. I didn't want to admit that you weren't like all the others. That you were selfless and kind, willing to jump into a fight that wasn't yours, to stick your neck out for four guys you knew nothing about and who had treated you cold from the start. Not many people or wolves would do that. Most have strong self-preservation instincts, especially when it involves situations that can lead to danger or repercussions. You stood up to Jackson and Trig for Zavier, not even knowing them, barely knowing him, and only seeing what they'd done. You took what had happened and rolled on without complaint, having to clean up messes that weren't yours. You were promised chores in the kitchen and didn't throw a fit when Zavier told you it wasn't happening. You volunteered to make Koni dinner for no real reason except that it was his favorite food. And ..."

And? I breathed in, my head swimming in his words, in his praises. But I still didn't understand completely.

He gazed at me, studying my reactions for a moment. His eyebrows furrowed the tiniest amount as his eyes scanned my face. "And you stopped Nima from touching Zavier that night while he was starting a flare. And before that, he told me you had asked him ... That you wouldn't touch him without him saying yes."

I tipped my chin down, starting at my feet and considering his last words. He'd stressed them differently as if they meant more than all the rest. And then I thought about what he'd said in the cabin, how he'd spoken about that night before, about consent. Next, my mind went back to their admissions in the kitchen about their transitions. Elijah had said he'd been alone in a dark basement.

Stud. That was the final nickname. His nickname.

Oh my God.

3

The apple fell from my hand onto the floor. I wanted to vomit. My stomach churned as I stared at him, the breakfast I'd eaten hours before rolling around in my belly violently as my mind conjured thoughts of what may have happened in his past, things so horrid that my body wanted to expel everything.

I swallowed thickly and took a deep breath, trying my hardest to gain control over myself.

Elijah blinked at me, and the corners of his mouth turned down a bit, obviously seeing my mood shift, possibly seeing the realization that I'd come to. There had been no hiding my reaction when the pieces clicked. I was struggling too hard to keep my food digested to care what my face had looked like.

"Ah." His voice was a whisper. He cleared his throat as he bent to pick up the apple. "You just went really pale. Are you sure you don't want something else? Hang on," he said, leaving my side then tossing the apple into the trash before dipping into the pantry. If he knew what I'd been thinking, he made no further mention of it. He returned only a few seconds later with a few energy bars clutched in one of his large hands. The other reached out to me.

I stared down at it as it hooked mine and entwined our fingers.

"You said you wanted a nap. Can I come with you?"

My eyes traveled up the body that had stepped right in front of me. Tipping my head back to meet his eyes, I looked deeply into them, seeing what he was offering. More. He had made the choice to open for me. I'd been so worried about how to approach him before, knowing that he was as different as the others. With him being a bit more silent, more reserved, I thought it would take more time. But now …

"Yes. I'd like that very much," I replied, squeezing hold of his hand.

We walked the entire way to the cabin connected that way. His long fingers wrapped around the back of my hand in a firm grasp, but he didn't pull or tug me along. He let go when we climbed the three steps, watching me enter and almost hesitating before following. After I removed my parka and stomped and kicked off my boots, he stomped and stayed at the entry, as he'd done so many times before, hesitating again.

"You don't have to stay. I understand if you'd rather go back to your own cabin and—"

"No," he said, seeming to snap out of his thoughts. He extended his other hand to me, holding out the chocolate energy bars. "I want to stay. Promise you'll eat one of these soon. If not now, then after the nap."

I took hold of them and set them onto the circle table while he unlaced his boots and kicked them off. When he finished, I stood there dumbly, still unable to gather my wits.

"Can I lie down with you?" he asked, dipping his head a bit as he looked toward the bedroom doorway.

"Yeah," I said, reaching out for his hand, still unsure how I should handle the situation.

He took it and let me lead him into the back bedroom. "Sorry it's not made. The guys left earlier than me, and I was too tired to care when I left for chores."

He blinked at the bed, which had since grown into four twin beds pushed together. He inhaled, and I couldn't stop myself from shivering at the sight. I knew he was taking it all in, the smells of the guys and me together. The potent smell of sex still lingered from our early morning quickie before they'd each had to leave.

"If it's a—"

"No, Teagan." He chuckled a little with a sigh. "You're so nice, so sweet." His eyes dipped to meet mine. "This is fine. It's perfect, actually. It'll help me."

"I don't understand."

"I'll explain. Can we?" He nodded toward the beds.

"Yeah," I said, crawling onto the beds first and turning on my side as he settled in beside me.

He lifted one of the blankets over us and wrapped an arm around my back, pulling me closer against his chest. "Is this all right?"

I inhaled him, letting his leathery scent invade my senses. It was warm and welcoming. The little bits of citrus hit me too, the bursts of freshness like invigorating shots to my mind. "More than all right." I burrowed into him.

"I agree," he said, his warm breath spreading over the top of my head as he spoke into my hair.

My hands were pinned between us. I opened them and started to explore, shifting them over his chest.

His muscles tensed beneath my touch, and his entire body stilled.

"I'm sorry," I said, wincing at my stupidity and eagerness. I had a feeling what had happened to him, and the thought of it hurt. But being in this position, being pressed against him, I fell into a comfortableness that made me forget all too quickly.

"It's okay. It's okay." The repeated words were breathy, and I wondered if he was trying to reassure me or convince himself. After a moment, he spoke again, his smooth tone back to normal. "Maybe just let me touch you if that's okay."

"Yes." I kept myself as still as possible, resisting the urge to explore him more, surrendering that control to him.

"I'm trying … I have some things I've been working through. It's why I've been hesitant with you, more so than the other guys have been. It's why I wasn't as interested to begin with. I can promise you it has nothing to do with you. You're beyond what I'd imagined." He let out a long breath. "There was no real concern again until now. I've been able to avoid girls, women, while living here. Kept my distance from any who stayed. None tried to force anything with me, like what Nima tried with Zavier."

I felt his arms tighten around me as he inhaled deeply, the bicep under my head flexing a little as he shifted his position some, and I prepared myself for what he was about to tell me.

"You, though … This past week and a half has really fucked me up. I told you that your smell calms me. Well, female scents have only repulsed me for a while. But yours … it enticed me." He chuckled, and I wanted to melt in his arms. The sound against his chest was deep and soothing. "You coming here was probably the worst problem I've faced in a while. I knew after you hit Jackson that there was no keeping you away. We all felt it, especially then, like fate had dropped you here to wreck us. That was the only way I could see it at first because I never planned to be with a woman again, sexually, I mean. I would have turned gay if that were an option, but I can tell you it wasn't. I love the guys, just not that way." He paused for a minute, considering. I held still, breathing him in, wanting anything and everything he'd give me.

"Loch probably told you we met after he fled the wolf fights up north." I nodded against his chest, and he continued on. "I fled my pack a couple of days before, crossed paths with him, and then we came here. My family was involved in some fighting. I heard them talking about it. I never saw that end of things, though. For me, there was a different kind of torture." He laughed bitterly and pressed his lips to my head for a moment. "Some wouldn't see sex that way, would think I was lucky … But most didn't know exactly what happened. I was used for years, before and after my transition. My family sold my body for profit. Visiting and local packs paid them to fuck me, whether it be for regular pleasure or during a female's transition, sometimes males too."

My fingers clenched his shirt so tightly, I feared they might break. Hate and anger coursed through me, quickening my pulse and my breaths. I felt sick all over again for him, knowing that I'd been right about what had happened when I wished to be wrong.

"Elijah," I whispered, tears rushing from my eyes. "I'm so sorry."

"Eli, okay? Call me Eli or whatever else you want to. Not my full name anymore from you, okay?"

"Okay," I answered, pressing closer to him and tightening my grip on his shirt so I wasn't tempted to wrap him in my arms. As much as I wanted to let his history go, I had a burning need to know more, the ending most of all. "Are they ... Is your pack still there?"

"No. When Loch and I found each other, I wasn't in a good place, wasn't in my own mind. I owe him a lot, actually. Both of us were fucked up in those days following, but really, if I hadn't met him, I'm not sure I would be here, alive. When I first escaped, it was because my mother"—he grit out the word in a harsh rasp—"had given me the wrong dose of tranquilizer before restraining me for the next client. I killed her and her two sisters who stayed there. I took off but felt guilty for not waiting for my father and the other mates of their pack. So I went back and ended them too. I'd planned to return again, but I wandered farther south. That was when I found Loch and snapped out of the blinding need for revenge. It was good that I had because the police found the house around the same time we dropped off the information for the fight ring. It was on the news, written up as murders."

"So you ended who hurt you." I sniffled, trying to rein in my tears.

"Yes. Not everyone, not the countless women and men who paid. I blame them too. Not the young ones, though, the ones my own age at the time whose family brought them and paid. They were innocent, didn't know any different."

I lost it then, my sobs heavy and uncontrollable. "I want to hurt them, Eli."

"Teagan. My angel." He breathed deeply. "Fate didn't drop you here to wreck us. I know that now. It gave us an angel, one to heal us. I might have been lost forever if you hadn't come."

"I think we would have found each other somehow," I mused, letting him steer us away from the heaviness of his past. I would be his angel, be his light if he needed me to be.

"Maybe. But it doesn't matter now. You're here with us, with me. I know the guys have talked about you leaving, and they were laying it on me pretty thick."

"Did they push you?" I asked, suddenly tense about it all.

"No, no, they didn't. They just knew that I needed a little shove, I think. And after what happened the other night, seeing you and them ... I felt the same, knew that we need you too. So I guess we'll have to figure some things out between us, huh?"

"Yeah, I've told them how much you all mean to me, that I'm willing to stay here, give up what I have at home ... But yes, we need to talk more about it. I spoke to Rosie about things too."

"I can guess what she told you. She always reminds us this place isn't forever. But she'll give us the time we need. So don't be worried about that right now, okay?"

"Okay."

"Good." One of his hands played with the ends of my hair while the other trailed down my back with long, smooth strokes. "This is unbelievably comfortable. You feel so good tucked here with me."

I chuckled lightly. "You feel great too."

"I'm close to passing out. Are you still all right with sleeping for a bit?"

"Can't think of anything better."

4

"Look at this," a rasped voice cut into my sleep. For a moment, I thought I was dreaming. And it sure was a good one, soaked with the smell of leather and citrus but surrounded by all The Four. All of us in a big bed together.

"Damn," a clipped voice said from somewhere close.

"Fucking hell. That looks so peaceful. Lucky fucker," another voice piped in.

Zavier. Loch. Koni. My mind sorted through their voices without needing to open my eyes.

"Don't you fucking dare get into that bed, Stray," Zavier whisper yelled. "Not unless you want to catch a bullet in the other ass cheek."

I giggled silently, unable to help it.

"Beautiful, you are something, aren't you?" Loch asked, and I peeked my eyes open.

My face was still buried into Eli's chest, and the light had dimmed inside the bedroom, but I could see them standing beside the bed easily enough. I smiled and blinked up at them.

"Shh," Zavier said, smacking Koni in the chest with a soft thud since he was in the middle of the three of them. "Go back to sleep, baby. We're grabbing some dinner, but we'll see you later tonight."

I blinked again and pursed my lips into a kissy face before they turned and left the room. After a soft click from the front door and some hushed words sounding from outside, I sighed and settled into sleep, still nestled into Eli.

When I woke again, I was flat on my back and the room was almost totally dark. The main light of the cabin was on, slicing into the doorway.

Eli's breaths cut quick and heavy through the cabin's silence, making me open my eyes fully and turn my head to face him.

He was lying on his side, staring at me.

"Hey," I said, unsure about the intensity I could plainly see in his gaze. "Are you all right?"

"Yeah," he replied after another sharp breath. "I have nightmares a lot. The one I just had … it wasn't that bad. I could smell you. It made it better, made me sleep harder. I don't normally. A pin could drop and I'll wake up."

"Oh. Well, that's good then, right?"

"Yeah. Really good. Fuck. I feel great. My head … my thoughts are clearer than they usually are after waking up. Despite that bit of dreaming, I feel relaxed, which is really hard for me to do at night."

I kept still. "I want to touch you. I won't. But I had to tell you because I want to be honest about how I'm feeling too."

He sighed, and I saw a smile tug at his lips. "I'm glad that you want both, to be honest and to touch me. And I would love to tell you to touch me, but I need some more time, I think. Or I'm not sure. Maybe ... Fuck. I want you. I'm fucking hard right now. My body wants you more than it's wanted anything else. I need to feel you. To be inside of you."

"I want that too. You can," I said, almost begging him. If it were anyone else, I'd be embarrassed by how eager my voice sounded. But I felt that way because I knew how big of a change it was for him.

"Maybe if I ..." He glanced around the dark room. "I need more light, to be able to see you, to know it's you. Is that okay?"

"Yes."

"Can you undress while I do the same?"

I nodded with a hum as he lifted himself from the bed and moved to the corner dresser. As soon as he flicked the lamp on, I peeled off my shirt and bra. When he did the same with his shirt, I stared at his body, half highlighted and half shadowed by the new light. A dusting of dark hair covered his chest and its deep olive-toned skin. Like Koni and Loch, he had no tattoos. But, unfortunately, like Loch, he had some scars. Not as many, but they were there. A few on his neck that I'd known about and a few light lines running down his torso. I wanted to kiss down them, to show him I would cherish him and never hurt him. My fingers itched to reach out, but I moved them to my jeans instead, unfastening then hooking the waist. I kept my eyes on him while I left the bed and slid my jeans and underwear off with my socks.

He paused a moment, his hands hitched on his jeans as he watched me crawl back onto the bed. His lips parted as he took in my bare body then he continued undressing, bending over to push down his own jeans. When he stood back up, I saw his impressive cock for the first time, its shaft long and thick, curving slightly downward under its own weight.

"You're gorgeous," I said with a breathy sigh.

"So are you," he replied, biting down on his lip. "I haven't done anything in …"

"It's okay. I just want you to do what you feel good with. No matter what that is. Tell me what you want." I offered myself readily because I wanted him so badly. Whatever he was willing to give, even if it was to sleep, I'd take it.

"I'm used to being …" He rubbed at his neck, at his wrists. So, yeah, he'd been tied up or chained, like Loch. Only his had been for sex, and it hadn't been consensual.

I swallowed, pushing those thoughts away as quickly as I could.

"Maybe if you don't touch me. Let me touch you."

"Yes," I agreed as I lay back in the center of the beds. Since the short bedposts were close enough together at the foot and head of each bed, I reached over my head, stretching my body long, and wrapped my palms around the posts. It would keep my hands on something so I wouldn't be tempted to grab hold of him.

He flinched a bit and shook his head as if to shake a memory.

"Is this all right?"

"Yeah," he said, then crawled onto the bed with me. His hand pressed lightly to my stomach, and he leaned his face closer. "You are so beautiful, Teagan." His lips—his full and luscious lips—pushed down onto my mouth, their plumpness enveloping mine. After a second, they parted, and I followed his lead, feeling his tongue slip along my lower lip, tasting me slowly. I opened wider with him. His mouth slanted, and his tongue licked inside to meet mine.

He sighed into my mouth, and I felt his hand shift up my stomach, higher and higher until it covered my breast fully. It kneaded my soft flesh reverently. His body leaned in, his cock pushing against my hip.

I writhed a bit, the longing to touch him growing stronger by the second. Every sweep of his tongue, every touch of his hand on my breast was driving me wild.

"Angel," he murmured over my lips as his fingers pinched my nipple. His mouth tilted, and his kisses moved down my chin onto my neck. He sucked and licked and kissed farther, his body adjusting beside me as he traveled down.

"Eli. Oh," I replied in an exhale as I gripped the bedposts harder, digging my nails in, fighting the urge to thread my fingers through his thick hair.

He didn't stop until his mouth was over my breast. His tongue bathed my hardened nipple before finally taking it into his mouth. My body rolled beneath his touch. Staying propped on one elbow, he moved his free hand, sliding past my stomach, down over my pussy. He cupped me, then moaned against my breast as his finger dipped into my slickness and found my clit. His fingertip mimicked the actions of his tongue over my nipple, swirling and flicking. After a moment, that single finger slid to my entrance and pushed inside.

"Ah!" I cried out at the sensation and tipped my hips up, trying to chase his hand as his finger retreated.

That seemed to snap a tether inside him. He unlatched his mouth from my nipple and climbed down my body. His hands wrenched my legs wide, spreading me as he settled himself between them. His mouth was on my pussy within another moment, quick and forceful.

I cried out louder as his tongue began its assault, licking my lips, thrusting inside, then sliding up to my clit. He puckered against me there and sucked hard, drawing another loud cry from me. "Eli!"

"Angel," he murmured while he continued to lick. He pushed two fingers inside me and curled them. My muscles tensed and seized in response. "Fuck. This is so good. Your smell, the way you feel, how you sound …"

He hadn't stopped fucking me with his fingers, fast, fast, fast. His tongue continued to circle and sweep. My climax hit hard, my pussy clenching around his fingers as I cried out again, my body arching, my nails digging into the wooden bedpost to the point of pain.

"Yes. Oh yes. Why did I wait so long to taste you? My God, you're delicious." His mouth and lips made the most erotic and offensive sounds as he lapped up my juices and drank me down. "I wasn't sure I could, but I want to … I need to fuck you."

"Yes, please," I begged. "Please, fuck me."

He kissed my stomach as he knelt up between my legs. "I'm so turned on." His hand pumped down his massive shaft.

I groaned as I watched, wanting to suck him. Licking my lips, I murmured to myself, "Maybe next time."

"Maybe," he replied, watching me, reading exactly what was on my mind.

I spread my legs wider, anticipating the feel of him, knowing his big body needed the room and his large cock needed it too.

He leaned down and ran his tip along me, then slid his shaft up and down between my lower lips, getting wet.

He clamped his jaw with a groan. "Oh fuck. I'm not sure I'll last. I want to come all over you right now, just from doing this. From smelling you, tasting you, being on top of you."

"Please. Whatever you want." As much as I craved him buried inside, I would take it all. "Anything."

His fingers moved to my clit again and began rubbing my sensitive flesh there, building me up. He wanted me to go again, realizing he wouldn't last. The thought pinched at my heart, seeing how caring and thoughtful he was through this experience, where I knew he was struggling with his own thoughts and memories.

"Ah, ah, ah," I murmured, taking in every feeling, my body pliant beneath him.

When I began to pant, he pushed his thick tip inside me with a hiss. He paused for only a second before shoving himself in fully with a single, hard thrust.

"Ah!"

"Fuck!" He stilled instantly. "Shit, angel. I shouldn't have—Did I hurt you?"

"No," I replied, inhaling as my body relaxed around him. "I'm okay. I like it. You're so hard. So big." My body rolled, needing more.

He let out a raspy breath as if he were relieved he hadn't hurt me but also struggling to maintain his control. His fingers circled my clit again and again, pushing and building me up.

I panted. "Yes. Yes."

He pulled away, his cock nearly coming out before he slammed back in. This time though, he didn't stop, didn't wait. He went out and in again, harder. In two more strokes, I was screaming his name to the ceiling as I came. My body shook, my orgasm tearing through me so fiercely I could barely breathe.

He pumped inside relentlessly, watching me fall apart beneath him. His fingers stopped, and he bared down, rutting rougher and faster. It didn't take him long, mere moments after me, and he was roaring his release too.

"Teagan! Fuck. Ah. That's so good, angel." His body sagged as his thrusts slowed to a stop. He bowed his head as he caught his breath over me.

I kept still, my pussy vibrating with aftershocks around his softening dick. "So good." As soon as I loosened my grasp on the bedposts, Eli's head lifted.

His eyes shifted between my hands and my eyes, and then his lips curved into a sweet smile. I smiled with him, loving how calm and happy he looked, knowing it was all for me. One hand supported his body while the other grabbed mine and brought it up to his mouth. He pressed a tender kiss to my palm before placing my hand over his heart. "This is yours, completely."

5

We cleaned up together in the bathroom, then grabbed the energy bars he'd brought and ate them as soon as we settled into bed. It had been mostly quiet between us, only soft murmurs of appreciation, smiles, and heated gazes exchanged during those few minutes.

I snagged the bottle of water I'd left on the dresser and drank some down before handing him the rest. He took it, watching me as I lay back down.

"Thank you," he said, replacing the cap and tossing the empty container onto the floor.

"I should be thanking you," I quipped as he settled in beside me.

He chuckled at my joke, and my heart squeezed at the reality of it, at how comfortable he'd gotten with me. It felt as natural with him as it had with the others, and now I couldn't even think of being without him too.

"You know what I mean," he said, turning to me. His arm wrapped over my side, pulling me into him again like the way we'd slept earlier.

"I know," I replied softly, gazing up at him, my face slightly lower than his but above his chest this time. I kept my hands tucked as I had before, leaving them in relaxed fists so I wasn't tempted to spread them wide over his chest.

We'd remained naked, not bothering with the clothes we abandoned. He still wanted to feel my skin, and I wanted to feel his as well.

"I know we need to talk it over with the others, but I want you to know I'll follow you anywhere. I'm yours. It wasn't a lie."

I inhaled his scent and exhaled slowly, my eyes searching his. "I know you aren't lying. I'm just worried that I'm being selfish, having and wanting you all. Maybe someone else will come along and—"

"No," he said, cutting me off. "There's no one else. And there won't be for me. For us. The four of us knew we'd stay together, even before you came here. None of us had set goals for the future, though, or thoughts of coupling. We'd discussed things, about girls and all, just never made plans. The fact that you attracted all of us as soon as you arrived ... we just knew. It made sense. I thought it would be messy at first, especially when Loch took your stuff and donated his clothes. He told us that it was to make a point."

"Zavier said it was a reminder to keep you guys away."

He chuckled. "Yeah. So when you stood up for Z and seemed to strip us all down whenever you flashed your beautiful gray eyes our way ... I had a bad feeling there'd be fights, that we'd be ripped apart if you chose one of us. Z and Loch fought that night you ... uh ..."

"Gave him a hand?" I offered with a breathy giggle, thinking about giving Zavier the hand job in the bathhouse.

He tipped his head back and barked a laugh. When his body stopped shaking, he met my eyes. "Fuck, you are gorgeous. Yeah, when you gave him a hand. But that wasn't even really a fight. I think we all knew it was something different. So, yeah, I'm so glad you want us all. And believe me, we like it that way, wouldn't want it any different."

"Good," I said, letting out a breath. "I wasn't exactly prepared to give any of you up, anyway."

His arm squeezed me tighter. "So tell me about home."

Home. The way he said it, already solidifying it into his mind, already accepting that it would be the place we went after this. Home. So instead of treating it as being my own, I decided to share it immediately. It was ours. Our home. Even if they hadn't yet stepped foot on the property, hadn't yet seen it with their own eyes, it was ours.

"Well, we have twenty acres of wooded land not far from Greenville, Alabama. It borders a protected forest there. The house is an older two-story Victorian, with a turret and a wrap-around porch with Tuscan columns. Four bedrooms. A finished basement. It's had a bunch of updates done but still could use more, eventually. Aside from working at the restaurant, it's where I spent all of my time before coming here."

"Wow." His voice was as soft as the touch of his fingertips running up and down my spine. "That sounds peaceful. Beautiful. What was the name of the restaurant again?"

"The Back Burner. It's about ten miles from the house, closer to the highway. It's a standalone building with its own lot and parking. But it's a great location, so the lack of neighboring foot traffic doesn't hurt the business that bad. My Aunt Sonya manages the place. We had about twenty employees before …" When I hesitated to continue down that road, he leaned down to kiss my lips in gentle reassurance. I blinked up at him as he kept silent. "She hired some humans when the few who remained chose to leave. As far as I know, it's running just fine. I'm not sure if she would tell me otherwise, though. Not right now anyway."

"Sounds like your aunt is a smart woman, even smarter for sending you here. We owe her, and I'm looking forward to meeting her … and moving there with you. That is, if you're wanting us to come."

I lifted an eyebrow at him, scrunched my nose, and teased, "I suppose I wouldn't mind." After a moment, I asked, "Won't you all miss it here? Miss Rosie and Tim?"

"Sure," he said with a nod. "They're our family, in a way. But there are always more who need their help. Plus, it's not really that far from here, right? We can come visit easily enough."

I smiled and nuzzled into his neck. "Yes. It's not bad. I flew here, but I think it's less than eight hours by car."

When he shifted to tighten his hold on me, he leaned back a bit, grabbed my hand, then moved it up and over his back, settling my palm onto his skin, letting me hold him. I sighed deeper as he gripped me closer.

"We can talk to the guys later, but I think they'd be ready to leave right after your transition. That's what you had planned, right?"

"That was the plan, yeah, to return right away since my aunt is handling everything at home. She wanted me here for that and to hide. It made sense. Especially considering she would have had more to deal with if I had stayed and transitioned there, and even more than that if my Uncle Raif found out about my family's deaths and showed up."

Eli tensed up. "Loch told me about that. I hope you don't mind that he did."

"No, it wasn't a secret from you guys."

"I didn't think so, but I was glad he told me. It actually helped push me closer to you too. And I'm sure it's helped all of us with the decision to leave here, to go be with you and help you there, protect you."

I faked a gasp. "And if I don't need protection?"

He chuckled. "You don't, angel. I don't doubt that. I'm really looking forward to seeing you shift, see how much stronger you are. See your fur, your teeth, your gorgeous wolf body and the way you move and fight with it. But I also know it's always better to have numbers on your side. Also, there's no way we'd let you fight alone, ever again, whether or not you need the help. If you had to fight a mouse, I would still be there to cover your neck so the little fucker couldn't get at your throat."

Those few words were possibly the most heartwarming claim of devotion I'd ever heard. "I can accept that."

"Good, because you really don't have another choice," he stated, his rich tone dropping deeper. After a silent moment, he said, "We'll talk to the guys later, but I know they feel the same and will want to go right away with you. We can work more things out after we get there. Loch and Koni will need more schooling. I already have my GED. All of us have driver's licenses except for Loch. I'm sure we can pick up jobs easily enough. Or do you think your aunt will be open to hiring us at The Back Burner?"

A breathy laugh escaped me. "Wow, you are on it with the planning, huh?" He chuckled and pressed his lips to my forehead. "You're sure you're okay with jumping ahead so fast? You're getting my hopes up, and I want you all to be sure."

"There's nothing to worry about. We're coming with you. And it's exciting to me, to think about all of us living together, being with you. I haven't felt this way. Ever. I never thought much about a future after here. But the thought of having you and a place together …" He let out a long breath. "I think you get the picture."

"I get it. And I'm excited now, too. I think we might need to knock down a few walls to make a bigger master bedroom."

"Ha! Now who's the one jumping ahead?" His smile was contagious. He tipped his chin and pressed his lips to mine, a low rumble of contentment vibrating inside his throat. His hand roamed over my back, skimming down to the top of my ass before making its way back up under my hair to my neck.

I kept my palm flat and still on his back, not willing to risk disrupting his comfort.

A few minutes passed before he sighed then pressed a small kiss to my forehead. "I've got to get up. I'm on watch with Tim again tonight." He rolled out of bed, and I didn't mind the view, even if he was covering up. "I know it'll be tricky to get us all together to discuss everything. So if you talk to them tonight, tell them my thoughts."

"Okay," I agreed. "Not sure all of them are off right away, but I'll tell whoever is."

"Good." He finished pulling up jeans then slid into his white shirt, drawing the edge down over his stomach then looking at me. "I'm hitting the kitchen first. You want me to bring you something?"

"No, I'll go soon. Just want to lay here in your scent a little longer," I admitted and watched his eyes go wide before an enormous smile took over his face.

"I like that. I like my scent all over you. I'll see you in the morning then, angel." He leaned over the bed, and I sat up to meet him, sighing as his palms cradled my face and his mouth took control of mine with an all-too-short and extremely enticing kiss.

"See you then."

He winked and then disappeared into the main part of the cabin. After getting into his boots, the front door clicked closed.

But I wouldn't see him in the morning after all. I wouldn't see any of them until much later.

6

I was almost tempted to fall back to sleep, knowing that I would need the strength later whenever Loch, Zavier, and Koni returned from their boundary duty. Instead, I'd gotten up and prepared to get food, which was equally important. Refueling for another night of sex was crucial with these guys. My body needed the energy for their insatiable appetites.

Before I could leave the bedroom, loud bursts ripped through the night's silence. Gunshots. Again! They didn't sound as close as they had been when Koni was shot, but there was no mistaking the noise. I rushed around, flipping on my parka before slipping into my boots. Fear rocked through my body, making my muscles tremble. The thought of someone else getting shot had me struggling to breathe. I battled with my second boot and gave up on tying it when my fingers shook too heavily to hold the laces.

I wrenched open the door seeing a body shift into wolf form right before disappearing around the lake, into the darkness and woods. The rule of shifting directly in camp was pretty clear-cut, except in emergency situations. Hunters were considered an emergency. They were also important enough to warrant another unofficial rule, which I'd learned the night Koni had been shot. Everyone capable was to respond to gunshots in case someone needed help.

The silence that followed was deafening. Stepping out fully onto the porch, I glanced around and strained my ears for anything that might tell me what was happening out in the mountains. It was dead calm. My heart raced, and I struggled to keep my breaths quiet to listen even harder. I moved down the steps, walking farther from the cabin's light to see and hear more clearly.

Snow crunched not far away and repeated a few more times. Footsteps. Not rushed at all.

A faint whine came next, and that simple sound made my heart stop.

"Hello? Who's there? Are you hurt? Are you—"

Pain exploded inside my head, cutting off my words, my sight, my thoughts ...

My head thumped in an indescribable amount of pain, forcing me to wake. My body was folded in a fetal position across a seat. A car seat, I realized, my front tipped downward toward the leather backing. I glanced up at the roof and the rear window, seeing no stars or moon in the night sky. My feet hung over the edge of the seat, one foot colder than the other. I rubbed them together, feeling the uneven tread of one boot against the sole of my sock-covered foot. I was missing a boot.

Cold air. Silence. The car was still. Not running. The scent inside was distinctly male but biting and bitter, like acid in my nose.

Someone had hit me. Someone had taken me? As soon as those thoughts registered, I shifted my body then bit down on my lower lip as pain pounded through my head. Instinctively, I lifted my hand to find the injury, only to feel a sharp stab of pain in my upper arm, too, in one isolated spot, not radiating all over.

I held back a groan, trying to adjust my body. Howls sounded in the distance. Many long cries I knew to be calls of unity for anything from gathering to grief. They weren't happy yips, yelps, or barks.

How close was I to camp? Was I still at camp?

My eyelids drooped. My thoughts grew hazy.

"Come on," a voice murmured, making my eyes snap wide open to the darkness again.

Rushed footsteps followed, then a blinding overhead light inside flickered on as a door was yanked open at my feet.

While the car's engine turned over, a blurry person lifted my legs and slid into the back seat with me. "Go! He's already at his mark."

"Help," I said weakly as the light turned off and the car lurched forward, pushing my face against the seat. I wanted to scream. I wanted to kick. To fight. But I couldn't focus. My head hurt. My eyes were heavy, and my legs were too.

"Don't you worry, darlin'. You're gonna be just fine with us for now." The darkness spoke, and a hand patted my thigh before laughter followed.

Jackson.

"I said open up, bitch!" someone shouted, waking me and the monstrous pain in my head.

I shifted, feeling my face still pressed against the car seat, my legs still folded. My eyes opened, and I winced at the harsh daylight streaming into the car windows.

"We have your niece here. Your only family, right? Isn't your brother the one who got everyone slaughtered? Some pack legacy he left behind."

Oh no. Aunt Sonya? Was I home?

I shifted again, my head swimming with pain but also drowsiness that continued to weigh my body down. My mouth was a desert, dry and barren. I gritted my teeth, twisting around in the seat.

"She's awake," a voice muttered from the front. Not Trig. Not Jackson.

My eyes met Ford's as I turned fully. His hard stare cast over his shoulder. On the center console beside him lay two black hand-held radios—the two-ways from camp.

"Goody. Let's go, darlin'." Jackson's voice entered through the open window behind my head. The door opened a moment later, and arms reached in and tugged my body from the vehicle.

"Ah," I cried, my arms and legs flopping under their own weight, unable to match his quick, jerky movements as he dragged me out.

"Stand up," he ordered, and I felt something hard press into my temple.

"We were supposed to wait," Ford said.

"Yeah, well, he also told us no one would be here," Jackson snapped, hauling my body upward with one arm at my waist.

I wobbled, trying to get my feet beneath me.

"Christ. How much of that tranq did you give her? She's dead on her feet."

"What's the difference? She's about to be dead in a grave," Ford mumbled.

Jackson grunted and adjusted his hold. "Not our business what happens, especially after we leave."

"Could be useful since he hasn't fucking shown up yet." Another voice spoke. Higher pitched. Trig. "I wouldn't mind—"

"Fuck off with that." Jackson cut into his words. "We're delivering her. That's it. You want to risk adding more shit to your sentence if something goes down? We do this. Get the money and go. That's fucking it. You can get ass somewhere else."

"Think she's calling the cops?" Ford asked as pins and needles shot through my legs, my nerves sparking with sensation, adjusting to my upright position, or maybe simply waking up. Except for the raging headache, my body had been numb and asleep for hours.

With my legs holding weight and Jackson's grip at my waist, I settled into a shaky balance and finally lifted my eyes to the Victorian house I'd just told Eli about the night before.

The sun was high in the sky, so I knew it had to be midday or close to it. The bright rays beat down onto the gray house like any other normal day. I felt as if this day should have been cloudy, stormy, miserable. I'd felt the same in the days following my family's deaths. It was too bright and cheerful for death.

"I'm not opposed to killing her right now. I don't have the patience for this," Jackson called out loudly, and I saw movement behind the living room bay windows. "Step out with your hands up, or I end her right now and then end you right after. I'm sure Raif won't care if I did the dirty work. But if you do as we ask, you'll at least have some time to say goodbye."

"You took me for him?" I snarled through my teeth, finally getting an answer to what was happening. My body flashed hot. I was irate—at myself for being taken, and at Ford, Jackson, and Trig for this sideshow kidnapping.

"Ah. Welcome to the party, doll," he murmured close to my ear, digging a muzzle harder into my achy temple. Before I could ask any more questions, find out more specifics, a voice called from the house.

"I'm coming out. I know you don't want to be the one to harm her. Otherwise, you would have done it. But I'm no fool to throw more oil onto this fire." Aunt Sonya's southern twang rang loud and true, and then the door opened wide. She wore a white polo and black pants—her usual manager attire for The Back Burner. Her golden hair was wrapped into the top bun with a few tendrils hanging down to the sides of her tight jaw. Her cheeks were flushed with anger, nearly the same color as the red stain on her lips. She'd either left work early or had taken a lunch break to stop by the house. They hadn't expected her to be here in the middle of the day.

"Good choice," Jackson called back as Aunt Sonya held up her hands, exposing the shotgun she held and placing it down onto the porch. "Leave it and step down toward us."

Ford and Trig exited the car and slammed the doors as my aunt descended the steps and stopped on the stone walkway.

Her eyes found mine as Ford reached her and grabbed her arms to pin them at her back. "I'm sorry, Teagan."

I gritted my teeth at the anger rolling inside. I wasn't mad at her, though. It was everything else. "It's not your fault. It's mine."

"No," she said, wincing as Ford wrenched her arms harder at her back and yanked her around. "I should have had you use a false name, should have known that someone would know the leech Raif."

"Leech?" Ford answered with a growl. "That leech saved my life years ago."

Ah. So he knew my uncle. That had been the friend he'd mentioned, how he'd known about my father, my family.

"Well, congratulations to you," my aunt snapped, then turned her head and spat on him.

"Fucking bitch," he snarled, releasing one hand from her pinned arms and punching her in the side of the face.

She let out a cry as her head recoiled from the hit.

I stiffened as Jackson chuckled close to my ear. My body bucked in his hold, and I swung a heavy arm to strike him. My effort was shit. I barely connected with his chest.

He twisted me around and rammed the but of his gun against my face. My nose crunched and cracked, and a needle-sharp pain tore through me, adding more punishment to my headache. I immediately felt wetness leaking down over my mouth.

"I owed you that for the laundry cabin," Jackson said, dropping hold of my waist and grabbing my neck as he continued to walk us to the house. "Now, don't try anything again, or maybe I'll consider playing with you while we wait for your uncle to show."

I wrapped my hands around his wrist as his fingers squeezed harder, cutting off my air. I couldn't breathe, through my mouth or through my busted nose. My head throbbed from the pain and from the pressure building up beneath Jackson's tight grip. But none of those things were what my mind was focusing on. No. As bad as all of that was, there was something worse happening. I thought maybe I was imagining it or possibly adjusting to the warmer temperature of the Alabama winter sun. I wasn't. Whatever tranquilizer they'd given me was wearing off. And instead of feeling better about the numbness disappearing, I was wishing they'd given me another dose.

The pins and needles disappeared from my legs, replaced by the deep ache within my bones, the tight coil of my muscles, and the hot stretching of my skin.

7

No, no, no, I thought as Jackson, Trig, and Ford walked us into the house. Jackson released my neck as we entered, gripping my upper arm instead.

Trig had lifted the shotgun from the porch. He strode ahead of us, opening the barrel and checking for shells as he moved through the living room and disappeared into the back kitchen.

"Where are the rest of the weapons?" Ford asked, his beady eyes darting around the sparse room, searching.

"There are no more," Aunt Sonya said with a wince as he lifted her arms higher at her back.

"Bullshit. This is Alabama, and we're all wolves here. I know this place has more than a single shotgun. Tell us where or lose some teeth," he replied, spitting on her cheek with the words.

"Basement," I croaked out the answer for her, knowing there was no need for us to fight them on it. They would find them with a quick search, anyway. After watching drops of my blood hit the hardwood floor at my feet, I added, "I have to use the bathroom."

Trig reentered the room and gave a nod to Jackson before opening the basement door and disappearing again.

Jackson huffed an irritated breath. "Since I'd rather not sit near you smelling of piss. Where?"

"Off the kitchen," I replied, then took a ragged breath. My muscles quaked as I struggled to keep control—of the pain, the stress, the heat ... the anger.

Ford shoved Aunt Sonya forward through the doorway first, and Jackson moved us after. He shuffled us past the dining table, over to the small door beside the mudroom. While he peered inside the tiny bathroom, I watched Ford force Aunt Sonya down into a dining chair.

"Don't try anything," Jackson warned. There was no room for him to join, but he wasn't as stupid as he looked. He didn't bother shutting the door, leaving it open enough for his body to fit despite remaining outside. He eyed me, lifting a brow as if waiting for me to protest.

I pushed my jeans over my ass and eased back onto the seat, using my parka to shield him from seeing anything.

He chuckled and pointed his eyes toward the kitchen. "I wouldn't take you for modest since you've let those four assholes have your body."

I clenched my teeth at his comment, biting hard to stop from replying. Tears stung my eyes at the mention of The Four. They had to have discovered me missing by now, had to know I wouldn't have left on my own. But would they realize what happened? Would they care enough to worry?

Stop it, Teagan. They cared. I knew they cared. They were probably worried sick. And that thought made my chest hurt, my heart ache. Would they come for me? Would they even know where to come? That, I didn't know.

As soon as I finished, I shed the parka and removed my only boot, needing to cool my body. Sweat leaked from the pores of my boiling skin.

"Come on." Jackson yanked me from the bathroom, not letting me flush, wash my hands, let alone clean the blood still trickling from my nose.

"Yeah, they have a decent armory down there. A few rifles, Glocks, Sigs, some knives," Trig said, leaning his shaved head through the kitchen doorway and tossing something to Ford. Just as quickly, he disappeared again. "Off to check upstairs."

Ford checked the roll of plastic strips inside his hand and separated two long strands from the bunch. Zip ties. He tugged Aunt Sonya's hands behind the high-backed dining chair and secured her wrists.

"Sit," Jackson instructed me, releasing my upper arm while keeping his gun pointed at my head.

I dipped down in the seat beside Aunt Sonya, and Ford went about securing my wrists too. I writhed, barely feeling his bruising grip as another wave of heat and pain rolled beneath my skin, spreading through my body.

The thin plastic bit into my wrists with the slightest movement. My arms were so stretched and tight that I wasn't sure if it was their position or how they were reacting to the change churning deep within.

"Where the fuck is he? He should have been here fifteen minutes ago!" Jackson shouted, stalking around the corner to the mudroom to look out into the backyard and the surrounding forest.

"I'll go check the perimeter," Ford replied, standing from the seat he'd taken and removing the two-way he had inside his back pocket. "I'll call my location before reentering."

"You okay?" I whispered to Aunt Sonya.

Her head turned, her big green eyes roaming over my face. "I'm fine. Are you? You look ..."

I shook my head, not needing her to say what she could plainly see. That was the last thing I wanted. How might they react to me having a transition flare? There was a chance they wouldn't care, but that wasn't a good enough reason to call attention to it. I squirmed in my seat, my nerves pinching, my muscles coiling, and my bones throbbing. There was no relief this time. The Four weren't here to settle between my legs and ease my need. I rubbed my thighs together absently, thinking of their fingers, their mouths, their tongues, and finding no friction from my jeans or underwear.

Aunt Sonya growled her displeasure as Jackson walked back into the kitchen and opened the refrigerator.

"There ain't shit in here to drink. What the fuck?" He smacked the condiments around as if something new would suddenly appear.

Neither of us bothered to reply. There was no reason to explain that no one was currently living here.

"Alcohol," Jackson said, pointing the gun at Aunt Sonya.

"Dining room," she replied with a head tilt that made her wince. One side of her face was entirely red now, not only from rage but from the strike of Ford's fist.

"Don't even think of shifting. We'll end her before you have time to attack." Jackson tramped across the floor and pushed through the swinging door into the formal dining room.

"I'm going to fucking kill them all," I said, my voice gravelly from pain and rage.

"I'm with you," she whispered.

"Have you seen him?"

"Raif? No. I haven't seen his scarred face since he was cast out those years ago. Your father never liked your mom's brother. But when Raif skipped her funeral then showed up here trying to challenge him at his weakest moment … Well, you probably don't recall much. You were only seven, and your brothers kept you away from the chaos that night. He lost, obviously, and your father, even in mourning, bested Raif, scarring his face more the telling him to never return."

I clutched my hands together, wracked with pain and the truth of the past. "My father never told me all of that. It would have taken seconds, and he never bothered."

"He never thought it important enough to bother you with, Teenie. He never wanted to clog your mind with worry, especially over somebody who was never meant to be part of your life, our lives."

"But see, that's the messed up part. He is now, right? And honestly, it all involves someone who meant more to me than anyone else—my mom. As rotten as he was, Raif was mom's brother." I huffed a pained breath. Letting the past upset me now was stupid. There was no reason to dwell. "Dad didn't take what I might want into consideration. Just like everything else."

"I know," she said with a sigh. "He made some bad decisions with you. But I did too. I should have come around more, should have spent more time with you, especially when your father stopped. I could have pushed him harder to include you."

"It's not your fault. You aren't responsible for his actions. For any of their choices."

"I have some blame in it all. See, I'm the one who frequents the vampire bar. Purgatory. Where I took you for the supernatural meeting before camp. I've always been an outsider of our pack, more of a loner my entire life, but I've always kept involved in the community to stay informed. At times, I had more information than your father. I'm the one who told him about the Marked Soul. I'd heard about what was happening with the reapers and passed on the information. That led him to meet with the vampire Fallon, who had planned to take the Marked Soul's blood, hoping to harness it for their benefits, make them stronger. She convinced your father it would help you as well."

"Don't. You didn't make the choice to fight. He did. Even if you told him, you didn't make that choice. He was the one so ashamed of his runt daughter that he sacrificed his pack over a weak promise from a power-hungry vampire."

"It's because he loved you, Teagan."

"I'm sure he did ... in a way. But focusing only on what I wasn't instead of what I am ... Well, that's not the love a child needs or deserves, is it?" I grunted and struggled to contain a cry as my bones popped beneath my skin.

"Oh honey," she said. "You're right. He was blinded by his need to have the best, to be the best alpha, to set the example for his pack. He did wrong by you, Teagan." Tears slid down her cheeks as she looked over at me.

"Well, look at you." Trig's irritating voice cut through the pain radiating in my head. I hadn't even heard him reenter the kitchen from his search of the house. "It's no secret what's happening with you, runt girl. That sweat on your pretty skin. Those tight muscles and clenched jaw. You're hurting right now, huh?" From behind the chair, his hand wrapped over my shoulder and slid down the front of my shirt to my breast.

Nausea rolled my stomach. Between the pain, his repulsive scent, and the thought of him touching me, I wanted to vomit. I couldn't see him, couldn't reach him. My hands were useless, but my legs ...

"Uh-uh-uh," Jackson said from the dining room doorway, a low-ball glass filled halfway with an amber liquid clasped inside his hand. He tutted with a shake of his head at Trig.

"What, man? I just wanted to feel these tits. They are fine. This little body ..." His hand squeezed again, and as much as it made me sick, my traitorous body also clung to the sensation, tightening my nipples and trickling pleasure over my skin.

I whimpered despite myself, my pain, my disgust. There was no hiding the way my body wanted the release, the relief that could come from an orgasm.

"You motherfuckers!" Aunt Sonya growled beside me, thrashing in her chair. Her golden hair tumbled out of its bun, falling around her face in a messy mass. "You want to get fucked? I do it all, little boy. Use me. Just stop touching her."

A radio squawked, and Ford's tinny voice spoke from somewhere near Jackson. "At the back. Coming in." He must have pocketed the other two-way outside.

"Oh! Auntie wants to play, does she?" Trig continued with a laugh. Jackson laughed too, obviously not bothered too much about Trig's groping. "Give me one reason to take your old ass over this tight little cunt right here? Seriously." His hand clutched my breast again as he spoke closer to me. "You smell so good. I bet you taste good too. It's no wonder those assholes at camp were smiling big after you arrived. You fucked them happy, didn't you, slut?" His breaths quickened, and I kept my eyes forward, not daring to look behind me at his smug, ugly face.

The back door opened and closed in the mudroom, and a new scent floated into the kitchen. Distinctly male, though not bitter like the others. There was a wooded smell attached to it that reminded me of my father and brothers. Familiar and ...

"What assholes?" A throaty voice asked. Not Ford's voice.

Aunt Sonya gasped. I turned my face in the direction hers pointed, seeing the figure she'd spotted by the mudroom doorway, Ford behind him. The male was larger than Ford, Trig, and Jackson by a couple inches, with a larger frame that usually came with age. Not overweight, only bulky. Though The Four were younger, his size rivaled theirs, but I could tell by his angled neck and shoulders that his muscle mass was far less defined. He wore simple jeans, a T-shirt, and had a ball cap seated low over his forehead with longer dark blond hair covering his ears. When he lifted his face enough, I saw the scars slicing his cheeks, lips, and nose despite the scruffy mustache and beard he probably grew to cover them. A carrier bag hung from one of his clenched hands.

"Raif, that's Jackson and Trig," Ford said from behind the man, breaking the silence that had taken over with his entrance.

Those hard eyes flickered around the room, taking us all in, stopping on Trig's hand still clasping my breast. He moved quickly, his hulking steps surprisingly silent across the old wooden floor. He stiff-armed Trig in the chest, pushing him away from me and backing him closer to Jackson.

The carrier bag dropped with a thud close to my chair.

"Ford, you told me there was nothing to be concerned with. What assholes is he talking about?"

8

Trig sputtered as Ford replied to Raif from the mudroom doorway. "There's no problem. He's only talking about the guys your niece was fucking at Midnight Moon."

"Guys?" Raif said, the word barely a breath as if he were considering something. "How many?"

"Oh, she fucked all four of 'em," Trig offered with a laugh, smacking Jackson's arm, which tipped his glass and spilled some of the amber liquid.

Jackson gave him a sharp glare, then set the glass onto the sideboard along the wall and muttered, "Idiot."

"Why does that matter?" Ford asked.

It was exactly what I'd been wondering. Why did it matter who I was with? He was planning to kill me so he could have the alpha spot of our demolished and discredited pack. Why care about my sexual habits?

"Look, man," Jackson said, straightening up. "We delivered her here like we said we would. We got lucky having that hunter distraction to work with. Otherwise, we wouldn't have had a chance.

So just give us our money, and we'll let you do whatever you were planning. We don't need to be involved with the rest."

"Unfortunately, yes, you do," Raif replied with a derisive laugh.

"No, we don't. We delivered. That's all we agreed on. We never said we'd stay for sure."

"You delivered, but you failed to consider how tied up she was. Those assholes of hers followed you here. So now you stay and end them, or you don't get shit."

What? They'd followed us? My chest heaved a breath as a spur of hope flickered somewhere within, a little ray of light amid the agony.

Jackson scoffed, possibly not believing him. "We agreed—"

"No, you agreed. You could have ended her for me there. But you bitch-asses couldn't handle offing a girl. Now, you've brought me this mess."

"You could have traveled there to end her yourself. You chose not to. So, yeah, still not our problem," Jackson shot back.

"You were considering my offer, a place here in my new pack after I dealt with her? That won't happen now unless we handle this."

"How do you know they followed? I wouldn't be so sure with those idiots. And really, could the pussy be that good to even bother?" Trig asked, staring across the room at the kitchen window behind the sink, looking out to the backyard.

The urge to end him was almost as strong as the pain inside. I'd never wanted to actually kill someone, but this day had changed that. I wanted to. Violently. Shifting my wrists and feeling the edge of the zip tie dig into my flesh, I grunted harshly.

"Because I spotted movement in the backwoods before I came inside. You said four?" Raif replied, paying my noises no mind.

"Yeah. Unless ..." Jackson mused.

"Unless? Spit it the fuck out and gear up, asshole. I doubt we have time to sit around and hold hands." Raif snarled. His hands dipped under his shirt, into the waist of his jeans, and he pulled out a handgun.

"Well, there were the guides there that her guys are close with, but I doubt they would leave their place," Ford answered for Jackson as he scuffed a foot over the threshold between the kitchen and mudroom, looking bored.

Trig picked up the shotgun he'd propped by the kitchen door, opened the break-action to check for shells, then lifted the barrel until it clicked back into place. It was the second time he'd checked if it was loaded. He was definitely nervous.

Raif's face turned and tipped downward, his eyes meeting mine for the first time. I knew what it meant. There was a debate happening in his head. He already planned to kill Aunt Sonya and me. He didn't see a niece. He only saw a wall that blocked him from having this house, the restaurant, and an alpha position of his own pack. But if The Four were here, it made everything more complicated, including our deaths.

"You look like her," he said, his rough voice taking on a softer tone. "When you were younger, you looked more like him. But now ... it's like I'm looking at my sister again ... before she married your asshole father."

I glared at him, having no desire to respond. Speaking required more energy than I had, anyway. I was writhing now and struggling to control even that as the pain commanded most everything.

Aunt Sonya had one, though. "If you loved her and hated him so much, why come back here and take what isn't yours? Why would you want to live in this house? Own a restaurant that was never yours? And murder your niece to take it all?" She growled. "Despite your obvious need to settle among past ghosts, did you ever consider talking to Teagan? Maybe she's had enough loss in her life. Maybe she'd consider a discussion of partial ownership with you. You are her family still."

I heard her, and I knew it was bullshit. If she had truly believed that he'd consider it, she would have never sent me away. She was biding time, hoping that whoever Raif had seen outside was in fact here to help us. I clenched my hands and tugged at them, no longer feeling the zip ties. My body was in too much pain. Tears streamed down my face. If I hadn't used the bathroom earlier, I was sure I would have pissed myself too. The agony was far too great to ignore or control.

Raif chuckled low and cast his eyes to her. "Sonya, Sonya, Sonya. Same old yappy bitch. You haven't changed one bit. Since you asked me so much, I'll ask you something. What makes you think I want to—what was it?—live among my ghosts inside this house and the restaurant? Maybe I don't. Maybe I want to burn it all to the ground so there's nothing left of Jin Wellis in this world, to include his bloodline." Those eyes cast an icy glare back to me.

"Please," she drawled, the single word dripping in southern sarcasm. "You never seemed stupid enough to take me for a fool. This place would have burned weeks ago. Years ago. What took you so long to come back here, Raif? Admit it. You were too scared to challenge my brother, afraid he'd rip your throat out the next time. I knew we'd only see you again when Jin died. Coming around after a funeral is your MO, after all."

"Fucking cunt. I will gut—"

"Wolves out front!" Trig yelled from the living room, having slipped out of the kitchen at some point. "Four of them."

More tears came as another surge of hope blossomed inside. It was true. They had followed us. They'd come.

Raif growled, and his body shook as he lifted his gun to my head. I closed my eyes, praying this wasn't the end.

"What the hell, man?" Jackson said, backtracking into the kitchen before he'd had a chance to see what Trig was talking about. "You can't do this now."

"And why the fuck not?" Raif bit out through his clamped teeth.

"We need them. It's four on four. If they realize she's dead, they won't hesitate. They will attack. With her alive, they're going to be more cautious. I've trained with them. I know their strategies. You'd be a fool to doubt them, especially Loch. He fights like no one I've ever seen."

The gun's hard edge fell away from my temple, and Raif huffed a breath. "Guess she'll get to suffer more of the transition, then she'll die first while you watch, Sonya." He twisted his body and called out, "You still have eyes on them?"

"Yeah, but they've split," Trig replied. "Two are headed around the side."

"There's no time to move her upstairs. One of you get up there and get eyes on the others. Take a shot if you have it."

"Take out the black wolf first if you can," Jackson said and rushed toward the front of the house.

Raif pointed at Ford, who was still in the mudroom doorway. "Watch the back."

My empty stomach flipped over, and I turned my head and vomited spit and bile onto the floor. When there was nothing left, I dry heaved over and over again.

"Maybe you won't even survive the change," he said, and I watched his boots back up then exit out into the living room.

"Hold on, Teenie. I know it's close. If you do it here, I'll be with you. Okay? Don't worry. We'll be together," Aunt Sonya said with rushed words to reassure me and possibly herself.

The chances of us getting out of this alive had grown with The Four's arrival. But the outcome still seemed dismal. I wanted to break free to attack Raif and the others. Yet even if I were loose, I'd be struggling to fight them while my body was fighting itself. Nausea continued, and I heaved again, spitting very little onto the floor at my side.

"Wait! Did you see that?" Trig's voice said.

"What?" Raif replied.

Trig shouted louder. "You seeing any more from up there, Jack?"

"What the fuck? I thought you said a couple moved to the side," Raif yelled from somewhere, his footsteps louder and clumsier now as he rushed around, possibly looking through windows. "There are four up front."

The first gunshot went off, loud enough to be inside the kitchen with us. There was no way for me to know for sure, though. Blood pulsed in my ears so intensely it clouded my ability to track sounds.

Raif called out again from somewhere close. After that, everything moved fast. More guns fired, and then Ford's body launched backward through the mudroom's doorway. Before he even hit the ground, his body shifted into wolf form, revealing a dull brown coat of fur. Another wolf appeared, leaping into the same space and pounding down on Ford. The wolf was not who I'd expected to see at all, but I recognized the shaggy brown fur immediately. Tim. I gasped a shocked, ragged breath despite the ache in my lungs. Tim's jaw latched onto Ford's throat, and their bodies jostled into the kitchen, flipping and spinning and knocking over the chair at the opposite end of the table.

Raif burst through into the kitchen from the front, halting in place as soon as he saw Ford and Tim tangled together, their jaws snapping and grabbing at each other's neck. He lifted his gun, attempting to aim. Hesitation crossed his features, and he released an irritated grunt. He didn't have a clear shot and was reluctant to take one. Ford meant enough to him to give him pause. It was either that or he simply didn't want to lose a number in this fight.

Gunfire continued elsewhere in the house. Ford and Tim snapped and tumbled some more.

"They're all advancing! I can't see them anymore!" Jackson's shouts sounded as if he were underwater. I shook my head, trying to stay focused, trying to be alert. My body killed all my thoughts, the agony seizing all my attention, narrowing my vision and threatening my very consciousness.

The aches hurt. It hurt so bad.

Pain. So much pain.

Raif's body stumbled forward. Something had struck him, shoving him farther into the kitchen. He hadn't been watching his own back. He reached out to catch himself on the sideboard, and when his hands hit, the gun flew from his grasp and launched to the sink, where Ford and Tim had tumbled beneath.

A gray and brown wolf leaped toward him, striking him in the back again and knocking him to the floor. Elijah. My nose was broken, but his scent had registered more clearly than my blurry view of his gray and brown fur. Suddenly, other scents flooded in as if my nose had reawakened while my other senses struggled.

More gunshots and screams came from the front of the house.

Tim and Ford tumbled toward the mudroom, Tim pinning Ford onto his back, jaws ripping into this neck. Ford yelped.

Raif jumped to his feet with surprising strength, knocking Elijah away as he scrambled toward the sink. Within a second, he had hold of his gun again. His arm extended and swung around as he turned to face me. The situation had gotten out of his control. They'd backed him into a corner. He knew it. So this was where it ended, where he ended me.

9

I could barely move as the gun inside Raif's hand swung in my direction. Though my body was engaged in its own war, muscles tightened and locked in a prison, it allowed me enough energy to let out a small cry and flinch the slightest amount.

The gunshot was a muffled explosion, so close and so final.

Instead of hearing my own cry, I heard my aunt's at my side, her wail tunneling into my ears louder than all else. But what came next would haunt me until the day I died.

A wall of gray-brown fur passed over my eyes, blocking my view of Raif and the gun before colliding with me and knocking us to the ground. There was a yelp mixed with a whine, and I knew ... I knew it had hit him instead of me.

No! Eli.

That was the last thought my mind had before the coiling surge of energy within me snapped, and my torso elongated. The zip ties around my hands broke under the pressure of my ridged body, my muscles stretching and seizing. I unfurled on the ground beneath the weight of Eli's warm mass of muscle and fur.

And then my skin ripped wide open.

I screamed as the transition peaked, rage and heat and pain cresting into something primal. It commanded control and threw me into the change, my human body giving way to the animal. There was no doubt in my mind that I was seconds from death. I couldn't convince myself otherwise. The intensity was too strong, too violent, too ... everything.

Bones snapped. Skin ripped. Muscle twisted. And then it was all ebbing, the throb inside my head and in every cell of my body tapering into a well of numbness. I recalled from Zavier's change that it had all happened within minutes. I wasn't sure how long it had been, but it felt like hours.

And then I was blinking my eyes to the bright light inside the kitchen, to the movement of limbs and shadows. My ears twitched at all the sounds. Breathing, panting, screaming, whimpering. The scents barreled in at once. Male and female. Musk and floral. Wood. Jasmine. Dirt. Leather. Citrus. Blood.

Eli.

My body surged, and I pushed onto my feet—my paws—not bothering to think of the change I'd known to happen. Because my eyes met Raif's at the same time as another wolf of white and gray struck him. Aunt Sonya. Her lithe wolf body bounded into the air at Raif and collided with his shoulder as he attempted to aim his gun. I hinged back and leaped at him too.

He shifted while I was midair, changing into a wolf with a scarred face and blond-brown fur. His body twisted, trying to escape Aunt Sonya unsuccessfully. Her teeth clamped down on his front leg. And when he snapped at her, he left his throat exposed to me.

I didn't hesitate. After what he'd done to my family, what he'd done to me—I had to stop him right here and now. All of my instincts kicked in, driving me on like second nature. Deep down I knew what to do, how to be a wolf. Everything my father had taught me sprung to mind, too, all the lessons I'd obsessed over when I was younger, hoping to please him with learning ahead of my transition. And despite not knowing then exactly how it would feel to break free from the human form and live within a wolf, it all seemed to click anyway.

There was an automatic connection with the others in the room. I felt their emotions. I heard their breaths, their noises. I could see and anticipate their movements by watching, hearing, and smelling their cues.

And Raif felt trapped. His wolf eyes locked on me, seeing my intent and knowing that he had no means of escape. He wasn't fast enough.

My teeth sunk into his neck with a punishing bite. I felt his tension, heard his heart race, and smelled the fear roll from him as I adjusted my hold around the channel of his throat and clamped down harder, drawing his blood and crushing his only path for oxygen.

A whine escaped as the last of his breath left his mouth and nose. Those wide eyes lifted to the ceiling and then stilled. His breath stopped first and then his heart.

The surrounding noises had silenced during those moments. Though as I released my hold on Raif's neck and backed away from his limp body, another gunshot pierced the air, followed by a deep scream. In the next moment, the kitchen doorway darkened again, this time by Jackson.

He had remained in human form, and he no longer held a gun. With his bloody arms lifted in surrender, his body backed into the room. Three wolves entered after, one at a time. Black, then gray, then copper-brown. All of them growled and snapped at him, their lips drawn back to bare their teeth.

Jackson's face turned, and his eyes shifted down, locking with mine. "You got the others. I'll leave. You'll never see me again." It was a plea for mercy.

Fresh anger rolled from me, directed solely at him.

His eyes dropped to my side, to Raif's discarded handgun. In the next second, he dove, ending his chance at any mercy. Loch jumped up and latched onto Jackson's throat. His teeth pierce through human skin with little effort. And as he clamped down and gave a single rough shake, it was over. Jackson's body dropped to the floor, blood gushing out as soon as Loch released his hold.

I felt someone else's pain, smelled their blood tingeing the air, but it wasn't from who we'd just killed. It was Eli. I pushed around Aunt Sonya to where Eli lay behind the table. Some blood seeped from his stomach, staining his beautiful fur a dark shade of red.

I crouched down with him, peering into his attentive eyes before licking at his mouth. With a whine, I nosed at his chest and looked up at the others. Their bodies and their soft yips made me feel safe, told me he was going to be all right. There was an unequivocal need to stay with him, so I nuzzled closer into his side before licking around his wound, begging it to heal.

He'd saved me.

"All right, Teagan," Rosie's voice entered the room. "Let me have a look at him, beautiful girl." Tipping my head, I saw her standing in the mudroom, head of pink hair pulled into a low tail. She smiled softly as she looked over my body, my new form. She moved closer and called over her shoulder, "Keira, Mike, Vic, can you help Tim take out the trash, please?"

Keira? Mike? Vic? Before I could think about their arrival, they all appeared behind Rosie with a newly shifted Tim.

Keira offered me a broad smile. "Ooh. Aren't you pretty? I knew you would be."

Tim, Mike, and Vic gave smaller smiles and tugged her to help them with the bodies. Dead bodies. The thought hit me suddenly, and my body shivered, my fur shaking with the movement.

Fur. Despite it all, my body felt good. So relieved and relaxed after the transition. I felt incredible inside my new skin.

Aunt Sonya barked, nudged me with the tip of her nose, then padded out of the room.

"Boys, it's over now. Everyone's fine," Rosie said to the others as they moved closer to Eli and me.

Koni crouched in close first, his narrow snout leaning down and licking my mouth before being shoved aside by Zavier. His broad gray and white face dipped down, too, poking his nose into Eli's back before his tongue licked out to kiss my mouth too.

"Come on, now," Rosie said with a laugh. "You know she won't be able to change back for a bit. Shift so you can help the others if they need it, please."

They moved away, leaving Loch standing there watching. His large black head and hazel eyes took me in. I studied the lines of scars at his neck and face, his dense fur unable to hide the pinkish lines fully. He moved in and gave a soft whine. But its pitch I knew to be more or a greeting than a note of sadness. I lifted my face higher as he pushed his snout against the side of mine, nuzzling me a bit before he licked along my mouth as the others had. With a shake of his head when Rosie eyed him, he turned and left too.

"Elijah ..." she said, running her hands over his stomach and around to his back. "There's an exit wound here. There isn't much bleeding. But stay this way for a while, heal a bit now so it doesn't cause more damage to your human body when you shift." She stood and watched Tim and Vic as they dragged Ford from the mudroom. When she glanced down again, her eyes met mine. I moved to stand, wanting badly to speak to her, to thank her and the others for coming, but she held up a hand to stop me from moving away from Eli. As if she knew what I wanted, she said, "There was never a second thought, dear. We were honored to come help you. We hope you realize that because they've claimed you, we have too. You're family now, even if we don't live around the corner."

I dipped my face in response, and she smiled in return.

"I'm going to talk with your aunt about us staying the night after the cleanup. And before you say anything"—she winked at her joke—"we do have to leave early tomorrow. Being last minute, we can't stay any longer. But this is a lovely place, Teagan, so I expect an actual invite to come visit for vacation soon."

If I could laugh, I would have. Well, actually, a few puffs of air pushed from my mouth and fluttered my cheeks. I supposed that was close enough to one, especially when Rosie chuckled in response.

Vic and Tim had already cleared out Jackson and Ford. Tim returned another time for Raif, scooping under his armpits and heaving him out through the mudroom.

"All right," Rosie said, turning to Keira and Mike, who had dragged Trig's body from the living room through the kitchen. "Line them outside. I'm sure the wraiths will be here soon."

Wraiths? Oh, how had I forgotten? Wolves who had transitioned could see wraiths and reapers. Vampires and some psychics could see them too. Also, witches who drank the potions they made called Sight, which enables them to see supernatural beings and their traits. I'd heard it worked on humans to a degree, too.

But even though I'd learned this all before, I had yet to see it with my own eyes. I'd gone to the vampire bar, Purgatory, with my aunt before going to camp. I'd seen the Favored reapers my father had fought in their human form. But I hadn't seen their true form.

"Go watch," Zavier said as he, Loch, and Koni returned to the kitchen in human skin, all of them pulling T-shirts over their heads. "I told you I couldn't wait for you to see everything, even something as morbid as a soul being reaped. I finally saw a few wraiths the other day. They came for a hiker. It's incredible."

I had a feeling it was quite a sight to witness. But I also couldn't shake the unease, knowing that the wraiths and Favored here had been the ones to kill my father, brothers, and many others. Even though I'd seen the Favored as humans, and even if the pack's death had been my father's fault, I couldn't help my hesitation.

Eli whined a little, and the others looked at him then at me. He could sense my discomfort, and they could too.

"Zavier will stay with Eli. I'll stand with you. Koni too if he wants," Loch said, walking around Eli and me and moving toward the mudroom. "We'll stay close to the door. It's better that you do, anyway. We don't want you being tempted to run into the woods until we can go with you."

I licked Eli's mouth one more time, then stood and followed Loch. Koni trailed behind. We propped the door open to the expansive yard out back and the bordering woods not far away.

As we looked down on the others lining Jackson, Ford, Trig, and Raif close to the house, Loch and Koni's hands found my body, their fingers slipping into my fur with soft strokes.

"Beautiful," Loch murmured before dropping down to sit at my side. He pushed his face against me and inhaled deeply.

"Babe," Koni said, mimicking Loch's movements on my other side. "You really are so beautiful. Fuck. I'm so glad we got here." His face nuzzled against me, and what sounded like a soft sob came from his throat.

Oh fuck. He was going to make me cry, wasn't he? I wanted to thank them all so much and couldn't talk.

A yelp and a whine escaped my mouth, but it didn't feel like nearly enough as their hands and faces continued to push into my fur, hugging and holding on.

With no other way to say it, something deep rumbled inside my throat, and then I opened up and released a howling cry.

10

We settled in for a while, watching and waiting. It took longer than I would have expected, but I supposed there were lots of deaths happening all the time, and they were kept pretty busy most days and nights.

A few dark clouds rolled through the bright afternoon sky. I thought I was hallucinating at first, and then I realized it was what we'd been waiting for.

Loch and Koni, who had been sprawled over me on the small back porch for several minutes, straightened up.

Aunt Sonya had returned from giving Rosie, Tim, and the others a proper tour of the house and was busying herself with business calls while waiting with us. As soon as she noticed the wraiths, she hung up with her assistant at the restaurant. "That's why it took so long," she said, eyeing the sky.

"Why?" Koni asked her what I'd desperately wanted to.

She looked back at us and gave me a tiny, sympathetic smile, recognizing this might be hard to see for the first time. "It looks like one of the Favored has come with the wraiths. Probably knowing that it was multiple wolves and that it happened here at Jin's old place ..." She trailed off and stared at the sky expectantly.

Sure enough, with the presence of the wraiths and reaper close, wispy white strands floated up from the dead bodies.

The dark streaky clouds dropped closer but stopped over the house and began to circle while the largest one dove toward us. Just before reaching Aunt Sonya and touching the ground, it shifted into human form. A Favored reaper was something between an ordinary wraith and Death himself. They not only managed the wraiths and all the deaths, but they were also peacekeepers of the supernaturals in their specific area. They worked with others and made sure no one stepped out of line, which is how my father had gotten our pack killed.

The Favored was a hulk in human form, bigger than The Four, and they were nothing to laugh at. Even though I'd been numb at the vampire bar meeting, I'd seen them before going to camp, and I remembered noticing this specific one with his shaved head of light brown hair, full lips, and scruffy five o'clock shadow.

He wore dark jeans, a fitted black T-shirt, and a pair of scuffed leather boots. His silver eyes studied the scene, tilting his head around. All of them had those silver eyes. I recalled how it had unsettled me at Purgatory.

"Sonya," he greeted her in a natural husky tone and with a tiny tip of his chin.

Aunt Sonya eyed him right back. She wasn't nearly as short as me, but she certainly looked it alongside him. "Shade. Thanks for coming."

He smiled, and it might have knocked me down had I not been already lying on my stomach. They smiled? That was a surprise. The fact that he was good-looking didn't help either. But it was that scary kind of handsome, especially considering he was technically dead.

"Well … Not like we have a choice when four more wolves die after only a month."

She nodded, and his silver eyes cut to me. I felt Loch and Koni both stiffen at my sides, their hands stilling on my back, preparing for anything. Shade smirked at them as the wraiths continued to circle above.

"You remember Teagan?" Aunt Sonya asked, watching him observe us.

"Teagan," he greeted me, and I whined a response, immediately regretting how pitiful it sounded. I followed it with a bark, which made him breathe out a light chuckle. His eyes cut back to Aunt Sonya. "Right. So, I suppose your fears about the outcast came true then."

"Yes," she replied, crossing her arms. "Raif had these others take her from Midnight Moon for him and planned to kill us both. He didn't expect Teagan's friends to come help."

"Understood. Since Raif was unsuccessful and Teagan has transitioned, will she be alpha as planned?"

Aunt Sonya looked over her shoulder at me then answered, "I believe so."

"You have another week to decide if you want to rebuild your pack here or dissolve," he said, eyeing me briefly. "The vampires are reassessing their houses to finalize their own decision on an area leader. We'll have another gathering then. You can announce your news there if you choose."

Aunt Sonya nodded again.

Without a glance from him, the wraiths swooped in and sliced through the wisps, tearing the souls from the dead. I stared in awe but also in sadness, picturing the same happening to my family too.

When I glanced back at Shade, his eyes were already on me. "I am truly sorry for your loss, Teagan. We admired Jin. He did well by his pack until that night. I hope you've found some peace after what happened, and knowledge too, for leading your own pack."

He peered at Loch and Koni, then cut his eyes behind us, where someone's feet shuffled in the mudroom's doorway—I guessed Zavier by the fresh rain scent wafting out to me. Shade's eyes moved farther, and mine followed, seeing Keira, Mike, Tim, Rosie, and Vic walk around the corner from the front of the house. They stopped, obviously wanting to check things out but not disturb.

The wraiths continued into a spiraling circle above, awaiting his command.

"If your friends plan to stay, inform them of our life here. I think we've lost enough wolves for a while."

He shifted into a cloud of blackness and soared into the sky with the wraiths rolling behind him.

"Well, he sure is interesting," Rosie said, walking over to Aunt Sonya. "We've encountered reapers in our area, but we aren't close with them."

Aunt Sonya scratched her head thoughtfully. She'd left her hair loose after having shifted back, and while it looked lovely, I couldn't help but notice more gray hairs shining from within. Her face also held a tired look, her eyes heavy with dark bags below them. I needed to step up now that I was back. Staying here, managing the restaurant, and handling the fallout of the pack's death had taken a toll on her. There was no way I could walk away from her again. As much as it pained me to think about, if The Four chose to leave, I would have to let them go. They hadn't spoken up when Shade had inquired about them staying. Maybe they thought it best to keep quiet, not insert themselves. Either way, we needed to talk together. All of us. I needed to know for sure.

Aunt Sonya cleared her throat. "Yes, the Favored here are quite an anomaly and a bit different than others. For the most part, as long as everyone follows the basic supernatural rules and don't kill humans or other kinds without purpose, they leave us to take care of our own."

"Well, that's good, I guess." Rosie looked over to Koni and Loch at my sides. I recognized her questions, her looks ... she was fishing for more information about the area her boys might call home from now on.

Tim turned his face toward the bodies. "I suppose we should handle these. Will there be a problem burning here, Sonya?"

"No. We should be fine. Not many travel our road, and you can't see the house clearly from the road, anyway. There's a burn pit behind the storage shed there. A wheelbarrow too."

"Great," he replied to her, then looked between the two women. "Have we found out where to grab some food and a few beds?"

I blinked. Then barked and stamped my paw.

"Okay, dear. Your aunt had offered earlier, so as long as you're fine with us staying here for the night," Rosie said with a laugh.

Loch's and Koni's hands roamed over my body again, touching me, feeling me. The contact made me want to be with them so badly, but I knew I'd stay a wolf for several hours, no matter how much I willed the change. The first transition always lasted longer to give the body time to adjust and adapt.

"And you're more than welcome to eat at the restaurant, or I can call in an order and pick it up. I'm beyond grateful that you came here to help her, to help us. I see why Teagan cares for all of you. Thank you for taking care of her."

I hadn't needed to tell her that. She could see in my short time at camp that I'd bonded not only with The Four but all of them too.

"It's been our pleasure, truly. She's become very special to all of us." Rosie's smile beamed between us.

"Let's get this done then, guys. Give me a hand, okay?" Tim asked.

Loch kissed my nose before joining him, then Koni did the same. Zavier appeared from behind me and said, "Eli's asleep for now. We'll be back soon."

I watched them set about their tasks then retreated into the kitchen. Eli was in the same spot, spread out and asleep. Blood coated the floor and his fur, but his wounds had stopped bleeding. Looking around at the mess, my body shivered. Broken zip ties were beside the chairs. My bile vomit remained there, too, thankfully not smelling nearly as bad as I'd thought it would. The smoky scent of gunfire hung in the air, and I barely contained a whine. I wanted to cry. Eli had been hurt, almost killed. Same with Aunt Sonya and me. Any of the others could have been too.

I lay behind him, licking his neck a few times before resting my head on his side.

As thoughts of the day drifted, the world around faded away and exhaustion took hold quickly.

11

"Wake up, baby." Zavier's voice spoke close to my ears as his scent filled my nose. More of their scents followed, heavy and heady and comforting.

More noises filtered in, high, far-off pitches and whispers from farther away, somewhere else inside the house. It took a moment for everything to flood into my mind, for me to realize that I was back at home and that everyone had come here to save Aunt Sonya and me, and that I had transitioned. I was a wolf. And with the potency of the scents and sounds, I realized I was also still in wolf form before cracking open my eyes and seeing my paws and the gray fur along my front legs.

"We carried you upstairs for some privacy," Loch said, drawing my attention to the side of the bedroom. My bedroom. Loch was seated in my desk chair, his legs stretched out and his eyes on me. His usual hard stare was more contemplative than anything else.

"This room ..." Koni spoke from the doorway, his hip propped against the frame as his gaze traveled the space. He dug his hand into a bag of corn chips and popped one into his mouth with a quick chew. "Gotta say, it mostly fits you. The books. The white and yellow colors. I thought there'd be a punching bag somewhere, though."

Zavier laughed from the wide sitting chair in the corner of the room. He lifted a bottled soda for a quick drink, and I licked my lips. With a beam of sunset light casting onto the wall at his side, his eyes seemed to twinkle. He looked from Koni to me, and his eyebrow and lip piercings caught the light and twinkled too. "They have one in the basement gym."

"There's a gym?" Koni replied. "Shit. I need to check it out."

"That's what you get when you're too busy eating to notice your environment." Elijah's voice came from behind me as a hand tightened around my stomach.

My heart leaped. He shifted back to human? I had to see. So I writhed inside his hold, twisting my body awkwardly and rolling on the bed.

My eyes locked onto his gorgeous face, seeing the olive skin healthy and glowing in the room's golden light. I yipped. The excitement of seeing him looking so well and rested was more than I could handle. He chuckled at my reaction, and I quickly licked his face, his mouth. But it wasn't enough. I stood upright on all fours to look over his body sprawled out on my bed, then leaned over him and attacked his face some more with my tongue. It might have looked indecent and ridiculous if I were in human form, but this was the only way I could kiss him right now, so I wasn't holding back.

The other guys laughed as Eli let me have at his face, not fending me off.

"Easy there, beautiful," Loch's said, his tone soft. "He still needs another shift before fully healing."

At that, I backed off Eli's body, looking down to make sure I hadn't stepped on his stomach, which was now covered by a T-shirt. Though the edge of a bandage was visible with a sliver of skin at the top of his jeans.

"Everyone is downstairs," Zavier said. "They've eaten and are settling in for the night. Your aunt brought plenty of food for tonight and breakfast, plus extra, seeing how big some appetites are." He cast a glare at Koni, who stuffed more chips into his mouth with a shrug and a chuckle.

"It's still kinda early for you to shift back yet. But we wanted to wake you to see if you'd try or see if you'd like to go run with us for the first time," Eli said, his hands pushing deep inside my fur at my belly and side, stroking me.

Oh, his touch felt so good. It made me want to shift immediately. I let the thought dig in, willing my body to make the change. My muscles tightened and my skin tingled, but nothing more than that happened.

I huffed a breath and leaped from the bed. If I couldn't change, I supposed trying my body out properly was the next best choice.

"All right. Let's do this," Loch said, getting to his feet.

Koni smiled brightly at me from the doorway. "Hell yeah. This is gonna be fun. We haven't explored anything outside of camp in a while."

"Too true," Zavier agreed, standing from his chair in the corner. "But we stay close this first time since we haven't been out to do a thorough check. Especially with it being Teagan's first run."

They all nodded in understanding and stripped off their shirts. Eli was the first to shift, doing it on the bed. Loch was next beside me, his massive body becoming the black wolf within a moment. He shook himself, then stretched long.

"It's too fucking crowded in here," Koni said with a laugh. "You lead, babe. We'll wait until we're outside."

I did as he suggested, walking to the stairs then trotting down into the living room. Eyes and bodies turned and looked our way.

Aunt Sonya held a stack of pillows, which she handed off to Keira beside Mike and Rosie. "I'm getting them all set up in the other rooms. Given this is now your place, I figured you might want the master bedroom. It has more ... space." Her eyes cut behind me to the guys.

"Sounds great," Zavier answered for us. "Thank you, Sonya."

So polite he was.

"Of course. It's the least I can do for you all," she replied. "If you're heading out for a bit, there shouldn't be much to be concerned with. Just be cautious since no wolves have been active around here for several weeks. I haven't had the time to monitor the entire area."

"Don't keep her out long, boys," Rosie said, winking at me. "Between last night and today, all of you have been through plenty enough and should really take it easy."

"No worries," Koni answered. "We're just going to stretch the legs a bit, see if Teagan can keep up."

I growled playfully, which earned some laughs.

Keira smiled at me, hugging the pillows in her arms. "Have fun! We'll talk in the morning before we leave, okay?"

I dipped my head in a nod and walked into the kitchen and out through the mudroom. Despite the fresh smells of food and cleansers my aunt had already used to clean the mess, the others lingered. Blood. Gun smoke. Death.

After pawing at the door and unsuccessfully opening it, Zavier leaned in and threw it wide with a breathy chuckle. I bounded down the steps, out onto the grass, then turned and watched as Eli and Loch followed. Zavier and Koni shifted as soon as they descended, shaking as they settled into their wolf bodies.

Tim and Vic gave a nod and a wave from where they were standing near the shed. They had been tending the fire, which looked close to burning out.

Without warning, something nudged my rear end before biting and tugging on my tail.

I yelped and spun, preparing to attack whoever had bitten me. Koni's copper-brown body flinched back, then he ducked his head and shook his ass into the air playfully. The others leaped, landing on him and nipping at his ears as if they were attacking him for me. With several barks, they all looked at me and sprinted toward the woods behind the yard's clearing.

Tim and Vic laughed loudly enough for me to hear, but I didn't turn back to them. I stood still for a few moments, listening to all the nearby sounds, inhaling the scent of Alabama in winter as the sun dipped into the horizon and daylight faded.

Then I ran.

Several hours later, I was exhausted beyond measure and completely sated. My limbs were weak from exertion, my mind hazy from an overload of information. The Four and I had explored the area, keeping within a certain range for safety. I understood them easily. Their movements. Their sounds. And even their emotions, which I didn't fully grasp how but could feel inside, could sense what emitted from their bodies. We'd returned to the house, and with everyone else already sleeping, we retreated into the master bedroom. Since my father's bed was nowhere near large enough, and the thought of lying on it was not appealing anyway, the guys got my cues and pushed it to the far end of the room after they'd shifted back into human form.

I still couldn't change. Whether it was because of exhaustion or simply that my body wouldn't allow it yet, I was too tired to stress or care. After they piled blankets on the floor, I promptly laid down. They cuddled up with me immediately, placing hands and heads on my body and fur, expressing sighs and murmurs of contentment that warmed me to no end. They were with me.

12

I woke to a grumble inside my stomach, my body begging for food. But it was also aching in a new way, one that was like the transition but far less intense. It was a dull throb deep in my bones, my body knowing it was ready, needing to shift. As I opened my eyes, I realized only Elijah was in the room with me, lying at my side. He was already awake, his sleepy eyes watching mine focus on him.

"Hey, angel." He licked his lips and blinked slowly before pushing up onto his elbow. "I heard your stomach. You ready to shift and get something to eat?"

I felt a stir deep inside with that ache, and I concentrated on the change, willing it to happen. It came quickly, my body seizing up as my muscles stretched then coiled. My bones creaked, and my skin curled in on itself. I expected it to feel worse, to be doubled over or to vomit from the stress of it all. But that didn't happen. Within a simple few moments, my body twisted on the blankets, and then I was human again, naked of fur though still with the clothes I'd had on during the transition.

"Hi," Eli said, moving closer to me. "How do you feel?"

Tears slipped from my eyes, a buildup of emotion crashing into me without warning. I turned to him, pressing myself against his body. "I'm so sorry about everything and so thankful y'all came, but I ... Why did you jump in front of me? You could have died!" My cries were muffled some by his chest and shirt, but he understood well enough.

"Oh, angel. How do you think I felt? He almost killed you! I wouldn't let that happen. I couldn't lose you. We couldn't lose you."

"But ... but ..."

"No," he said, his arms tightening and lifting me on top of him. "No, buts. It's done now. I'm fine. You're fine. We're here with you."

"I know. So happy you are, and that you're okay. I'm so relieved."

"I know," he soothed, his hands caressing my back.

We stayed that way for a few minutes until there was a soft knock on the bedroom door right before it opened.

"Ah, welcome back," Loch said, walking over to us and dropping into a crouch to kiss my lips. "Glad to see you, beautiful. You feel okay?"

"Yes." I sniffled, and he eyed Eli.

"Everything crashed down," he said for an explanation. It was then I realized I was on top of him. He'd pulled me over his body, which was a big step after what he'd been through. I'd known when we had sex that he needed to be on top, needed to control the situation. Something had changed. Maybe it was the threat of death, the chance of loss.

Loch nodded. "The others are packing up. Your aunt had to leave last night then check in with her assistant this morning. She just returned."

"I should get up." Loch helped me stand from Eli. I looked down at my clothes from yesterday, taking in the bloodstain at the front of my shirt from my broken nose. Instinctively, I reached up, feeling its tenderness.

Eli stood upright, eyeing me. "Doesn't look broken anymore. Does it hurt?"

"A little sore, but not bad. I feel okay otherwise." Glancing down again, I winced. The clothes from the other night were still filthy. I needed a shower, but I knew everyone was leaving and I didn't want to waste a single minute. Especially if The Four decided to go too. I couldn't think that way, though. I had to accept whatever they chose.

My stomach rumbled again, and Eli and Loch both chuckled. Eli grabbed my hand. "Come on, angel. Let's get you food."

I let them lead the way to the kitchen where all the others were gathered, not feeling strong enough to lead myself. When we entered, Koni and Zavier walked over to me immediately, pushing between Eli and Loch and squishing up against my body.

"Hey!"

"How are you feeling?"

"Teagan!"

The kitchen seemed to buzz with greetings as everyone inside noticed our entrance.

I smiled at them, looking around the table where some sat and along the counter where others stood. "Hi. I feel good, thank you. And thank you all for ... so much." Tears stung my eyes, but I blinked them back. "I really wish you hadn't needed to come here to save us, but I'm so grateful that you did. I'll never be able to repay each of you for your help. Just know that I will do my best to do that. Whatever you need, I'll try my best to help."

Aunt Sonya beamed at me from beside the refrigerator. Rosie did the same at her side.

Tim, Vic, Mike, and Keira nodded from their seats at the table.

"Do y'all really need to leave so soon?" I asked.

"Unfortunately, yes," Rosie replied. "Everyone at home can fend for themselves, but things still need to be done as usual."

"Mike and I have a test to get back to," Keira said, and my stomach rolled. When she saw the look on my face, she added, "Don't you dare worry about that. We are ready, right Mike?"

Mike's eyes widened, and he let out a long sigh. "As ready as we'll ever be."

"I wish you the best with that. I hope that one day ... maybe you might consider ..." I bit my lips together, not really knowing how to invite them.

"Are you saying what I think you're saying?" she asked, lifting an eyebrow.

"If you're looking for a place, a pack, yes. You. All of you," I admitted with a nod, then looked at both Vic and Mike as well, who lifted their brows and smiled in return.

Keira shifted her long wavy hair over her shoulder to glance at Mike for a moment, then turned back to me. "Since you and the others in this room have been the only people I've gotten along with, we might just consider that offer."

I chuckled with her as the others looked on.

When they started talking to each other, and Rosie and Aunt Sonya started to talk as well, I looked at The Four at my sides. "I know we haven't been able to discuss everything, but ... I wasn't sure if you wanted—"

"Ooh! Are we invited too?" Koni asked, raising his eyebrows and giving me a goofy, sarcastic grin.

I huffed a breath and teased, "Maybe. You might need to bring your own food, though."

"Ouch!" He grabbed his chest, then leaned down for a quick kiss on my cheek.

I felt Loch's and Eli's hands roaming over my back and ass from their positions behind me—not sure which had what—while Zavier leaned closer to my side and dipped his face down to press a kiss on my neck. He straightened but tipped his head to meet my eyes. "Baby, you couldn't get rid of us even if you wanted to." I had to laugh at his attempt at mimicking my Alabama accent. Others had heard and chuckled too. "Seriously, we aren't going back to Midnight Moon. No offense, Rosie."

"None taken," she replied. "Though, if you'd rather keep your clothes instead of donating them to the office pile, you'd better come for Christmas next week." Her gaze moved to Aunt Sonya.

"You don't need them to start at the restaurant right away, do you? I think they might need to take a little break first, considering …"

I gaped at the women, who had obviously discussed all of this without truly knowing. But maybe they had known, anyway. Someone squeezed my ass, and I looked around at The Four. They each smiled brightly.

Yep. They'd already talked about this too. I should have felt a bit sidelined, but I couldn't be mad. Honestly, I couldn't be happier about all of it.

"No," Aunt Sonya replied, her smile as broad as the guys'. "I need to get things sorted anyway, so after Christmas will work perfectly. They can settle in with Teagan in the meantime while she decides her alpha status."

"You're more than welcome to join them for a visit," Rosie added. "We'd love to have you come too."

"I'll see if I can make that work," Aunt Sonya replied noncommittally. She was busy here, and I had my doubts she'd be able to leave for any amount of time.

"I'm looking forward to learning the kitchen," Eli whispered behind me, making me smile. All of them working at The Back Burner and living here with me … it sounded like heaven.

"Teagan, we'll go through the paperwork this week sometime too, yeah? The deeds and all, meet with the lawyer again." Aunt Sonya said.

"Yes. We can do that."

Tim shifted in his chair and looked up at the clock on the stove before standing. "Well, I think it's about time for us to head out. We have everything in the van?"

"Yeah, it's all loaded," Vic said, standing with him. Keira and Mike did as well.

"It was good to meet you, Teagan. I'm glad we could help. Take care of these boys, okay?"

"I will. Thank you, Tim," I replied as the guys moved with him into the living room to say goodbye.

"You are beautiful, you know," Keira said, pulling me into a hug.

"You are too. Good luck with the test. And I'm serious about the invite."

"Good. We'll talk more about it when you come cook for Christmas, I guess."

"Yeah." I chuckled, perfectly okay with doing just that. "See you."

After Mike and Vic flashed me smiles and said goodbye too, they moved into the living room with the others.

"I'm so happy for you and the boys, Teagan." Rosie held open her arms, and I leaned into her for a hug, inhaling her flowery scent that seemed so much clearer now.

"Thank you for everything. I'm forever grateful."

"Thank you for loving them. They are so happy with you, and I'll forever be grateful for that, Teagan."

"Call me Teenie, if you want," I said, pulling back with a grin.

She tipped her head and laughed. "I consider it an honor, Teenie. See you soon."

Aunt Sonya and I were the last to move toward the living room as the others filed outside.

She let out a relaxed breath and wrapped an arm around my shoulders, pulling me close. "Proud of you. And before you even think about it, it has nothing to do with your transition or those boys."

"Yeah?" I asked, unsure why she would be. I hadn't done much. I'd even dropped the ball with helping her after my father's death.

"Yeah," she replied, walking us to the front door. "You are intelligent, confident, and have become more comfortable with yourself. The fact that you are unapologetically choosing to be with those four, taking your own path even if it is out of the ordinary … that is braver than I think you realize. I also heard how you dealt with things at camp. Despite all that's happened, and maybe because of certain things that have, you have a strong character, Teagan. So yeah, I am damn proud of you."

"Thank you. And I'm proud of you for handling everything alone when I completely shut down. I am really sorry for that. I should have helped."

"Don't be sorry for that. I'm not. You had to mourn, honey. You needed that time to grow and to reflect. Even though there was distance between you and your father and brothers, you needed that time to get through their loss and to find your true self. I think you have. And I'm not sorry for that."

Tears ran freely from my eyes as we stepped onto the porch. I wiped them away and quickly waved to the others as they got into the minivan. The Four were on the pathway, giving Rosie last hugs, then waving goodbye as she climbed into the passenger seat last. As soon as the van turned and drove off, disappearing down the driveway, The Four jogged up the porch steps to us.

Aunt Sonya rubbed the side of my arm and held me tighter for a moment before releasing her hold on me. "I'm going to go too. I have a bunch to catch up on. We'll talk more in a couple days—about work, alpha announcement, and everything else. You guys get settled in here. Call me if you need anything."

My stuff. "I don't have my phone."

"It's here," Koni offered.

"Rosie had us grab it in case we got split up, since the rest of us don't have phones," Zavier added.

Aunt Sonya nodded then walked down the steps. "We'll work all of that out soon." She moved to the side of the house, and after a few moments, her black Civic drove off down the driveway, leaving The Four and me alone.

I turned around and bumped into a solid chest, hit instantly with déjà vu.

13

All of the guys' gazes dragged down my body slowly, their already tipped faces moving a bit more to accommodate their traveling eyes.

I looked like utter shit. My clothes were a mess and stinkier than I cared to admit. But their stares pierced me as they had the first night I'd arrived at Camp Midnight Moon, assessing my body from my sock-covered feet and back up to my messy morning hair, which probably still had some blood in it too. Their lips didn't curl this time. I'd wondered then if they were disgusted, repulsed, or simply annoyed, having smelled that I was a runt. It may have been a combo of it all, though I'd learned since then there were other reasons too. The main of which being that they were attracted to me and my scent and immediately hated me for that, knowing I was about to change their lives.

"You done with the eye fuckin'?" I asked, my lips tugging upward as I repeated what I'd said to them that first night.

Loch's gorgeous hazel eyes blinked once. His lips twitched before spreading into a full grin that made his hard face soften and my panties catch fire. "Feisty runt," he said, repeating his words from that night too and placing a hand on my shoulder.

Koni, Zavier, and Eli laughed at my sides as I reached forward and placed my palms on Loch's broad chest and up to his thick, scarred neck, something I'd itched to do that night despite the unease hovering around us.

"Eye fuckin'?" Eli said with a chuckle, joining in the game.

My eyes met his soulful browns before moving to his luscious lips and sexy chin dimple. Then I glanced at Zavier and Koni, who had been silent that first encounter even though they were ordinarily more talkative than the other two. Zavier's brown and blue eyes met mine. He licked his tongue out over his pouty lower lip piercing then bit down. None of them had shaved in a couple days, but his jaw remained the scruffiest. Strands of his long top hair fell all around his face, not having any product to keep it back. I gazed at Koni next, my eyes eating up his beautiful copper-toned skin, angular jaw, and high cheekbones. The pointed tip of his nose moved as he sniffed the air.

"You stink, babe," he said, bringing my eye-fuckin' of them to a screeching halt.

A laugh burst from me, and they joined in, watching me as I doubled over. When I stood upright again, I snorted and covered my face, which only made them laugh harder.

"Like I'm the only one?" I asked, scrunching up my nose at them. We all stunk.

"Dibs on the master shower with Teagan," Eli said quickly, grabbing my hand and yanking me toward the door before the others could protest.

And protest they did.

"What?!" came from all three as they followed.

"No fucking way," Zavier grumbled. "I want to wash her."

"Fuck no," Koni added. "That's something we haven't done yet either. Dammit."

"The shower isn't big enough for all of us at once. It'll barely fit two," I said, letting Eli pull me up the stairs while the others rushed up behind us. "We'll have to redo it."

"The bathroom and room too," Loch added from the back. "We need more space. We'll have to knock out a wall or two."

"Dibs on Teagan's shower," Zavier said as we reached the top landing. "After showers, grab the other mattresses and bring them into the bedroom. We'll make do for now."

"Ooh, like a den?" I said, giggling at the thought but also feeling warm and tingly all over. This was the beginning for us, the start of our life here. All of us together.

As we passed by my old room, Koni shoved Zavier out of the way then launched himself inside to get to the bathroom first. Loch disappeared down the hall to the bathroom my brothers had shared. Eli ushered me into the master bedroom.

I was struck with how empty it was but also glad for it. Aunt Sonya had come in while I was gone, had cleared away most of my father's items, donated the useless stuff and clothes, and boxed the sentimental things to store in the basement.

I looked at the space in a new light. It was still my home, but now it was mine and theirs. Ours. There was no empty and numb feeling when I stood inside the walls. I only felt a tinge of sadness at what once had been. From here on, this place would be happiness. That, along with pure excitement about the memories we would make together, made me smile so big my cheeks hurt.

Eli turned the faucet handle inside the boxy walk-in shower. He stripped his clothes off in a rush then removed mine, taking more time, more care, kissing random places as he did. He led me in and under the stream. His fit muscles flexed as he squeezed shampoo into his hands and began massaging it into my hair. He helped me rinse. And while he soaped up a washcloth, I applied conditioner. His dick hung heavy between his legs, growing thicker and longer as he cleaned me. I wanted nothing more than to touch him, but I kept still while he ran the cloth over my skin. He washed gently over my arms and breasts, down my back and stomach, then he dipped down to do my legs and finally my pussy and ass. When his fingers slipped inside my lower lips and moved across my clit, pleasure coiled deep inside my belly, my body begging for more.

He grunted, and I knew he wanted more too, but he refrained. His hands backed off, and he quickly soaped himself while I rinsed. I watched his hands roam his body, longing to touch him the same way.

"Can I?" I asked hesitantly.

"Yes," he replied, handing over the cloth and scrubbing shampoo through his hair, keeping his hands occupied.

He'd gotten most of his upper body done already, so I dropped to my knees in front of him and washed his legs and feet first. When they were done, he finished rinsing his hair and peered down at me. Water cascaded from his head onto my neck and chest. I grabbed hold of his erect cock with my free hand and ran the soapy cloth over him with the other.

He hissed, and his body jerked a bit, but he kept his eyes pinned on me. I knew he was fighting off the memories, needing to see me to know I wouldn't hurt him, use him. Because of that, I focused on the task, even though I wanted to take him in my mouth.

"Mattresses are down. That means all showers are over, right now," Koni said, stepping into the master bathroom completely naked, his long wavy hair still dripping.

Eli and I both laughed. He finished rinsing himself while I stepped outside onto the rug.

"Did you even wring your hair?" I asked Koni as he wrapped a towel around my body. Lifting my hand, I pinched some of his wet tendrils.

"Kinda," he replied, then bent in front of me to smooth the towel over my body.

Eli grabbed another towel and dried himself behind us. After he vigorously rubbed it over his head, he gathered my hair and began squeezing its excess water too.

Koni stopped moving the towel at the bottom of my legs, his eyes level with my belly button. He groaned, leaned his face closer, then inhaled deeply. "Much better. I can actually smell you now and not those dickheads or guns or blood. I can smell this sweet pussy."

"You better not start in there," Zavier shouted from the bedroom.

Koni stood with another groan, this one irritated. I laughed and grabbed the towel from his hand, moving it over his head to soak up some water from his hair while Eli finished with mine.

We walked out into the bedroom that way. The queen-sized bed was still flush against the far wall, but they had removed the mattress and placed it on the floor where we'd slept on covers the night before. Three other mattresses were added and pushed into the opposite corner of the room. They had moved all other furniture to accommodate our new floor bed.

"This looks cozy." I released my hold of Koni's hair and tossed the towel back toward the bathroom.

Eli did the same behind me, and my limp, damp hair fell down to brush my bare shoulders, making me shiver.

"Beautiful," Loch said, holding his hand out for me to take. When I stepped closer, he dipped his face to the side of my neck and pressed an open mouth kiss there. "I was fucking terrified. I've never felt that way, even before. It was like someone had ripped my heart out."

"Yeah," Zavier agreed, moving in closer, running his hand down my side and cupping my ass. "Baby, we were freaking the fuck out when we couldn't find you. I'm so glad we got here."

"I am too," I admitted. "I was so scared that I'd never see y'all, that I wouldn't be able to say goodbye."

"Never going to happen again," Koni murmured, kissing my shoulder.

They had surrounded me, touching me in different places. Loch in front. Eli in back. Koni and Zavier at my sides. Their calloused hands and fingertips trailed over my skin, pinching my nipples, slipping between my legs, between my ass cheeks. All of them were hard, their muscles tense, their cocks erect and jerking lightly as they caressed my skin.

I turned around to face Eli, wanting to fulfill my craving from the shower, needing to have him in my mouth. "Eli, can I touch you? Can I suck you?"

All of the guys reacted with tiny grunts and groans. Eli included. His jaw tightened, the muscle there ticking a bit before he replied, "Yes."

"Back up first, babe," Koni said, and I felt all their hands brace me as they walked me backward onto the mattresses.

I knelt before Eli, staring up at his eyes as I ran my palms up his muscled thighs. His gorgeous lips fell open while he watched. With one hand, I cupped his balls, tugging a little, feeling their weight. With the other, I took hold of his heavy cock and gave it a long stroke, loving how he felt. I also loved how he was letting me touch him, how he was moving on from his past with me.

His hands slid over my face, fingers trailing into my hair to hold it away for a better view. I kissed his tip then licked the underside of his shaft before opening wide and taking him into my mouth. He moaned, and the sound had a direct line to my pussy, like a shot of pleasure through my body. I smiled around him, delighted that he was enjoying it.

"Fuck, baby," Zavier said from my side. "You are so gorgeous eating his dick. Your mouth is magic."

I could see him and Koni at my sides stroking themselves. I could hear Loch doing the same behind me. The sounds and sights were such a turn-on. My body rolled as I sucked Eli deeper and pumped his base. His hips jerked, and I felt him throb inside my mouth.

"So good, angel," he murmured to me.

"Mmm, babe," Koni said with a moan, jerking himself roughly as he watched.

I released Eli and reached out to my sides, taking hold of them.

"Fuck yes," Zavier said as I grasped him and stroked hard. "Loch, move around front. Let her suck you too."

I tipped my head back a little, watching Loch do exactly as Zavier suggested.

He stepped around and pushed in close to Eli, holding himself out for me. I bobbed my mouth on Eli a couple more times then opened wide for Loch. He growled when I licked the underside then sucked him in. "Oh God, yes."

I worked them that way and switched, giving turns in my mouth and in my hands. Their hands roamed over whatever they could reach—my hair, shoulders, neck, and face. And the sounds they made had me dripping wet between my thighs, had me rolling my hips in search of relief.

Seeing my desire building, Zavier said, "Oh, baby. I've got you. I wanna make up for your transition. I wish I'd been able to eat this pussy, to fuck you so hard through it. But we're here now. Everything's better." He slid around behind me, moving my legs apart and settling his head and shoulders beneath me. He propped himself up higher with pillows so I could still kneel and reach the others. "Sit back a little, baby. Ride my face while you suck them." His mouth was on me immediately, his tongue licking a flat stroke from my ass to my clit. He moaned then started sucking relentlessly, eating at me, biting at me.

"Ahh," I cried out, unlatching from Koni's dick and moaning toward the ceiling.

"Look at you," Koni said, his eyes wide and flashing as he watched me rock on Zavier's face. "So fucking sexy. Damn."

I gazed up at the others, grabbing hold of Koni and Eli and opening wide for Loch. He slid himself in and thrust several times, the last time hitting the back of my throat. I swallowed through a gag, and he yanked himself out quickly with a sharp breath, close to coming.

The other guys breathed chuckles, and Zavier slipped two fingers inside me, working me into a frenzy from underneath. As soon as he rubbed them along my inner wall, an orgasm ripped through me, curling my toes and making me whimper.

"Yes, baby. Fuck, yes. I need to be in this ass again. Do you think you can take us in both at once?" One of his fingers prodded my asshole, teasing, while his tongue continued to lick at my sensitive clit and lips.

"I want to try," I admitted, honestly wanting to have them everywhere. There was nothing more exciting than being filled by them.

"This is a dream," Koni said. "Where are we starting? Fuck, I might come just thinking about it."

I giggled at his reaction and released his dick as the others chuckled too.

Zavier wiggled out from under me. "I think we all need to feel you first, baby." He leaned over my back and pushed me down on all fours. His blunt tip pressed to my pussy, and he eased himself inside. "Yes. Damn. So damn good." He retreated and shoved forward again. Spreading my cheeks, he pumped into me several times then pulled free.

Before I could complain about the loss of him, Koni had taken his place behind me. And in another moment, he was inside me. I moaned and grabbed hold of Loch, who was at my front still, taking him into my mouth.

"Yes, that's it," Koni said with a grunt, pounding into me, forcing me to take Loch farther down my throat. They worked me from both ends while Eli and Zavier watched and stroked themselves.

Koni jumped up, and Eli took his place, rubbing his tip along my lips then pushing into me with a growl. "You feel so good, angel. Oh." His hands hooked my hips, and he moved faster, pumping a few more times then letting Loch take over.

"Beautiful," Loch said with a growl of his own when he sank inside me. "I've been craving this. Craving you."

"Oh, yes," I agreed. "This feels so good. You all feel so good." I was panting after only a few of his thrusts, my climax building up again, tightening my muscles and tingling all over.

"Loch, you want her ass?" Zavier asked.

"I'm perfectly happy where I am right now," he said. I looked over my shoulder, watching his gaze shift up to my eyes from our connection, a wicked smile overtaking his face.

"Okay. Lay down. Baby, get on top of him," Zavier instructed us, and we complied.

I pressed my palms to Loch's solid chest, bracing myself as I sank down onto his cock. He clamped his teeth with a hiss, and I smiled down at him, loving how he reacted to me.

Zavier settled in behind me, between Loch's and my legs. His fingers rubbed along my ass, wet and slippery. He had found some lube somewhere, but I wasn't even about to ask him where. His finger entered me as I rocked back and forth on Loch.

"Yes, baby. Oh, this ass is so tight, same as that pussy. You feel this? You like this?"

"Yes, yes, yes," I chanted, already so close to coming again.

"I think you're ready for me. I'm going in alone first, okay? Get you used to it," he said, and I whimpered and bit my lip. "Pull off of Loch and keep sliding over him, rub your clit on his cock."

"Okay," I replied, doing exactly that. Loch's hands slid down my sides as I slipped over his shaft.

Zavier's tip pressed to my asshole, harder and harder, stretching me until it popped inside. He released a guttural groan. The sensation rocked through me, so much feeling everywhere.

"Good girl," Koni said from my side, watching and stroking himself. "Fucking hell. This is incredible."

"It is," Eli agreed from in front of us. "You're so sexy."

"I'm going farther," Zavier said, then shoved himself inside.

My clit throbbed against Loch's dick as it jerked beneath me. The pain of stretching was tolerable and was muted by the pleasure of it all. Zavier stopped when he was fully seated, then rocked out.

"Oooh!" I sighed, the feeling so strong and delicious.

"That's it, open for me, baby. Oh, yes." Zavier thrust in harder then picked up his pace, in and out, sliding me back and forth over Loch. "That's so fucking good. Okay, you ready to try us both?"

"Yes, oh," I said, barely hanging on to my release. I dug my fingers into Loch's skin, and my eyes rolled back.

Zavier helped lift me, keeping himself inside as Loch positioned below. Zavier helped ease me onto him. The pressure was indescribable and unimaginable as Loch's dick slid in inch by inch.

We all groaned and grunted, everything so tight we were losing our minds. I knew I was. "Oh god! Loch! Zavier! Ah. I'm so full." I heaved several heavy breaths with both of them deep inside.

"Easy, baby," Zavier said, and I knew both of them needed a still moment too.

Then he bent me forward more, my breasts rubbing along Loch's chest. "Loch, touch her clit."

That did me in. Zavier started moving in and out of my ass, and Loch pumped up from below. As soon as his fingers found my clit, I came, pulsing and convulsing in euphoric waves, screaming my pleasure.

"Yes, baby."

"Fucking gorgeous."

"Yes. Yes."

Their voices were garbled inside my head. I didn't know who had said what because I completely lost it, the sensation blinding and deafening in the most glorious way.

They were relentless, their bodies moving and thrusting from behind and below. It wasn't long before Loch's mouth took mine, rumbling a throaty growl while he spilled himself inside me.

"I'm coming too," Zavier said, slamming into my ass. "Fuck. Fuck. Fuck. Ah!" He slowed his strokes and kissed a trail down my back while Loch continued to kiss my mouth.

"Our turn," Koni said, jumping behind me. I pried my mouth from Loch and chuckled. "Fuck, babe, I don't mean to sound like you're a ride or anything, but seriously, I've never been more excited in my life."

"Eli, you good with being bottom?" Zavier asked him while I lifted off Loch.

Eli looked at me and bit his lower lip. Before I could tell him not to worry or force it, he answered, "Yes. I want this. I want you on me, angel." He slid beneath me while Koni adjusted himself at my back.

I rested my hands on Eli's chest calmly, looking into his eyes as I sunk down onto him. His cock felt so good sliding inside. They all did. So big and strong. I leaned down to kiss his lips.

"Ready for me?" Koni asked, his slick tip pressing against my ass. I hummed my reply into Eli's mouth, not wanting to let him go. My eyes remained open, locked with his because I knew he needed that. He needed to see me, to connect, to know …

Koni's cock pushed in fairly easily, my muscles already relaxed and eager for more. "Oh fuhhhhhck. You feel amazing. This is so, so tight and hot. Damn."

Zavier had disappeared for a moment and returned with some towels. He and Loch both choosing to kneel on the mattresses and watch. They were getting hard again.

I moaned at that, seeing my effect on them, taking all the pleasure in it. When Koni was fully inside, he and Eli both began moving fast, unable to control their urges for more.

"Angel," Eli said as I pushed up a little. His hands found my breasts and my nipples, then one traveled down as Loch's had before, reaching between us to rub my swollen clit.

"Yes, babe. Oh yes," Koni shouted, riding me, thrusting more forcefully, spreading my ass cheeks farther apart while he pounded down.

I screamed as another orgasm erupted and splintered through me. My spine tingled, and my leg muscles seized up.

Zavier and Loch stroked their cocks faster as they watched, kneeling up closer, looking ready to come again already. Fuck.

Eli grunted from under me, his body jolting, hips thrusting upward, coming so deep.

Koni let out a roar and gripped my ass hard as he did the same, spilling into me with a few final thrusts.

"Baby, I'm going again," Zavier panted the words as Koni pulled away from me. "Roll off Eli, baby. I'll wash you, but I want to come on your body."

I lifted off Eli and flipped onto my back as Zavier and Loch leaned over and stroked themselves close to me.

"Fuck. Ohh," Zavier said with a moan as his thick string of cum sprayed onto my stomach. I smiled up at him, thinking of how I'd watched and helped him the first time in the bathhouse.

Loch tensed up on my other side, his large hand pumping his cock. He shot his load all over my breasts, hot and thick too, marking me.

I licked my lips and sighed as I watched them come down from their orgasm high, their eyelids heavy, their mouths open as their breaths slowed.

"We need to do that again in a little while," Koni said from somewhere in the room. The sink in the bathroom turned on, and he and Eli returned right after.

These men. My men. My wolves. They'd claimed me, and I'd claimed them. They were mine, all mine, here with me forever.

"I love you four so much," I said as Zavier and Loch grabbed the wet towels and wiped me off, beaming as they did.

"I love you, too," they all echoed almost in unison. I met and held each of their eyes as they cleaned up.

"Do you want to shower again?" Eli asked, running a hand over his sweaty forehead and into his thick hair that was mostly dried, with wet chunks and puffy patches mixed together.

Koni smacked him on the chest, then looked at me and said, "Dibs on being your soapy partner this time if you do."

"Can we just lay down for a bit?" I asked, smiling up at him, my eyelids getting heavy. They had worn me out. It probably had to do with my body adjusting to shifting earlier too, but still.

"Baby, you haven't eaten yet," Zavier said.

"Later, okay?"

They didn't argue for spots, only stretched out around me. I used Koni's waist as a pillow while Loch laid his head on my chest, lying the same direction as Koni above me. Eli curled against one side, and Zavier lay a bit lower on the other, his face against my thigh. My hands moved to Eli's and Loch's heads, my fingers threading into their shorter hair, scratching my nails lightly against their scalps. Koni's fingers worked through my hair the same way, and Zavier's hand roamed my leg.

"I was so numb before," I admitted, closing my eyes at my new contentment. "I never expected that to change when I got to camp or even when I first saw you. I thought I'd be alone forever when I returned here, that no one would want me when my family hadn't either." Though I felt them tense up as if they wanted to reply, they remained silent as I spoke, listening to my thoughts. "Never in a million years would I have imagined finding someone to want me, to love me, let alone four of you. I'm so thankful I did. You saved me in more ways than one."

Their murmurs and touches followed right away, replies of feeling thankful too.

"And I'm thankful you gave Z that hand job," Koni said, and I barked out a laugh.

"Christ," Zavier muttered, and I knew if I hadn't been between them, he would have hit him.

"Also for the fried chicken," Koni added with a breathy chuckle, which made me reach behind my head and smack him myself.

"Hey! Is that all I'm good for?"

"No, babe. That was just the start. From there, you claimed us and saved us too," he replied.

"That's fucking better," Zavier said. "And he's right. You saved us too."

"You did, beautiful," Loch said.

"Yes," Eli agreed.

And though I tried to hold back my tears, they came. There was no numbness to block my feelings anymore. I had found my family. And now that I was no longer an unwanted, a loner, or a runt, I would claim my alpha position and our pack area, with my new family standing by my side and helping me lead.

Cassa Daun lives in Florida where she actively avoids the steamy days by staying indoors, writing steamy romance stories.

<u>Books</u>

Marked Soul series (Reapers)

Bone

Shade

Blood

Ash

Midnight Moon series (Wolves)

Runt

Stray

Bait

Stud

Sanguine Heart series (Vampires)

Vessel

Vagrant

Villain

Vigilante

Printed in Great Britain
by Amazon